CONSCIENCE AND THE GARGERYS

CONSCIENCE AND THE GARGERYS

HUGH SOCKETT

Waterside Productions

ISBN-13: 978-1-958848-42-5 print edition
ISBN-13: 978-1-958848-43-2 e-book edition

Waterside Productions
2055 Oxford Ave
Cardiff, CA 92007
www.waterside.com

For Tom and Janet

CONTENTS

INTRODUCTION

The Victorian Era saw the growth of the British Empire such that by 1900 it contained almost a quarter or the world's land mass and four hundred million people, backed by the country's overwhelming authority on the oceans and control of lands far and wide by effective armies or subtle means of political control. If it was the empire on which the sun never sets, as one wag put it, that was the case because God could never trust the English in the dark.

Rudyard Kipling coined the phrase 'the white man's burden' in his poem encouraging America to conquer the Philippines, a hymn to racism and white supremacy. Yet for many people in Victorian and Edwardian England the pursuit of 'empire' was also seen as a Christian civilizing force, as opposed to the pioneering lust for wealth.

Members of the Gargery family carry the burdens of conscience, challenges to their duties and responsibilities in terms of dilemmas, how to interpret a duty and how to determine its limits. Matters of conscience are not merely personal, but professional for individuals in the law, the military or business, and for women seeking status and independence.

None of the characters are modeled on any individual, alive or dead, with the exceptions of John Singer Sargent, Winston Churchill, the Marquess of Salisbury, Arthur Balfour, MP, Emily Hobhouse, General Bindon Blood, Edmund Knox, MP, John Atkinson, MP, and Sir Thomas Lea, MP. Pip Gargery, son of Joe and Biddy Gargery is the only survivor from Dickens' *Great Expectations.*

I have been immensely privileged to have my friend, John O' Connor as a reader and critic. His careful work is a constant companion to my writing and my gratitude to him is immeasurable. As ever, my wife Ann has been a constant loving support.

1896

I

"What happened to me da, Mam?"

"Bastard Prods killed him, Seamus."

"Why, Mum?"

"Because they'se bastards, Seamus."

"What did he do, Mum?"

"He was helping poor Catholics like us to get together with the new landlords, Seamus. Them Prods hate our guts and want to keep us down."

"Why, Mum?"

"It has always been them against us, back so far as they've wanted our land."

"When I grows up, I'll get them for you, Mum."

"You do that, Seamus, you do that, though you'se be having to look after the little 'uns too. Jesus, Joseph and Mary, what will become of us?"

Tears flowed down her cheeks and soft howls of grief resounded in the tiny mud-walled cottage that counted as home. The brutal murder of her husband Seamus O'Sullivan the week before was a terrible heart-breaking blow. Her son, also Seamus, was only thirteen and she had five younger children to care for. What could she do? The boy was not yet old enough to take his father's place in tending their land. Would the new landlord help?

A knock on the door heralded an older well-dressed balding Englishman with wisps of grey-red hair sticking out around his ears as he had a bandage around his head. He stumbled through the door, walking with a stick and obviously in some pain.

"Oh, Mrs. O'Sullivan, Marguerite," said the man quietly, "I am so dreadfully sorry about Seamus. I am Pip Gargery."

She continued to sniffle and young Seamus looked at the Englishman with ill-concealed hostility as the other children clambered over the boy, frightened by this stranger with a limp.

"I'm the representative of the Jaggers Trust, the landlord here in Clumber. Your husband was with me last Monday night at the Lodge, tossing around some ideas. He left to come home and the villains set on him with a vengeance. He was a fine man whose company I enjoyed and whose ideas for the community should make you proud."

"Thank you, sir, you must be the man Seamus talked about a lot and said he thought good times were ahead. But what happened to you? No one said you'd been beaten too."

"I'm afraid I was too late to help Seamus. We shared a wee dram together and as he left, he was ambushed. I heard the dreadful commotion at the Lodge gate and I ran down the path where they set on me too. I was unable to get back into the Lodge for my revolver in time. July seems a bad month for Ulster."

"How bad is you?"

"I have a gammy leg from service in the Crimea and they cracked a couple of my ribs so I am in constant pain, but I also got this nasty blow on the side of the head which gives me somewhat of an ache, I fear, but enough about me. On their behalf of the Trust I am giving you twenty pounds now, and then you will receive three pounds each month. Here is a bag for you containing the first twenty sovereigns. This will make it possible for you to feed your children and yourself until your son Seamus here is able to work the land or earn money. Use it wisely."

"Oh," said Marguerite beginning to weep, "how kind, how kind, I had no idea of what would happen to us. I'd thought I'd go either to my cousins in Moville or in Buncrana, but they're no better off than me."

"Take care. I can only promise this money to you if you remain here on the Trust's estate."

"I understand and now we will stay, but when will they stop hating us? My Seamus often said we Irish needed to fight. After that bastard Colonel died and that nice woman inherited, we all saw hope."

"Of course, she sold the plantation to the Trust whose mission is the relief and education of the poor. I promise that we will do just that, though I cannot say how much I will be able to be a part of that work."

"Thank you so much, sir. If I took my bairns from this part of Ireland now, would you want this bag of sovereigns back?"

4

"No, I was only speaking of the three pounds a month."

"I see. Them sovereigns is not blood money then, is they?"

"Of course not. The Trust was in no way responsible for Seamus' death, but we have a responsibility to all our tenants."

"I've a mind to go south somewhere like Cork, Mr. Gargery. Mebbe I'd take them to America with this money though without my man, that'd be harsh. We dreamed of that, you know. Lor' bless us, I don't believe any soul I know has ever had this much money in their whole lives. I only saw a sovereign once before and now I have twenty. P'raps in a city I could get a position. My daughter Anya would care for the youngsters then. I am so confused."

"Think about the possibilities and the Trust will be able to help, I am sure. If you all want to go to America, we will pay your passage. Do you have relatives there? Think about it. But I must go as I am on my way back to London. I must also say, Mrs. O'Sullivan, that the funeral last Tuesday was solemn and wonderful."

That was enough for Marguerite, who collapsed in tears on a chair, as Pip left the home.

"Oh dear, oh dear, we all did love him so," she cried, at which her children came over from young Seamus and covered her in their embrace.

Meantime, Pip's wife Harriet and Aaron Levy the lawyer were waiting at the Lodge after hurrying across the Irish Sea to Pip's bedside when they heard of the attempt on his life. The Lodge was as old as the main house itself, built at the entrance to the Clumber Plantation and was serving as the base for the Trust's work because the main building had been destroyed by arsonists in January. After three days, however, Harriet was anxious to leave as she saw the place enveloped in clouds of hatred and ill-will. She wanted to get her injured husband back to London and he was quite ready to go, to report to the Trust if nothing else. Whether he would return was uncertain. 1896 had become a very strange year for her.

"Do you think Pip will continue to want to work here, Aaron?" Harriet asked, stretching her hands out over the burning peat fire to get herself warm, while waiting for Pip to conclude his visit to Mrs. O'Sullivan.

"I don't know after this attack. He is not a man to walk away from a fight, but the whole context seems intractable to me, and it might feel like that to him."

"I suppose this Lodge will be a sensible home and an office for the work of the Trust," she added inconsequentially, "but God save us from another mission!"

5

"I understand. Good, here he is now."

The three of them then began their journey in the old carriage from Clumber to the train station in Londonderry. They left with a shared sense that this assault and murder demonstrated just how difficult the Trust's ambition of building a working community of the tenants was going to be, primarily because its ideas would be under constant assault from outside forces, shadowy figures of the night, but the future would now be up to the directors of the Jaggers Trust back in London to determine.

They were settled on the boat and were having dinner before leaving the Lough for the journey to Liverpool and conversation turned to comparisons.

"It strikes me that the Irish have been persecuted by the British, like the slaves they rounded up from Africa. Getting wealthy from dominating poor people."

"And not unlike my people, Pip." said Aaron.

"How do you mean, you are Jewish, am I right?"

"Yes Harriet, I am. Moreover I am very fortunate indeed. As a family we go back to Cromwell's time in England when my ancestors came from France. They brought with them enough treasure to avoid poverty and they decided to seek a quiet life, outside a Jewish community. In those days, of course, Jews were blamed for the death of Christ."

"Oh goodness me, yes. Of all the claims I heard growing up as a preacher that was the most unfortunate. I suppose what followed has been the persecution of Jews, but fortunately I am a nonconformist, so I am not required to believe such things."

"The long-standing effects of that calumny, Pip, are to be seen most clearly in Eastern Europe. My Jewish ancestors had fled from Poland to France and then settled in what was then a remote village called Sheffield and over the years they became as local as any other Yorkshire folk. But down the generations my ancestors worked hard and eventually my father became a well-loved doctor, so it was easy for me to become a lawyer. Our relatives who chose Hanover to settle in after leaving Russia still live in. tight-knit communities established all those years ago because they are so despised."

"In some ways like the Catholics here in Ireland."

That conversation faltered before they retired. It had rained throughout the journey to Belfast and continued the following night and day in Liverpool. The fine soft rain of the western part of Ireland gave way to more incessant rain but fortunately, the overnight boat crossed the Irish Sea quite comfortably, notwithstanding the weather, so they all slept well.

As the train left Liverpool dock on its way to Euston station in London, Aaron seemed to be dozing. Pip sighed and turned to Harriet:

"What should we be doing over there? The Trust has the resources to act in such a way as will benefit the people at Clumber. But how?

"For my part, darling, the Trust is in the maelstrom of Irish politics. This centuries-old problem will not be solved by the Trust, but by politicians. The Trust should hand money over to the tenants and be done with it, and that should not be on your conscience."

"I fear she is right, Pip," said Aaron stirring, "I know about landless peoples, about how force dictates lives, about how Jews fled pogroms just as the Irish want to flee starvation and oppression. The cultural and political forces are too great for our small incursion into Irish complexities."

"Put it like this, my dear, are the police there even concerned about the murder of a man in a group they despise? Police are the arm of the state and are not protective of all the citizenry, and the London government does not rein in these aggressive Protestants of whatever class, let alone the absentee landlords. Did the police even talk to you?"

"No, Harriet, they did not, and I agree that they will not put themselves out for a Catholic peasant. We could arm the tenants, of course, but more violence is no solution."

"Another possibility is to pay all the tenants to emigrate to America, Canada or Australia, those welcoming beacons to the oppressed across the globe. The Trust could simply pay their passage."

"Seamus' widow dreamt of that, Aaron, but that is difficult for her with her five children. What follows their emigration? What would the Trust do with the land?"

"The Trust would simply hold it in perpetuity, Pip. It could pay others to keep the grass down, and maybe just plant hundreds of trees. So much wood has been cut down for fuel across the north of Ireland, that would be a project of restoration."

"Maybe," mused Harriet, "all these solutions could be combined. Suppose half the tenants left. Then the Trust could divide the vacant land among those who decided to stay. Maybe too, it could quietly equip those remaining with modes of defense. Meantime, the Trust could pay the remaining tenants a living wage and pay them to plant trees."

"It will not be to your surprise, my dear, to know that my conscience is seriously conflicted. Unlike Gladstone, I do not see a mission in Ireland but, willy-nilly, I do feel a responsibility to Seamus' memory at the very least. Yet at this time in my life, do I really want to become embroiled in a situation wracked with controversy, violence and hatred? Am I just over-rating myself, seeing myself as a kind of minor messiah? What on earth would be my motive for continuing there?"

"It is really not my place to say this," said Aaron quietly, "but I think that a project like this, however large or small, is not the destiny of the older man, but of a younger soul who could conduct such a responsibility with zest and for a long time. It is always a problem for men of conscience to define the limits of their obligation, but their physical abilities must be a consideration."

"I am the last person, to stand in the way of your ambitions, darling Pip, but you have already conducted one mission and it would be much more sensible for you to pay attention to poverty in the East End of London than in the wilds of Ireland."

"Perhaps, perhaps. The Trust had long inconclusive discussions about what to do last year. Our problem reflects the human dilemma: We know we must do something morally speaking, but we have no idea what to do in practice."

For the next few days, Pip and Harriet spent the days quietly at their home in Chiswick as he convalesced, the pair of them in mutual agreement not to raise the vexed problem of Ireland.

Albert Pirrip picked up a newspaper as he walked from Old Square down Kingsway then on to the Strand, noting a piece about Charlotte Cooper who had recently won the Wimbledon Women's title again. He had wondered whether a tennis lawn could be created at home in Essex or at Numquam, the house where his mother-in-law Nellie lived, but his interest had flagged. He suddenly realized it was July 14th and he was recalling those hectic months he spent in the Paris Commune when, as he passed Simpsons, a cab stopped and John Sargent got down. Broad smiles of recognition were immediate with that look of pleasure when old friends meet.

"Albert, is it you my friend, how very good to meet you even by chance?"

"John Sargent, well, well," and they shook hands. "You realize it is Bastille Day?"

"I did indeed, and over breakfast I was recalling those splendid days in Duran's studio."

"I have seen so much about your success, I am truly amazed and delighted for you, but I am also grateful for your persuading me that my talents as a painter were slim, to say the least."

"I have been lucky, you know; although that portrait of your step-mother came to the Gallery after she died, it has me drowning in commissions. But what of you? You seem prosperous?"

"I am. I inherited my grandfather's business in the timber trade and how have two bases, one in Hackney and one in Chatham."

"They do very well by the look of you."

"Oh indeed, indeed, and I am blessed with children."

"Ah, marriage is a state I have yet to enter, but tell me, what happened to that beautiful woman you lived with in Paris, Elizabeth, if I recall her right?"

"Indeed, she married Timothy Egerton, a diplomat and I think he is at the Paris Embassy."

"That is good news, as I am bound for Paris tomorrow, I'll try to see them."

"See them? Why?"

"I corresponded with Estella your step-mother from time to time and she badgered me to get a commission to paint Elizabeth's portrait."

"Oh you should, she needs to be captured for the ages to dwell on her beauty."

"Should I brave a call on Mr. Egerton?"

"I see no harm at all and mention me if you wish."

"Well, thank you Albert, indeed thank you, but I am going to be late for lunch here with Lord Cloverdale whom I am going to disappoint. He wants his portrait painted, but I cannot possibly do it this year, especially if I am to paint Elizabeth."

The pair exchanged cards, shook hands as firmly as good friends do and parted, Sargent into the restaurant for his lunch.

Three days later John Singer Sargent was pacing his room in the Hotel Westminster in Paris suffering from a double bout of anxiety. Impulsively, he grabbed a piece of the hotel writing-paper, wrote a swift note, and called the bellman to have his letter delivered. He was always nervous before an exhibition of his work, due to open on the Saturday but that was immediately beset with worry about the note he had just sent to the Honorable Timothy Egerton, Counsellor at the British Embassy. John was a man of passion, not merely in his exquisite work but that very passion was too often thwarted by a fear of personal relationships especially with women, other than his family. Nonetheless he

9

savored the memory of the beautiful Elizabeth Fitzroy as she was before her marriage, playing the piano in the Music Room at the Embassy. He had to wait two days for a reply.

Timothy Egerton had been enjoying a brilliant career in the Foreign Service and was widely expected to be nominated for one of the plum Ambassadorships, perhaps St. Petersburg or even Berlin, or possibly be brought back to London as an Under-Secretary. Since their arrival in Paris in 1893, the Egertons had cultivated an artistic set of friends and Elizabeth had continued to foster her talents as a pianist such that musical soirees were frequent in the Embassy Music Room and in some of the grander salons in the city.

Timothy put his official valise on the table after a long day at the Embassy and embraced his wife Elizabeth who had come out of the drawing room to greet him:

"Good evening, Timothy darling," she said, catching his arm as they walked into the room, "Charlotte and I had a brief conversation with Henrietta Dalrymple and her daughter who were taking the air in the Bois today. She's a splendid woman, don't you think? Don't forget we are due at the Meyers for dinner, darling, le quatorze juillet."

"I had not forgotten. Interesting, is it not, my dear, that our closest friends in France are of Jewish descent, though their families have been in the country for a couple of hundred years? They are such wonderful patrons of the arts which gave us the entrée into that world."

"I knew some of the Impressionists when I was here with Albert, mainly in cafés, I might add. Now I feel a real affinity with Sarah Meyer, you know. We have children of a similar age, musical talents and interests and very interesting husbands," she said smiling at him.

"But it is your music too, darling, which must create a bond. I have listened with awe to the two of you, and I am always in rapture when you play Mozart's 25th together or any Beethoven sonata of course."

"Isn't that Mozart such a magical piece, especially the waltz melody in the second movement. I find the way she plays her fiddle there quite breathtaking."

"I almost forgot. I had a strange and obviously hurried note today from that artist fellow John Sargent who said he wanted to meet. I replied that he should call next week."

"How interesting, he's an odd cuss, but that portrait of Estella was wonderful and maybe he will ask you about my portrait too."

Sarah Meyer had invited Elizabeth to give an after dinner recital to a group of eighteen of her friends in her opulent home on the day that all over France people were celebrating the storming of the Bastille. The Egerton's barouche had to make its way through the noisy crowds from the Embassy to the mansion just off Les Invalides. Sarah greeted them with her usual extravagance:

"My dearest Elizabeth, how wonderful you look, quite enchanting, and Timothy trés gallant as we French would say."

"Enchanté, chère Sarah," replied Elizabeth and Timothy added his own greetings in his formal English style.

It was no surprise that most of these friends were fluent in English as well as German as they were part of a highly cultured bourgeoisie. In a matter of fifteen minutes or so the Meyer's drawing room was full, and Timothy noticed immediately hushed conversations among the Jewish men, Isaac Mendelssohn, a distant relative of the famous German composer, Solomon Ashkenazy a banker, and Isaac Sinzheim a dealer in the fine arts.

"Now then, gentlemen, why this private discussion?" Said Timothy, approaching the group.

"Not private, my friend," said Isaac, putting his hand gently on Timothy's shoulder, "after all that terrible miscarriage of justice, we have been getting some information that it is now admitted that Alfred Dreyfus has been wrongly imprisoned and that his fellow officer, one Esterhazy, is to be tried for the offences for which Alfred was convicted."

"That is good news, surely. I must confess I was taken aback by the harsh sentence, and the whole business seemed to an Englishman to be a travesty of justice. I thought that it was obviously false as what serious spy would commit an incriminating letter to a wastepaper basket?"

"You must understand, Timothy," said Solomon, "that here in France there are conservative elements, especially in the army who resent Napoleon's opening the country's public offices to people of our race and religion. Of course this hatred of Jews goes back to the falsehoods propagated by the Christian Churches about the killing of Christ."

"More than resent, Timothy," added Isaac, "one hears of even well-endowed Gentile families that would expel us or even put us in some kind of ghetto. This affair with Dreyfus merely provides an opportunity for that kind of sentiment to be expressed."

"But we must dine, gentlemen," interjected Abraham, Sarah's husband, "perhaps we can discuss this further after dessert."

However, the women around the table insisted on opening the discussion.

"We do our best," said Sarah, "to keep a low profile in Paris, apart from our husbands' work and status, and we keep our religious practices as concealed as is possible, for we are well aware that those of us in the diaspora across Europe meet waves of resentment, anger and hatred. Of course there are exceptions. Offenbach, for instance, was enormously popular during the Empire."

"It certainly is uncomfortable for us, Sarah," said Elizabeth. "After all, Lord Roseberry is married to a Rothschild which has not stirred up waves of anti-Jewish sentiment in England. We have had a Jewish Prime Minister in Benjamin Disraeli. Timothy has had one or two Jewish colleagues. We have welcomed Jewish immigrants and there is no obvious discrimination against them, though there may be fights and whatnot among the poor working classes."

"It is so difficult for us," said Martha Ashkenazy, "here we have a circle of friends with common cultural pursuits, but poor Jews of the kind you refer to are as likely as we are to meet torrents of prejudice which we feel a responsibility to combat. I wonder too whether you move in a circle of English friends who think as you do, and that there are anti-Jewish sentiments in England you do not come across?"

"That may well be so. I suspect that the deepest prejudices come within institutions that are cliquish and where high intelligence is not a perquisite for success, like the army," Elizabeth said laughing and there was general amusement around the table.

"Timothy, is there any outside pressure that might influence the case of poor Dreyfus?"

"Do you mean diplomatically? Frankly, Abraham, I doubt that very much as I am sure my branch of government would regard it as an intrusion into France's internal affairs which we would not welcome into our own. As you can imagine diplomats do discuss all aspects of French life, and while there was considerable surprise at Dreyfus' original conviction and the harsh sentence, we felt that any attempt to intervene could make matters worse. I also am afraid, as Martha suggested, that English society is not as pure as one might hope in the way it regards Jews."

"I remember the total defeat of the French army when I was a young woman and my father was a diplomat here. I suspect that institution is still reeling from the humiliation," said Elizabeth, "and probably blaming Jews for it."

"I have not heard any talk like that," said Sarah, "but you are right to think that such falsehoods would be constructed."

After dinner, the party withdrew to the drawing-room to hear Elizabeth play two of Mendelssohn's Songs without Words, as a tribute to the hosts and the company, before ending with Beethoven's Tempest Sonata which she delivered with such verve that everyone was astonished at her virtuosity.

In the carriage back to the Embassy, Timothy was a little morose:

"What must it be like to have achieved so much over generations and to be so discomforted in the land of your birth?"

"I don't know, but I hope my playing gave some comfort."

"Oh my darling Elizabeth, you are such a tower of strength, of beauty and of talent, I am as humbled as I was when I first heard you play all those years ago."

"I love you too, my dear. I feel so fortunate with you and our beautiful children."

"We are fortunate indeed."

Two days later Timothy received a message in a diplomatic bag recalling him to London urgently and indicating that this would be a permanent re-assignment. He was to be in at the Foreign Office within the week with the result that Elizabeth was left in Paris to superintend a move to London that was a little unsettling for her, though Henry the eldest would not be at Cambridge till October, and Oliver at Eton by September, so she had some help and her daughter Charlotte, the youngest child was always a splendid supporter of her mother.

Nevertheless, it was a matter of great excitement for them all to return home for a commission as yet unknown. Timothy managed to reply to Sargent before he left telling him to contact them when he was back in London. The Egertons would miss their cultured French-Jewish friends enormously and there was no chance to say goodbye en masse, so Elizabeth spent a day writing an affectionate note to them all.

"We will have them all to London when we are settled," said Elizabeth on Timothy's last night, but he was already asleep.

The previous April, Malcolm had been posted to South Africa and had left England at the beginning of May. However, the ship's engines ran into trouble in the Bay of Biscay and had to put into Gibraltar for repairs. With new parts being sent from England the delay ran into three weeks and while the Rock was interesting in its way, Malcolm spent too much time kicking his heels and gazing at the famous monkeys. He was tempted to go into Spain, but he didn't know the language, the country was of little interest and the library in the Navy Mess did not contain anything worth reading.

As a result it was not until early July that he arrived in Port Elizabeth, bronzed and fit after weeks basking on the deck in the ocean sunshine. He loved the sounds and smells and the light of the veldt, but he was back in a different corner of South Africa. Once disembarked he was met by a young corporal who showed him the way to his superior officer's room where he was given some letters including the latest from Clara in which she emphasized that her pregnancy was going well. Then his superior officer arrived, accompanied by a large dog of a breed that Malcolm had never seen which promptly made itself comfortable under the desk, ignoring Malcolm completely.

Brigadier Henry Motely-Millard was a man of military bearing, a large moustache which curled around his cheeks but without reaching his ears. Of medium height he was quite stout, a sign of his over-indulgence over many years. Near retirement he was the type of military gentleman who bored guests to death over a dinner party, retelling of some combat actions in which he had played a part, if not a central one, and others in which he was loath to let fact control fiction.

"Ah, Gargery. I have heard a great deal about you and I am sorry you lost your eye. Dashed inconvenient, what?

"Indeed it is, sir."

"At least you have the other one. I knew a man in the Sudan who lost his eye in an action and, damn me, if a large bird didn't fly down and make off with it."

"Very unfortunate, sir, but it would be of no use to your friend, but useful for the bird."

"That's rather callous, isn't it, Gargery?"

"I suppose so, sir."

"Now I have been here not more than six months and what with the Boers and the native-johnnies making a fuss, I am not sure what HMG wants me to do, except be in reserve if needed. Your orders are to act as a kind of spy-cum-liaison officer, trying to interpret what's going on and I will forward anything you come across to Capetown and London."

"Right, sir. I will walk around the town to get the lie of the land."

"Good man, Gargery, good man. You'll have a couple of men to assist you and a small office in the Fort here. As you can see, this was a Napoleonic War construction and only you, me and a few other officers can be based here and the main barracks are near the Port. Most officers live in accommodation in the town. I anticipate reports on anything that you think worth our attention from time to time. We have made an uneasy peace with the Boer but he's a clever fellow and very demanding, and I would not be at all surprised if we did not have another shindig before long."

"Really, sir? That would be a pity, I think. This is such a beautiful country from what I have seen."

"Indeed, it is very different from the New Forest of England my ancestral home. I suppose one could get to like it."

"I should let you know, sir, that my wife and children may come here from England, and that I will take a house to accommodate them."

"What? Your wife here? Are you sure? I know some of the young officers want to create a social set and no doubt your wife would assist in that. But there are dangers here, Gargery, real dangers. By the way, Corporal Jackson will tell you where your accommodation is."

"Thank you, but I think the dangers here are preferable to a long separation, especially as we have not been married two years."

"Ah, well, that is very brave of her, if she decides to make the trip. My good lady is at the family ancestral pile outside Winchester. My son died young and my daughter Sophia married a clergyman in Belfast when I was home on leave. Interesting experience, don't you know, giving away one's daughter."

"I am sure. Talking of Ulster, my wife inherited a large estate south of Londonderry which, she did not need and it was bought by a Trust to ameliorate the shocking conditions of the tenants."

"Catholics, I suppose."

"Indeed, but God's children nevertheless."

"I suppose so, but that religion seems mumbo-jumbo to me. Give me the good old Church of England any time. But we must get back to work Gargery. I am glad to have you on board. We need men of your caliber in this colony."

"Thank you. Tell me, sir, that is an impressive dog of a breed I have never seen before."

"What? Old Duke? You'll need a dog here, Gargery. He is the only friend I have. He is like the boer-hound which some Boers have, or so I am told. His type was bred by a native tribe for hunting lions. Quite clever actually: They didn't fight the lions but just harassed them. As you might guess Duke is strong and he had this ridge down his back. I never saw his like in England. In some ways he is a very soft lovable creature, always with me, lying at my feet or on the floor of my bedroom. Yet he can be extremely fierce in guarding the home: The appearance of any quadruped nearby can send him in convulsions of barking and racing around. Have you ever kept a dog, Gargery?"

"No, I really have no acquaintance with them."

"Then you should get a pup as soon as your wife and children arrive, for protection of course. This is the kind of dog who will be wonderful with children but will bare his teeth at any perceived threat."

"Thank you, sir. I'll get your advice when the time comes if I may. Perhaps your man would now direct me to my office?"

"Glad to help," and he shouted 'Jackson' with a voice that frightened the starlings in the courtyard of the Fort.

Corporal Jackson led Malcolm to a pokey little room to use as an office but it had the saving grace of a glorious view toward the mountains, not the sea, although he intended not be bound to an office desk given the curious and obscure contours of his assignment.

His first lonely days were spent exploring Port Elizabeth wondering whether it was really sensible for Clara to come and bring the children there. Walking down from Fort Frederick in brilliant sunshine to the Donkin Lighthouse and Pyramid he remembered hearing that the founder of the city was a Sir Rufane Donkin who had named the port after his wife Elizabeth some thirty years before. The view of the sea and the town was indeed magnificent. The noise of building was continuous, as the Port was beginning to expand, not merely from the demands of settlers, but from the Government's need for a stable well-garrisoned port in the uncertain relationships with the Xhosa tribe and with the Afrikaners as the Boers called themselves nowadays.

One evening at the end of his first week, in the middle of a long letter to Clara about the voyage, his love for her and his first impressions, he wrote:

'I have also made time to walk around this town which, while it has numerous British soldiers, its population is largely new settlers and the descendants of those who arrived in the 1860s. On Castle Hill, new houses seem spacious enough, though nothing is as grand as the Down Street House in Mayfair.

The weather here is beautiful, if windy. The beaches are sublime and the views of the sea in a class of their own. How different it is from the stones of dear Aberdeen! If people are to be believed, this part of the

Eastern Cape has an enviable climate with the sun shining constantly, rather different from the stench and fogs which enveloped London.

What we would surrender in comfort, we will gain in a climate for good health. I miss you all, my darling. While I am somewhat nervous about it, and while I know we said you should come, why not come with the children for just six months when the baby is born? Don't risk being at sea before that and having any difficulty on that score. I will take a house and we can see what happens and make decisions about making this neck of the woods a permanent home, depending on what I am ordered to do and how much we enjoy it.

As you know, my greatest wish is for us to be together."

While cautious about the possibility, he hoped desperately that she would come and stay till his stint was done. He knew it made sense for him to settle in first to assess the situation, its advantages and obstacles, though she would not initiate a visit until her baby was born. Walking through the small City Center he noticed a large house in Clyde Street which seemed vacant. There was a notice on the door which directed him to an address further along the street. A dog barked in the background as a wizened old lady opened the door, spectacles falling off her nose, her hands and fingers riddled with some bone disease or other, but her eyes sparkled and she seemed very friendly.

"I am enquiring about number 7, I was wondering whether it might be for sale or rent."

"Yes, young man, it is. Come inside. I am Ella Makepeace."

"I am Captain Malcolm Gargery of the Gordon Highlanders, though my posting here is not with my battalion."

"Welcome to South Africa, then. Number 7 was built by my grandfather after he came here in the 1820 settlement, but my husband is dead, my children are gone, I am old and it is far too big for me. A cunning old boy, my grandfather, he bought several houses in the street."

"How good for you if I may say so. However, I have been sent here by my commanding officers because I know something of South Africa. My parents were missionaries in Barotseland when I was a child. I was at school in Capetown and later worked in diamonds. However, number 7 is very pretty and looks substantial, I must say, from the outside."

"Here is the key. Look for yourself," she said somewhat abruptly, "as you're a military man, I am sure you are reliable. I must get on with my weaving."

"I should just mention that my wife and three children and probably her maid will come from London as I expect to be stationed here for a year or more. At least, that is what I hope. My word, this is so different from getting a home in England or Scotland where agents are involved."

"No agents here, though I did hear one was starting in the town. If you wish, I can help your wife with choice of servants when she arrives. I only keep a cook nowadays. There are plenty of natives willing to work for us, you know."

Captain Gargery and Mrs. Makepeace signed a lease dated July 27th, 1896, for three years at sixty pounds a year, and by the following week Malcolm had bought just enough furniture and trappings in the expectation that Clara and the family would come and he also hired two local maids on Mrs. Makepeace's instructions. Clara would want to make her individual mark on the house, and decide on servants, though whether she would be satisfied with the emporium in the town after those in Oxford Street was another matter.

Number 7 was much like many a townhouse in London, with a double front, windows and doors in the Georgian style. A small library and the main drawing room were to the right of a wide hall, decorated, he felt, too loudly for his taste. At some point the house had been extended to the side, not to the back, so there was another sitting room, a kitchen, and two additional bedrooms above. Thus the main bedroom had windows on to the street and on to the garden, which was a blaze of tropical plants and flowers, most of whose names he did not remember, except a huge bougainvillea cascaded over the back of the house, a jasmine across the rear garden walls, and birds of paradise in every flower bed. She will make this a treasure of a home, he thought, with the confidence of man whose utter devotion to his wife brooked no rival.

He returned to his office in the late afternoon and to his great surprise there was a formal letter from the Headquarters of the Regiment informing him of his promotion in rank to Major. He smiled broadly, looking at the mountains and thought immediately just how delighted Clara would be. He would wait to tell her.

Major Malcolm Gargery, well, well!

II

Elizabeth Egerton and her daughter Charlotte came back to London a week after Timothy, and they were thrilled at the London posting because they could open up their Chelsea home which enabled the family to settle quickly, and the beautiful Summer weather in London was a delight. Her sons Henry and Oliver had decided to visit Rome first, so the unpacking was overseen by Elizabeth and Charlotte though the servants had already done enough for the home to accommodate Timothy.

Timothy came home the evening they returned looking very grim. The usual greetings were tense as he said:

"I can only tell you a very little about my commission, darling, and I decided to wait until you had returned, rather than write. I was called to a Downing Street pow-pow for my precise instructions when I arrived. I am going to have to travel to St. Petersburg and probably to wherever the Sultan's entourage is located this summer, but I can say no more than that, except that it is an assignment of the very highest importance."

"I understand, darling, and I will read of Foreign Office activities in the newspapers and no doubt there will be gossip."

"Dear God, no, I hope it is kept totally secret. This is no ordinary assignment."

"Oh dear, is it dangerous?"

"It could be, I suppose."

"Then meantime I will re-establish links with our friends in England while you are away as we have not lived in London for so long."

"I forgot, my dear, with all that has been going on. You remember that artist fellow Sargent asked to meet me in Paris just before we came to London. My colleague Sebastian Cholmondeley told me Sargent had asked for our London address and a note came here before you arrived saying he would like to call."

On the second Saturday in August, the maid introduced Mr. Sargent. Timothy was buried in secret papers in his study, but curiosity got the better of him when he heard the artist was announced.

"Very good to meet you, Sargent, your fame precedes you. What can we do for you?" Said Timothy as he led the artist into the drawing-room.

"Welcome, Mr. Sargent, I recall your listening to me playing the piano in the Embassy long ago, am I right?"

"Indeed, Mrs. Egerton, it is one of my most pleasurable memories of Paris."

"Be careful with your flattery, Mr. Sargent."

"I will, I will, but there is more to come. I missed you recently in Paris, but no matter. As you know, I have been quite successful in painting portraits of gentlemen and gentlewomen, though one of them caused such a stir in Paris some time ago that I hesitated to continue, but I recall the impact that painting of Beth Morisot did of your face within a body that was not your own, that I resolved then at some time to paint your portrait. Now that I have tracked you down to London, I am offering my services."

"That is so splendid," said Timothy, "I have had it in my mind for some time to have my wife's portrait painted and let me show you where I think it could hang. Ever since we saw Estella's portrait in the National Gallery when we last lived in London. Now the time has come. You see Sargent, we have only this elderly painting of the Scottish Highlands above the mantel and I want my wife's portrait to be in its place looking down on our dinner conversations."

"What an excellent place to hang it. I'd like to paint her at her piano with perhaps sheet music on her lap, not a full-length portrait as there is not enough space there for that."

"That will be wonderful, Mr. Sargent," said Elizabeth, "I will be happy to start when you are ready."

"I will need five or six sittings here and then in my studio when I have the canvas going."

"What shall we say," said Timothy, "seven hundred guineas?"

"Good heavens, no, five hundred will be ample."

"I will write a note. Let me just add that I am extremely preoccupied with a Foreign Office matter, so you will make all the necessary arrangements with my wife."

"Entirely satisfactory, Mr. Egerton, I will call within a week to determine the first sitting, if that will suit Mrs. Egerton."

"Indeed, I look forward to your call," she said, conducting Sargent to the door as Timothy had hurried back to his study, locking the door behind him which raised the artist's eyebrows.

"It must be a very secret matter."

"It is, and that is as much as I know."

"I would like to make a start in mid-August with the idea of completion for Christmas?"

"That would be lovely, but what shall I wear?"

"Your choice completely, but I like being challenged by fashionable and complex clothes, but you will be seeing yourself on the wall, so something that you love, I surmise."

"I know exactly the garments."

After several visits to Eaton Square, Sargent had completed a variety of sketches, coming perhaps more frequently than was necessary so that he could sit and adore this beautiful woman. He had not revealed that he had begun applying oil to canvas after two sketches, but he needed her to sit for him properly. That would come in late September. Their conversation was always lively, but Elizabeth had a presence which he found difficult to penetrate such that anything remotely close to the personal was impossible.

She had such natural elegance, he thought, with her dark hair now with very slight touches of grey, offsetting the brilliance of her eyes. That elegance gave her this aura that kept even the most daring of men at bay, as if any attempt at courtship would simply be a disaster and a courtier would be banished. Yet the temptation lived regularly in the minds of many a man who met her, because the prize of her assent would be beyond compare. Not that she would ever contemplate any such betrayal, bound up as she was in the deepest of love for her husband.

Albert Pirrip was very proud of his position as a man of business, the proprietor of Pocket and Pirrip, Timber Merchants of Hackney and Chatham. The Chatham firm that he had bought needed his close attention as he did not have as reliable a staff as he had at Hackney. As a result he was spending long days at work and travelling daily from Numquam by carriage. He was attracted by the possibility of the new automobile that some of his acquaintances were considering, but for the moment, he had business only on his mind.

His marriage had drifted into a languid partnership with his wife Victoria. She had become an anxious wife caring for her husband but he was beginning to view her as a constant nag. Her initial hope that taking on a business in Chatham could bring her responsibilities beyond the home had not materialized as he failed to create the opportunity.

"Albert, my dear, the children and I have to wait for dinner till you get home from Chatham. Could you not leave earlier?"

"Time and tide wait for no man, my dear, my business here demands my care."

"I know that but you will make yourself ill with it if you're not careful."

"You like spending the money I earn, do you not Victoria? It is not as plentiful as air, you know, and someone has to bring it home," he replied with a growing sense of impatience.

"Yes, and you know I am very grateful and the children too. Sometime soon we should talk about Philip. He's eight and we should put his name for admission to that good school in Rochester I've heard about and he could be a boarder there when he's older."

"I must see to that soon. Yet another responsibility as if I did not have enough."

"You've remembered we are bound for the Cottage this weekend with my brother's family."

"Oh dear, is it that important? Should a family of property and station mix with a blacksmith and his large family?"

"He is my brother, you know."

"Alright, I do like going to the Cottage where I lived with Joe and Biddy when I was a child, it is the present inhabitants I don't like."

"I don't know, Albert, you've become such a snob since my mother died. Just think what she would have said to you if you'd said that to her."

"But she's dead, isn't she?"

"That's unkind. I'll tell you what she would have said, she'd have told you your father grew up in that cottage before he met the old convict and had his great expectations and your grandfather was as proud a blacksmith as ever was, and that you should stop being so superior."

"Alright, woman, alright. We'll go. I'm off for a smoke and then bed."

He retired to the library, now commandeered as his study, put on his blue velvet smoking jacket, poured himself a whisky and sat down with a large cigar. Albert now saw himself as a man of parts with a considerable degree of smug self-satisfaction. While Hackney was a village and his firm there as one of significance on the River Lea, Chatham was a much larger field for his ambitions. He worried now about appearance and status as he had never done before when moving around Paris with his louche painter friends.

A week later at the Cottage, Horatio Fletcher was at his anvil building a small iron gate for a customer in the village.

"Dad," said ten-year old Arthur, the eldest boy watching him work, "how come we sing so much?"

"Tradition, my boy, tradition. My father was usually to be heard singing old songs as he worked."

"I don't remember him really."

"He brought up your aunt Victoria and me to sing, with your grandma Nellie of course. When we was all in the cart, we'd always be singing. I think it was because my mum and dad had had some very rough times, so they sang to show how good their life was."

At that moment, Arthur's mother Beth appeared. Beth Horsfield, often called Bets or Betsy by her man, was a native of All Hallows who married her husband after a solid romance and a long engagement, celebrated raucously in the Three Jolly Bargemen among their numerous friends from the village. She was so proud to be married to a blacksmith because it was a trade which gave her status. She was a woman of country stock with a build that indicates that labor not leisure was her main preoccupation. She had only mild enthusiasm for the Fletcher tradition of singing, and she came out of the cottage carrying her four-month-old baby, Georgiana.

"Now, Harry," she said, abbreviating her husband's name which she thought was a mouthful, "my love, have you forgotten your sister and her brood are coming over tomorrow with that fancy husband of hers?"

"I'd stop, darlin' but ain't it a luvly day for an old bird like me to sing. I forgot they was coming. Oh crikey, we'll make the best of it, I suppose, Bets," and he put down his hammer and took the baby from her.

"Coo, coo," he said, holding the child so her could look her straight in the eye, "how's my little Georgie then," and the baby responded with a pronounced gurgle of pleasure.

"I'll put out plenty of vittels and we'll open that keg of ale," said Beth, "if his lordship can stoop low enough to drink our beer."

"I don't know what's up with that Albert, he used to be a proper fella fond of a lark before he got into that Chatham business. Still, if Victor loves him, that's good enough for me."

As the Pirrip family rode in their carriage the following morning along the well-worn track from Numquam House to the Cottage, Albert said to his wife:

"I have a plan, my dear,"

"What's that?"

"I am going to gather some acquaintances together and found a club for gentlemen in Chatham. Gentlemen of the town who are not in the Navy are never invited to those elegant mess dinners they have. I see these officers in their splendid uniforms and shining medals on occasion when I leave my office, and I think 'why should I not be invited?' Navy people do not know what makes the world go round which is the lot of the hardworking men of business like myself. I plan to have a lunch with Martin Gadabout, the grocer, and ask him what he thinks of my plan."

"I suppose that will give you more of an excuse not to come home for dinner."

"No, my dear, my thoughts are for a lunch club, though of course it may expand as we grow," he replied knowing full well dinner was the object for such a club and for other less worthy entertainments.

The Pirrip family descended from the carriage, all beautifully dressed according to fashion, a sign of Albert's wealth. Beatrice was nearly eleven and much like her mother and grandmother in looks. Nine-year old Philip was still small for his age, not yet quite struck by that earthquake called puberty, and finally there was four year-old Ellen known as Nellie, who had just had her birthday.

Their hosts, the Fletchers, were typical of rural folk who had profited from medical discoveries and inventions so that the child mortality which had marked much of the mid-century now seemed under control. Arthur was the eldest was ten, Betty after her mother was almost eight, Charlie was seven, Dottie do-dah, as they called her, was five, then there was Ernest at four, Frank at three, and Georgiana. Nor was this number necessarily the limit as Beth was as strong as an ox and in her early thirties.

"How luvly to see you, Victor," said Horatio, grabbing his sister with tree-trunk arms and using the nickname he had given her since her birth.

"And you too, Harry darling," replied Victoria, breaking from her brother's clutches.

24

"How d'ye do, Fletcher," said Albert, deluding himself that his voice was not patronizing, but Beth saw through him.

"How d'ye do, Beth," he continued as she moved toward him.

"You'se put on a bit of weight since I last saw you, Albert. Eating too much eh?" said Beth, coming close and pretending to punch him in the stomach, "my mum used to say men wot put on weight aren't getting any."

"What do you mean, Beth?"

"Leave it alone, Bets," said Horatio.

"The cottage looks nice," said Victoria quite aware of Beth's comment which was too near to the bone, so she was anxious to change the subject.

"Yeah, see, wot with all these kiddies," Beth went on, "we needed more rooms, so Harry is building rooms out the back, so there'll be four bedrooms and a big downstairs room."

"We saw you had started when we were last here," said Albert.

"So you did, did you?" said Beth with the slightest sneer.

Albert started off in the direction of the marshes, indulging himself with nostalgia as an alternative to conversation with his wife's relatives, remembering his walks with his grandpa, Joe Gargery the blacksmith, but he returned quickly, important as it was for him to retain self-control.

"Victor," said Horatio, "we like having all these kids as long as business is good and we can support them."

"We thought it would help 'em do their letters, see, so we call 'em our alphabet kids," Beth said laughing, "I could never remember it, just like my 'rithmetic tables, so help me!"

"What do you mean?" Asked Albert.

"Well, think about it, A is for Arthur, B is for Beth, C is for Charlie and so on."

"Christ knows what we'll do when we to X," said Horatio laughing, "don't know any X's meself."

It was no surprise that the cousins from the different families looked at each other with curiosity but found little common ground. In particular Charlie and Philip fostered their instant dislike to each other with a fight at the back of the house in which Philip was floored with a deft right-hand blow from Charlie. The Fletcher girls saw the Pirrips as stuck-up, reciprocated by comments about dirty hair. Arthur ignored them all and went back to the Forge where he often watched his father for although he was still at school, he anticipated becoming a blacksmith. Anything to get away from his cousins.

After the visit was concluded, both adult couples seemed to recognize there was little point in them trying to behave as if they liked each other. The only tie was between brother and sister, Horatio and Victoria. Albert was contemptuous of the whole family, as if someone of his station could not possibly mix with a family that was so far beneath him. What Beth thought of Albert consisted of a stunning variety of country epithets, mostly animalistic which she expressed to her husband. On getting home, Victoria went to her bedroom, unable to make out why her husband was changing so much but determined to keep up with her brother and to make her children like their cousins too, not an easy task.

A weary Captain Alec MacPherson was dozing on the train from Euston to Aberdeen trying to recover from the experience of his ship from Bombay ploughing through a dreadful storm in the Bay of Biscay, arriving at Southampton with more surface damage than had ever been seen on a troopship.

It was not a journey he wanted to make. After his unenviable task in Aberdeen he would stay with his parents in Edinburgh and spend time with his sister Jeane before returning to his wife Cecily and his tea plantation near Darjeeling. He had been obliged to return from India to regimental headquarters to formally resign his commission, and his journey had been unnecessarily delayed, as he thought, by various administrative tasks he had been set.

The morning after his arrival, he called on Colonel Duncan Urchadan at the Gordons' Barracks in Aberdeen to begin the process. As he walked across the Square, he remembered that Urchadan was somehow related to his friend Malcolm, but he could not work out the connection.

"Come in, MacPherson, I am pleased to see you but I have your recent letter in front of me which surprised and disappointed me in equal measure. You have proved an excellent officer, so I am saddened by your decision to abandon us to whom you owe a great deal. Please explain."

Alec stood nervously in front of the Colonel's desk after their salutes.

"This was not an easy decision as my conscience was troubled by the debt I owe to the Regiment. I enjoyed the military life greatly in India, but after I was moved from the North-West Frontier to Delhi and Simla, there was an unending round of social life without much military activity. However I met my wife Cecily there, born in India, and her father is a tea-planter in the Darjeeling area, a strange man who keeps two elephants. As a result of my marriage, I decided to acquire a tea plantation a short distance from his, and saw that would involve my resigning my commission, although I did not realize that would demand returning to Aberdeen to complete the process."

"I cannot stop you, of course, Macpherson. However, Britain is a mighty growing empire, and she must be able to marshal large numbers of troops to any country in her colonies if she is to protect her wealth. The Regiment cannot afford to lose officers of your quality. It is a blow for us too when officers like Malcolm Gargery or Tom Hesketh get wounded badly enough to make combat duties impossible."

"Yes, I heard about them."

"Tom had lost a leg. As an intensely active man, sitting here in Aberdeen behind a desk is not his forte and I expect his resignation at any time soon. Malcolm lost an eye, but he is in South Africa in a liaison role as he lived in South Africa as a young man."

"That must be hard on his wife and children, Colonel."

"No, I heard that she is taking the family, lock, stock and barrel to live there if that is the right phrase to describe a splendid family," and they both smiled.

"To return to my situation," Alec continued, unnerved by not being asked to sit down, "I have found this a difficult decision. To be frank, I joined the Regiment more with a sense of adventure and as a relief from my dissolute life than with a strong sense of duty to Queen and Country. I do believe that my investment of my assets in this plantation and my attachment to my dear wife is the direction for my life. But I do feel pangs of conscience about my decision."

"I am not interested in your damn conscience. I see no reason to go further with this discussion. I am a busy man," said Urchadan reaching in his desk drawer for a prepared document indicating Captain Alec MacPherson's resignation from his commission as an officer of the Gordon Highlanders. Duncan inserted the date, August 15th, 1896.

"Sign this: I will witness it. Collect any belongings you have left here and, unlike those who reach a retirement age, you should not henceforth use your military title."

They shook hands and wished each other well. Mr. Alec McPherson left the Barracks and hurried to the station for a train to Edinburgh.

The mid-year meeting of the Board of the Jaggers Trust for the Relief and Education of the Poor planned for early June was postponed to September. Once again it turned out to be interesting but inconclusive. Before the meeting began, expressions of relief, thanks and good wishes for his recovery surrounded Pip.

After Clarence started the meeting, Pip began: "Lady and gentlemen, I need not rehearse the circumstance of Mr. O'Sullivan's murder or of the assault on me. Clearly we could continue our present plans, that is, to build a self-supporting community of our tenants. However, we wonder whether the astounding turbulence of Irish affairs is not best left to the politicians for when anyone tries to contribute to the solution of Ireland's problems, there is always more turbulence. Nonetheless we have some alternatives to suggest.

"The first is that we simply pay the passages of tenants who want to emigrate, no doubt with a small amount, and offer what land is left to be divided among those who remain. I gather that Lord Palmerston paid for the villagers on his estate in County Cork to emigrate to New York, so we have a fine example. If that was acceptable, we might then pay the remaining tenants to plant trees all over the estate, perhaps even including the vacated land, the object being to restore a part of the forest which once graced that land. In addition, we might quietly arm those who remain for their own protection with revolvers at least and perhaps rifles as well against those members of the other community who would destroy them.

"Arming them could sound like treason," noted Aaron, "I am sure it would be seen as such in Irish courts, dominated as they are by the Anglo-Irish, though I do not think there are laws against having arms. That would need investigation, but they are probably forbidden to Catholics."

"Forests don't grow overnight, you know," said Clarence, "my father planted a hundred trees thirty years ago and they are no more than six feet high now. I'd be sure they'd be destroyed long before they matured."

"The idea of paying them to emigrate seems sound to me, but I am not sure whether we can be confident that would be within the Trust's legal charge."

"I suppose that might be contained within the idea of relief, Aaron," said Pip, "but I think the more important question is this: Given the context of the ferocity of politics about Ireland here in England and across the Irish Sea in the four provinces, is whatever we do the right thing to do?"

"A question going right to the heart of the matter. Nothing seems to get anywhere with the politics," said Adam, "so an initiative like ours, whatever it is, would be valuable."

"I am torn," said Harriet. "I must confess first that I disliked the country and the people intensely in the few days I was there. As a woman everyone

28

seemed to me uncouth whether they were rich or poor. It was as if their cultural and religious animosities have degraded them all; as if hatred were the dominant human sentiment across the land, certainly not love. We should intensify our work here in England. Ireland is a distraction to the work of the Trust."

"I appreciate that sentiment, Harriet, what a pity it is that Malcolm and Clara are not here to advise us," murmured Clarence.

"While my attendance at the Board has not been exemplary, do we know why they chose not to attend?" said Albert apologetically.

"Albert, you must have missed it. Malcolm has a new posting in South Africa."

"Oh, goodness me, I had completely forgotten that, so my apologies to them as well."

At that moment, Hamish and Mary arrived.

"I am sorry," said Clarence with a smile, "I have been derelict in my reporting to you that our friend Mr. Justice MacDonald would be delayed by court business but he insisted that Lady MacDonald and he attend."

"Thank you, in fact Mary and I have timed our arrival at the right time as I see the meeting is ready to adjourn to The Cheshire Cheese."

As the laughter subsided, Clarence suggested an extraordinary meeting two weeks hence to determine a precise course of action with regard to the Clumber Estate and to hear of progress in the Trust's other activities. He promised to brief Hamish over lunch, frustrated as he was at the Board's inability to decide what to do.

"How is your business these days, Albert?" asked Mary as lunch was concluded, without attempting to disguise her prying.

"The Walthamslow firm I inherited goes along under its own steam as the managers are simply excellent, loyal, efficient and well-paid. I recently bought a timber merchant's business in Chatham which demands my attention, but it means we can live at Numquam."

"Oh, really, that delightful house of Estella's near the marshes?"

"Yes, indeed. I love it and oddly the house itself has put behind it those terrible events, the murder of Estella's mother in the garden and the vicious assaults on my mother-in-law Nellie by that recruiting sergeant in the dining-room."

"Yes it is a strange thing, is it not, Albert, a house can seem, so to speak, as if its inhabitants are merely tenants, helping it live through to those who follow. I liked the house immensely too, and I also remember a delightful time with

Estella's League of Women, and how the joy of that occasion was annihilated by the news of Jude Brandram's drowning. Poor Honora, his mother."

"Talking of sons, Mary, what happened to your son, James?"

"James? He met an American lady when he was studying at Edinburgh and they went off to America with some fancy idea about going round the world. He sends us cards and letters from wherever he is. I did not realize I had bred a nomad, but if you encourage your child to be independent, you should not then be surprised by his or her choices."

"I admire that greatly for that is exactly what Estella and my father gave me."

"Yes, but you were near enough to visit Old Pip and Estella regularly. I have no wish to spend any time of my life on an ocean liner to visit him. Life is too short."

Hannah rushed from the dining room to the tiny room upstairs at the front of the house where her husband Tom was sitting gazing at the River Dee, "Tom, Tom," she said entering the room breathless, shaking a letter, "Clara is going to South Africa with her three children when her baby is born in the Autumn."

"Good Lord. Lucky old Malcolm, I'd say."

"But is it not very dangerous down there?"

"I am sure Malcolm will make sure they are safe. There is peace at the moment, though how long it will last will depend on the Boers."

"It all seems quite mad to me."

"Like Clara, you must not upset your dear self in your condition. You've been having a hard time with your aches and pain, and there is still four months before we name our own baby."

She stood beside him, kissing his forehead gently.

"I do envy Malcolm you know," he said, "the loss of an eye would not incapacitate him from action in principle or in fact whereas losing my leg has made me simply an encumbrance for the Regiment. Everyone is very kind, of course, but I was a soldier, a man of combat, whereas now I fight only with paper and ink."

"Darling, I know. I have been more than content to stop pursuing medicine to share a life with you. But I wonder whether we should not find some other way for you to exercise your talent."

"I think of that all the time. I do some instructing of officers but it does not tax my energy or my imagination."

"I had a long letter the other day from my father mainly worrying about my pregnancy, I suppose losing my brother Lachlan and then my mother makes him very nervous about my condition."

"I am not surprised as he loves you dearly."

"Have I told you about Clara's inheritance and, indeed about the Jaggers Trust?"

"You have indeed: Their Irish adventure seems a complete mess from what you have said."

"My father is also very perplexed about what the Trust should do, enhanced by his injuries there and the murder of the tenant. I wondered if you might find philanthropic work of interest."

"I must give that some thought. I suppose I could resign my commission and we could start some ventures here in Scotland, although the Irish situation is an interesting one, certainly."

"Let's go down to London for a week and talk with my father and the others about the possibilities."

"I'd like that."

After messages had been exchanged between Aberdeen and Chiswick, Tom and Hannah arrived for lunch after an overnight train journey in a carriage which contained compartments set out as bedrooms, a novelty they much enjoyed, though Tom's sleep was fitful, as always. Like many an amputee, in his dreams he would be riding a horse, rushing down a hillside, loving his wife, walking toward the mess for dinner, always on two legs.

When the Heskeths arrived, Harriet and Hannah embraced cordially as if there had never been the ructions which had emerged when the Gargerys returned from Africa, much to the surprise of Pip in particular. All that now seemed buried, as they sat down for lunch. After various conversations, including shared delight at the knowledge of Hannah's baby to be, Tom launched the conversation about his future.

"I was in the service of my Regiment, but my incapacity makes it impossible for me to do more than work at a desk and do some instructing work of young officers. It was an empty sort of life for me who enjoyed combat as a soldier. I could not expect promotion, of course, and even if it came my way, it would be gratuitous."

31

"I can understand. It took me some months, even years, when I returned from the Crimea to come to terms with my gammy leg and discover that I could still preach. Indeed, some people saw me as a hero, which I was not, but it encouraged them to hear what I had to say. Otherwise I would been ignored."

"I do not believe that, Pip," said Tom, almost as an aside, "but Hannah has told me of the situation the Trust has inherited in Ireland."

"It was Clara's heritage. The Trust bought it from her."

"Yes, and I am wondering whether I might resign my commission for philanthropic work and perhaps the Trust would employ me on some appropriate project."

"My dear Tom," said Pip with delight, "that is such a splendid offer, and I am sure the Board would welcome your participation with open arms. As a matter of fact, we have a meeting later this week to assess, once again, where we are with the Clumber responsibility. I will write a note to Clarence Smythe, our chairman, to ensure you are invited."

"Marvelous. Your Irish situation fascinates me, I suppose, because it seems on the cusp of serious combat and demands a strategic approach. I'd love to conduct an in-depth analysis of the problem, but I suspect you have already done that."

"How interesting, and no, we have not done that. We have jumped from idea to idea but been moved by events as much as plans. Perhaps you and I can take some time this afternoon on the full details so that you can think about the possibilities before the Board meets."

"You will not need me, will you," said Harriet, "as I thought Hannah and I might visit Oxford Street to examine the shops for items in respect of this forthcoming child, and of course, to look at clothes that will be useful to her over the next months."

"I would love to do that," said Hannah, "the shops in Aberdeen are fiercely Scottish, and the emporia in London will have much wider choices."

III

A flurry of telegrams between London and Port Elizabeth announced the arrival on August 10th of Susanna Eleanor, Clara and Malcolm Gargery's second child, with names which had been determined before Malcolm left for South Africa. Her birth facilitated decisions about his family so that Malcolm was excited by the later message that the family would travel on the SS Hawarden Castle arriving on September 21st in East London, not Port Elizabeth, both growing towns on the Indian Ocean. On receipt of this latest wire, Malcolm rushed down to the port to check the day and time that the ship would leave Tilbury and the time of its arrival. As he left the telegraph office, it dawned on him that she had bought six passages not five, presumably that meant she was bringing Matilda.

Malcolm booked himself into a hotel near the docks for the night of September 20th, and as he had been told the ship would arrive overnight, he booked sufficient accommodation for six on the train which departed at noon for Port Elizabeth, to arrive there in the late afternoon. He hardly slept but read a little book called Plain Tales from the Indian Hills by a man called Kipling that one of his colleagues thought he might enjoy as he had been in India. He arose early and hastened to the docks.

He scanned the gangplanks at either end of the ship as it docked, catching sight of Clara carrying Susanna, and George, Alice and Andrew holding hands as they carefully threaded their way off the ship. Pushing through the crowd, he managed to get close to his family as they reached the end of the gangplank. Anxious not to block the path of other passengers, he hurried them all back from the ship, reaching out to hold their hands before embracing them.

"Oh, my darling," he cried, throwing his arms around Clara, cooing at the baby in her arms.

"How wonderful to be here," she said, clasping him tight.

He picked up Alice first, then each of the boys in turn, kissing them all fervently.

"Malcolm, meet your daughter Susanna Eleanor," said Clara, "but the children think we should add Elizabeth to her name as we are coming to Port Elizabeth."

"Splendid. I agree. First things first, I must get porters for your luggage. Our train to Port Elizabeth leaves at noon. But wait, I thought you would be six."

"Yes, Matilda is with us. She is overseeing the baggage for us but will be down as soon as that appears. My goodness, darling Malcolm, you look so well."

"This sunshine is such a boon, windy though it is by the sea. You will adore the climate, my dear. I have not yet swum in the ocean but the children will love the beaches."

"Where will we live? Have you booked rooms in a hotel?"

"No, I have a surprise for you."

"A house?"

"Yes, and I think you will make it quite lovely."

Much later that evening, the cart arrived at number 7 Clyde Street with Matilda and all the copious amounts of luggage Clara had brought with her. To say the new arrivals were ecstatic about the house would be an understatement, for three of the children had their own rooms contrary to their expectations, and Clara's bedroom was large with a splendid rear view toward the port.

"You're a genius, my dear, quite simply a genius. We will have a delightful time here. I have brought furniture in the ship's hold so it will be here directly."

"How did you manage all that as you left so quickly? No matter, I want you to meet Mrs. Makepeace the owner who lives at number 14. She has been here most of her life and her grandfather built this house and her father completed it. They used the only models they knew, so the house seems to be a copy of houses they knew of in Bury St. Edmunds. I have yet to find more staff, a cook for instance, so we can eat at the Cecil Tavern, presumably named after Rhodes and Mrs. M. said she would help you with that. You can decide about the servants she hired for me. The food here is excellent, if simple, but how is everyone at home?"

"Five weeks ago, goodness me, did it take that long? I saw your father and Harriet. They had a letter from Hannah saying that Tom and she might be coming to London to stay. Perhaps you didn't know she is pregnant."

"Yes she has written to tell me that and another Gargery will do no one any harm," and they both laughed, "but I know my father will worry himself sick till the baby is born."

"I am sure he will, but they also said they thought Tom was losing interest in the Regiment and might think about other avenues for his talent."

"Good show. He's a fine fellow, wasted at a desk in Aberdeen."

Later that week Malcolm and Clara visited Mrs. Makepeace who was delighted to welcome a woman of such class to her home.

"The fact is," said Mrs. Makepeace, "that fellow Rhodes has attracted to South Africa a bunch of n'er-do-wells, criminals and gold-seekers, whereas in my young days we were all farmers, most of us unable to find good work in the old country. The Boers call these riff-raff uitlanders, but now they are up to no good, I fear. So, my dear, I am glad to see more military men arriving."

"I assume you find development here not to your liking then?"

"To be honest, I wish we were not arguing with the Boers. They have their own territory and want to be left alone with their farming and their religion and that damn man Rhodes with his mines and railways has offended the Boers and encouraged London to send the army to support his wealth."

"Do you think that's the case, Malcolm?" Asked Clara.

"I think Mrs. Makepeace is largely correct. I saw just how grasping these uitlanders, as the Boers called them, were for gold and riches. That gave Rhodes power and influence. Now it is not my place to ignore the Empire's desire for more colonies, or to protect those they have."

"Oh dear, I hope I have not brought our young family into a war arena," said Clara.

"No, darling, even if there is fighting, it won't take place here."

"We need advice on another matter, Mrs. M.," said Malcolm, "I have been told by my commanding officer that we should get a dog as a pet for the children certainly, but also for protection. Do you have views on the matter?"

"I have given up keeping a dog, too much trouble for an old woman, though I suppose it would be a companion."

"My Colonel has a large dog with a ridge down its back."

"Ah, yes, superb animals. An old friend of mine outside the town breeds them. I can put you in touch with her when you are ready."

As they left, Clara said, "why the sudden interest in a dog?"

"We do not know this town, Clara, and a dog can be of service for protection as well as a distraction for the children."

"We've only had dogs in the country, never in town, though one does see them in Hyde Park from time to time."

"When we are more settled, we should take up Mrs. M's offer."

Within a month after her arrival, with Mrs. Makepeace's advice, Clara had kept the staff, added a third maid and a Xhosa cook with a name that was unpronounceable to the English ear and voice, so Clara and she agreed on Marjorie.

"Why did you choose that name?" Asked Malcolm. "I suppose it is alright as she won't be Marjorie Gargery which would be a mouthful."

Clara laughed heartily and said:

"I only hope Marjorie and I reach an understanding. I understood English servants, but Marjorie will be a challenge."

The furniture began to appear from the ship the day after their arrival, so accommodation in the Tavern was only needed for a night. Clara had guessed Malcolm would find a suitable house for couches, beds and bureaus, desks and bookshelves, all of which had been finally extracted from the hold of the ship and brought to Number 7 Clyde Street, a home soon alive with the sounds of a happy healthy family and that special joy which excites those engaged in new adventures.

Whistling a country dance song to himself as the sun was rising, Bill Youngman rode quietly up the lane on his elderly nag toward Numquam House with the newspapers, now delivered from London on train overnight. The beautiful gates made by Horatio's father Fletch opened at a touch. The drive was perhaps one hundred yards long and on the left halfway to the house stood the old elm tree, an unusual sight for the marshland area, with rhododendron bushes in a line up to the house shielding it from the lane which curled around behind it.

Once past the elm, on the left a grass lawn extended up to the gravel area in front of the house. From the front of the house the rose garden with its extensive arbors were notable too for the stone memorial to Mollie, Estella's mother. Estella had never regarded Miss Havisham as a mother, just a guardian and she had met her natural mother by accident and they began to live together, but Mollie's dark and miserable past caught up with her and she was murdered in that rose garden at the entrance to the orchard, with its apple, plum and cherry trees.

To the rear of the house were the stables and various other small outbuildings. It was a substantial property which Albert had enjoyed most of his young life as

Estella was his step-mother but he now saw the house as an appropriate dwelling for a successful man of business. He was not a man to dwell on the past.

On the dining room table an hour or so after Bill had left, the September 15th copy of the Telegraph lay awaiting the perusal of Albert Pirrip, timber merchant, of Chatham in the county of Kent. His wife Victoria was at breakfast and she greeted her husband as she had done daily since their marriage:

"Morning my love, how was your night?"

He replied with his own morning greeting which had become more formal since his self-elevation to prosperous businessman:

"Very satisfactory thank you, my dear."

Victoria gazed at her husband during breakfast, still troubled by the person he was becoming. She saw not the beautiful young man of their early meeting but now the successful gentleman of trade, slightly corpulent, his face betraying a fleshiness which was a sign of aging. He had recently returned to drinking coffee with his breakfast rather than Indian tea which used to be his staple. Coffee reminded him of the intense life of French cafes where painters would sit for hours drinking wine or absinthe meliorated by the calming effects of the nut of the arabica cherry.

He had almost finished his breakfast when he turned to the obituary columns which daily lent him a sense of gratitude that his name was not amongst those whose life was recorded in descriptions of their careers. To his surprise, there was an obituary on Timothy Egerton who, as he remembered with some regret, had married the loving partner of his adolescence, then the beautiful Elizabeth Fitzroy.

He was equally surprised to see that Timothy had taken his own life, though no details were recorded. Rather the obituary itemized a sparkling career, with the expectation that he would have soon been appointed to one of the jewels of the British Embassies.

"Darling, you will recall my telling you of my youthful engagement with Elizabeth, she who was a Fitzroy."

"Did not her father die in Greece?"

"That's right. I met him in in Paris, but the newspaper is recording the death by suicide of her husband Timothy Egerton who must have been bound for greater things in British diplomacy."

"That is simply awful, Albert. Just imagine. She is only your age, probably with children, and now bereft."

"Indeed, would you be upset if I went to his funeral? I feel that the past that we had makes it incumbent on me to express my condolences in person rather than by letter," and he realized that asking her permission rather than just telling her they would both go was an indicator of the state of their marriage, though he could not tell precisely now that state might be described.

"Of course, my dear. I am sure she would appreciate that gesture and you might discover more about the man."

"That is generous of you. I wonder whether this death has anything to do with a young English diplomat who was suspected of treason when we were at an Embassy reception with my stepmother and her friend."

"What was that?" said Victoria wondering vaguely why she was being so generous, since she was as confused as her husband about the state of their marriage.

"Did I not tell you?"

"I don't think so."

"Elizabeth and I were summoned from the Embassy Garden during a large party to meet the Ambassador and we were asked for details of a man's behavior which we happened to have overheard. He was obviously communicating information to a notorious gossip and spy, a large boisterous lady as I recall. I don't know what happened to him in the end. Anyway, the funeral is at St. John's, Smith Square tomorrow at noon."

"You should go, my dear. You will be able to go there and back in a day," she said, consciously assuming that this re-acquaintance carried no implications for her marriage.

The churchyard was packed with all manner of men who looked like civil servants. Their wives appeared long-suffering from being espoused severally to a cadre of men whose chosen work was now the result of intense competition, not the nepotism of former years. Albert noticed one or two men who were obviously French civil servants, but also John Sargent was in the congregation though he hurried away after the service. There was also a group of elegant Frenchmen and their ladies too whom he thought must be Jewish.

He had arrived early in a cab, watching these crowds and he lingered outside on the church steps as the cortege arrived, led by Elizabeth, her two boys, Henry and Oliver, and her daughter, Charlotte. Elizabeth did not seem too downcast but looking around her as she walked slowly up the steps with her children behind the coffin. She caught Albert's eye and nodded in recognition without smiling.

Sir Henry Stewart Arbuthnot, Under-Secretary at the Foreign Office, read a rather long eulogy which was merely a record of his service without much attention to the man's character. The occasion felt perfunctory to Albert's mind because the mourners from the Foreign Office were keen to get to their next meeting, or more generously, because they hoped Timothy's suicide would not cast too long a shadow over the work at this high office of state.

As the service ended, Albert slipped outside hoping that he could grab a word with Elizabeth and, as the coffin with its six pallbearers passed him, she stopped and turned to him as, saying: "Ride with me to Highgate." To his great astonishment, she added, "I need to talk with you. I have asked my children to accompany Timothy's parents as they are so distressed."

As he walked alongside her down the short path to her carriage, the guilt of his infidelity in Paris was uppermost in his mind. No wonder their relationship had broken up after his behavior. The hearse led by two black horses with their traditional plumes started off as Albert held Elizabeth's hand to help her into the carriage.

"This such a surprise to see you, Albert, but I am so grateful as I hope I can trust you whatever happened in the past. I must say I have not spent any time in my marriage with regret for our rupture."

"My dear Elizabeth; I too am happily married."

"That at least is a blessing for you."

"I am so sorry at Timothy's death, especially as you have the children to care for and his death was such that it creates its own mysteries."

"No, it does not, in fact I am surprised it did not occur earlier."

The carriage rattled along the cobbled streets past King's Cross on its way to the cemetery and up the hill to Highgate.

"What do you mean?"

"There is nobody I can share this knowledge with and I did not know how I was going to able to cope. And then you appeared."

"This must be some awful secret."

"It is. I believe that Timothy had been inveigled into some treasonous activity, not out of any commitment to some idea or other I might add, perhaps because he found it exciting, or so I thought. We certainly did not need money."

"What was this activity?"

"I don't really know, but six weeks ago, indeed since he started back in London in this senior position, he has been buried in work. Recently he returned from a diplomatic mission to St. Petersburg to meet the Crown Prince and then to Constantinople where he talked with the Grand Vizier. After that he became increasingly morose but he had already begun to drink copious amounts of brandy of an evening."

"Oh my goodness, he must have been in great distress."

"No one knew about this. He went to work with the same countenance and attitudes as was his custom. That simply disintegrated when he walked through the door of an evening. He was profoundly intoxicated when we went to bed. He seemed to have fallen asleep one night last week, but he turned over and in a trembling voice, slurring over his words, he said that he thought he had found out something that put him in great danger. I asked him what he had discovered, and frankly I had become very angry at his drunkenness quite apart from his risking a catastrophe for all of us."

"Did he enlighten you?"

"No, he cried himself to sleep. I could not rest at all and when I asked him about it the following day, he said he must have been drunk and I was to ignore it. I knew, of course, he was dissembling. I really cannot believe he committed treason, but it seems the only explanation for his suicide," at which remark Albert was silent as he did not know the man.

As the hearse and the various carriages arrived at the cemetery gates, she said,

"I would have wanted him to be buried in the family grave in Dorset as a churchyard grave but that is nigh impossible after his apparent suicide. His brother and sister will be coming here after the burial, I am sure, but please ride back to the house with me. I really cannot stomach a reception, so one has not been arranged and I am sure friends will understand. This committal will not take long."

Indeed, it was soon over and within the hour the carriage finally arrived at a splendid house in Eaton Square, the Egerton's home. Albert was just taking his leave at the door when two men came up to Elizabeth and he heard one of them say:

"Mrs. Egerton, we are from Scotland Yard. This is Detective-Inspector Monroe and I am Chief Inspector Strayman. We have avoided talking with you until your husband was buried but we do now need to talk with you about him."

"Of course, may my friend Albert Pirrip accompany me?"

"Did he know your husband?

"No, Mrs. Egerton and I knew each other long ago in Paris and we have just renewed our acquaintance."

"Then I don't think you will have anything to contribute, sir," said Monroe with a steely glare, "and we need to talk with Mrs. Egerton in private."

"Goodbye then, Albert," said Elizabeth, "please be sure to keep in touch."

"Indeed, I will."

Elizabeth showed the two policemen into her drawing-room and asked her maid to bring in tea. She was somewhat forlorn in her black dress, but after taking off her hat and veil, there was revealed to the men a woman of great beauty.

Inspector Strayman began the conversation:

"We are here, Mrs. Egerton, to conduct follow-up enquiries on the death of your husband. The Foreign Office is anxious that we pursue rigorously the circumstances of his death so that the Diplomatic Service can be assured that his decision was in no way influenced by affairs of state or other matters in which he might have been implicated either by intention or not. Please forgive us if our questions seem impertinent."

"Inspector, I am as anxious as the Foreign Office to find out why Timothy decided to end his life, so I will anticipate difficult questions. You are probably aware that my father was a diplomat in Paris and Athens so I do know something of the work of diplomats."

"We were not told that by the Under-Secretary, but that is valuable to know."

"First," Monroe asked, "were your relationships with your husband good? Might there be any semblance of a cause for his decision located in his marriage to you?"

"Good gracious," and she laughed, "I see what you mean by impertinent! No, I have been profoundly fortunate in a mutual loving marriage, and I am sure any of our friends would confirm that. I know Timothy would agree, if he were here," and she turned away for a moment to hide her discomfort.

"Recently, however, had he changed in any way?"

"Ah, yes indeed, and it was a source of great concern to me. When he returned from a diplomatic visit two months ago, he began drinking, heavily at times, which was quite unlike him. Indeed, before those visits he was a sober as a judge. He seemed fine in the mornings after his drinking at night. He left for King Charles Street with his usual insouciance, but when he walked through the door of an evening, he went immediately to the decanter and by dinner-time he was intoxicated."

"Did you ask him why he was engaging in this uncharacteristic behavior?"

"Of course, each evening."

"And he never responded?"

"No, except that one night in bed he turned to me, still drunk, and said he was ruined."

"Nothing more?"

"No, he just turned over and slept."

"So you are confident that he did not take his own life for any conceivable domestic reason and that his remark about ruin must therefore apply to his work as a diplomat."

"Absolutely."

"Now," said Strayman, "this request is a further intrusion on your privacy, but please bear with us."

"Go on."

"We have searched his office in Westminster and we would like permission to search his study here if we may."

"Of course. I should say that from time to time he would say just how valuable it was to be able to leave his work behind him when he was at home, except of course when there was any emergency and he would bring home his valise with papers which he worked on in his study and then take them back the following morning."

"Please show us to his study."

Elizabeth got up from her chair asking the men to follow her, and they walked across the hall to a library at the front of the house, the walls lined with books all expensively bound and ordered. The desk was small, but almost bare apart from a photograph of Elizabeth on the desk. There were two large comfortable armchairs and on small tables and on the walls were family portraits, many being photographs in the modern idiom. One or two objects betrayed his diplomatic assignments, but the room seemed to the police not to hold anything beyond their expectations.

"Mrs. Egerton, is there a safe in this room?"

"Of course, Mr. Monroe, let me show you."

She went to the desk, opened the right-hand top drawer and took out a small key. Moving to the wall beside the fireplace, she took down a portrait of her mother to reveal a small safe built into the wall and then handed the key to Strayman.

"It contains money and a variety of significant family documents, and I am sure there is a copy of his will in there and probably mine too. But I will leave you to your search."

"Not yet," said Strayman, "we want you to witness our emptying the safe."

Elizabeth stood to one side as Strayman opened the safe slowly to reveal a small strong box and a large bunch of papers. The strong box was not locked and, on opening, it revealed family papers including wills and a box with collection of sovereigns, half-sovereigns, guineas and several five-pound notes as well as currency from several countries including Russia and Turkey which Monroe laid out on the desk.

"We kept household cash in that box for paying the cook and other servants or for reimbursement for those who purchased things for us, as the gardener does with plants."

"So you were accustomed to use the safe?"

"Indeed, I was constantly using it for the household, probably far more than my husband."

Most of the papers Strayman pulled from the safe after that concerned family business, title to the house, birth certificates, wedding certificates, various stock certificates, newspaper cuttings of family events, the bric-a-brac of a household's significant documents.

Underneath them was a manilla folder, labeled 'Top Secret' in an unruly hand, containing documents which seemed to be diplomatic to Strayman and he glanced at Monroe with the inquisitive look familiar to those in his profession.

"Thank you, Mrs. Egerton, we will take these papers with us as they seem to be the property of Her Majesty's Government. Their significance is not for us to determine and they may be inconsequential."

"I have no need of them, to be sure, so do I need to stay? I am extremely tired after this morning and need to rest. Roberta will show you out when you are finished."

"That will be fine, Mrs. Egerton, we do need to examine the contents of the desk."

She left in somber mood and walked upstairs to her bedroom. What on earth could he have got himself into was the main question running around in her mind as she lay down.

"Mamma," said Charlotte, rushing into her room, "there are two men rummaging around in Father's study."

"I know, darling. They are men from your father's work who are retrieving any documents which are connected to the Foreign Office, probably to hand on to whoever will be taking up his position."

"Are they policemen?"

"Probably, as your father was an important man at the Foreign Office."

"That's all right, then."

She clambered up on to the bed and Elizabeth held her tightly, wanting to weep but unable to do so.

When she awoke around dawn the next morning, she felt utterly exhausted and lay in bed for a long time pondering the situation. The inevitable speed of events had overwhelmed her. It was just over a week since the news of Timothy's suicide had been brought to her by his senior whom she knew only by reputation. She got up hurriedly deciding to talk with her eldest son, Henry who was about to return to Cambridge for the Michaelmas term, and after completing her somewhat elaborate toilet and a small breakfast, she called him down from his room where he was preparing for examinations.

"Mamma, we have suffered this terrible misfortune. Suicide brings out all the darkest suspicions in people. A College Fellow killed himself last year, drowning himself in the Cam and it raised many a speculation as to why."

"I fear so. I am sure many a soul is thinking my marriage was on the rocks whereas nothing could be further from the truth."

"I know, I know. There will be some who believe he was secretly homosexual, like the don I mentioned, and we all know that would be patent nonsense. My father was an extremely attractive man and you were like a god and goddess together to us children."

"Thank you, darling Henry, those two speculations are very wide of the mark."

"Another favorite of the gossips will be that he had a debilitating illness obviously contracted through working in uncivilized countries like the Ottoman Empire but there were no signs of that, were there? Only one possibility that I can conjecture might gain some currency."

"What is that?"

"That he did not commit suicide but was murdered by government interests or at the behest of a foreign power. Might he have betrayed them, or have been in their sway?"

"They have told me firmly that it was suicide, Henry, but I have racked my brains to understand why."

"Have they yet told you how? Was it poison or a self-inflicted wound of some kind?"

"No, no. Oh dear, why not? I try to stop thinking about it, which is horrendously difficult. At this moment, I feel betrayed by him and by the Government."

"You do have friends, of course, but I am very pleased that you feel able to talk with me, especially at such a time. The loss is such that I feel I have suddenly become an adult."

"Darling, I would not confide in anyone else, though I have had some discussion with Albert Pirrip whom I was very close to years ago in Paris, a relationship killed by his infidelity."

Relieved by talking with her son, she sat in a chair in Timothy's study after a quiet lunch.

Whatever the thoughts of others, what did she feel? That it was inexplicable, but it could not be. Apart from his recent aberration with strong drink, she thought, he had never seemed in any way out of sorts. People do not kill themselves for no reason. In this chaotic aftermath and prompted by Henry she wondered more seriously as to how he had actually done it. Then floods of remorse overwhelmed her that she had not been able to comfort him but had been angry at his drunkenness.

Suddenly she started up from the chair.

Perhaps indeed Henry was right. Perhaps he was murdered.

Perhaps the killer was protected because Timothy was in such a high office.

Perhaps it was announced as suicide to protect someone.

"I must get advice from lawyers," she said to herself out loud as she walked into the hall, "Emma's husband Clarence drew up our wills so I must see him directly."

"Ever so sorry, ma'am, were you callin' me?" Called out a maid's voice.

"No, Roberta," and she stopped there, seeing no reason to explain anything to her staff.

Elizabeth had just finished dressing and was walking down the stairs to prepare to leave to try and see Sir Clarence Smythe when Mr. Sargent was announced.

"I must apologize profusely for not letting you know I would call, and I am simply overwhelmed at your husband's death, Mrs. Egerton, and I wanted to express in person my profound sorrow. Manifestly his death has forestalled your coming to my studio to complete the portrait, but I am obviously going to find it difficult to do that while you are in mourning."

"Thank you, I appreciate that and of course you must come when you feel able. I suppose I may look a little different than I did on your sketches."

"Since you mention it, I am anxious that we wait a little while, how can I put this without being indelicate or impertinent, oh dear..."

"I know exactly what you mean, Mr. Sargent, until I am over my grief, is that it?"

"Yes, well, you now look quite different from the lady of my sketches. I am reluctant to complete the painting as if nothing had happened to you. Yet I am also not keen to paint your face in your grief."

"No indeed, we hardly want a painting of a grieving woman staring down at the dinner table."

"May I suggest, then, that I put the canvas and the sketches away for a while, perhaps a year, but until you feel ready for it to be completed."

"Have far have you got?"

"Oh dear, it is virtually complete. I had a little trouble with the way the music sat on your lap and that would have been the major task. The head and shoulders is complete."

"Then you must keep it like that, just as Timothy would have wanted. I will come to your studio soon and bring some music for you to complete the portrait."

"You are so brave, Mrs. Egerton. I feel quite strongly that it is some of my best work and I believe that your husband would have been delighted."

IV

Albert was especially perplexed about how Elizabeth might respond to such a tragedy. After a week or so, he decided to call on Mary MacDonald who had been close friends with Estella his stepmother and with Charlotte Mudge, Elizabeth's aunt years ago. He had seen her recently at the Board meeting where they briefly discussed his business.

She was pleased to have a visitor and welcomed him into her drawing room.

"Did you see that Timothy Egerton had died?" He asked.

"Forgive me, who is he?"

"You remember my friend Elizabeth, Charlotte Mudge's niece."

"Indeed, was she not your loving partner in Paris? Oh yes, now I remember, Estella told me that you had found other pastures at the time but then married Nellie's daughter Victoria."

"Indeed, but Elizabeth is now in some difficulty."

"Really? How so? I recall just how delightful and beautiful she was."

"To be sure that is true. However, her husband was a diplomat who committed suicide in his office not a fortnight ago.

"How awful. Now then, I do remember reading of that tragedy quite recently, but I did not know it was her husband."

"In the last months after his visits to Russia and Turkey, he apparently became morose, started drinking heavily."

"Dear me, how very sad."

"I was wondering whether you might meet her and take her under your wing if it seemed appropriate?"

"Let me discuss this with my husband. I need to be sure that she is not in any way a party to whatever his malfeasance was, if there was any. From what I know of her I certainly doubt her participation in anything underhand. However, you will appreciate that the wife of a High Court judge cannot do anything that might even have the appearance of evil."

"I do, indeed. I do not believe she would in any way be implicated."

"Nor me. Was Elizabeth not that wonderful pianist?"

"Yes, she was most accomplished: What a memory you have! I know of her circumstances because she insisted I ride with her in her carriage from the funeral to the cemetery and then back to her house as she wished to confide in me as someone who knew her but was not close to her husband."

"I see, so you were gone completely from her life after Paris, not in any way in her social set, but familiar enough to her if she was unable to express her feelings to anyone closer to her."

"You are correct. We had three wonderful years till I smashed our relationship by getting involved with another young woman. After this tragedy, she will be very lonely."

"You clearly have her on your conscience, given your infidelity."

"I suppose so, but, as I was about to leave her the other day, two Scotland Yard Inspectors arrived to ask her some questions."

"Goodness gracious, that does sound suspicious," said Mary. "I will talk to Hamish and let you know."

Pip continued to be very depressed in the early autumn worried about his daughter Hannah's pregnancy and the insoluble Clumber problem which had stalled since O'Sullivan's murder, and Harriet shared that mood, if less intensely.

"I simply cannot overcome this dread at Hannah's pregnancy, mixed with the sheer delight at having another grandchild."

"Look, dear Pip, there is no reason under God's Heaven, as you might say, why she should not give birth as the vast number of women do. I've asked Mary to call this morning as maybe she will have insights into the Clumber problem," and as the bell rang, "there she is now."

"It is so pleasant to see you both again," said Mary later, "I especially wanted to discuss with you the plight of Elizabeth Egerton as well as Clumber."

"Why?" asked Harriet. "Did you know her, Pip?"

"Indeed. She was the niece of Estella's friend Charlotte. But what has happened, Mary?"

"You will know it has been announced that Timothy committed suicide in his room at the Foreign Office. The inquest has not been made public, which is itself enough to arouse suspicion, I must say. Her only confidant has been Albert Pirrip, your namesake's son, Pip, for reasons I find rather odd. Albert has asked me to visit with her as she must be very lonely and he told me what he knew. In recent weeks her husband, always a sober fellow evidently, began to drink unusual amounts of whisky each evening and in a semi-stupor said to Elizabeth that he was ruined. I shared the information with Hamish, but because of his position as a High Court judge, he did not want to have any knowledge and certainly no involvement in the situation."

"That I can understand," said Pip.

"So, I am at a loss as to know how to comfort her when I see her. I will either call later today or tomorrow."

"I am sure you will be of immense comfort, dear Mary," said Harriet.

"The problem is how far I should delve into their marriage. Why did he kill himself? Was it something in their marriage? Albert thinks not, giving his drunken statement about being ruined. But then might he have been murdered? She did not want to see his body, but it seemed as if she was not allowed to, or rather someone in authority convinced her that she should not. If he was murdered, and this is conjecture, could it be the hand of a colleague or a killer at the behest of a foreign government for he has recently been in Russia and the Orient?

"My inclination is to stay away from searching for reasons with her."

"But Harriet, is this not the only way to offer her comfort? Her loneliness is surely wrapped up in contemplation of her husband's death, so mere formal sympathies will be meaningless too."

"Except that she might find comfort in just having someone to talk to and you know me well enough to know that I am very inquisitive," at which Pip and Harriet smiled in recognition.

"My problem is direction," Mary continued. "I could listen, ask questions and offer comfort through such a conversation or I could be more direct, encouraging her to demand explanations and inquiries. Albert told me that police had arrived at her house to question her."

"It is actually simple enough," said Pip. "Was it suicide or was it murder? If so, why on either account? To ascertain which, one would need to know exactly how he died. That may be difficult to establish as the Foreign Office could be very anxious to conceal any of the means that caused his demise."

As they were finishing lunch, they heard a carriage draw up and then a few minutes later, the maid introduced Albert.

"Albert, my dear man," exclaimed Pip, "how good to see you. Mary has told us of her conversations with you about Elizabeth."

After an exchange of greetings, Albert said:

"It is indeed a tragedy for her and her children."

"I am planning to see her today or tomorrow as you suggested, Albert, but if we are to help her, we need to get beyond speculation and to find out first whether it was murder or suicide."

"I had a brief note from her this morning, saying she was soon going to consult Clarence Smythe as he is an MP."

"What an excellent idea," said Harriet. "He has the status to demand from the Foreign Office information on Timothy's death. The very least he could do as an MP would be to table a question to the Prime Minister, making the whole matter public. Is that not so?"

"Oh my goodness," said Mary, "that really is a capital idea. Now I do have advice to offer her as well as comfort."

"Did the Smythes know the Egertons?"

"I don't know, Pip," said Mary. "Hamish and I chatted with Clarence at a Foreign Office reception some months ago, and his wife Emma was there too, but the Egertons were not mentioned."

"Now," said Harriet, "before you leave, Mary, do you have any thoughts about the situation in Ireland, the Clumber Estate, I mean?"

"Yes. After that Board meeting, I think the Trust should sell the estate and be done with it all as it is nothing but a confounded mess."

So much for that, thought Pip.

Elizabeth called at Old Square but Sir Clarence was out of town. That following day, she received a note saying that Sir Clarence Smythe would be pleased to meet with her. He would be in court for the next two days, but Friday the 9th of October would be excellent at any time during the morning. Her nights continued to be fitful, and she seemed very tired and she knew well that women in their mourning attire were usually an object of pity.

On the way she called at Mr. Sargent's studio and was quite stunned. She wept copiously when he took the sheet off the canvas and tears began to flow from his eyes too. It was truly a magnificent portrait and she felt keenly embarrassed at seeing it. She moved to stand close to him, and he put his arms around her shoulders.

"I don't know what to say, John, may I call you John, it is quite wonderful and I am thrilled that I look so content and so happy as it will be a constant reminder of how I used to feel and it will always help me come to terms with Timothy's passing."

"I too am more than delighted that you approve of it. I will have it framed and sent to you if I may."

"Indeed, and in a few months I will have it hung and invite my friends and you to dinner to see it in place."

Leaving the studio, elated at her portrait, she arrived in her carriage at the Old Square chambers to meet Clarence and was shown into his office by Robert Gillingham, the newly promoted Senior Clerk at Courtisone and Jaggers.

"Good morning, Mrs. Egerton. Now your message said you wanted to discuss with me the death of your husband. Was this about his legacy or some other matter?"

"You will not have seen anything in the newspapers about his death then?"

"No, I read about it, but I am puzzled as to what I can do for you," he said as she raised her widow's veil revealing a face of exceptional beauty which he seemed to recall he had seen somewhere before.

"Might I share with you some detail?"

"Please do."

"Timothy and I met when he listened to me playing the piano in the Embassy music room in Paris where my father was a diplomat. We married twenty years ago and we have two boys, one at Cambridge and the other at Eton, and Charlotte is my daughter. In fact Timothy and I attended your wedding when we both returned to London after his junior post in Paris."

"Ah yes, that was a day on which I found concentration difficult, it passed in a blur, and I thought I recognized you. You are a pianist too, to boot. You sound to have had a very romantic life, Mrs. Egerton."

"Yes, I suppose so but through my aunt I also got to know Estella Pirrip and her set."

"You knew Estella as well?" he asked with some astonishment.

"Indeed."

"So you'll know the Sargent portrait of her in the National Gallery."

"Certainly. As Albert was then trying to become a painter, I met John and various other painters in Paris whose names now escape me. However..." and here she refrained from telling of her own portrait.

"Go on."

"A senior official from the Foreign Office called on me last month to say that my husband Timothy had been found dead in his office, apparently it was a case of suicide. They impressed on me the importance of discretion as questions about the suicide of a senior person in such a prestigious Government office should not be allowed to get to the newspapers, an intimation I understood, though the suicide itself was announced which puzzled me as I have been considering the matter recently."

"I see."

"I was not anxious to view his body and indeed I was not allowed to. The Foreign Office people originally insisted that the funeral be very private, with only a couple of Timothy's work colleagues, but then for reasons unknown to me, they changed their minds and it was a grand affair. Two police officers came to talk with me afterwards and they searched his desk and safe and they took away documents which they said were government property."

"What were their names?"

"I think they were Monroe and Strayman."

"Presumably Inspectors or Senior Inspectors?"

"Indeed. Yet was it really suicide, or was he murdered? If suicide, why? It is simply a mystery to me, except that, after his visit to Moscow and Constantinople in June, he began drinking heavily which was not his habit. He did say to me in a stupor that he was in great danger and if it was not stopped he'd be ruined."

"So the Foreign Office merely said it was suicide but did not give you the cause of death. Did you get a death certificate from a coroner?"

"No, I didn't as I assumed that the need for secrecy overrode such detail and I was not informed of the inquest which must have also been a state secret. I have therefore come to seek your advice because you are my MP, though not my lawyer. I would like to pursue the matter with the Foreign Office, but I cannot do so without either legal advice or representation."

"Of course, of course, and as a Member of Parliament, I have other means than the Law to discover how he died and extract an explanation from the Government."

"I can understand the general need for secrecy as I am the daughter of a diplomat, but that is different from being kept in the dark."

"Indeed. I am sure I can dig out much more detail from the Foreign Office on this very curious matter. I know Lord Salisbury quite well though he is not in my party, and I will see what I can get from him first but I will then search around and make some enquiries."

"Thank you, Sir Clarence, thank you. It is a great relief. You will let me know your fee."

"Oh no, Mrs. Egerton, as this seems to be a matter of state, I regard it as my responsibility as an MP, rather than just a lawyer. But may I ask my wife to put your name on our guest list? We like to hold dinner parties regularly."

"I will be in mourning for another two months, but thereafter I would be most pleased."

As she left, he felt quite stunned by her, the color of her eyes, the way she held herself, the delightful movement of her lips. He shook himself and returned to his desk but was unable to get the woman out of his head the rest of the day.

"Robert!" called Clarence walking towards a very distinguished looking man with fashionable whiskers and moustache in the foyer between House of Commons and the House of Lords. Bob Salisbury had been Prime Minister, and though Clarence was a Liberal, they had spent time together, although very little socially. He was now at the Foreign Office.

"Clarence," said Lord Salisbury, "how very good to see you. Were you at Newmarket last week?"

"You know, Bob, I've not been racing since Beresford won the Gold Cup in '94. No time what with the Commons and my law practice."

"I thought of you as the Prince buttonholed me and said he needs to find yet another lawyer. It is possible he will be cited in a divorce case."

"Goodness me, well, I suppose so, but I am not that anxious to raise my profile."

"I won't mention your name then. Is there anything I can do for you?"

"I have been approached by a Mrs. Egerton whom I know only through friends."

"Oh dear, not Egerton's wife."

"Indeed."

"All I can tell you at this juncture is that we are holding an internal enquiry."

"I need more, Bob. The man is dead. Was it suicide or murder? And why has his wife not been permitted to see his body or a death certificate? She is my constituent, you know. What are senior police officers doing nosing around at his home? I am acting primarily as an MP, and I don't want to table a question for the PM. Then speaking as a lawyer, unless there is some overwhelming reason which you must share with me in confidence if it were a matter of national security, I must ask you for more than this on behalf of my client."

"You will know more than I do at the moment, Clarence. I will do this for you, provided I have your complete confidence and that we will decide mutually what Mrs. Egerton is to be told."

"I agree provisionally but it will depend on the content."

"Quite so. I will ask Harry Montague to be in touch. He is Head of Security at the FO."

"Oh, to be sure, I know Harry. We were at Cambridge together, so I can meet him at the Athenaeum. Tell him five o'clock."

"I will."

That evening, Clarence enjoyed the walk from Westminster to the Club. He was actually feeling rather pleased with himself that he had told a peer of the realm, the Marquess of Salisbury no less, to fix an appointment for him. That the noble Lord accepted it was an indication that the Foreign Office was very deeply concerned about the Egerton suicide. However, Harry Montague was standing in the foyer chatting with a man he knew only from his speeches in the Commons when Clarence arrived handing his silk hat and coat with a fur collar to the porter.

"You know Arthur Balfour, don't you Clarence?" Asked Montague.

"I have admired your speeches, sir, though I disagree with most of the content."

"I think that is true of most of you on the other side of the aisle," said Balfour, "especially on this damn entanglement with the Boers. I was telling Bob, he's my uncle you know, that we will never get your party to agree to a common policy."

"Oh, Bob's your uncle? I didn't know."

"Arthur," said Harry, "I need a private word with Clarence if you don't mind."

"Not at all," and Balfour withdrew.

"Clarence, old boy, how good to see you. Uncle Bob tells me you need some information about Egerton," and they smiled with memories of summer evenings in their youth.

"That's right," said Clarence asking a waiter for a whisky as they sat down in large comfortable armchairs in a private corner of the colossal main room of the Club with its ornate chandeliers and gilded ceiling.

"I'll tell you what we know and what we are doing, but, for the moment, we do not want to trouble Mrs. Egerton with what we are discovering."

"Let me say this," said Clarence, "anything to do with national security is safe with me. At the same time, this good woman does need to know about the death of her husband, by suicide she has been told."

"We told her that for national security reasons. In fact, he was murdered."

"What? In his office? How on earth could that happen to a senior government official?"

"Precisely. That is our puzzle."

"We know this. His secretary said that he did not arrive at the office until after lunch. His lunch appointment that day was with a member of the Russian Embassy, Count Igor Chernishevski, who was recalled to Moscow suddenly the day after Timothy's death. That raised our suspicions, though Egerton's reports also suggested a turbulent recent visit to Russia and Asia Minor."

"Good heavens."

"Yes, but the plot thickens, for earlier that morning, he had also met with an attaché at the Embassy of the Ottoman Empire, one Mohamed Yildirim whom we believe was newly arrived in London so we did not know his name. We are not even sure whether he is a mere envoy from the Grand Vizier or an addition to their intelligence staff, or both."

"But you must know how Egerton died."

"Indeed, a slow-acting poison. That might be Aqua Fontana or Canterella, we don't know yet, but we have yet to discover which. There's been a delay, but analyses of Timothy's blood are now being conducted, samples which were drawn from his body before we released it for burial. If it was this poison Aqua Fontana, then an expert could make it work immediately or delay it for weeks, even months. Symptoms are complicated too: We don't know whether there are any, and his secretary reports that he had no symptoms of anything, except his usual hardworking self."

"Great Heavens, how miserable."

"Cantarella, so we are told, acts immediately which rules out the Aqua Fontana in a preliminary way, but whether our chemists are expert enough to find which poison it was, or whether it was some other brew we do not know. Whichever it was, his face was very badly disfigured. I am sad to admit that one of our men fainted on seeing it in the morgue and another vomited all over the corpse. I must say I have never seen anything so gruesome. That is why we protected Mrs. Egerton from seeing it."

"I can see the wisdom of that but do you have any sense that the murderer was acting under orders?"

"None thus far. To establish that, we are examining his dispatches and reports much more carefully to see if we can glean anything. We know details of his mission abroad, of course, but I am not able to tell you about it. Safe to say, the matter is very delicate indeed and I want you to know that the papers will be sealed for one hundred years."

"I understand."

"Let me just say just this. A great deal of government money was involved but I will also tell you this in the most complete confidence. We are coming to believe he was murdered by someone close to him in the office, probably in the pay of a foreign government."

"I suppose that seems fairly obvious once you say it."

"The police are taking care of the detective work but identity and questions of motive are left to us."

"Now this is all very interesting, Harry, but I do think it is now appropriate to tell Mrs. Egerton that her husband did not commit suicide. It is bad enough for her loving husband to die, but to believe that his death was self-inflicted carries with it a burden of shame if not guilt. Not least, she had the man buried in the cemetery not in the family graveyard plot as the clerical establishment would object to a suicide being buried in consecrated ground."

"I had not thought of that. However, I have cleared it with Bob that she can be told that he was murdered. But she must know it is an official secret and that for any information about his death that escapes into the public arena she will be held legally responsible. I need hardly say that applies to you."

"She has three confidants that I know of, Sir Hamish MacDonald and his wife and a very old male friend of hers, Albert Pirrip. Can they be told?"

"As I said, it is the public arena that worries us, not merely for the reputation of the Foreign Office but as a matter of our diplomatic relations with those two countries. This Pirrip fellow will need watching and warning, probably warning before watching, eh?"

"I will talk with her tomorrow and see Albert myself. One last thing. Was all this a test of his character?"

"Oh, indeed, he was an exceptionally brave servant of the Queen and I am sure that will be recognized with a posthumous award in due course. We hope the Queen can be persuaded to meet Mrs. Egerton privately."

"That at least will be something for her to treasure, Mrs. Egerton I mean, not Her Majesty."

At that Clarence rose from his chair smiling, he shook hands with Montague and left.

V

Albert's wife Victoria was more than eager to discover the outcome of her husband's meeting with Elizabeth Egerton, and she confronted him on a Sunday morning so that he could not wriggle out of her questions pleading his need to get to work.

"It is a mystery, my dear," as he spelt out the details, "she does not really know whether it was suicide. It could have been murder."

"Very interesting, but how was she after all these years?" she said coming straight to the source of her concern. "It must have been strange to talk with a woman whose body you once knew intimately. Did you harbor any sort of desire for her?"

The tone in which Victoria asked the question contained a strong hint of jealously couched in mild aggression, and to Albert her voice began to sound like Nellie her mother.

"No, my dear, that was very far from my thoughts," he said in a dismissive tone.

"But why did she choose to confide in you?" She asked, beginning to bristle further at his feigned indifference, "you have never shown much conscience about anything, why now? Why did she not send you away with a flea in your ear? I would have done if I had a former unfaithful lover who appears on my doorstep with condolences. She would think you were anxious to be forgiven, that your desire for her was still there."

"Stuff and nonsense, Victoria, arrant nonsense."

"But does this visit conclude your relationship or are you going to be rushing down to London every week to sooth her troubled brow?"

"Such jealousy does not become you, my dear."

"Tell me, Albert, you wanted her, didn't you? Just be honest with me. It is so much easier than dissembling."

"All right, meeting her did stir memories of our love together, but I did not behave as though I was anything more than a confidant and she certainly offered no encouragement: And no, I did not want her."

"Tell me this. If you had comforted her, just by putting your arms around her, and she had responded, what would have happened?"

"But no such thing occurred."

"That's not the point, Albert," she said, getting increasingly upset. "I'd bet she would have turned to you; you would have kissed her and thereafter, recent widow or not, you've have found yourself in bed with her."

"Your imagination does you credit, my dear. You have had only me as a lover, I believe, so you cannot understand how the memory of intimacy never really leaves you, especially if the relationship lasted for any length of time."

"What do you mean?" cried Victoria, her fanciful suspicions now beginning to feel real, "do you mean you think of her as your lover even now?"

"No, I did not mean that. I meant simply that one cannot obliterate any past experience that easily from one's consciousness."

"Does this mean you think like an adulterer, or remember the bodies of women you have had as conquests?"

"Of course not."

"I see you now in a quite different light, Albert. I'd wager that if you had the opportunity with her, you would take it."

"That is a mistaken supposition. I know she has gone to meet Sir Clarence Smythe for advice and counsel so there is no need for me to meet with her further."

"But you go to London to your silly Board meetings. You'll have plenty of opportunity that you can conceal from me."

"What can I do to convince you I am not being unfaithful and that I have no desire to do so?"

"Nothing, I suppose. While I did urge you to go to meet her, your absence raised all kinds of visions for me, of you with her, that I thought I was going out of my mind. After all, your step-mother was a philanderer."

"Nonsense: Estella had a loving affair with your mother Nellie, but that was it and my father Old Pip was dead by then."

"Really, I remember someone telling me she and Harriet had been bed-fellows as well."

"That is a lie, but what has that to do with me? I could easily turn the tables on you in this matter. Your mother was a whore, you know."

"How dare you say that to me? How dare you? She was a victim of brutal men, and once my father appeared in her life, apart from Estella, she was as faithful as the day is long."

"This mutual recrimination is too upsetting. I am going into the garden."

"Go then, I hate you, I hate you," and she burst into tears and rushed outside to sit down in sight of the memorial to Mollie while he wandered around in the rose garden and stayed there for a few hours, trying to grapple with his wife's attack.

When her children returned from school in the late afternoon, Victoria was still burning with jealousy and anger back in the house such that she found it difficult to conceal her temper. Unused to this, the children went into the garden:

"What's the matter with Mum?" Beatrice asked her father.

"I am not sure, Bea. She was worried by my going to London, I think."

"That sounds very silly to me."

"Don't you dare talk about your mother like that. Say that you are sorry, now, this instant."

"I am sorry, Father."

"I should think so too."

At that he returned to the house with the children to find Victoria in the drawing-room weeping. He put his arms around her.

"I am sorry I upset you, dear," but he did not know as he spoke those words whether he would get a volley of invective or a similar phrase of sorrow in her reply.

There was silence for a few minutes as he stroked her back.

"I am sorry, too. I just love you so much, Albert. Any hint that you are not mine drives me mad."

"I know, I know. I do love you and, let it be said, I also like you."

"Oh, darling," she said turning to him for a kiss.

As he left for his business the following morning, he knew that their marriage would never be quite the same again, whatever the reconciliation. Was this expression of her jealousy just an outburst of her love for him? Certainly it was an indication that mutual trust had been disturbed and he could not tell whether it was his meeting with his old love Elizabeth or a general frenetic jealousy that was the cause. Would she react like this with any woman but Elizabeth? Presumably not because of their history. Of course, she was right to be suspicious about him as Elizabeth had matured into an outstandingly beautiful woman and his memory of possessing her young body so freely magnified his desire to recapture this woman now in the prime of her life. He wanted her and conscience be damned.

For Victoria the solid ground of her marriage felt to be shaking under her feet. Female intuition should never be discounted and it is a property that eludes most men completely. His expressions of love had become too formal, too worn, too false to be real, she thought. She was convinced that Albert's record as an adulterer was being taken out and dusted down if not with this woman, then some other unknown. At least he did not work with women, as far as she knew.

While these accusations might have been off the mark, she saw their exchange as a pre-emptive attempt on her part to make him realize how much he would be putting in jeopardy if he strayed. She knew Albert could not comprehend the fullness of her relationship with her mother Nellie and how the intimacy between the two left the daughter with a very profound understanding of men. Whores know everything about men after all.

It was also dawning on her that, stuck out here in the Kentish marshes, she had no friends. She resolved to promote her relationship with her brother Horatio and his wife Beth, if that were possible. She shivered at the thought of loneliness but, like her mother, she would not be browbeaten, so a couple of days after the altercation with Albert, she rode over in the trap to see her brother's family.

Six of the seven alphabet children were at the school in the village and Beth had walked with the baby Georgina to the village, so she was alone with her brother Horatio. He was working fiercely, shoeing a horse from the Buzza stable. Old Man Buzza was long gone, but his two sons, Herbert and Alfred had kept the stable going. Alfred was standing waiting for the shoeing to be completed.

"Hallo, Victor, how lovely to see you, stranger," said Horatio.

"Crikey," said Alfred with a leer, "you'se come up all fancy, ain't you, missy?"

"You mind your own business, Alfred Buzza," said Victoria, using the mode of address which she thought this country bumpkin would understand.

"Here she is, Alfred," said Horatio, handing the horse's reins over. With a smirk at Victoria, Alfred put a shilling in Horatio's hand, jumped into the saddle and rode away at a gallop.

"So what brings you 'ere, Sis?"

"I'm really lonely over there at Numquam, you know. I didn't realize till I had this row with Albert."

61

"With Albert? What about?"

"He's seeing an old girl friend from when he was in Paris and I'm jealous."

"Is it serious?"

"No, I don't think so. I just resent his never being with me. I don't really think this old flame would want him, but her husband's just topped himself, so who knows?"

"If it's serious, I'll come and beat him up, you know. No one makes my sister feel unhappy, not even her husband."

"No, I don't want that."

"I'll be honest wiv' you, Sis, I never really liked the bloke. When you was here last, he was really stuck up, I thought, and I was glad when you all left. Bets thought he was 'orrible, and your kids wasn't much better."

"Tell you what," said Victoria, "I'll get him to come one evening to the Bargemen, and p'raps he'll soften up a bit."

"I wonder what Mum would have done," said Horatio pensively.

"I am not strong like her, but if he was her husband, I think she'd have just given him a whack and told him to bugger off if he didn't want her."

"That's right: You should think about doing that, Sis."

Beth returned soon after that conversation and they had a pie for lunch spent reminiscing about the old days which brought tears to Victoria's eyes when they remembered the antics of their mother, Nellie.

"Didn't we half love our Mum," said Victoria with tears in her eyes.

"She was such a treasure, she was," said Horatio.

Clarence left the Club and walked down to the Embankment in a quiet autumn evening, then up through the Temple across Fleet Street toward Lincolns Inn and Old Square. The office was closing when he arrived, so he packed up a couple of briefs in his valise. He was satisfied with progress so far in the matter of Timothy Egerton, but he felt he was being regarded as mildly hostile by Lord Salisbury and by Montague almost as if he were prosecuting counsel and they were witnesses. He told Robert to let Mr. Pirrip know that he needed to talk with him after the December Board meeting and to let him know if he did not plan to attend. He also began to wonder whether the Government might be sued for damages for exposing Mr. Egerton to such danger.

He called a cab and was set down outside Mrs. Egerton's house in Eaton Square and as he approached the door he heard the strains of that melancholy Waldstein Sonata echoing through the door. My goodness, he thought, she certainly is accomplished.

Mrs. Egerton welcomed him with a great smile and invited him into the drawing room. The piano was in the bay window which explained why he had heard it so easily and he was again mildly overcome with how desirable she was, what beauty, what elegance and what experience lay behind the black attire.

"Do you have news, Sir Clarence?"

"Please call me Clarence. You play wonderfully, I should say. I could not help but hear you as I came to the door. I do have news, I do indeed. It is not happy, I fear.

"Then please call me Elizabeth. Please take a seat."

"I have spoken to the Head of Security at the Foreign Office," and he hesitated.

"Please continue."

"I cannot find the words to avoid hurting you, Elizabeth, so I must just say it straight out. Timothy was murdered."

She clasped her hand to her mouth in horror without weeping, which he had not expected.

"Murdered? By whom?"

"They do not know."

"How?"

"He was poisoned."

"Oh, my darling, how could they do this to you?" and then the flood of tears started.

He got up from the chair and sat next to her, putting his arm around her shoulder but she did not respond by moving toward him. After a while she composed herself, saying:

"How dreadful for him. No wonder, I suppose that he knew he was in danger, life-threatening danger which he saw as being ruined. No wonder he could not tell me. No wonder he took to drink. How awful for him, my precious husband. I could have helped him, you know."

"I doubt that, Elizabeth. He was representing the country on a very difficult mission, though the details will never be revealed. The man I talked with, one Harry Montague, told me he was an exceptionally brave man, referring to the circumstances of his death."

"Harry Montague? We have dined with the Montagues. Timothy knew him quite well. I am not surprised he was courageous for his country. I would love to know how."

"Harry gave no indication that he could ever tell you or me. All he was prepared to say was that Timothy had met with an envoy of the Ottoman Empire in the morning and lunched with a Russian diplomat before returning to his office where he died and that a great deal of money was involved, but there is much more to it, I know. Papers about Timothy's murder will be sealed for a hundred years."

"So, he was not murdered in the office, the poison could have been inside him for a while?"

"They are examining his blood for two types of poison, I forget their names, one slow-acting and one fast-acting. Of course, Harry asked me to express his profound sorrow not merely for Timothy's death, but for the way the Foreign Office felt they had to behave. The circumstances were such that they had to tell you immediately that he had died, but at that point they could not tell you he had been murdered, for reasons of state. Explaining that it was suicide was for them an obvious step to take."

"My God, my God, what a hell he must have been in, poor lamb."

"I fear so, Elizabeth. You are asked, nay you are ordered to keep this information to yourself, though Harry understood that you would want to tell those of your friends who knew of Timothy's death. Their concern is publicity. They hardly want it splashed over the papers that one of their senior men had been killed in his office, poison or no poison."

"I see. I have only confided in Albert and he asked Mary MacDonald to visit me and she called yesterday, and she had talked with Pip and Harriet."

"I am confident that all of these friends will be discreet."

"I feel almost betrayed by the Foreign Office, Clarence. It occurs to me too that he could have been buried in his family grave not in Highgate Cemetery as he and I wanted."

"That had occurred to me too, Elizabeth, and it is a serious matter. Would you allow me to talk about this with Lord Salisbury if you would like his body to be moved?"

"Please do. It may seem odd, but Timothy does not deserve the implicit stain on his life which being buried as a suicide conveys."

"Now I hope I have been of some help, Elizabeth, and Emma and I really would be very pleased for you to dine with us, probably in a small company with the MacDonalds and the Gargerys."

"That would be delightful. While I am in mourning, I am also beginning to be very lonely, so were such an occasion to be soon, that would be a comfort."

"Next week, perhaps?"

"Indeed, if Lady Smythe is not put out."

She accompanied him to the front door, her arm in his.

"I cannot tell you how helpful you have been, Clarence. I value it more than you will ever know."

He looked at her and smiled broadly.

"It is indeed a great pleasure. But there is one more fact you should know. The effects of the poison was so dreadful that they decided to protect you from seeing his body."

"How dare they? How dare they?" she cried and rushed upstairs to her bedroom as Clarence let himself out quietly.

Sir Hamish MacDonald was at the desk in his chambers, reviewing the judge's documents in a forthcoming bigamy trial. He was conscious of being very self-satisfied to be at the summit of his profession and widely respected both for his compassion and his judgment. It was All Hallows Eve and while as a Scot he was aware of 'ghoulies and ghosties and long-legged beasties and things that go bump in the night' from the Litany, he disliked superstitions or anything that could not be buttoned down to a scientific explanation.

At times, he would contemplate his marriage and see himself as a man of immense good fortune. Mary was a continuing delight and a marvelous companion of great intellectual and emotional strength, so far away from the life he might have lived as his early desire for men not been stilled. He had several long-term friends and none of them knew of those proclivities of his of many years ago. He was a very contented man.

Robert knocked at the door and asked whether he would meet with a Mr. Pryce-Howard from the Foreign Office.

"Good morning, sir," said Pryce-Howard as they shook hands.

"How can I help?" asked Hamish.

"It is a matter of immense national importance and Lord Salisbury has asked me to approach you first."

"Pray, continue."

"The Foreign Office wants to bring a case against one of its staff, but the case hinges on top secret evidence. I know we must seek the Lord Chancellor's advice and I am sure that he would ask us whether we had been in touch with one of Her Majesty's judges, for the trial must be in camera. Many judges hold that no trial should be conducted in this way in the belief that it compromises the defendant's freedom. The Courts can be seen by some to be the secret tools of the Government of the day. We would wish to know your feelings on the matter."

"I am not against in camera proceedings in principle. However it should be used only with regard to that part of the evidence which could affect national security. The public has a right to know that a man is a defendant in a trial, and the defendant himself must be aware that his case is public as of right except for that top-secret evidence."

"The difficulty is that the charge is not one of treason, but of murder."

"Good gracious, I thought you were talking of treason. What national security evidence could there be relevant to murder?"

"Motive, sir, motive. We would anticipate defense counsel insisting that the motive for the murder be understood by the Court, whether it is honorable or not."

"Can you enlighten me a little?"

"Not easily. Or at any rate, not yet. This is the Egerton case, I should say. We believe that the person in question was being used by a foreign government to wreak revenge on Mr. Egerton, and that this person conducted the murder."

"What might be the alleged motive of the putative defendant?"

"Money from the foreign entity of which the deceased was aware, and jealousy leading to treasonable activity."

"That sounds very formal."

"Yes, sir. We could simply charge the man with treason and that would then have to be in camera, yet there are strong feelings that he be charged with murder as it is the murder of a colleague in situ that has so incensed the Foreign Office leadership and anyone who knew the victim who was the epitome of goodness, charm and integrity."

"Either way, if found guilty," said Hamish, "the killer would hang, but there is not an either/or here. Charge him with treason and then you might or might not need to bring evidence of the murder, am I right? Putting the murder to one side, and I say that advisedly as one never can, do you have enough evidence of treason?"

"We do. He has been watched for three years now."

"Then would you tell your seniors that they should put their feelings behind them and instruct their counsel only to bring up Egerton's murder if they believe their treason case cannot stand on its own two feet? Then the whole sordid business will be in camera as legal convention dictates with regard to treason. H'mm, this Egerton case," said Hamish in contemplation, "let me see, he died in September, I think, and it is now January. A long time, eh?"

"You surmise correctly, sir."

"Yet I suppose four months is not that long in a case of this kind. I have not met Mrs. Egerton, or if I have, it was when she was a child. But my wife has been offering her some comfort at the urging of friends. I want to avoid any sense of being parti pris, so another judge must conduct the trial."

"I should add that when we have a conviction, we will not be able to brief Mrs. Egerton on the whole affair and the papers will be sealed."

"I am sure she will not appreciate that. However, if I may I can now get back to my bigamy trial papers and bid you good day."

"I am sure Lord Salisbury would wish to convey to you his profound thanks for your counsel."

At her husband's urging Lady Emma Fotheringaye-Smythe was planning a dinner party and the discussion on who to invite between them was as lively as might be expected.

"Emma darling, I am sure Mrs. Egerton will be pleased to know that a widow like herself can still find her own place at the dining tables of the upper class through such an invitation."

"Of course, Clarence, and I am sure she is still greatly distressed."

"I did not know her, of course, but when she came to see me in my chambers, I was quite stunned by her exceptional beauty, though," he said laughing, "that is not why I told her she would be a pro bono client."

"I look forward to meeting her certainly, Clarence, but I do want this to be a top-drawer occasion. Obviously we will ask Hamish and Mary."

"Yes indeed, and is not your cousin Alfred Bishop of Darlington or somewhere in the North?"

"He would be able to come, I am sure, and his wife Dorothy is a very strong personality as I recall. I will ask my brother Henry Eustace and his wife, Sarah, and I thought we ought to have military representation with Bindon and Cecilia Blood. That would then be the MacDonalds, the Bishops, the Archie Smythes, the Bloods making ten with us, though we need to find a man and we have no politicians, and of course Mrs. Egerton."

"Interesting, isn't it, Emma? We always think of couples in terms of the man and his wife as a kind of attachment. Would we ever invite a woman of stature and anticipate that she would bring a husband to a party as husbands brought their wives?"

"Apart from the Queen herself, no."

"I do think table imbalance is unacceptable this time, not least because it would indicate to Elizabeth that a complementary man was neither necessary and desirable, and in any case, that could be seen as a gratuitous insult to her widowhood. So, we must find a substitute for husband, but not someone who could possibly be thought of as a match."

"I agree."

"What about that up-and-coming firebrand of a journalist, that officer who has written well about India and who had vague connections to my father? Winston Churchill, I mean."

"A capital idea. I know him vaguely through politics. His father Lord Randolph Churchill had sought my father's legal advice, I know."

"I am sure Elizabeth will not have met him and he can hardly be regarded as any sort of suitor to her."

"He would also bring the views of a younger generation to the table on whatever will be discussed, which is very good for us, however distasteful it might be. But, should we do this before or after Christmas? My inclination is to leave it to the New Year."

"That is probably best, Emma, as I want to be sure no one has a conflicting engagement."

Albert was leaving his office in Dock Road, Chatham. It was a wintry December evening but he was warm in his fur-lined overcoat and his new fur hat suitable for the winter as the North wind whistled incessantly off the North Sea through the streets of Chatham, ushering in a Siberian cold. With four men of his acquaintance the Gentleman's Club was being formed, although premises had yet to be acquired. Last to leave for the day, he stood outside the gates of Pocket and Pirrip, feeling enormously self-satisfied and preparing to light a cigar which he drew from a leather case, a Christmas present last year from his children, preparing to walk to the stable to wake up his coachman and ride home to Numquam.

Lighting a cigar in the wind was proving impossible but suddenly he heard a woman's voice, "Can I help you, sir?"

He turned around and saw a woman under the street gaslight, not more than twenty, shabbily dressed, but with deep brown eyes which reminded him immediately of Elizabeth.

"I've got lots to offer, anyfink really. I'se so cold on a night like this and there's not bin a boat in today. I'd help you with your smoke if you only wanted that, too."

"Come with me," he said, realizing immediately that there was no one in the building. He grabbed her hand, turned back to the gate and unlocked it. He led her along the yard to his office door, unlocking it with another key. The room was warm as the coal fire had not yet burnt itself out.

"What's your name, m'dear?" He said, taking off his coat and putting his hat in a safe position on his desk, and then holding her hand, drew her down on to the couch.

"Millie Smith, sir, and I haven't bin in a place this warm for months. You can take your pleasure with me. I sees you're a rich man so I knows you'll treat me fair. Just do what you like," said woman, gradually disrobing, her slender figure with large breasts impressing him greatly.

"Oh my, you are a pretty little thing, aren't you Millie, how come you're on the street?"

"I'm not from these parts, I'se from Lewisham, that's near London. I got married but my husband wanted to beat me all the time, so one morning I took all the money I could find, got meself to Victoria and ended up in Chatham."

"When was this?"

"One month past."

"So you're new to the game."

"Well, I've had several sailor fellas since then, but yes, I suppose I am."

"Tell me about them; I like to know these things."

"Oh no, sir, I couldn't really,"

"Alright just tell me about one."

"Well, he was only my second since I came to Chatham. Big man he was, said he'd sailed the seven seas and his wife had left him. But then, though he'd just got off the China boat, he was so gentle with me, not like most of them, and when he was done, we lay there and he just cried. I'd 'ave you for my wife, if I wasn't a sailor, he says."

Ignoring what he thought was a pathetic tale, Albert said:

"Do you have a lodging?"

"No, sir, I live on the street cos no one takes me in. Cor, it's so nice and warm in here even without my clothes."

"I am usually here in the morning before anyone else, so when we are done, you can sleep here. I'll give you money for a room if you're really nice to me. I can teach you all kinds of things which you'll enjoy," said Albert with a slightly menacing look.

"Oh you'se so kind, I'm past caring what men do to me and yesterday I thought I'd throw myself in the water."

"Well, now, stop that nonsense and let's begin."

Afterwards he smiled with satisfaction as he watched her dress, wondering whether he would make her his whore as he had enjoyed himself mightily and she was adept, so he thought, at her new-found profession. For the moment, he'd think about it, but he generously gave her five sovereigns which overwhelmed her, being used to a trade only in shillings and pence without anywhere to live. That money made a lodging possible on the morrow.

They bade each other good-night and he left her on the couch, asleep.

On the way home he felt no conscience about either his infidelity or his consorting with a whore, rather he was proud to have been so generous as befits a rich man like himself. He also realized how easy it would be for him to enjoy Millie's company in Chatham regularly for he could use his premises after business closed, not go to hers which would obliterate any tittle-tattle. When he got home, Victoria and the children found him much more cheerful and friendly before a late supper was set out for him.

"I've been thinking," said Victoria, "shall we go to the Bargemen one night? I'd like to see the changes Josh has made and we could meet my brother there. I think you'd enjoy it."

Albert felt trapped. He could think of nothing worse than an evening in that smoke-filled den, but he needed to humor his wife, especially after his evening's entertainment.

"Of course, my dear, as long as we don't spend too long there: I'm dreadfully busy at work, you know, and need my rest."

"Oh, God," Victoria thought to herself, "what's he up to now?"

Clarence walked through the foyer to the dining room in the House of Lords searching for the Foreign Secretary, Lord Salisbury whom he saw at a table with several of his peers. He told the butler to ask the noble Lord if he could have a private word. Glancing toward the door, Lord Salisbury saw Clarence and excused himself.

"What can I do for you, Clarence?"

"It is a matter of mild urgency. As you told me, Egerton was murdered and did not commit suicide. However, given the Church's attitude to allowing suicides to take up space in their precious graveyards, he had to be buried in Highgate Cemetery as a result. You can imagine that fact itself was a distressing matter to his widow and indeed to the wider family whose grave is in Devon, I think."

"What can I do about it?"

"As she sees it, your Office has besmirched his memory and his work with the stain of suicide which we all know is quite false and lives with him in that secular grave. I am asking you on her behalf to arrange for Egerton's body to be transferred to his family grave, presumably with an appropriate very private funeral, only with her and her children perhaps."

"I see. I don't think anyone in the Office had foreseen that and it is intolerable. The honorable course of action is for us to arrange an exhumation and a new funeral. I will order this but it must be a matter of the utmost secrecy. For a man who so graced his profession and put himself in such danger, we can do no less."

"May I convey your decision to Mrs. Egerton?"

"You may. Harry Montague will arrange everything with her. She may invite immediate family and I will have Canterbury come and deliver the final rites."

"I am sure the presence of Archbishop Benson will be of great comfort."

"Clarence, I am grateful for your help. The Office has no experience of its staff being murdered in its buildings, and I will have Harry write a detailed memorandum in the event of such killing taking place in the future.

1897

VI

The Board of the Jaggers Trust for the Relief and Education of the Poor was to have been convened for their half-yearly meeting in December to consider their ownership of the Clumber Estate in County Londonderry, but too many members of the Board were indisposed with influenza that seemed capture most of the population in London over the course of the winter.

A date for the meeting was finally set for January 15th, but blizzards enveloped the country from Aberdeen to Kent, making travel difficult, even in London. The result was that it was not until Valentine's Day 1897 that a meeting was finally held.

Pip and Harriet were about to leave for the meeting when a maid came in with a wire.

"How wonderful," said Pip reading the message, "talk of an angel. Hector Thomas Hesketh has arrived safely and mother and son were doing well."

"You see, my dear, she is in fine fettle."

After congratulations and cheerful renewals of acquaintance were circulating around the room in Old Square where they shared their good news, Sir Clarence began the meeting by pointing out that the choices open to them on their Irish involvement were different from those considered at the time of the purchase of the property from Mrs. Clara Gargery, for since then the plantation house had been burnt to the ground, their representative Mr. Pip Gargery had been attacked, and one of their tenants Mr. Seamus O'Sullivan, had been murdered.

He then went on to say:

"Before we consider the agenda, I want us to recognize the presence of Mr. Tom Hesketh formerly of the Gordon Highlanders and invite him to explain why he has joined us today."

"Thank you, Sir Clarence. The wounds I sustained in a campaign on the North-West Frontier are such that I can no longer engage in combat on behalf of her Majesty, and while my regiment is loyal to me and uses me as an instructor and on regimental administration, I do not see myself spending the next years of my life in that kind of employ, so I have resigned my commission. Mr. Gargery is my father-in-law and philanthropic work is attractive to me."

"Thank you, Tom, and we are delighted to have you with us and please join our discussions. The time had come to determine the fundamental issue from which other choices and decisions would follow, and given the atrocities and the political context in which our venture in Ireland is set, do we wish to retain an active philanthropic effort or should we choose the line of least resistance and cut our losses? I should add that we have the resources to do whatever we choose. I would like each of us to address the issue in turn."

"I am not one to run away from difficulty, Clarence," said Pip, "but we are like babes in the wood in understanding the antagonisms that beset Irish culture. I was astonished in the short time I was there just how little I knew about Ireland and its history. The problem for the Board, however, is that we now have the Clumber Estate and its future on our collective conscience."

"Conscience be blowed," murmured Albert, controlling a cough and with his voice a low grumble, but then loudly "as a man of business, I look on this as a matter of benefit and cost. I understand our situation, I am for reducing our presence. We should just give the land away, retaining perhaps a small piece of the estate, and have the peasants stand on their own two feet. It is their country."

"Have you no conscience, then?" Asked Aaron Levy angrily. Though the junior lawyer in the Chambers he was known for speaking his mind and he continued, "these people are subject to such constraints that it is immensely difficult for them to stand up against their oppressors, for that is what they are and it is our duty to help them and that is was this Trust is for."

"I had thought," said Harriet quietly, "that we might involve the one institution which seems to hold some sway in Ulster where the major cultural problems are located, and that is the Roman Church."

"How involve?" asked Clarence.

"By giving them a large part of the estate."

"Now that would be like a red rag to a bull, Harriet," said Hamish, "the Protestant community there, as I understand it, roots most of its hatred in bizarre theological assumptions about Catholics, hence the 'No Popery' mantra."

"Like Pip, I am not one to throw in the towel," added Simon Brandram, "though I am well aware that I would not be a person to do anything more than sit on this Board. The legal problems are complex; we have a fiduciary responsibility to husband the resources of the Trust and giving away the land we have bought seems legally complicated."

The discussion continued with the Board seemingly split between the 'involvers' and the 'retreaters,' between those who would pursue an active course and those who wanted a path of least resistance leading to distancing from Irish affairs.

Tom had not yet spoken, but he now began:

"I can see the merits of both sets of arguments and it is not my place to put my preference before you. It does seem to me that you need much more information to determine a strategy. I would be prepared to undertake an enquiry over there, and I am not yet clear what has been done thus far."

"That's a wonderful offer, Tom," said Pip. "Before he was killed, O'Sullivan and I had begun to put together a scheme for the community to work together. We listed every tenant and their attitudes from the committed to the wary and I have our notes at home. We talked with Father McGowan the parish priest as his influence was considerable."

"As I listen to this discussion it strikes me that no attempt has yet been made to conjure any support from the Protestant community for such work. You had some unsatisfactory intercourse with Londonderry lawyers, I believe, but I think you must enter discussions with the Protestant community's leaders to be effective."

"How sensible, Tom," murmured Clarence, "it has never occurred to me but I do know Edmund Knox, representing Londonderry City as he is a barrister at Gray's Inn. Hamish, you must know John Atkinson, he's a bencher at King's Inn and isn't he Solicitor-General for Ireland? Sir Thomas Lea I don't know, but he has been utterly opposed to the use of the Irish language in schools, as I recall. These two are MPs for the county."

"My goodness, how obvious is this as a development," said Hamish. "Clarence, let's us have the three of them to dinner at the Athenaeum to solicit their support."

"Let us hope," said Mary, "that these men of distinction will be able to influence those who actually live in the county. I would not be surprised to learn of a fissure between the nobility and the ordinary Protestant man. But Tom might discover that."

"Do I conclude from this," said Pip, "that we are delaying once again any positive actions in deference to Hamish and Clarence dining with the MPs, but thereafter asking Tom to visit Clumber and develop a strategy on the basis of our initial enquiries? Do you think Hannah would accompany you, Tom?"

"I don't see any reason why the two proposals should not run in tandem. With only one leg I would need personal support if I were to travel there, and I am sure Hannah – and Hector of course - will come, and I am eager to get my teeth into something."

"Then you should join us when we meet the MPs, Tom," said Clarence. "That would give you information, I am sure. I will write to them today. To summarize then: Tom, Hamish and I will meet with the MPs for the area. Independently of the outcome, we will support Tom in an in-depth enquiry, given that Malcolm, Pip and Aaron with Harriet have done what they can in their time there and we would all value such a report. "

That afternoon, Clarence drafted a letter to the MPs explaining that he was Chairman of a London-based Trust which had recently acquired the Clumber Estate in Londonderry and that he would be very pleased to meet with them to discuss conditions there and what the Trust might consider doing.

Each of the three men accepted the invitation, more to be entertained than with any expectations, though Sir Thomas Lea thought privately that interfering do-gooders had no place in Ireland. Nevertheless, each MP thought it would be sensible to find out what was afoot.

Elizabeth was surprised on Monday by a letter dated February 25, 1897, from Buckingham Palace in an envelope bearing the Royal Seal which read:

'Her Majesty is appointing Timothy Henry Tatton Egerton to be a Knight Commander of the Royal Victorian Order posthumously for his gallantry in the service of the Crown.

You are commanded to receive the Order at Buckingham Palace on March 15th, 1897, at 3 o'clock in the afternoon.

No guests will be permitted to attend and the appointment to the Order will not be made public.'

This was a rather abrupt command, she thought, but at least she had two weeks to prepare. She had been thrilled by the private funeral in Devon just before Christmas and was gratified that the Archbishop had taken the service, a particular honor for Timothy. Her three children were especially pleased as they saw that their beloved father's reputation was restored.

Elizabeth promptly took a cab to Bond Street that afternoon to equip herself with the appropriate dress, hat, gloves and other accoutrements to attend Her Majesty. She decided to tell no one, not even her children or her maid, so when the day came, no one in her household knew where she was going.

Her carriage was stopped at the gate to the Palace, the guardsman admitted her on verifying her identity, and the carriage drove under the arch into the forecourt of the Palace and circled around to the main entrance. An usher in royal livery opened the carriage door and asked very politely whether she was Mrs. Elizabeth Egerton to which she replied affirmatively and she was led up the grand staircase and into a room with a grand piano overlooking the garden. She noticed numerous elaborate decorations celebrating the Queen's Diamond Jubilee that month.

There she waited for a few minutes before a tall man in morning dress came in and introduced himself as Sir Marmaduke Stewart-Campbell, Equerry to the Prince. The Queen, he said, was indisposed and the Prince of Wales would conduct the ceremony. He described the procedure to her, which was brief and then asked if she had questions. She had none, so he led her into a larger very ornate room with tables and mantelpieces covered in Sevres porcelain. On a small dais stood the Prince of Wales in front of a herald in full dress and an usher holding a cushion.

"Your Royal Highness," said Sir Marmaduke, "may I present Mrs. Elizabeth Egerton, widow of Timothy Henry Tatton Egerton."

"Welcome, Mrs. Egerton," said the Prince.

"Please step forward to receive the award, Mrs. Egerton," said Sir Marmaduke.

She did as she had been instructed kneeling on a footstool embroidered with the royal coat of arms. Looking up at the Prince, she saw him turn to the usher with the cushion. He picked up the medal, a white Maltese Cross with a blue ribbon, and placed it around her neck saying:

"The Queen commands me on her behalf to present to you this medal indicating membership of the Royal Victorian Order, which is the acknowledgment of the gallantry of your husband Timothy Henry Tatton Egerton in the service of Her Majesty.

"Her Majesty has further commanded me to express to you her most grateful thanks for your husband's service to the country but to the Queen personally, and to express her most profound condolences to you."

The Prince then held out his hand to help her stand.

"Good Heavens," he said, "it is you. I was not certain. Did we not meet very briefly in Paris years ago and were you not somehow related to my shooting chum Camberley? Am I right?"

"Yes indeed, sir, I remember the occasion well, but I think you have my aunt in mind."

"Probably," he said, but then turning to the steward, he said:

"Let me dispense with the formal matter first. He then stood at attention and said:

"The Queen has asked me to explain why your husband deserves this particular honor, posthumous though it is. I should add quietly that Lord Salisbury does not agree that you be told this, but Her Majesty has overruled him. Your husband discovered a wide range of nefarious activities by foreign powers, among which was to a plan to assassinate several members of the Royal Family including the Queen and myself. On behalf of the family, we are much indebted to your husband and we hope this is some small recognition of our gratitude."

"Thank you very much, your Royal Highness, and I am most grateful to know those details, though I confess I am not that interested in foreign policy, but the safety of Her Majesty is of great concern to any of her subjects."

Dismissing Sir Marmaduke and the officers, the Prince then said, "now we will have some tea," and taking Elizabeth's arm, he led her into a small anteroom with a settee and two very ornate chairs embroidered with Scottish royal emblems, on which they both sat as a flunkey served tea and cakes.

"Is your aunt still alive?" He began.

"I fear not," Elizabeth replied, "her first husband died in an accident and then she married Percy de Vere and went to live with him in Pompeii where he was engaged as an archaeologist."

"I did not know that. Very sad. And what was your husband like? Is it impertinent of me to ask about him?"

"Not at all. I was very fortunate. We had a very close relationship and until this problem began three months before he died, we felt we had a charmed life."

"Now, my dear, you must not look backward. You are still a young woman, I can see, and moreover one of great beauty and charm. I wonder if you might come to a soiree I am having next week. There will only be me and two of my most favorite ladies whom you will meet. It will be a chance for you to relax in an informal setting."

"I am honored by the invitation, your Royal Highness," said Elizabeth, later astonished by the speed with which she found an excuse, "but I am about to leave the country and stay with friends in Paris and then go to Athens for Christmas, both places where my father was at the Embassy and I met friends there I now feel able to renew the acquaintance."

"That is unfortunate indeed. You see, Mrs. Egerton, I am a passionate man and much enjoy close relationships with beautiful women which, between ourselves, angers my mother. I would like to see you within my intimate circle."

"Again, I am honored, sir, but I feel I must decline. I am still unable to consider any sort of attachment to a man or a group. I know I will come out of my grief eventually."

"Ah well. It has been a pleasure to speak with you," and he got up abruptly and left the room, and she too got up quickly from her chair at which the flunkey led her out down the staircase to her carriage, without finishing her cake or her cup of tea.

She had heard rumors about the Prince's flirtatious behavior and it was surely not long before he would be King. She was not dazzled by the invitation, not least because she found him most unattractive, ugly and dissolute for all his finery. She giggled quietly to herself as she entered the carriage wondering how on earth such a fat man could actually make love to a woman.

Yet now she had a royal secret.

That Saturday evening the weather was glorious, one of the days in early May which gives such charm to an English Spring. There were now benches outside the Three Jolly Bargemen and it had changed greatly since Victoria was last there. Josh was running both pubs, this one and the Blue Boar. He had become not exactly wealthy but with enough to be able to think that one day he could stop filling beer mugs and get away from the tedious chats with the odds and sods of customers who frequented his establishments.

"Oh, it's lovely," said Victoria, as they went into the bar. The old dirt floor was tiled. The bar was now a beautiful wooden construction with bottles on shelves, all in a gorgeous cherry color, with glass and mirrors behind the bottles which gave the bar a pleasurable light from the newly installed gas lights.

Albert and Victoria approached the bar as Josh cried out: "Good heavens, you's Nellie's child, Victoria, ain't you?"

"That's right, Josh, I'm surprised you recognized me."

"And this your husband?"

"Indeed," said Albert barely able to conceal his disdain, "I am Albert Pirrip."

"Pirrip, Pirrip, now where have I heard that name?"

At that moment, Sid Butterworth called out from the settle:

"That's Joe Gargery's nephew, ain't it, Old Pip's son, what was a Pirrip? No, he wasn't his son, as I recall, but his nephew, but I heard tell his first wife was a tyrant, Mrs. Joe as everyone called her."

At this, Albert began to soften, pleased to be recognized.

"You Butterworth then?" Said Victoria, "but I thought you was drowned in that boat disaster."

"No, no, that were my older brother, God rest his soul. That were, ooh, ten year ago or was it twenty, but then he were the eldest, nearly seventy he were, and I'm almost eighty-year-old now. Can't think what keeps me going."

"It's the ale, Sidney, that's why I sells it," said Josh to general laughter.

At that moment, a down-at-heel man of uncertain age came up to the bar. As Victoria thought about it afterwards, he seemed to be invisible when they came in, but he manifested himself with a slightly threatening manner. Victoria backed away as he approached because he exuded that kind of smell unique to a man who works with pigs.

"You behave yourself now, Samuel Hubble, I don't want no trouble," said Josh.

"I ain't here for no trouble. I thought I heard the name Gargery."

"You did indeed," said Albert, "Joe Gargery were like my grandfather. Why do you ask?"

"He had a wife, didn't he?"

"Biddy? Sweetest creature, she was, lovely woman," said Josh.

"I must be wrong then; I thought his wife's name was George or summat."

"You're right," Sid called out, "that was his first wife, wot was Old Pip's elder sister, always called Mrs. Joe. Fair dragon of a woman, she was, quite unlike that Biddy that Joe married when she was gone."

82

"I remember my father Pip once telling me that his much older sister was beaten and died later. But what is it to you, Mr. Hubble?" Asked Albert, becoming intrigued by this history, like every customer in the pub.

"Well, see it's like this. My mother, bless her memory, well she was expectin' me when Orlick he wot was my real father went off. They was not wed, like they should have been, though they were going to be, but he was a bad lot, my father, Mum said. If he wanted a woman, he would always be trying to get her."

"What was his name again?" Asked Sid.

"Orlick, it was, Orlick, never called anything else. She told me he was my father and that he had disappeared off the face of the earth, I don't have his Christian name but she later married Ebenezer Hubble so I was then called Samuel Hubble and my mum was Maggie."

"Why is this a concern of mine?" Asked Albert, now irritated by Hubble's manner.

"Well, as you mentioned Gargery, I thought you'd like to know what my mum told me about Orlick and Mrs. Gargery, the first one."

"Go on, then."

"She called me to her bedside one day afore she passed and told me all she knew about my father. Afore that, I didn't even know his name. She told me all sorts of stories but especially about how he imagined that this Mrs. Joe really loved him, though she was very harsh with him."

"Get to the point, man," said Albert, tiring of the conversation.

"Now he did odd jobs for Joe Gargery from time to time and she said Orlick's fancy for this woman in the cottage next to the Forge tempted him something dreadful."

"What do you mean? Do you mean Biddy?" Asked Albert, the color in his cheeks rising as he remembered her kindness to him.

"No, no, no, the first wife, Mrs. Joe, I mean," said Hubble with some frustration.

"My mum said that she was like a tyrant with Joe, always on her rampages, but worser to Orlick. Anyway, says she, this Orlick comes home one a'ternoon, battered and bruised, telling my mum he'd had a go at Joe's wife while Joe was out in the village with this young fella Pip, so, said Orlick, he thought he'd try his luck."

"For what?" asked Albert.

"To have his wicked way with her," said Hubble, "this was the kind of man he was. Terrible, terrible, really. Mum said he had told her that that Mrs. Joe, her that was so nasty to him, she needed taking down a peg and he was going to have her to let her know wot's wot."

"Good Lord," said Albert, "that really is terrible, not just that he wanted her but that he told his woman that he did."

"True enough, my friend. But that Mrs. Joe, Mum said, she weren't having any of it and she was a strong woman, and he hadn't reckoned with that. She hurt him so bad with her rolling pin that he ran off."

"What an animal," said Victoria who did not know and was not connected to anyone in the story was still deeply shocked at the way this Orlick thought he could have any woman he wanted.

"I think that Orlick was a brute," continued Hubble, "even though he was my real father, but I was brought up with Ebenezer as my dad."

"Is that all?" said Albert wanting to get away from this man.

"I'm not finished yet, so listen. Two days after he had been sent packing by Mrs. Joe, she was hit on the back of the head something dreadful by someone else and she was like a cabbage, and everyone thought it was Orlick, but it wasn't. When he heard about the beating, he was frightened because he had a go at her in the days before she was hit, he knew he would be blamed so he disappeared that very day and was never heard of again. In the end, Mrs. Joe died from the bashing in her head. Though he didn't kill her, Mum said, it was still a wicked thing to do to go for her."

Albert took Victoria's arm after this tale ended, and indicated he wished to leave, and indeed, she was only too pleased to get away.

"Interesting, isn't it, Victoria," said Albert as they left the Bargemen, "did you know that under English Law a husband can force himself upon his wife as her consent is seen as irrelevant, given her marriage vows."

"But Orlick was not Mrs. Joe's husband, was he? Whatever the Law, that tale is quite disgusting."

Next time, she thought, we'll go to the Bargemen with Horatio and Beth.

As the Bishop said grace Elizabeth still had her experience at the Palace at the back of her mind. However, the food was excellent, all kinds of sweetmeats, turkey and joints of lamb, a feast indeed and dinner conversation was sparkling with Mary MacDonald proving an excellent foil to Winston Churchill's ebullience. Clarence and Hamish were circumspect in their comments on racing, the theater and other leisure pursuits of which they were almost entirely ignorant.

This was the dinner party that Clarence and Emma had planned six months ago, and one thing had led to another in the Smythe household such that invitations were not sent out until the end of April for the party to be held on the 3rd of June. Bishop Alfred seemed keen to engage Elizabeth, realizing that the way she dressed, though always in the height of fashion, represented her imminent release from mourning, though his wife Dorothy stared at him with the slightest degree of menace when he ventured a little too far into enquiries on her personal situation.

But it was General Blood who unwittingly lit a fire, directing his question to Clarence and Hamish:

"Now tell me, you are both lawyers, what do you make of these notions that women should be given the vote? Dolly and I agree, I think, that the time is not yet ripe. I mean, Dolly keeps me in order and is a jolly sensible sort, aren't you, m'dear, and I'd be sure her vote would be as much value as that of some tinker from Manchester."

The proverbial fly on the wall would have noticed that hackles were rising around the table, though as yet the said fly could not determine who thought what.

"I have heard that the Government is considering introducing a bill on women's suffrage," said Clarence, "in the next session, I believe."

"Might that be to get more votes?"

"General," said Elizabeth, "you say the time is not ripe. I say it is well past time."

"Oh, do you support the proposal then, Mrs. Egerton?"

"Of course. Many women of my generation do not, however, as they think that politics is the preserve of those unruly drunken fellows in the House of Commons with whom they do not wish to associate. I see obtaining the suffrage as a right removes the stain in society of women being of lower status, a position with which my dear husband agreed."

From the head of the table, Emma nodded sagely.

Churchill was listening to this conversation and intervened:

"Forgive me, Mrs. Egerton, I have thought about this for some time. A woman voting would be contrary to natural law and the practice of civilized states. Saving your presence, most of the women wanting to vote are from an undesirable class of women. Women can discharge their duty to the state by marrying and giving birth to children. Their husbands adequately represent them."

Mary MacDonald who had been bantering with Churchill all evening exploded with anger.

"Mr. Churchill, tell me, which is it? Are you ignorant or are you stupid? Given your remarks, I find it difficult to decide."

"Neither, I hope, Lady MacDonald."

"Let us assume that you are neither until proved otherwise. The claim to natural law is immediately disproved as a matter of fact by the many powerful women who have graced civilization from the outset, the present monarch to name but a few. Who would dare not to attribute to her anything but intellect, courage and determination? That it is the practice of civilized states to exclude women from voting is proof positive that such states have yet to become civilized."

She stopped there, being in great danger of shifting from being forthright to downright rude.

Emma picked up the conversation.

"I do not know, Mr. Churchill, what you regard as an undesirable class of women, but I suspect that each of the women around this table want the suffrage; should we therefore be included in your category?"

"I must say I am puzzled," said the Bishop, "as something of a theologian, while God created men and women with different natural abilities, it would be unwise to assume from that, as many do, that His intention was to create the one as superior to the other. Yet I still share your sentiment, Churchill. Children have to be brought up and women are naturally able to do that. Most men are logical, stable and even-minded, whereas women are, I believe, too emotional, even fickle, present company excepted ... "

"I would stop there if I were you, Bishop," said Hamish laughing, "lawyers and judges can produce hundreds of examples of men who are also fickle, emotional or what have you, and certainly to suggest there is something about men, qua men, as being logical and stable is mere wishful thinking. As a reason for keeping women from the vote it is of dubious quality as an argument. Traits of character are evenly distributed among the population, men and women, good and bad."

"I assume that married women around this table took a vow of obedience at their marriage," said Churchill.

"And what, precisely does that show?" asked Emma, holding up her hand to restrain Mary from answering, fearing that her friend might bring an undesirable level of acrimony into the conversation, "many husbands might encourage their wives to vote, as General Blood has just shown, they are able to choose whom they think would govern well, without making it a matter of obedience, a matter that is moot in a secret ballot anyway. In all honesty that cannot be a rationale for denying women the vote."

"My dear Lady Emma," said Churchill, "you will be suggesting next that women should be members of Parliament."

"Indeed it might well come to that."

"Steady on, darling," said Clarence, "that could be a bridge too far."

"Why?" asked the Bishop's wife Dorothy, now getting energized by the conversation. "The way many men behave in Parliament indicates not just that it is something of a circus, but more like a nursery. Women would be like mothers in the Mother of all Parliaments," and she smiled a little smile at her clever remark. "I do think, however, that there is something to be said," she went on, "for the idea that women's nature is feminine, quiet, loving, restrained."

"Come, come, Dorothy," said Mary, "that is simply what you have been told to believe, not what you might yourself choose to be."

"Yes, my dear," said the Bishop, "You should be more careful."

The volcano that was Mary MacDonald exploded at that remark.

"You see, Bishop," she said, her voice rising, "men like to treat women as if they really were inferior, disqualifying them from entering conversation of merit rather than permitting them to discuss the trivial."

"The time has come," said Emma, "after this heated and interesting conversation, for us to leave the men to their cigars and port."

"Come, ladies."

"Well," said Churchill graciously, "I thank everyone for this stimulating conversation and I see that I must marry a woman who wants the vote as it is clearly an element in strength of character."

"Be careful, Mr. Churchill," said Emma as she walked round the dining table toward the drawing room, "you might fall in love with a woman of equal strength, and that would be something you would need to get used to. On the other hand, you could marry some empty-headed aristocrat whose only quality would be to breed offspring like herself."

"Yes, I suppose I should marry a woman with my mother's strengths."

"And what are her views on the matter?"

"Temperamentally for, politically against, socially on the fence."

VII

The July sun was setting and the rear garden in Clyde Street was almost in the shadow of the house. Clara was sitting quietly there with the children playing around her wondering what the summer in this Southern Hemisphere would manifest. She need not have been concerned for the climate in Port Elizabeth was always tropical and usually mild but it was not known as the Windy City for nothing.

Malcolm returned home just as Matilda brought out a decanter of white wine and glasses on a wooden tray.

"I am developing a taste for the wine here," said Clara.

"Let me see," said Malcolm examining the bottle, "I chose half a dozen cases from the Constantia vineyard in Capetown, the oldest such grower in the country, recommended by the Brigadier. I heard a remarkable story today, my dear."

"Another one?"

"Oh indeed, I am building up a picture of the history of this land which continually reveals its complexity.

"This took place in 1815 at Slachter's Nek, which is somewhere in the Cape Colony. A farmer was summoned to a magistrate for mistreating his African laborer, note, not a slave. He refused, retreated to a cave where he was killed by colored soldiers sent by the magistrate."

"Good heavens, that seems a little hard, poor man."

"But a couple of his neighbors started a rebellion against the British Colonial Authority. Apparently they were disgruntled by the way the Authority ignored the farmer's complaint but treated Xhosa people leniently. It was said that the Xhosa had stolen hundreds of cattle."

"Go on."

"The rising was put down, of course. Twenty rebels were tried and five sentenced to be hanged."

"No Authority takes kindly to rebellions, do they," said Clara, "and I suppose the animosity is great and, as Voltaire would have put it, you hang rebels *pour encourager les autres.*"

"Absolutely, but my acquaintance was really telling this story for my amusement!"

"Why?"

"At the execution of these five men, the platform collapsed on which the men were lined up to have nooses round their necks. Spectators pleaded for their lives, but the official responsible then hung them separately. I must confess, I found it not at all amusing, and I think he expected me to laugh. The story-teller was one Rudolph Botha, a rare specimen."

"How come?"

"He's a Boer who is not a farmer but a trader, as he comes from a trading family near Antwerp and is a recent immigrant. He identifies with the Boers in the Transvaal and the Orange Free State but he tells me Kruger and others rule with a rod of iron in terms of their religious rules and ancient customs."

"What was he doing here in Port Elizabeth?"

"He sees huge opportunities in the expansion of this city since the building of the railways. He's mainly trading in French and German wines, and he believes people like us will prefer European wines. Botha also explained to me that slavery to which Boers had become accustomed since their forebears from Holland arrived two centuries ago was a major part of the reason why they trekked north."

"Of course," said Clara, "our government abolished the slave trade wherever the flag flew, so that would have been a blow to the Boers, but why he should find such a dreadful incident amusing astonishes me."

"Yet, I don't understand enslavement by Boers: The so-called justification from America was that slaves were crucial to the economy because tobacco and cotton required large amounts of labor to grow and harvest them. But as far as I know Boers are cattle farmers, importing their wheat. Why would they need slaves, not the odd gardener or maid?"

"I am glad my own family have done little investing out of England on a matter of principle, as far as I know," Clara commented.

"Me too. My mother's investments, now mine, are all tied up in Scottish enterprises, as befitted bankers."

"Oh, there's the bell for dinner," said Clara.

"Good, I do love having the children dining with us, young though they are."

"Of course, dear Malcolm, we are on our own in this country, with no family relatives, so the more we all see of each other, the greater all our ties will be."

"On another matter, darling, are we going to have another baby soon?"

"I was about to tell you, I think so, but it is only the first signal I have had and I prefer to wait for two such signals to be sure. We should give him or her a least one name typical of this colony."

It had become the Gargery custom here in South Africa to dine with their children, not simply because they had no friends but because they were anxious to support them wholeheartedly in a strange land. Malcolm had not had much trouble convincing Clara that this was desirable, remembering with regret his own separation from this parents. Moreover, it was essential to teach the children how to behave at dinner, but also to have longer conversations with them than would have been the case in London.

"Would you like to go to school, George?" Asked Malcolm.

"Oh yes, but is there a school near us?"

"Yes it is very small, about twenty young boys and it is run by a Mrs. Enderiprist. Your mamma has met her and thinks she would be a good teacher."

"What would I learn?"

"Well," said Clara," you can read and write already, but it would give you the opportunity to make friends."

Conversations continued with the children as they did not go to bed till until the sun had gone down since it was difficult for them to sleep in the light. Eventually, the children were sent upstairs and the couple went out into the garden, hand in hand, walking together in the twilight.

"So, my dear, we have been here a while now. Are you enjoying it?"

"Immensely, and with my contacts with men like Botha as well as my travels outside Port Elizabeth, I have got a clear picture of the politics which, I feel, are inevitably going to lead to a second war."

"Will that affect us?"

"In general, yes, but the prospect of fighting around here is most unlikely. My main worry is that my services might be required elsewhere, perhaps in Capetown."

"We will go where you are, darling. I am determined not to miss a moment I can get with you."

"That warms my heart. I'd dread being on my own now that our life has become so wonderful, but the political problem we face is that the Boers in their states hate the pioneering people, like Rhodes, with a vengeance. The diamond trade I worked in rested on mines in Natal. In the last few years, diamonds and gold have been discovered in the Transvaal and we, the British, are bound to want permissions to extract these very, very valuable stones and metals. I would not dare predict what will happen, but my best guess from my conversations, and I have said this to the Brigadier, is that the Government needs to anticipate the Boer starting the fighting. I am not sure that we have enough troops in the country to repel them."

"Do you think we ought to return to England, and you give up the Gordons?" Asked Clara.

"That depends. I don't anticipate fighting around here as I have said, though I am sure the port would be more alive than it is with soldiers arriving. We will just have to see how it works out."

"Yet while I am enjoying our life here," said Clara, "I don't know for how long. In so many ways I am quite content not to have any social life, apart from my regular coffee mornings with Mrs. Makepeace. I love teaching my children and tinkering on the piano. I love the sunshine, the garden, but most of all, as I said, I love being with you, and I cannot tell you what a relief it is that you are not going to be in combat."

"I share all those sentiments, darling. I have got used to my eye-patch, although I still hanker after a glass eye. I am concerned that my socket will close completely and not have the room for one. I'll make it my responsibility to discover whether one may be available in this colony, but I expect it can only be done properly in London."

"Do that, please. But darling, there are times when I miss London and our friends there. I am very anxious for the children growing up here and what it will be like in their future. I feel we are somehow pioneers, so we lack the accoutrements of civilized life – galleries, theater, concerts and that is a form of deprivation for the children."

"That had not occurred to me, I'm afraid, probably because for much of my life I grew up here. I constantly reflect on is the number of different races there are here and how they are treated. Apart from those of European stock, Dutch, English, Scots, there are the Cape Malays, folk brought here from south-east Asia. There are some who are clearly from India that I recognize and then there are the indigenous people and I suppose those are fewer and refugees, perhaps, from their tribes."

"I do not see them as much as you do, of course, though I have noticed differences. To be open about the matter, darling, I am torn. I was brought up to believe every race except the Europeans are either children or savages. But when I see a mother with her child, whatever her race, I see her with the same sentiments and behavior that I have as a mother."

"Indeed. I vividly remember Tom Hesketh's conversation when we were on that boat coming back from India. We were discussing what it felt like to kill a man, and how after the first time, it became much easier. But then he said that he'd look at the men he shot and thought that they had wives and children and how he was destroying a family."

"I suppose we grow up with our racial and social views and they are very hard to break, I am very glad I brought Matilda with us, not because I would not employ a girl who was not white but because I would find it difficult to treat Marjorie in the same way as we do not share the understandings that I have with Matilda. I don't know why."

"We share with Matilda a common background of being English, whatever the class differences. It is those little understandings as you put it which make life easier. Why do we put the forks on the left? You would have to teach all those little things to, say, a Muslim girl from the Far East. I am fortunate, Clara, in two ways. First, my father was a preacher and it was drummed into me early on that every person is one of God's children. Second, while my parents were at the mission, I was working with all kinds of people, not just European, in the diamond trade."

"Did your father and mother see Africans as children in the Mission?"

"Oh no. They regarded the men and women as their friends and as children of God and treated them without distinction. I only spent two separate weeks with them the whole time they were at the Mission and I did not go when Harriet was there. But we had a meal on three different occasions with African families and it was clear that there was no master-subject relationship. My mother learnt to cook all kinds of dishes, helped by African women and my father tried to learn crafts Africans used to build the small church at the Mission."

"I suppose a Christian faith should diminish one's prejudices."

"Tom's notions are with me constantly. I fear that a war always makes soldiers and those at home feel superior to whoever is the enemy. I wonder if my ideals will be tested again if a war with Boers comes, which it surely must. That applies to nations, I suppose."

"Let us hope war is postponed," said Clara. "Now I had put this at the back of my mind, but don't you think it would be good for the children if we had a dog?"

"I had put that aside too. I will talk to my Brigadier as I think that breed had much to recommend it."

"Pip darling let's go away for a couple of days, Brighton or Bournemouth, for walks on the beach or near the sea, anywhere. It is mid-August and the weather seems set to be fair."

"How about north Kent, my old country? I'd like to visit my father and mother's grave, it's been too long."

"Let's do that later after we have planned a visit, see the Pirrips and the Fletchers, and stay longer. From there we could visit Canterbury and there is that famous oyster eating-place at Whitstable too."

"That is sensible, it would need planning. I will send a wire to the Grand Hotel in Brighton. Joseph can get himself to school."

The couple took the train from Victoria the following morning, had lunch in a small café on the Eastbourne Road and were back in their room for a rest by three o'clock. It was cloudy and threatening with rain, so there was little incentive to explore the beach or the pier.

Harriet undressed completely as Pip struggled with the studs on this shirt. Naked, she went over to him and helped him. He smiled:

"You are so beautiful," he said, "though we are both getting old."

"I have never stopped desiring you, and I loved you from the start all those years ago in Salford."

"Life has been full of adventure for me," and he led her by the hand to the bed, stumbling slightly from his limp. He would admit that he was not as physically compact as he had once been. Sagging skin around his chest, almost bald, a developed pot belly and a face starting to wrinkle heavily.

She too had slightly sagging breasts, but her skin was free of wrinkles or the blue marks of old age where her limbs had bruised. They lay caressing each other and began to enjoy each other more perhaps than they had done since that erotic engagement in her rooms in London when his wife Susanna was alive. Intimacy in Africa was as rare as the moon at midday.

They lay together afterward and he said:

"Why have we stopped doing this? I mean, we have not stopped, that is true, but we rarely enjoy this kind of intimacy."

"I don't know. At night we are often simply too tired and want to sleep. In the morning, well; there's Joseph rattling around so we are not alone."

"Unlike now. The hotel is protecting us from the outside world."

"I want more of this, my darling, rather than Ireland," she said stroking his arm, with his head on her breast, "I know you are as fiercely engaged in this Irish activity as you have always been with any project that comes your way."

"I don't want to go back to Ireland, Harriet," he said abruptly.

"Good. I cannot tell you how glad that makes me. It has been a dreadful worry for you after Seamus' murder and the conversations with the Board. Tom is obviously willing to go, but how about Hannah and the baby?"

"Whether or not he goes depends on what the Board wants to do and I don't see any collective commitment emerging, do you darling?"

"No," she replied, "we have four lawyers on the Board, and they should be able to rule in or out the option of paying the tenants to emigrate. That does seem a far-fetched view of the word 'relief.'"

"I agree. I think we should go back to the original idea. Give the land to each family, though in ancestral terms this is merely to return to them what is theirs, give them a small stipend, say ten pounds to get them going, and hire as many as needed to plant trees on any spare land."

"Now that would be something Tom might do for a year, Pip. Of course he might be prepared to farm the land that is vacant himself."

"Possibly, but what does he know about farming?"

"Don't suggest it, or he might find it attractive. I feel like a drink and dinner, don't you, old man?"

She rolled on top of him, kissing his neck and then his chest, going down his body to his wounded leg which she caressed with such loving care that it led to more of the same.

The weather had cleared; after dinner they strolled on the stony beach in front of the hotel, and other couples called 'good evening' as they walked. She suggested that they should get to know the children of their friends, but they postponed further discussion. The pier beckoned, but the band had stopped playing as it was nine o'clock, so they returned to the hotel and slept the sleep of the gods.

Walking along the beach the following morning, Harriet began:

"We really don't know the children of our friends well, do we? Joseph is fourteen years old now, but he is becoming very scholarly, interested in pursuing classical studies at a university and while he chats from time to time about school acquaintances he has not asked if he can invite one home, nor has he been invited. I am of a mind to hold some sort of gathering whereby the children of our friends get to know each other. It is now some time since Malcolm and Clara went to South Africa, but as we grow older, there will be strength for all of them in not merely being vaguely acquainted but real friends who can share their life and experiences."

"What a marvelous idea. We could hire a small steamer and have a party on the river, or we could entertain everyone at home. Of course, we would ask their parents as well, but it would primarily be for the children.

"But who are these children we might invite?"

"Let me think of them all, said Harriett, starting to count out the children on her fingers. "Of Malcolm and Clara's children, George is eight, and Alice is five, and Andrew must be two years old, and there's the baby Susanna."

"But they are in South Africa," said Pip.

"How silly of me, of course, I wanted us think of all our friends. Put those distant Gargerys aside. You know Clarence well, and Emma and he have four children. The youngest Elizabeth is eight, Alexandra is twelve, Sophia is sixteen and coming out next year, and then there is young Clarence now almost nineteen and I believe already studying law at Cambridge.

"Albert and Victoria family have Ellen at five, Pip at ten, and Beatrice almost twelve.

"Then Mary told me about Elizabeth Egerton's children, Henry who is nineteen and at Cambridge, young Oliver at fifteen and Charlotte at twelve, nearly thirteen.

"Then of course there is Tom and Hannah with Hector, but they may be in Ireland."

"Who else?"

"The Simon Brandrams. Felicia was murdered of course, but they have Jude who must be near twenty. The Masterson children we do not know, and they are much older."

"Good heavens, darling, where on earth do you get all this information? I had no idea."

"Each time a child was born I received a notice card and I have kept them. I really want all these children to grow up as friends and support each other, although I am sure they won't all come, especially the older ones. Without the Gargerys in South Africa, that makes twelve in all.

The children's party finally assembled on Valentine's Day and it seemed a success. Afterwards Harriet and Pip sat with a whisky in their drawing room discussing the event. London had lived up to its reputation for weather, the evening being cold and blustery.

"Did you notice how Joseph and Sophia had immediately paired off?"

"Yes, the four older children also seemed very good friends. Excellent social practice for all of them."

"The younger Pirrips were used to being on their own," said Pip, "but they seemed to enjoy themselves. Albert and Victoria seem very prosperous and it was so good of them to travel up from Numquam. Did you notice her rings and the quality of his dress coat? Timber must be a profitable trade."

"I noticed how civil the young people all were to each other," said Harriet. "Sometimes boys will tease girls in occasions like this one. Alexandra, for example, has a bit too much puppy-fat which might make her a target, but when one listens to her you can almost tell that she is the daughter of a famous lawyer and a very gifted mother."

"Bullying seems to come naturally to boys before puberty. Then their minds and bodies focus on the opposite sex," said Pip, "and the transition is somehow innate, though I don't remember it myself, probably because I did not come into contact with any girls, living in the marshes, until I was in Chatham as a farrier."

"Many boys imitate their fathers. I cannot imagine young Clarence or Henry being anything but courtly gentlemen in their homes."

"No, precisely, and when younger, those boys have both been to schools where there are bullies they probably admired, are terrified of, but would not dare imitate them at home," said Pip.

"Perhaps such schools which do not educate girls with boys provide a setting for boys to rut with each other like stags on a mountain."

"We have such a fine son, Harriet, have we not? I am sure it would never have crossed his mind to be rude or impertinent to girls."

"Yes, Joseph makes us both so proud. I wonder how much these Egerton children have been affected by their father's death. This is obviously a good topic for the League of Women. I had intended to ask Antonia Penoyre about it, as she is supposed to be the convenor."

"Should we make this party an annual event?" Pip asked.

"I am not really attached to Guy Fawkes and all that, so next year it would have to be a Christmas party.

Clarence's knowledge of Ireland was limited to what he read in the papers though he had listened conscientiously to the Commons debates on landlords, rents, rebellions in Ireland. Before the Irish problem came to the Trust with Clara's legacy, he had tried to avoid entanglement with Parnellites in the House. He found his position sitting on the Irish fence very comfortable and making no demands on his energy. A clerk in the Commons had arranged a committee room for the meeting with the Londonderry MPs but it had to be postponed on various occasions as one or other of them had used various tactics of delay, and the summer, a long period when Parliament did not sit, had also intervened. So it was October, nearly nine months after the proposal at the Board that the meeting was convened.

"Let me begin," said Clarence, "by thanking you gentlemen for meeting with Major Hesketh and myself, and let you know why. Sir Hamish MacDonald is detained in Court and sends his apologies. I am Chairman of the Jaggers Trust for the Relief and Education of the Poor, a wealthy philanthropic organization created from the will of Nathaniel Jaggers."

"Was this the same Jaggers who appeared in Lord Binding's case? That was a disgrace to treat a distinguished peer of the realm in that way," said Mr. Atkinson.

"I am sorry I do not know what you are referring to, sir."

"Let me you tell you then. Jaggers so upset my father's old friend Arthur Binding by getting his civil case appealed three times, leaving Binding virtually bankrupt and all because of some altercation with his brother-in-law Dingleberry, a nincompoop don from Cambridge."

"H'mm," said Clarence, "that sounds like Jaggers if I grasp his reputation, but may I proceed?"

"The estate at Clumber in County Londonderry was willed to a Mrs. Clara Eustace, grand-daughter of the owner…"

"And a damn fine gentleman he was too, and a good friend to Londonderry," interrupted Atkinson again. "Family descended from one of Cromwell's New Model Army, you know. Henry Fitzcuthbert was one of Ulster's finest, a brave soldier and an Irish patriot."

"Didn't know the man, except by reputation. Is it right he was a prodigious lover?" said Sir Thomas Lea, "I heard he sired a few Catholic fillies in his youth."

"May we proceed, gentlemen," said an exasperated Clarence, while Tom Hesketh realized this was unlikely to be a useful exchange.

"Mrs. Eustace was surprised by her grandfather's generosity but had no special interest in the estate and, to cut the story short, she decided to sell the property to the Jaggers Trust for a modest sum in part as a charitable gift. I should add that she is a wealthy woman and found the idea of the estate not to her liking."

"Why did she not put it on the market?" Asked Knox. "I know there were several buyers around the County and in Donegal who had their eye on it well before Fitzcuthbert died."

"To be frank I think she thought the Trust could handle the tenants better than she, as she saw the extreme poverty there which she wanted to be ameliorated."

"She should have put managers in there," said Lea, "what about Cunningham the bailiff? I remember Henry talked about him as a good man."

"He emigrated to Australia, I believe, with financial support from Mrs. Eustace."

"That's an odd thing to do," said Lea, "wanted him out of the way, I suppose, but what does the Trust have in mind for the estate? I would not advise anything too controversial. We men of Ulster know well that you English do not understand our situation at all. Not at all, at all," this repetition being a common phrase in Irish parlance.

"Oh no, Lea," said Atkinson, "the English in general understand nothing about the four provinces not merely Ulster. Those of us whose families have lived here for generations know our cause: Never surrender the country to Popery and that means getting rid of Fenians."

"English ignorance," added Knox, "is found in the do-goodery that arises from people like you who do not understand that the native Irishman is close to a savage."

"My experience of Irish people is limited, I must confess," said Clarence.

"Mine is perhaps greater," said Tom, "I have come across many a soldier in my time from different parts of Ireland and they make excellent disciplined fighting men," to which there was no reply from any one of the three MPs.

"Gentlemen, I would like to achieve from this meeting, if not your support for our plans, but at least no active hostility. Since Mrs. Eustace inherited the estate, the plantation house was burnt to the ground. Then since the Trust took over, one of the tenants was brutally murdered and a member of the Trust Board was attacked in the same affray. I hope I can rely on your support if only to condemn such acts of violence."

"I am sure we would not wish to condone violence," said Sir Thomas Lea, "provided it is unprovoked. A provocation would include any attempt to destroy the natural order of society in Ulster."

"I very much doubt whether our plans would do that. Let me give you an example of one of the many options we are considering. As with Cunningham, the Board might pay as many of the tenants as wanted to emigrate. The land released would then be planted with many hundreds of trees, such that many animals might return to their natural habitat, not least providing areas of woodland for hunting and shooting."

"You know," said Atkinson, "it really is an Ulster tragedy that far too many trees have been cut down over the years, the need for wood being so important, but forests for hunting and shooting would be welcome, however long it took to grow."

"Another option," said Hesketh, "is to offer tenants a choice between emigration and giving them title to the land."

"That is where you need to be very careful, Major," said Sir Thomas, "ownership of land carries with it some voting rights and God save us from having heretics on the electoral roles."

"For my part as a devout Protestant wishing evil to none," said Knox, "I am not opposed to philanthropic work and would not be hostile to it."

"I agree," said Atkinson, "but please keep us informed of your plans so that we are able to give public support where it is desirable. I am based in Dublin and I am somewhat indifferent to Ulster."

"My support is guarded," said Sir Thomas, "I do not believe your Trust can contribute much to a historical situation in which there is an established hierarchy and a set of social conventions in place. I mean you no ill will, mind, but please do not give me reason to be your opponent."

"Little is likely to happen in the very near future anyway," said Clarence, "and Major Hesketh is going to do some exploration and research."

With that the meeting broke up and Clarence and Tom both sighed with relief.

"Now I know why there is truth in the old notion that in argument the Ulsterman states his position and turns his back," said Tom.

At that Clarence smiled grimly and said, "I don't envy you, Tom. Just make sure Hannah and your baby are safe."

"I will, and if I need a Maxim gun, I will call on my friends in Aberdeen to supply one. Oh, and by the way, I am no longer allowed now to use my military title."

"I knew that, but I thought it might impress those dullards."

VIII

Hamish and Mary were surprised by Churchill's vehemence about women's suffrage; he was on the wrong side of history as Mary put it. Although she sensed the danger that the campaign might eventually become more militant if men like Churchill continued their intransigence, the attainment of the suffrage seemed to her to be a matter of when, not if. The idea of women actually fighting for their rights excited her in some ways, at least until she viewed the matter in the calm light of a cool day.

In the various meetings and parties for tea and dinner over Christmas 1896 and the New Year the original guests at the Smythes' dinner party regaled their friends with the claims of this political firebrand Churchill, with the result that the question of the franchise became a staple of discussion throughout the Christmas period. Indeed an interwoven theme in such discussion was the subject of marriage. Did the presence of the word 'obey' in the wedding ceremony extend to a wife's vote? Or did the secret ballot make that question redundant? Would the ability of women to vote be a central measure of their independence as a member of the polity with full rights? Voting and marriage were intertwined topics as Churchill's outburst had made abundantly clear.

The matter of marriage was raised in a case before Mr. Justice MacDonald in a stark and different form, one which occupied the attention of Mary too, for it raised questions about the contract implicit in marriage vows, tangential to matters of independence. For Hamish was preoccupied by a bigamy case. Nor was it that of a bigamous man but a woman who manifestly was someone who had taken her independence by the scruff of the neck. Mary was therefore highly intrigued as to the outcome, and so were her friends, Harriet in. particular.

The clerk called on all to rise as Hamish walked into the court. It was mid-December 1897, and in the dock was a woman by the name of Cynthia

Blackstone, aged thirty-five, of Streatham in the County of Surrey, who pleaded not guilty to the charges.

As the case for the prosecution began Hamish asked:

"To which husband does the surname Blackstone belong, one, two or three?"

"As we understand it," said Sir Ralph Standby, the Crown counsel, "she is using Blackstone as her name, but her maiden name is Naylor. If your Lordship pleases, I understand that the term may not be legally correct although that still has to be demonstrated."

"Quite so, Sir Ralph, the Court will call her Mrs. Blackstone. Please proceed."

"Cynthia Blackstone lived in Coventry in the Midlands. At the age of twenty-one, she married Thomas Bladon Cooperston in the church of St. Mary, Coventry according to records there. Mr. Cooperston was fifty-eight at the time, and a shopkeeper well known to the people in a quarter of that city, purveying groceries. The wedding took place on February 28th, 1896.

"M'Lud," Sir Ralph continued, "if your Lordship pleases, there is no need for me to ply questions to the defendant or invite witnesses to the stand to verify a situation which public documents clearly display. When lawfully married, the defendant undertook the ceremony of marriage with two other persons, one in a Welsh chapel to Daniel Jones in August 1896 and a third in a Registry Office in South London to Richard Andrew Blackstone in November 1896. I present to the Court Exhibit A which contains the necessary documents in certificates of marriage of Cynthia Blackstone to Thomas Bladon Cooperston, Daniel Jones, and Richard Andrew Blackstone respectively. I have added the death certificate of Thomas Bladon Cooperston, but as your Lordship will see, that untimely event took place after the second marriage and the death certificate for Daniel Jones which took place after the third marriage. Nevertheless, while only one of the three individuals whom Mrs. Blackstone married is still alive, the charges of bigamy stand as the exhibited documents reveal."

The examination of the documents completed, the Crown rested its case.

After the jury had passed the documents around, Hamish called on the defense counsel.

"Mr. Droitwich, you represent Mrs. Blackstone, am I right? I will not look kindly on attempts to prolong the defense to evoke sympathy for the defendant, given the public record."

"I understand that fully m'lud, but I hope that my examination of the defendant will not prove too onerous for your Lordship," a remark that Hamish felt verged on the impertinent, but he let it pass, though Mary in the Gallery thought it dreadfully rude, as did Harriet sitting next to her.

"Call Cynthia Blackstone to the stand," said Droitwich to the Clerk of the Court at which there were murmurs around the court as she took the oath, for she was a most attractive slim woman with striking blond hair and very intense blue eyes in fashionable dress with a large hat.

"Mrs. Blackstone," began Mr. Droitwich, "would you tell the Court about yourself before your marriage to Mr. Cooperston?"

"Yes sir. I was born and bred in Bethnal Green, that's in London, but when I was older, we all moved to Coventry and I tell you I was glad as I was fed up to the back teeth with London."

"Now tell the court about your marriage to Thomas Cooperston."

"Tom and me met first when we was passing in the street. I had dropped my glove, I didn't mean to, it just slipped out of my hand as I was thinking about my mum who had died the week before and I was hoping she'd gone to Heaven though she could be a bitch sometimes but I was hoping God would forgive her. That was January when she passed."

"Mrs. Blackstone, you must just answer your counsel's questions," said Hamish, thinking this woman has the mind of a butterfly, flitting from flower to flower, or topic to topic.

"Yes, your Worship,"

"You should call the learned judge 'your Lordship', said Droitwich.

"Sorry, your Lord Worship."

"No, just 'your Lordship' will do."

"Sorry Judge," said Mrs. Blackstone wanting to cut through the etiquette of the Court, "all this palaver makes me so nervous, I hope it does not show..." at which a woman's voice from the Gallery shouted: "Of course it shows, you trollop."

"Silence in Court," bellowed the Clerk and Mary and Harriet turned around to try to locate the woman.

"I must warn those in the public gallery that I will have offenders ejected if there are any more interruptions," said Hamish, "please continue, Mr. Droitwich."

"Mrs. Blackstone, you were describing the circumstances of your meeting Mr. Cooperston."

"I had just come out from Cantilever's Millinery Emporium as I was thinking of making something nice for my dad's wedding, and I was on my way to my lodging."

"I thought you said your mother had just died," said Droitwich, unable to resist this irrelevance.

"Yes, she had, but as my dad said, no point in crying over spilt milk, so he asked Mrs. Clappermouth, she who was the widow next door but one if she would, and she said yes, much to his surprise, and she says why wait, I knows your Maggie's not yet cold in her grave, but she won't mind as she was a good friend to me."

"Thank you for the explanation," said Droitwich, "but were you employed at the time?"

"Yes, sir, I was a shopgirl at Misanthrope's."

"What then happened?" continued Droitwich.

"Tom was ever so kind that afternoon, taking me to a coffee shop. I remember it as if it were yesterday. He was so sweet, a proper gentleman, though I knew he was much older than me, but you know, Mr. Droitwich, love falls where it will. It were a whirlwind romance really."

"So he asked you to marry him?"

"Oh yes, only two weeks to the day after we first met. We'd been seeing each other every day at five o'clock on the dot at Lucy's Coffee Shop like I said and he popped the question there. He had a nice grocery business where I was going to help, me being a shop girl, but we had to live in the house with his sisters. I'd asked him why he'd never married and he said his sisters would not let him."

"Liar, liar, liar," came from a woman's voice in the gallery, and there was a commotion as a middle-aged woman seated just behind Mary and Harriet and wearing an extravagant hat was removed. Harriet started to giggle and Mary asked her gently to control herself, though she herself found it difficult.

"But you were prepared to marry him with that knowledge?"

"Of course, 'cos I loved him. I never met them sisters before we was wed, but they were so nasty to him, well, Connie was the worst, but the younger two Dottie and Fannie they were as bad to me."

"How long were you married before Mr. Cooperston was taken ill?"

"Only three days and nights, poor lamb. The first night we was both dog-tired after the excitement of our wedding, and there was a terrible row with Connie too."

"So three days is the answer to my question."

"You take the words out of my mouth, Mr. Droitwich, and on the second night after a big row with Fannie, we was walking in the park and I asked him if we could go to Brighton for a honeymoon, but he said no as he was worried about his shop."

"So it was third night of your marriage that he fell ill."

"Yes, poor lamb."

"Trollop, whore, strumpet," cried another woman's voice such that Mary and Harriet were alarmed by the ruckus just behind them as the woman resisted a burly official removing her. Another scuffle in the Gallery ensued, and yet another middle-aged woman was ejected.

"Oh my gawd," said Mrs. Blackstone, pointing to the Gallery, "that's Fannie Cooperston."

"I hope that's all three of them," whispered Harriet to Mary.

"As long as they have not brought reinforcements," Mary replied.

"Please focus your attention on my questions, Mrs. Blackstone; you were saying."

"Well, yes, on the second night my Tom, bless his heart, could not, you know, could not, I shouldn't say it really, but he couldn't do it, poor lamb and I told him, I said, Tom darling, don't worry, we'll get it right soon."

"I see, and on the third night?"

"I don't want to say what happened as it's too private to me and it was very sorrowful, but he was ready, and I was too, but then this strange look came in his eyes and he just flopped on top of me in the bed, and Christ, was he heavy, but I managed to get out from under, and there he was unconscious. I had to call for help."

"Do I understand from your account, Mrs. Blackstone, that your marriage to Mr. Cooperston was never consummated?"

"What do you mean?"

"I mean, did you in fact never have relations with Mr. Cooperston?"

"Well, the sisters were his relations, though what with my mum dead and my father marrying, and my brothers God knows where, I didn't have any relations."

"No, Mrs. Blackstone, I mean sexual relations."

"Oh dear, I'm surprised you should ask about dirty things like that in public, Mr. Droitwich, but the answer is no and I don't thank you for asking."

"Let us move on," said Droitwich, increasingly puzzled as to how to handle this woman. Hamish too was slightly baffled by her answers, while Sir Ralph was quietly reading briefs and Mary and Harriet were having difficulty restraining their giggles at the defendant who reminded them so much of Nellie.

"So," said Droitwich, addressing the jury now, "Cooperston fell ill of the apoplexy the third night of the marriage, and the marriage was not consummated."

"Mrs. Blackstone, what happened when your husband became so stricken, paralyzed and unable to speak?"

"I had to call his sisters to help. The following morning, before the doctor came, Connie told me to leave and gave me two hundred sovereigns," at which there was a gasp from the Gallery, "and I was glad to get away from those three bitches who had been so nasty not just to me, but to my Tom. I took their money and was glad to go."

"But you were aware that Mr. Cooperston had not died."

"Of course, when I was leaving, I went into his room and gave him a big hug and he squeezed my hand ever so gently, though he didn't open his eyes and he couldn't speak."

"Tell the Court now about meeting Mr. Daniel Jones."

"I moved down to Mumbles in Wales and found a little cottage for rent as I had the money. Anyway, every weekend, I'd walk along the beach and sit watching the kiddies playing on the beach. Daniel found me quite pretty as he'd come and sit next to me regular. He told me his wife was dead and he had no children. I felt sorry for him, all on his own, with only his cows for company, so later I told him I'd live with him if he wanted, no thought of marrying him as he didn't seem interested in that, rather he just wanted company."

"Which month was this?"

"Must have been end of June."

"Can I assume we will hear Mr. Jones's testimony?" Asked Hamish.

"Regrettably no, m'lud. He died in an accident with a new threshing machine at the end of October 1896 when all was being safely gathered in, as the hymn goes."

"Of course, that is in the Exhibit, but Mr. Blackstone is well, I trust?" asked Hamish which caused ribald laughter around the court eliciting another trombone-like bellow from the Clerk.

"Indeed, three months after Mr. Cooperston's apoplexy," said Droitwich once again addressing the jury, "the defendant made it clear to Mr. Jones that she was prepared to offer him a woman's favor which he accepted. The defendant moved into Mr. Jones' home at his farm outside Crickhowell in June 1896."

Turning back to the defendant, Mr. Droitwich then asked:

"Was this a happy state of affairs?

"Oh my lord yes, and he was as strong at his age as I think a young twenty-year old would be, so regular such that I never understood why he and his old lady never had children."

"Then that August, Mr. Jones offered you his hand in marriage."

"Well, I told him I thought I was having a baby, not surprising after what we'd been doing, so he rushed me down to the chapel in Abergavenny and we was wed."

"And there you made your wedding vows?"

"Yes, though I did not understand a word of what the preacher said as it was all in Welsh."

"But you were not expecting a child, were you?"

"As it turned out, no. I mean, a woman knows, don't she, when she's expecting, and I thought that I must be expecting and my body told me I was."

"But there was no child."

"No, but do you want me to explain why?"

"That won't be necessary, but did he at any time ask you whether you had been married?"

"No, never."

"But you knew you were married to Cooperston."

"No, I wasn't married no longer, see. My poor Tom couldn't do it, it wasn't consecrated, no, that's not the word, you know the one where he hadn't done it, consummated, that's right, my marriage to old Tom wasn't a marriage any longer, was it?"

"But legally it was."

"Not in the sight of God though, was it, how could it have been a real marriage when we hadn't done it? But Daniel was so upset when I told him it were a false alarm, and he told me I had trapped him into getting wed, all I wanted were his money, which was not true."

"When did you tell him?"

"As soon as my body told me I was not expecting."

"Compose yourself, Mrs. Blackstone, did your relationship with him change?"

"I'll say: Something terrible. He took me in the kitchen and beat me with a stick on my bum twice a day sometimes. He made me sleep in the cowshed for a week, but I cried so much, it upset his bleeding cows, so he brought me back in the house and set me up in a bedroom in the attic with the maids, so my marriage was over, he'd had enough."

"When Mr. Jones asked you to marry, did you tell him about Mr. Cooperston?"

"No, like I said I didn't as my marriage to him was over as it wasn't consummated."

"That does not matter in the eyes of the Law, as I told you earlier."

"Well, I know that now, don't I, or I wouldn't be standing here, "she said caustically. "Oh, I'm sorry, Mr. Droitwich, I didn't mean it."

"Can that remark be struck from the record, m'lud?" asked Droitwich pleasantly.

"Strike the record and continue."

"If it pleases your Lordship," said Droitwich, anxious to bring a sense of calm into the proceedings, "Jones was a farmer of such means that his household comprised a housekeeper, three servants and several farm hands. The defendant had not been required to do anything in the household at the farm, so she was left much to her own devices, and as she was very lonely especially at night in her little attic room, she began to take regular walks on the hills near the farm without her husband in the early Autumn."

"Let me be clear. Which year was this?"

"Thank you, m'lud. That would be the autumn of last year, 1896."

Turning again to the defendant, Droitwich asked:

"Mrs. Blackstone, how did you come to meet Mr. Richard Andrew Blackstone?"

"Dick? You mean my Dick? I never knew his middle name was Andrew, isn't that a thing? Well," she said, pulling herself together, "he was with a group of friends on a walking tour early that October, and they was living at the Lamb in Crickhowell. I first met Dick out on the Beacons."

"How long was his group in Crickhowell for?"

"A week, but I met Dick his first day out with his friends and asked if I could walk with them, and we got talking and laughing and flirting a bit. Funnily enough, I found out later that my poor Tom had died later in that very week I was with Dick, poor bugger with those sisters."

Mary and Harriet were now open-mouthed at these extraordinary revelations, looking at the woman in the dock with unrestrained admiration mixed with horror.

"Please tell the Court, Mrs. Blackstone, how did your relationship with Mr. Blackstone develop after Mr. Jones banished you?"

"First of all, that Daniel Jones did not care what I did. He put me out like I was the cat being put out at night, and he was not bothered what I did or where I was. I stayed overnight at the Lamb with Dick most nights that week and Daniel didn't notice."

"Did you tell Mr. Blackstone about Mr. Jones?"

"Why should I? He had kicked me out of his life. My marriage to him was over. When we was wed Daniel said that he would give me all his worldly whatsits, that's what they told me he'd said in Welsh, and keep me for better for worse, but he had stopped doing all that, and I was really upset. Sod 'im, I thought, two can play at that game. I had no one to care for me till my Dick came along."

"So you then went with Mr. Blackstone to his home in Streatham after his walking tour was over early in October without telling Mr. Jones."

"Yes, and I told Dick a little while later that I was expecting his baby which was no surprise to me or him. That was November, and we got married in the Office, not in church."

"You knew you were breaking the Law, but he did not."

"Law, law, law that's all you people think about! Tom couldn't do it, Daniel threw me out, and only Dick cared for me, bless his heart. I think the way it happened and the way I was treated, I didn't do no wrong, and I wanted my baby to have a father and a proper name. So, yes, I married him, and bother the law. You see ... " and here she hesitated.

"Go on."

"I know bigamy is wrong, but I had always thought it meant that for a woman it was when you had two husbands at the same time, or for a fella when, you know, you had one wife in London and another in Bristol and be to-ing and fro-ing between them. I didn't think I was doing bigamy once Daniel threw me out. I was never with one of them when I was with the other like a bigamy person would be."

"But you made religious vows to him."

"He broke the vows first, didn't he? Once he did that, why should I keep mine?"

"Thank you, Mrs. Blackstone, that will be all. Call Mr. Blackstone to the stand."

None of the women in the Gallery thought that Mr. Blackstone would be anything but a desirable mate. He was handsome with a disarming smile, a strong red beard, and was dressed for his appearance in court as any gentleman would.

"Mr. Blackstone," enquired Droitwich, "were you captivated by Mrs. Blackstone when you encountered her in Crickhowell?"

"Oh, yes, indeed, she was a real poppet. I found her quite enchanting, beautiful and full of just regular common sense, though I admit that I did not know she was married when we were together at the Lamb Inn."

"When you slept with her, you mean."

"Yes," said Blackstone with a slight blush.

"So do I assume correctly then that you had no knowledge whatsoever of her marriage to Cooperston or to Daniel Jones?"

"I fear not. I understood she was living at a farm with a dull old farmer but that he had stopped desiring her company, though I did not know why and frankly, I did not care."

"So she deceived you in that respect."

"Not quite deception, she failed to tell me of her marital situation."

"How did you discover that?"

"When Farmer Jones realized she was missing, he had hired an investigator to look for her, one Samuel Endweary, sometime that November if he told me aright. Jones had apparently sent out search parties but gave up assuming she was either dead on the Beacons or elsewhere.

"How did he come to hire Endweary?"

"As I understand it, Jones went to the Lamb for a Christmas drink and told the customers about his missing wife and everyone began to laugh loudly and Dai Evans, the landlord, told him that she had gone off with me, to which Jones did not take kindly. He recruited Endweary, who later enquired at the Lamb but Dai refused to give him my address, as he was not a policeman, so he spent the first part of this year searching for us."

"Once Endweary tracked you down in May of this year he told you of Mrs. Blackstone's marriage to Jones, and you had been married since the previous November?"

"Yes, just after our baby arrived, early I'm afraid, he told me and I was surprised and I suppose I was very hurt. I did not ask Cynthia about his claim, for with the new baby I was anxious not to upset her. London police arrived two weeks later to arrest her, presumably on advice from Brecon, and the magistrate granted her bail because of the baby, but sent her for trial."

"Sir Ralph, do you wish to cross-examine?"

"No m'lud, my case rests in the Exhibit, and the Court has had quite enough melodrama for one day."

"I suppose it is not necessary to hear from Endweary."

"No, we do not need his evidence," said Sir Ralph.

"Pray proceed then, Mr. Droitwich, to address the jury,"

"Members of the jury, Mrs. Blackstone has shown considerable courage in revealing to us her state of mind and body during these so-called marriages. Here is a woman whose sensibilities are more attuned to matters of the heart and body than to the problems of the law. At the time, she believed two things:

110

if a marriage is not consummated it ceases to be a marriage, and if one party to a marriage breaks his or her views, that releases the other party from the commitment.

"I must point out to you, however, that in none of these three relationships does Mrs. Blackstone show one jot of malice. She is not a conniving woman, or a woman so filled with lust that she wants two or three husbands at once. My learned friend has argued that the document in the Exhibit speak for themselves, but Mrs. Blackstone surely deserves some mercy at your hands."

"The court will now adjourn and we will resume tomorrow," said Hamish quite anxious to discuss this bigamy case with Mary.

"I assume," commented Mary over dinner, "that she had initially been anxious to marry to get away from dire home conditions."

"I suppose so, but she offered this interesting explanation as to why the institution of marriage with its rules is complicated. If the husband breaks his vows, does that release the wife from hers?"

"Morally, I certainly think so, and Harriet and I were enormously impressed by her. You realize, don't you, Hamish, that she is the victim here, poor woman."

"But she has broken the law twice, Mary."

"Maybe, but she is unable because of her social situation to fulfil herself and her needs. A rich woman could take lovers by the handful and not be affected in terms of her status or situation."

"One law for the poor, another for the rich?"

"Absolutely. Obviously she is going to be found guilty, Hamish, but what on earth is the point of sending her to prison?"

"I agree, my dear, but my hands are tied by custom and law."

"I find one aspect of this so interesting. Presumably the only reason why the state, as opposed to the church, should be interested in marriage is the property rights the act contains. Of course, the Church has embellished all this with 'holy matrimony', to exercise its own control over us sinners. Why not ask Blackstone whether he would forgive her as the other two are dead?"

The following day, Hamish took the prosecution's line, and summed up for the jury by simply rehearsing the dates, adding that while the Court had heard Mrs. Blackstone's evidence at length, the documents demonstrate her bigamy.

"So, members of the jury," he concluded, "in the eye of the laws, the defendant entered into two unlawful marriages one with Mr. Jones and one Mr. Blackstone. You must now retire to decide on the defendant's guilt or innocence.

The jury then returned promptly with the verdict Mr. Justice MacDonald thought was necessary on legal grounds. Mr. Droitwitch then asked permission to recall Mr. Blackstone to the box where he indicated that, as the two former husbands were dead, he was prepared to accept the defendant as his wife, especially as he was now a father.

The judge then sentenced Mrs. Cynthia Blackstone to a term of a suspended sentence of six months in prison and bound her over for ten years. The details of the case were widely broadcast in the popular press and the mercy shown by the judge was praised by many women, including Hannah Gargery who, for all her Presbyterian predilections was becoming more attached to the cause of women.

"Was justice done?" asked Hamish that evening.

"You're becoming quite a wise old owl," said Mary.

"You know, darling, I really began to like her very much. I found her answers to Droitwich quite endearing, very straightforward, but showing a woman of real character not one to be browbeaten into submission by anyone. I much enjoyed her reasoning on why she felt she was not a bigamist, as I said last night. The question of breaking the vows is a serious point, my dear. If we think of a commercial contract which, like an oath, is basically a promise, no one would argue that if one party breaks such a contract, the other is committed to fulfilling their obligation under the said contract, would they?"

"That must be true, Hamish, the problem is that 'for better, for worse' phrase which must have been quite new when Cranmer or some other divine wrote it. I know it is obvious, but your case brings out just how a woman can be treated, especially by that Jones man, and how her assertion of independence alarms all and sundry. As usual, it is women who suffer from laws written by men for men, and Mrs. Blackstone should be seen a heroine in the long struggle women have to endure to get equality."

"I so admire your fervor in these matters, Mary, and I hope that our civilization will gradually put these matters to rights."

1898

IX

By the Spring of 1898, life for all the Gargerys had new challenges. Malcolm and Clara Gargery had settled into life in Port Elizabeth, though British relationships with the Boer Community in the Transvaal were very unsettled. Malcolm's liaison responsibilities extended beyond the confines of the garrison stationed there to the higher commands based in different areas across the whole of the Cape Colony.

Pip Gargery had become committed to the Trust's work in a variety of activities in London's East End while his wife Harriet Gargery was intent on re-establishing the League of Women, given the increasing talk about votes for women, and she had begun to lay the groundwork with the women who had been involved.

Yet it was the Clumber Estate and its future that occupied the attention of the Board and particularly Hannah and her husband Tom. The meeting with the three Londonderry MPs had convinced Clarence and especially Tom that here was a project that was worth his time, so the Hesketh family had crossed the Irish Sea to Clumber. After Tom told Hannah of the meeting with the Irish MPs, they were both enthusiastic to seek to counter this patent bigotry, however minor their efforts would be in comparison to the politics of Home Rule. Yet the birth of their son Hector had been a delight for both of them and was not seen to count against involvement in Ireland.

Hannah realized that Harriet, no longer her nemesis, would be a good source of advice about Clumber as she had gone with Pip to the African interior. The comparison struck her forcibly and she realized there was a sense of mission present in both activities. The two met one afternoon for a walk along the river near Cheyne Row.

"Harriet, I need to talk with you about this Clumber venture."

"I will offer what I can, although I privately think Ireland is a matter for politics not philanthropy."

"I know, but you ventured to Africa with my father and I guess that was quite a trial for you."

"Indeed, it was. I went for no other reason than that I loved him and wanted to be with him. I was in a state of funk rather than terror for him, for Joseph and for me. The very idea of it was difficult to comprehend, but I thought he needed my support there. After all, your mother and he had been partners and I tried to offer as much support as I could, though without her religious zeal."

"That is a very interesting perspective for me. I was worried that my strong active husband might sink into depression since the Regiment simply can't offer a man with one leg any worthwhile challenge. Even with a prosthetic replacement which I hope will come to fruition, he could still not return to combat duties. I know administration of all kinds bores him to death. This Clumber assignment must succeed, as it gives him purpose and challenge."

"The situations are not that different then, Africa and Ireland. Of course, you are much nearer home. But one matter will challenge you as it did me. You are almost cutting yourself off from your friends, and I suspect that it will be difficult to create friendships with Protestants who will think anything done for Catholics a betrayal. They are so unlike us."

"H'mm, I had not thought about that. It will mean writing lots of letters to keep up with my friends both here and in Scotland. For you that was not possible, I suppose."

"No indeed, the mail took so long, but it did mean that Pip and I were, so to speak, on a desert island. It was not all sweetness, light, sermons and friendships with the local population, as there was some hostility to the Mission, you know, as there is bound to be for you."

"I see. I need to be aware that my relationship with my husband will be very intense and close. I suspect that I will have to find something to do which complements his work."

"That can be very frustrating. In my case, I tried to teach the children English as the local language had no script and the dialect was tough to understand."

"This is so helpful. I think I must regard our presence there as living in a foreign land. I must not assume anything about social behavior, language, attitudes or relationships."

"What about young Hector, and presumably those as yet unborn?"

"I will make certain he has friends to play with as he grows older."

"One other matter, Hannah. Pip and I both realized soon after we arrived back at the Mission together that we had had enough. I would counsel you both to fix a period, say, two or three years for your stay and that you persuade the Board quite soon to start looking for a successor. When the time is up, you know, there will be plenty of work for Tom and you back here in London."

"That is useful too, as I think Tom perceives this as an open-ended commitment. I must get him to define its length."

"Do not misunderstand me, Hannah. I would not do this, even if I were younger, but I admire Tom's interest and I can see he needs something to challenge his talents. I will support you both in any way I can."

"Thank you so much, Harriet. I do hope you will come and see us with my father of course at some convenient time."

"We will, I promise, not least to see our grandchild, if you are happy to regard me as a grandparent."

"Of course, of course."

The Hesketh family settled at Clumber in the March of 1898.

Harriet told Pip one morning in mid-April that she was going to find the Penoyres, deciding simply to call at the Putney address she had obtained from Honora a long time ago. On a sunny April afternoon, she walked up the river which circled around to Barnes Bridge. Trains crossing the bridge disturbed her with their proximity as they rumbled past, but she was on the footpath alongside the tracks which gave her quick access to the west side of Putney and the walk to number 7 Lower Common was quite straightforward.

This was a splendid very large house, quite new, set back from the street but with a charming view across the Common with All Saints Church on the eastern side. That too looked quite new, though Harriet was ignorant of ecclesiastical matters. It was not typical of her to call without either being invited or sending a note indicating her intentions, but she surmised Antonia was no specialist in etiquette.

A perambulator was set against a large bay window to the right of the front door with its large porch and pillars. Harriet raised an oak-leaf brass knocker but as she did so, the door opened and Antonia shrieked:

"Harriet, it is Harriet, isn't it? How wonderful to see you!"

"Oh, Antonia, what a lovely welcome."

"Come in and sit in the garden with us. This weather is surprising for the autumn."

Together they walked quickly down a capacious hallway through a massive conservatory and out into the garden where Aubrey was lying on a rug and, as far as Harriet could count before she was given a chair, there seemed to be at least four children rolling on the grass, playing with hoops, wielding tennis rackets and in one case attempting cartwheels. The youngest child was naked.

"Darling," said Antonia, "this is Harriet Middleham."

"Well," said Harriet, "no, actually I am now married to Pip Gargery."

"Really, wonderful, how come?"

"His wife Susanna died in Africa where they were missionaries. He had yellow fever too and returned to recuperate. We met again, married and we returned from there some time ago now."

"Pip and Susanna, h'mm. I don't recall them. I suppose we must have met them at that party."

"She did come to the Numquam meeting with Estella, but she and I were then, how can I say this politely, not the best of friends, yes, not the best of friends will do. That was long ago."

"Ah," said Antonia, "were you his lover?"

"Dear me," replied Harriet, "the short answer is yes, but it is very complicated. He and I were very close for four years when we were young and neither of us were married. We then met by accident and had a couple of days together when his marriage was in difficulty."

"How lovely, was he not a preacher? Did the wife guess?"

"Yes and yes, but that is all water under the bridge, I am glad to say. I am even quite reconciled to his two children, both married, one in Ireland, the other in South Africa. I have a son, Joseph."

"Is Pip his father?" Asked Antonia with a grin.

"No, though their relationship is now one of father to son. I went to vacation in Paris and had an attachment to a painter who was eventually uninterested in my bearing Joseph, so I returned to London before he was born."

"How exciting. I always thought you might be a bit of a rascal. I so admire women who are just tired of miserable conventions, are completely independent and choose their own way of life. We try to do that."

"Indeed, for a long period of my life," said Harriet, "I was a free lover, though nowadays, I am older and much in love with Pip."

"A free lover? Aubrey and I wonder how one would conduct oneself with that stance to life, for I assume you don't bed any male in sight, do you?"

"Good Lord, no. Free love does not mean a loss of integrity in a relationship, rather it implies not being bound by the conventions of relationships between men and women. But what about you?"

"We are very happy indeed. Aubrey came into an inheritance from his brewing family, so we bought this house as it was being built and live a life of leisure. We do not have servants either, as we want the children to grow up both free and responsible."

"You are very fortunate."

"Yes, but no one leads a charmed life, you know. I have not had time to revive the League. Aubrey was very ill for almost a year and as he now ingests some new potion or other he is much recovered. You can tell which year that was because we did not have a child."

"Goodness me, that is a challenge. How many do you have now?"

"Six, Aubrey and Rex are the eldest two boys and they are staying with their grandmother in Hertfordshire, and these," she said pointing to the youngsters rolling around the garden, "in descending age, are Charles, Margaret, Estella, and Ellen the baby. I love having children and now we have an equal number of boys and girls we may stop," and, she said addressing her husband, "may we not darling?"

"Perhaps, perhaps," he replied with a soft growl, "though I doubt it."

"To move to more sober matters," said Harriet, "I have been meaning to be in touch to see you and ask about the League of Women. There are various movements concentrating on votes for women, and those are all very desirable. Can we do something more, to get beyond the formal political emblems of freedom like voting or owning property to get at the drudgery and despair which haunts the life of many women?"

"I was most interested in such activity when I was a young woman, but with six young children I do not see how I would be able to contribute. I should have resigned from the League long ago, but as no one else that we knew seemed ready to be involved, especially after Estella died, I neglected the responsibility and let it drift. So, I am sorry, Harriet, I truly am, but you must count me out."

"I understand and I sympathize. I am no model of virtue in terms of working for good causes. I spent time in Africa with Pip trying to bring Christian values to the people in a large village in the bush. I did a little, helping women, but my heart was not in it."

"There is a line between general support for a cause and active prosecution of it. I would gladly give money to causes I supported, but my family comes first. Is that selfish?"

"I don't think so. Of course, I am much older than you and I have plenty of leisure time. Those who are privileged have an obligation, if they believe in a cause, to promote it. My conscience is rattled from time to time when I see that I only talk about good causes, but rarely act on them. I have no excuse."

"Oh conscience, now there's a thing! Our dilemmas are not really such as I would call them matters of conscience, partly because they don't keep us awake at night which I believe exemplifies a matter of conscience. So I would gladly host a meeting here once in a while for discussion on extending the suffrage, and I could bring in my women neighbors, most of whom on the Low Common I have met. If that counts as promotion, then I might do that, but either way it is not on my conscience."

"Conscience apart, there are so many matters particular to the lives of women which men do not countenance. So remedying that distress rarely creeps to the top of the political agenda. The expansion of education is always publicly considered by men in terms of a nation's needs for prosperity, not as a relief to women for the burden of bringing up their children."

"Interesting remark that. Aubrey and I spend our lives bringing up our children which I realize is an immense privilege as most people lack the wherewithal. Or, more likely, a parent is so much involved in other matters that they spare no time for their children."

"Do you do anything different from the ordinary parent? Discipline them? Teach them to read? Teach them good manners?"

"I don't know that we have any worked out scheme and to be frank we started to read books about raising children, but that was a fad. I suppose that French philosopher Rousseau was the most influential but we like the idea of the kindergarten. An adult needs to get out of the way of a child's growth."

"Do they go to school?"

"Good heavens no!"

"So you don't teach them to read?"

"You mean to a set timetable? No; we read stories to them and they see us reading. The older ones have all asked to learn to read and did so very quickly. Each child will in its own time. More of interest, they are all so different by temperament and interest. Charles there is fascinated by anything mechanical, not surprising for a boy, but then Margaret follows him. I see them both becoming engineers."

"And personal cleanliness?"

"Oh dear, I hope I don't shock you with this. We simply do not do what we were taught to do, again keeping out of their way. With the babies, we use napkins, but they soon get the idea from watching us."

"Watching you?" asked Harriet in astonishment.

"Yes, when we use the water-closet or the chamber pot, one of them usually comes to watch and they soon pick up the idea. I know that sounds odd, if not disgusting, but all that early training you and I had is so unnecessary. We pride ourselves on not being prudes, but we draw the line at them being with us in bed."

"I am sure that is wise. So modesty is not a virtue?"

"I don't know, Harriet. We see it as an exciting experiment. We provide clothes, of course, and they learn to dress as early as possible, that is, when we stop dressing them.

"So far, as a large family we learn social habits like taking care of each other, having conversations around the table. The urge to intervene is always with both of us, so we try not to. I suppose where, as a mother I might have said 'Stop that!' I now always try to ask a question."

"What do you mean?"

"I'd say, 'do you think that is a nice thing to do?' or something like that to get them to think about their actions rather than being told."

"You are both very brave, Antonia. Your children cannot live in the cocoon of your family for life and it will be their eventual interactions with the world outside that may prove a challenge."

"You are right, of course, and just before Aubrey was ill, we had begun to think about it."

"What was his illness?"

"He had pneumonia, badly. Doctors were surprised that he survived. His health is now a difficulty. We have even considered moving to a sunnier climate where there is less rain."

"We would miss you, but health is vital. They say that a mountainous environment is excellent for diseases of the chest."

"Switzerland might be a good move, but who wants to live with the Swiss?"

"Right, my dear, can I search out women who might come to a revived League and meet here in your lovely house?"

"You won't mind, will you Aubrey?"

"The more women we can convince of our pioneering efforts, the better," said Aubrey, and Harriet was struck by how unusual it was for a man not to insert himself into the conversation.

"Expect to hear from me, Antonia. Goodness me, how do you remain so beautiful and desirable with all those children?"

"I'll tell you one day, Harriet," said Aubrey, laughing contentedly.

Elizabeth Egerton was in her living room feeling particularly miserable after breakfast one May morning, not least because the rain was beating on the windows and London was a grey soggy mess. Sir Clarence Smythe was announced, and Elizabeth rose hurriedly from her chair to greet him.

"How are you, Elizabeth? I think you are looking much better than you were after those terrible times around Timothy's death."

"Yes, I do feel better on the whole, though today I'm in the dumps, I must say. I am very glad you called, however, as I want to have you as my lawyer. You and Emma have been so kind, and I inherited Timothy's lawyer, John Petersmith whom I have always disliked and avoided if at all possible. I propose to write to him with my instructions on the subject, if you are willing to accept me as your client."

"Nothing would give me greater pleasure, but was there anything that requires my immediate attention?"

"I suppose I should review my will and my assets as I am considering emigrating to America. Timothy and I were very happy when he was posted there. We visited the West Coast for a holiday and the weather is idyllic. I'd fancy a bustling town called San Francisco, but I am not sure I could live in an earthquake area. There would need to be arrangements to make about transferring everything into dollars, if I finally do decide to leave."

"That is a most profound shock, Elizabeth. Yes, profound indeed."

"Why Clarence?"

"This is far too difficult to say coherently, but in my mind and in my heart I am developing a loving attachment to you such that I would be mortified if you were out of reach."

Elizabeth looked at him in amazement. How could anyone think of her, a dowdy widow, as an object of love, especially such a handsome man of great distinction?

"I don't know what to say to that, Clarence. To begin with, your wife Emma is becoming a good friend to me. I think you are a most attractive man, but in the abstract, so to speak. It simply never occurs to me that I might love anyone after Timothy, certainly not Albert who was my lover when we were young."

"I know, I know. Yet I cannot bear you not knowing how I feel if you are seriously planning to go to America as you seem to be. This is completely out of character for me, you know, but I am just totally and completely preoccupied with thinking about you, and I also know this is as imprudent as could be. I feel I had no choice but to burden you with my love for you."

"I am immensely flattered, dear Clarence, but you must know that anything more than friendship with you is quite out of the question for me. It is true, I confess, that I do miss the intimacy Timothy and I had, but that is the widow's lot."

"That need not be yours, you know. We could be very discreet."

"Clarence, my friend, there is no such thing as privacy in affairs of the heart. We would be discovered, even in the unlikely circumstance that I felt able to agree."

"You will consider it then?"

"No, Clarence, I fear not. Be my lawyer and my friend without the complication that would stain my friendship with Emma with deceit. Go away now to your Chambers and think of some legal matter or other but please, please put me out of your head, as I don't think your conscience could cope with infidelity."

With that she took his arm and walked him out to the front door, where they shook hands and he looked at her as an infatuated schoolboy with mournful eyes would gaze on an unattainable beauty.

Elizabeth then walked slowly upstairs smiling to herself at Clarence's intensity, glancing into her children's bedrooms and longing for them to return from school. She returned to her drawing room, sat down at her Steinway and indulged herself with a couple of late Haydn sonatas before lunch.

After lunch, she was about to take a walk, when Albert was introduced.

Sitting down next to her on the large settee and looking at her closely, he took her hand said, "How are you, Elizabeth? I need your comfort."

Goodness me, she thought, was this going to yield another proposal from a married man?

"For some reason Victoria has got it into her head that I am in love with you and she lost her temper recently when I told her of our meeting and my solicitation for you after Timothy's death."

"Precisely what has that got to do with me, Albert?"

"You have completely upset my equanimity. Meeting you showed me yet again just how foolish I was to neglect you all those years ago in Paris. Your very presence reminds me of our intimacy and how we relished each other's bodies. As I looked at you when we first met recently, I went over our time in Paris and I remembered that you neglected me as much I neglected you."

"Wait, please Albert. Are you really making me responsible not merely for our break-up in Paris but also for your present state of mind with regard to me?"

"I know you can't help it, Elizabeth, you are so damn lovely. You arouse my most tender feelings and desires which have long since disappeared from my marriage. I dream of you constantly and I know we could become lovers, restoring what is properly ours. I need you, my darling Elizabeth."

"Stop, stop, stop. As you seem to be a tortured soul, let me put you out of your misery. I thank you for your support in my troubled times, but I would never, ever, consider any kind of relationship beyond friendship with a married man, least of all you who has betrayed me once."

"No, no," cried Albert, throwing himself on top of her and attempting to kiss her which she resisted fiercely. A struggle ensued in which she was just able to wriggle out from under him, stand up and ring the bell for the maid.

A disheveled Albert got up from the settee, while Elizabeth said to the maid:

"Mr. Pirrip is just leaving," while Albert mumbled an apology and meekly followed the maid to the front door.

The maid returned:

"Is there anything I can get you, Ma'am?

"Yes, a cup of tea and an unmarried man," at which the maid giggled and left.

Elizabeth sat down awaiting her tea trying to comprehend a day in which two men had presented themselves to her as her lover, though in different ways and for different reasons.

"What on earth are they thinking?" she said out loud.

Then to herself she said, "I must share these episodes with someone, but who? I can't talk with Emma, obviously. I don't really know Mary MacDonald, but my Aunt Charlotte always spoke highly of her. I will send her a note."

The Hesketh family had travelled to Ireland shortly after Hannah's meeting with Harriet in March. It was a fine cool afternoon in June 1898 when Tom and

Hannah took Hector in a perambulator with its high wheels and canopy up the hill to the remains of Clumber House, destroyed by fire when Malcolm was there. The flower beds which nestled around the house had recovered from the collapsing stones, broken glass and wooden windows. The buds showing earlier on the rhododendrons were now in flower, and the fruit trees in the old orchard had begun to lose their blossom. An elderly bay tree was the closest to the house, which stirred in Hannah's memory the Psalmist's phrase on such trees flourishing, but one side of it was charred from the fire.

"I wonder," said Tom, "whether we could clear this site completely, certainly not restore the house but use the stone that is left elsewhere."

"What a good idea. We could extend the Lodge, I am sure, and have tenants do the labor, even use what is left over for their cottages."

"We must think about it. The Lodge is indeed quite small, though comfortable and it could do with another bedroom and an administration office."

"Are you getting used to this strange country, Tom?"

"Yes, though I am comforted by having a defined three-year period which you insisted on, bringing me down from five years. We'll be having a break in London soon as I am sure we will get news of the prosthetic for me, and I must make a list of what we have done to include in the report."

"We have achieved a lot in two months, you know."

"Yes, I think we have," said Tom. "Clumber tenancies on the estate are now free, and the costs of maintaining the estate are covered by the Trust. We have attacked poverty through the monthly payment to tenants. We have not had any protest about this from the other community."

"On the health side," said Hannah, "we have already improved the prospects of everyone on the estate, whether it be nits in children's hair or a changing diet. The physical strength and mental health of every man, woman and child is quite apparent to those who knew them before. The wives and daughters have some basic health education, such as hand-washing, using napkins for babies rather than letting them run around naked."

"Father McGowan told me all that generates more goodwill than the financial payments."

"I wish sometimes I was fully qualified as I am really only acting as a doctor."

"That does not matter, you are not required to deal with pneumonia or anything very serious."

When they returned to the Lodge, they found three women sitting on the grass outside having a cup of tea before heading home. There was Mrs. Darcy, the housekeeper from the destroyed main house, and Colleen and Beth, the housemaids there. who assisted with the housework.

Conversation between the five of them had helped Tom's research into family legend and lore. When they returned from their walk, Mrs. Darcy got up and hurriedly brought out a chair from the Lodge for Tom, and Beth brought out another for Hannah. There was now a significant level of mutual confidence because both Tom and Hannah liked the women and treated them with great respect, unusual for these women in their lives at Clumber. Tom was certainly the first man they had seen without a leg, but they soon got over their curiosity and the presence of Hector still their earlier and obvious speculations.

One afternoon a week later Hannah was chatting with Mrs. Darcy in the small kitchen about her life, whilst Tom was in the next room writing the report but he could overhear the conversation.

"Do you have family on the estate, Mrs. Darcy?"

"Oh, yes, Ma'am, my maiden name was Lynch, large family we was, six of us. I was eighteen when I married Sean Darcy, my husband, now long dead poor soul of a disease of his head."

"Would that be meningitis?"

"That's the word, taken terrible he was."

"Did you have children?"

"Only the one, Colleen, and then I came to work in the big house first as a maid, then as cook."

"So, did Sean die soon after you were married?"

"Lor, bless us, no. There was almost ten years, but I'd not been able to have another child. That was like my father, his dying young, but then I was never certain that my father Michael Lynch was my father, God rest his soul."

"What do you mean?" said Hannah with dismay.

"When he was a young man, the Colonel always exercised his rights, as he called them."

"I am sorry, I don't understand."

"Oh yes, it's been tradition here and on many estates in Ireland. The landlord takes any bride he wants to his bed before the husband. There's a French name for it, I am told."

"That's right - Droit de Seigneur," said Hannah scarcely able to conceal her disgust.

"Of course, the Colonel was much younger when he took my mother," she said, as the tears came to her eyes, "but my father never recovered."

126

"Oh, dear, I am so shocked," said Hannah as Tom came into the room, struggling with his crutches, his face burning up with anger having overheard the conversation.

"Mrs. Darcy, I have never heard of anything so terrible. And you say it has been a regular practice?"

"Oh yes, sir. There were some brides he didn't want, but some of them didn't have a choice."

Both Tom and Hannah were agog at this revelation.

"Them landlords could do anything, you know."

"What do you mean?"

"Ask old Mrs. O'Carroll. She's the widow on her own and must be well into her seventies by now."

"We've met her."

"Now her husband would not let her go to the big house the night of their wedding. The Colonel came to fetch her with his man. They beat him so badly that he died that night while the Colonel was having his way with his wife. She did not have a baby and when she was young, she used to say that she wished she had."

"Was there nothing you could do?"

"What could we do? The laws were against us all the time. They had rights, we didn't."

As this conversation ended, Hannah was weeping and holding Mrs. Darcy close to her. Tom had to leave the house, the anger still burning inside him, his crutch thumping on the gravel as he sought to cool his temper, as he now understood that remark made by one of those bigoted MP that the Colonel had sired a few Catholic fillies. How disgusting and uncivilized. The revelation vigorously enhanced his determination to discover everything about these tenants that he could.

He had not yet talked to Father McGowan in any serious way, so he clambered into the trap and set off to Claudy, though it was now toward evening, calling out to Hannah that he'd be back in a couple of hours.

The housekeeper showed him into the priest's study where he was working.

"Father, I need to talk with you."

"To be sure, Major Hesketh, I'd be delighted. I've felt it impolite to ask in our brief acquaintance so far, but how did you lose your leg?"

"I was wounded on the North-West Frontier so badly that they had to amputate it. I am used to it, and a London firm is developing a prosthetic leg for me."

"I suppose that will be a blessing."

"Perhaps, perhaps, though I'll have to learn to walk again."

"Father, as you know, I am here as the representative of the Jaggers Trust. My task is to report about the history and conditions on the Clumber estate so that decisions by the Board are fully informed. I have just come from a discussion with Mrs. Darcy, our housekeeper that has made me both angry and appalled."

"How come, Major?"

"Droit de Seigneur. I thought this was a practice of medieval princes like the Borgias, long since abandoned in civilized Europe, and here I find this evil Fitzcuthbert man, the former owner, guilty of forcing himself on young brides on his land."

"You're shocked, Major?"

"Why do you say that, Father?"

"I have never understood how it is that the English who live over there seem utterly oblivious to the evils inflicted on the Irish population by their kinfolk. My family originally came from Munster. They were starved out and the province then was laid waste by the English and some Scots so that they could be given title to the land."

"Did that happen in Ulster?"

"You need to go back at least six hundred years. The Statutes of Kilkenny were a failed attempt to impose English law and customs while making most Irish customs and the language illegal. It's getting near three hundred years ago since that King James brought over the heathen Scots to be given land that was the ancestral property of Irish families."

"Yes, we have been finding that out on the Clumber estate."

"The really strange fact, you know, is that Protestants treat 'King Billy" as their hero because he won the Battle of the Boyne, and Catholics toast 'the little man in green velvet' honoring the mole that killed that King."

"How so?"

"The king was killed when his horse stepped into a mole hill and threw him off."

"I'd never heard that."

"Yet, and this is what is stranger, what both the Protestants here and the English ignore is this. In the Treaty of Limerick which followed that battle, William and Mary guaranteed rights to Catholics including worship and land tenure. Though worshipped as a soldier, his political decisions were rapidly and completely ignored, God rest his soul."

"I confess my ignorance of all this. I have been brought up to believe the Irish were just continual trouble-makers."

"You know, Major, for all the evils that have been laid on our people, I feel sorry for the English and the landlords here. They have no conscience about their oppression in all its forms, and I know they will burn in Hell, and they do not see that is their fate. Now it is said that this right of landlords you discussed originated in Irish peasants offering their daughters to landlords to curry favor with them and it gradually changed into a right. No one is quite sure of the social history of this wretched practice and I think it is now largely abandoned. I am told planters in America use their women slaves as they wish. But that Fitzcuthbert, he truly was a devil of a young man."

"What can I read to learn about Irish history?"

"The only books I know are written in Irish and even they don't get at the truth properly, though I am told there was a history written by a Frenchman, Gustave de Beaumont by name, but I don't know whether it was ever translated into English. Now you've started by talking with your housekeeper, such a good woman. Ask others and you'll start to build up, family by family, the terrors of their existence. Ask them about the famine."

The conversation continued far into the evening as Tom received a powerful lesson in Irish history from a point of view that he, like most of his countrymen, had never properly been heard. No wonder the idea of Home Rule was such a contentious matter. He returned home late but it was still light in mid-June this far north. He collapsed into the arms of his darling wife whose loving comfort, he sometimes thought, simply kept him alive.

X

Elizabeth arrived in Cheyne Row the following afternoon to meet Lady MacDonald. Mary was becoming much like Estella Pirrip, a person to whom everyone went for advice or solace. Harriet was already there to report on her visit to Antonia.

"At last we meet properly, Elizabeth," said Mary, " though we were both at what I call the Churchill dinner. Really that young man seems unstable to me. I also do remember you from the time you were with your aunt Charlotte, and my goodness, what a splendid creature you now are. I hope you have not put the piano to one side."

"No indeed, I play whenever I can. Timothy bought us a wonderful instrument by a famous American firm Steinway which has robust tones and is generally quite beautiful."

"But do you know Harriet Gargery?"

"No, we have not met properly either. Let me see. You knew my aunt Charlotte then?"

"Indeed, and I married Pip after his first wife Susanna died."

"It is a real pleasure to renew our acquaintance. I have so many memories of my aunt and Estella here and in Paris, some good, some bad, but it was a wonderful time for me."

"Estella often talked about you and Albert."

"Albert is indeed a part of the advice I seek from Mary," said Elizabeth, "but I am sure with what I may call your provenance as known to my aunt, that you are capable of keeping a confidence," she said smiling generously at Harriet.

"I assume that you want help or advice of some kind and I hope it is not legal, for, even though my husband is a High Court judge, I know nothing of the law."

"I am sure you will both know of the murky circumstances surrounding Timothy's death."

"Indeed I do as Hamish had to recuse himself from giving the Government any advice as he knew you sufficiently well and he is a tiger about any conflict of interest."

"Why was Hamish consulted?" Replied Elizabeth with some alarm.

"I am sorry, I am not allowed to say. Suffice it to say that it was on some legal matter on which the Foreign Office needed clarification."

"Nothing to do with Timothy, then," said Elizabeth persisting with her questions.

"No, I can safely say that it was not."

"Oh dear, My husband's death seems enmeshed in varying webs of secrecy so I suppose I just have to get accustomed to the fact that I will go to my grave not knowing what really happened to him."

This response so upset Mary, seeing the immense distress in this poor lady's countenance that she broke her husband's confidence.

"Oh, dash it all, Elizabeth, Hamish was asked whether he thought the proceedings against his murderer should be in camera in the trial, a question of emphasis on treason or murder. They had not decided which grounds of which to prosecute."

"Oh, thank you, thank you, Mary. Now I at least know that if they are considering treason the murderer must be an Englishman. But that is an important part of the puzzle, although I am sure they will never tell me his identity."

"I am glad my breach of confidence has brought you a smidgin of comfort, my dear."

"Let me introduce a more light-hearted topic," said Elizabeth. "I had an experience last week which is something of a puzzle, and I know you will treat what I am about to say as an essential secret too. This involves men you know, so secrecy really is of the utmost importance. You may be tempted, I expect, to tell your husbands but I would rather you don't, as will become clear."

"My goodness," said Mary, "what on earth is this that is so secret?"

"This first is a state secret. My husband was posthumously awarded a KCVO, and I was commanded to the Palace to receive it. The Prince of Wales presented it and afterwards gave me tea and invited me to a soiree with two of his lady friends."

"Good gracious, importuned by the Prince of Wales, eh?"

"I made some excuse about going abroad, of course, at which he promptly left the room. Yesterday I had two male visitors on the same day, both of whom professed their undying love for me. Both are married and to a greater or lesser degree, they seemed to conceive that their passion for me was somehow my fault. Now I expect to meet them again, not least as I am very friendly with the wife of one of them. The other man is Albert."

"How simply terrible of them," replied Mary. "That makes three men pursuing you, a matter of good or bad fortune, difficult to know which."

"Why is it that men take such liberties with women?" Asked Harriet. "All three of them are assuming that, as your husband is dead and you are obviously a woman of great passions, that you are in need of their sexual services. Widows are familiar with such behavior, I am told."

"Of course, how obvious, it is my widowhood and supposed need that makes me their target."

"Absolutely. I always found Albert something of a rake in attitude if not in behavior," commented Mary. "May I ask who the other aspirant for your body is?"

"That is such a sensible way to put it! Neither of them have any intention at all of leaving their wives, not even for me. Yet the other man surprised me."

"Wait, let me guess. It must be someone we both know, I think. Now it is not my husband," she said with a smile.

"Let me think, it could not be Pip as he is too old for that sort of thing," said Harriet. "Albert we already have."

"It can't be Malcolm as he is in South Africa," said Mary, "so is it Clarence?"

"Yes, it is, so you see why secrecy is important. I asked him to be my lawyer, not my lover! But he behaved with me like an overgrown schoolboy, or perhaps like a spaniel with his tongue hanging out," and they all laughed.

"I must say I am very surprised, but you know, Elizabeth, I have long since given up the task of understanding men. I know he is devoted to Emma and when he wakes from this dream of you, he will be very ashamed of himself."

"But Mary, I am not sure that I can continue my easy friendship with Emma as I am bound to be meeting him in their house."

"Nonsense, of course you should continue," argued Harriet, "I have a strategy for you to finish off his dream which you should implement with all the courage and finesse that you have."

"Really, what is that?"

"Well, I don't know if it would have the desired effect, but how about this?"

"Go on, I am intrigued."

"When you are next with Emma, I expect Clarence will know of your coming and he will either be there on some excuse, or he will make sure he arrives when you are there. Let us suppose that the latter is the more likely. You are there, having tea with Emma and Clarence enters. When he arrives, you get up, take him by the arm, and say something like this:

"'Emma, my dear, your darling husband came to see me the other day and I told him I am engaging him as my lawyer, upon which he declared his undying love for me which I thought was so sweet of him, such a gentleman, but we decided' - and here you can look at Clarence firmly – 'that we would just limit ourselves to a lawyer-client relationship.'"

"Oh, my goodness, I can see that demands some courage which I am not sure I have."

"You will know better than I how to effect that, but it is not insulting, it can be passed over as a joke, Emma will plague Clarence with questions thereafter, but you will have killed his childish dream."

"What of her?"

"Yes, indeed. What of Emma? I know. When you finish that, you take Emma by the arm, address Clarence and say something like 'aren't we lucky to have such a faithful man, your husband and my friend and lawyer.' The critical point is to assure Emma that you are her friend, first and foremost."

"And," added Elizabeth in contemplation, "that makes it clear to Clarence that he should stop this silly nonsense as well. Goodness me, I love the strategy, Harriet, and I think I have enough in me to carry it off. But of course, Albert is a different problem because of our history together."

"I have a view about those who are successful in trade or business as he is," said Mary. "I know Pip the elder was his father and Estella his stepmother, but there is something about trade which coarsens a man. Now they may be good to their workers as I am sure he is, but they tend to see the world in terms of manipulations and contracts. This leaves them without a conscience."

"That is interesting, Mary. When I knew this sweet artistic boy in Paris, he was lovable indeed but then got swept up with louche painters and was unfaithful. Whether that was a sign of wild oats or not, it broke my trust in him. Now when he appeared immediately after Timothy's passing I was glad of his support, but he had become fatter, you know, the sort of tradesman who smokes a cigar not for pleasure but as a badge of wealth. I knew I could never re-establish any relationship with him."

"What was he like when he talked of love?" Asked Harriet.

"Disgraceful as he tried to smother me and I had to wiggle out of his embrace, call my maid and show him the door."

"Now that is not the behavior of a gentleman," said Mary, "manifestly, my dear, you need to cut any relationship with him, and probably that means his family."

"That is not difficult as he has bought another business in Chatham, and the family live in Estella's old house. Dear friends, I am so grateful for your advice and I will let you know how it goes with Clarence."

"Oh, and I am thrilled by the other part of your encounter with the Prince of Wales," said Harriet, "that is, I mean I am thrilled at the medal."

"It was a surprise, but again a secret. I will probably never be able to wear it of an evening. Among other things, I was told, Timothy foiled a plot to assassinate the Royal Family."

"Good heavens, how extraordinary," and both Harriet and Mary were profoundly shocked.

"I don't suppose you know the details."

"Yet again, no, I'm afraid," said Elizabeth, "the whole ghastly affair is wrapped in these parcels of secrecy."

"On another subject," said Mary, "you told me that artist John Singer Sargent had painted your portrait."

"You know, I had quite forgotten, which sounds ridiculous, but it is true. I must send him a note and ask for the portrait to come to me quickly. Timothy had paid him before he died. I suppose the good man is waiting for me to be in touch."

"Probably, but we will be very interested to see it, won't we, Harriet?"

"He was about to complete it when Timothy was murdered. He arrived one afternoon and we talked about the possibilities. Should I be left that 'charming young woman' or, should I be painted as 'grieving widow', or should we wait a year for 'middle-aged rather dour woman?'"

"Oh my, what a dilemma," said Harriet laughing at the way she described the three possibilities.

"Not really, I decided on 'charming young woman' as Timothy knew me. I am not certain why I have avoided getting it, or indeed him not reminding me of its availability."

"Oh, surely, you were not ready to receive it, and he was not anxious to foist it on you before you were ready."

"Well, I am ready now after all these excitements and whenever I look at it, I will remember my beloved Timothy who wanted it so badly and would have admired it so."

The Pirrip children had grown to love Numquam. With its outbuildings and beautiful gardens and with a mother brought up to country life, they were encouraged to play in the grounds though their schoolwork was always the formal priority.

The old elm tree had become a base for the children's imaginations and their secrets in their Grandma Nellie's time with Beatrice, the eldest, dictating to Philip and Ellen the parts they should play in an evolving drama around the tree, featuring various knights of old and their ladies for whom the tree was a secret meeting place. It was also a palace and its lower branches facilitated the creation of quiet boudoirs, secret chambers and even a round table for the knights to converse and it even continued, though with less regularity as they got older.

The alphabet children came to Numquam on very rare occasions, even when their grandma Nellie was alive, but Victoria wanted to be closer friends with her brother's family, so the Alphabet children arrived one mid-morning, and Arthur, Betty, Charlie, Dottie and Ernest were sent out to play with their cousins in the Numquam garden, while the younger two remained in the house. Victoria obliged her daughter Beatrice to act as host to the visitors. Arthur Fletcher was a little older than Beatrice and unused to a girl, any girl, from his family or from school disregarding his conception of what was to be. Nevertheless, he remembered his father's warning earlier in the day, that he wanted no altercation with the Pirrip children.

"We've never done climbing before," pronounced Beth, "I wish we had a tree like this."

"What do you play at, then?" Asked Beatrice, as they sat together on a low branch, side by side, but looking carefully at each other as girls do.

"Dottie and I have finished with our dolls and a house our Daddy made for us which we kept in the shed so the boys didn't come and spoil it."

"We love playing in this tree and since we moved here permanently we play all sorts of games with knights and beautiful ladies, and witches and wizards as we climb up in the tree."

"I don't know why we only have two apple trees, " said Beth, "but no big trees like this one."

"I don't know either. Beth, do your brothers play with you?"

"Oh no, the younger ones run around playing soldiers, and we don't play with them like we used to."

The younger children, Ernest and Frank Fletcher with Ellen Pirrip had left the tree to explore the rest of the garden, and Ellen was thrilled by the opportunity to show her cousins around.

The slender lightweight Philip was moving easily as usual as he climbed up through the branches, and the more solidly built and older Arthur followed though he had little or no experience of trees, living in the marshes. Indeed Arthur was what locals called big for his age.

"Wait for me," he cried, "I don't know about trees."

"Oh, it's easy, just don't look down."

"Alright I'm coming, I'm coming."

The pair were now twenty feet off the ground and Philip was coolly watching Arthur clamber clumsily up toward him. As the older boy got near, he reached for the branch on which Philip was sitting and began to pull himself up, but the combined weight of the two was too much for the slim branch and it snapped, sending Philip crashing through the branches to the ground screaming. Arthur missed his footing too as the branch snapped and he followed Philip down through the tree.

Beatrice rushed across the lawn to the house and into the drawing room where the adults were enjoying a glass of sherry.

"The boys fell out of the tree," she screamed, at which Horatio leapt from his chair and was almost at the tree before Albert could get to the front door.

"Oh Christ, what have you done, Arthur?" he said to himself as he picked up his unconscious son.

"And what about this Philip lad, young Beth?" He asked.

"I don't know, Dad, they just both fell past us to the ground."

Albert came puffing across the lawn, followed by the two mothers.

"Arthur, Arthur," said Beth, patting his cheeks, "are you alright, son?"

Arthur came round, groaning, "my leg hurts."

"Philip my precious," said Victoria to her unconscious son holding his head and saying 'wake up, child, wake up, child' as if she thought such an exhortation would stir the boy.

Albert hurried slowly across the lawn to the stable and found the coachman cleaning the carriage:

"Take a horse and go to Dr. Withington in the village and tell him the boys have got serious injuries falling out of the tree. Ask him to come at once."

The respective fathers carried their boys back into the living-room at Numquam House to await Dr. Withington, Arthur was now conscious, but crying with intense pain, urged by his mother to be brave and he was fortunate to have a strong blacksmith to carry him. Philip was still unconscious. In circumstances like these, the tendency for parents to apportion blame was irresistible, though young Beth had been unable to explain what happened as she was engrossed in doll talk with Beatrice and conversation was difficult with Arthur's cries and four very nervous adults, anxious that Philip had not recovered.

"Has Arthur any experience of climbing trees?" Asked Victoria.

"No, we got no trees like that near us, so I don't fink he's ever climbed one," said Beth.

"Too right," said Horatio, "stupid boy to try that. I'd bet he was just trying to follow Philip."

"That's not Philip's fault," said Albert.

"That's not what I said, Albert," replied Horatio aggressively.

"Well, our children are always clambering about in that tree, and they've got used to it," said Victoria.

Before any serious rancor developed, Dr. Withington strode into the room, a tall angular sort of man who always seemed in a hurry and talked in a series of staccato comments:

"What's all this? What? Boys in trees? Dangerous what. Dangerous, very dangerous. Never did it myself. Too frightened. Hate scratches. Come here, screaming one."

"H'mm," he said as he felt the fracture in Arthur's leg. "Not surprised, not surprised; boys climbing trees; broken leg. Damn painful what? Needs setting. Young bones mend."

"Can you mend it?" Asked Horatio.

"Good God, man, not me: Needs an expert: Hospital in Chatham: Directly."

"What about Philip?" Asked Albert.

"Let me look. Nothing broken," said Withington, as he ran his hands around the boy's limbs. Big bruise on temple. Blue, very blue." He opened Philip's eyes and said: "Hospital for this child too. Brain injury shouldn't wonder. Concussion at least."

137

"Is it serious?" Asked Victoria now weeping.

"Serious? Serious? Are you serious, madam? Recovery uncertain. Maybe paralyzed. Expert needed. Before he wakes up, get both to Chatham. Good day."

With that diagnosis, the doctor left as abruptly as he spoke leaving behind the misery of all the parents and the mystification of all the remaining children bar Beth and Beatrice.

"Mum," said Beth, "it was a terrible fall. Lucky Arthur didn't land on top of Philip, wasn't it?" But her mother was too upset at Arthur's condition to take much notice.

Each father took his son in his arms and walked to the carriage. Holding them on their knees, the conversation took several minutes to begin, as Arthur was moaning and Philip was still senseless. The jolting of the carriage on the track to the small village hospital made Arthur's pain worse, but it awakened Philip, who moaned in unison.

"Philip, Philip, Pip my boy," said Albert, knowing enough about paralysis to pinch each limb in turn and ask if he felt anything.

"Why are you pinching me, Dad?" said Philip between moans, "it hurts."

"I wanted to know whether you had feeling in your limbs, my boy."

Philip opened his eyes but said he could not see anything.

"What? Nothing?" Said Albert, waving his hands in front of the boy's face.

But at that moment, the carriage came into the hospital yard. While the doctor had suggested Chatham both men felt the nearest very small cottage hospital was desirable, not least because a dose of laudanum would ease their children's pain.

Elizabeth received a message from Emma inviting her to afternoon tea the following week. She was nervous as she approached the house, but her expectation that Clarence would arrive later was dashed when she was shown into the drawing-room to find him there with Emma.

"It is so kind of you to invite me," Elizabeth said, ignoring Clarence as she embraced her friend. Then taking the bull by the horns, she walked over to where Clarence was standing, his eyes moist with puppy love as he looked at her, and she took him by the arm and led him to where Emma was sitting pouring the tea.

"I am sure your dear husband has told you that I have asked him to become my lawyer, Emma, but in return, the dear man has covered me with such pledges of love and devotion that I thought for one moment he had misheard me and that I had asked him to be my lover, not my lawyer," and she glanced at Clarence smiling broadly.

Emma continued pouring the tea, laughing gently.

"Oh yes," she said, "if there is a beautiful woman around, you can be sure that my husband will profess his undying love. I think he does it to bolster the law practice, but you never know with men, sometime someone will take him seriously. So just ignore him, my dear."

Meantime Elizabeth gripped Clarence's arm firmly so that he could not escape her.

"Surely Clarence," said Elizabeth, "you are not a man to toss your affections around like confetti, are you? Yet I suppose as a lawyer you do get deep into the confidences of your clients and that will lead to friendship and mutual admiration, will it not?"

Before Clarence could reply, Emma intervened:

"It is one of the delights of being a lawyer's wife that when he tells me about his clients, I find myself guessing whether it is his friendship, his professional etiquette, or his dashing persona that makes him so adored."

"Now then," said Clarence, "I feel I am undergoing some dreadful surgery at the hands of you two and I have not been put to sleep, so everything adds more pain to pain and then more pain."

"Well, my dear husband, a successful man always has and always will try to shield aspects of himself from his wife. But I love you and I know you have a fulsome heart such that you feel drawn to beauty romantically, so your protestations of love to dear Elizabeth here I would anticipate and admire. It is part of your charm to me."

"And I agree about the charm, Clarence, and I look forward to many years of mutual confidence, admiration and friendship with Emma and yourself."

"I will now leave you two then for conversation and hide away in my study," said Clarence, almost as if he was a wounded stag, "but on a serious note, Elizabeth, please come to the office at your convenience. I have already indicated to your lawyer Petersmith that I am his successor."

As he left, Clarence felt completely baffled. He knew he had been utterly outgunned but in such a clever way that any hope of enhancing his deep desire for Elizabeth had now been comprehensively annihilated. He thought Emma was unfair, though, as Elizabeth was the first, certainly not one in a long line of potential lovers. Lack of experience probably accounted for the clumsiness of his approach, but now he knew Emma would be watching so any such future attachments would be impossible. But then, he loved his wife profoundly, so why did he shame himself so? He sat in his study chair for a while, thinking about Elizabeth and trying to imagine himself as a philanderer. Once he faced that possibility governed by reason, he saw just how miserable his conscience would make him. Whatever his desire for her, he really was not that kind of person.

As Elizabeth was leaving after a thoroughly interesting and lively chat not merely about men but about poets and novelists, Emma embraced her, saying:

"I cannot thank you enough, my dear, that is a true sign of great friendship."

"And you are my great friend," said Elizabeth. She then stopped in Cheyne Row and delighted Mary with her account, but now Mary was in a quandary as to whether she should tell Hamish. After all Clarence was the senior partner in the Courtisone and Jaggers practice.

Elizabeth hoped Mary could keep the secret.

The discovery of the droit de seigneur practice in the past on some of the Irish estates, particularly at Clumber made Tom realize that he needed to read about Ireland as much as he could. He thus wrote to Hatchards, the century-old bookshop in Piccadilly, asking if they could find a copy of a book on Ireland by a Frenchman Gustave de Beaumont which he had heard about from Father McGowan. He did not know the title.

A month passed and he received a letter from Hatchards which pleased him greatly.

'Dear Major Hesketh:

We are in receipt of your letter of the 23rd inst.

We do have a copy of William Taylor's translation of de Beaumont's book, called Ireland published in 1839, which one of our staff found in our basement filed under Geography. It achieved a mild success at the time, but his novel about American slavery was much more successful and is still in print. That is called Maria. We would be delighted to send you that book as well, were you to be interested.

We are somewhat uncertain why the Taylor volume was not of more interest to the British reader, perhaps because de Beaumont's portrayal of Ireland was disturbing to the English mind.

Please let us know whether you wish to purchase both books. Our total charge would be three pounds and we would be glad to mail them to you at our charge.

Believe me, Major, our most sincere thanks in advance, and we remain your most obedient servants,

Harold Braithwaite, Manager.'　　　　　　London, July 7th, 1898

With the same post came a letter from Guy's Hospital in Southwark, London, apologizing for the delay but that the prosthetic leg for Major Hesketh was ready to be fitted.

Tom looked up from his mail at Hannah feeding Hector and was overcome with delight.

"Hannah, my leg is ready. We must all go to London as soon as possible, and there is also a letter from that bookshop saying the book on Ireland is available."

"If this works my darling, it will make such a difference to your life and mine. I can see you playing cricket with Hector when he is bigger."

"Indeed, but probably not football," he said smiling.

Later the following morning, the carriage from Clumber put down the Hesketh family at Londonderry Station for the journey to Belfast and therefrom by sea to Liverpool and train to London. As they were watching their luggage loaded at the station, a porter said:

"You'se Major Hesketh?" in an aggressive tone.

"Indeed, I am, sir," was the reply, "to what do I owe the pleasure?"

"Me auld ma, she used to live at Clumber afore she came to me and my woman in the city. She's heard you'se doing good there, ain't you?"

"We do our best, but how did you know it was me?"

"Well now there ain't too many one-legged soldiers around, y'know, in these parts," and he laughed long and loud.

"Thank you, sir, but having one leg is no joke, I can tell you," Tom's anger now rising at the man's coarse laugh at his expense.

"Ach, no, I's sorry, not to mean it that way, I's just glad you'se doing summat for us poor wee Irishmen."

At this apology, Tom nodded and hurried Hannah and Hector into their carriage.

"Odd, is it not," said Hannah, "can you imagine such a man addressing you in a London street, let alone a train station?"

"No, my dear. The English tend to be much more private unless they are in their own enclave of whatever sort. The social climate, I suppose one would call it, is so tense here that such interchange is rare and a high risk. I wish I could understand Ireland."

After they had settled into their first-class cabin for the sea-crossing, they went into the dining room to have dinner before the boat left, hoping to get to bed before enduring the rigors of the Irish Sea.

Sitting at the next table was a very well-dressed man who insisted on introducing himself as James McAfee.

"Do you live in Ireland then?" asked McAfee.

"Yes," said Tom, "I represent the Jaggers Trust which owns the Clumber estate near Londonderry. Are you going to England for business or pleasure?"

"I hope both, so I do. I own a carriage shop in Belfast, and I am minded starting a shop where I'd sell some of these new automobiles, as they's not known in Ireland, so they are. But I heard tell of a doctor in Dublin who got himself an automobile last month, first in Ireland so they say."

"I heard that too, a Dr. Colohan. We have thought of buying one too, but the machine needs petrol to run and that would mean buying it in containers which seems a great labor."

"Indeed, indeed. I knows this fella and he's from England, and he's telling me about how he first bought one in London, now what was the name of the place, yes now, it were Vauxhall. He started it up with its two pedals and that wheel, what do you call it, a steering wheel, that's right, but you could not touch the metal, says he, as the electrics would shock you.

"Anyways, he sits tight on the seat in the automobile, says he, holds the wheel and off he goes, driving it in the street avoiding the horses, people and whatnot, says he, when he sees a peeler with his hand up, but he didn't know how to stop the thing, says he, and he goes right past him and the peeler gives him such a look of surprise that anyone could do such a thing!"

"Oh, my goodness," said Hannah, "what a good thing he didn't run into anyone."

"That's exactly what he said, but he's gotten used to the machine now and knows how to stop it."

"Do you think these mechanical contraptions on wheels will last and outdo the horses? I mean the trains have taken over transport over long distances, have they not?" said Tom.

"I don't rightly know, says I, but he tells me there are so many horses in London now and they all need feeding and there aren't the fields around for them to be a-feeding."

"I think we really should investigate having an automobile while we are in London, Tom. For one thing, it would be so much easier on your leg."

"Begging your pardon, Major, how did you lose your leg?"

"Oh, a battle in India, but we are off to London to get a wooden leg."

"Now there's a thing, isn't it? Just to think of that. I don't think I'se ever seen a wooden leg."

"No indeed, I wonder what it will be like too, but this one was built for me," said Tom, so I hope it works."

"You've a real shopping list in London, then? A leg and a motor: Anything else?" Asked McAfee.

"Yes, a book on the history of Ireland written by a Frenchman?"

"I hopes he's a Protestant Frenchman or it will all be lies," and here McAfee launched into such a virulent attack on native Irish Catholics that Hannah felt deeply embarrassed and Tom equally angry at the man's vehemence. However, Tom recognized that discussion about Ireland with this man would lead nowhere so made no attempt to engage him.

XI

In his days on the judicial bench Mr. Justice MacDonald was usually faced with men and women charged with larceny, charges of serious body harm, murder, burglary and other crimes, the warp and woof of criminal behavior becoming endemic in a society undergoing rapid change through industrialization. He'd enjoyed the bigamy case as it was so unusual, and Mary had prompted him to see how the status of women in society was embedded in the person of Cynthia Blackstone.

It fell to him, however, to adjudicate a case in which two men, Harold Upton and Tom Featherweight were together charged as associates in the crime of burglary on May 3rd, 1898, at the home of Mr. and Mrs. Henry Basing of 13, Lansdowne Road, Tottenham in the County of Middlesex who were holidaying in Bournemouth at the time, and both men had at first confessed but that morning changed their plea to not guilty, presumably on Honeycutt's advice.

The Crown Prosecutor was Sir Archibald Hamilton-Dawes, a well-established lawyer, whose Chambers were also in Old Square such that there was a fraternal, if not an intimate relationship between judge and counsel. Counsel for the defense was a tiger of a man, George Honeycutt, Q.C., whose ferocity in cross-examination was legendary and who reminded Hamish of his erstwhile predecessor, Nathaniel Jaggers. How these defendants were able to engage a famous advocate like Honeycutt was a matter of conjecture, but as his fees must be exorbitant, thought Hamish, perhaps the wages of sin were being put to good use, or perhaps Honeycutt was working pro bono.

Sir Archibald opened the case by pointing out that the defendants had admitted the crimes to the police, but had this day changed their plea to one of not guilty. In the course of the first morning, he relied on two witnesses, Mrs.

Charmian Haworth and Mrs. Denise Cloudless, both of whom claimed to have seen the pair leaving the house in Lansdowne Road.

On his bench high above the courtroom Hamish thought the testimony of these two ladies was flimsy to say the least and was therefore not surprised when Honeycutt did not bother to cross-examine either of them. Sir Archibald then called Detective Sergeant Latterly to the stand, after presenting the written confessions as exhibits.

Latterly was the senior of the two detectives who had arrested Upton and Featherweight and he gave an account of interviews in which they had made their confession, and on the basis of which the indictment was served. This was a quite straightforward account of how the men had been placed in separate rooms and each had admitted responsibility. Clearly these confessions were the vehicle on which the prosecution relied, ignoring the women's testimony.

It was these interviews that sparked Honeycutt's interest, however, just as Hamish thought he was on the point of closing his defense and conceding defeat. This cunning lawyer raised himself slowly from his seat, looking around the Court as if he was looking for his wife, a waiter bringing him a beefsteak or even watching a game of cricket, but his silent theatrical movements put his audience on the edge of their seats with expectation. Then, in a severe mode, he said:

"Latterly, let me take you over the evidence that has been presented. In your gathering of evidence from the first witness, Mrs. Haworth, where was this undertaken?"

"She came to the station, sir, after we had made public our request for people to come forward and she volunteered her claim that she saw Upton and Featherweight leaving."

"I see, and we have heard that she was accompanied by the second witness, Mrs. Cloudless, her friend?"

"Yes, sir, they both came to the station."

"So as far as the detectives were concerned, these two are the only material witnesses, independent of the defendants' confessions."

"Yes, sir."

"But are these not two elderly women whose sight, and perhaps motive, are strange matters for a detective to rely on?"

"Yes sir, they were not certain of the time of day when they saw the defendants."

"You and your colleagues were thus convinced that to secure a conviction, you would need admission of guilt from the defendants, notwithstanding their recent plea of not guilty which of course enables us all to have a longer day in court," he said with a smile.

"Let us turn however to the evidence of Upton and Featherweight themselves. You told the Court that they admitted guilt under examination by you and your colleague, Detective-Sergeant Morrow, that is, that they had both been responsible for this crime."

"That is correct, sir."

"Now, this is of great importance. Were Upton and Featherweight together in the same room when they confessed?"

"Oh, no, sir. Sergeant Morrow interviewed Featherweight and I took Upton."

"Then tell the Court how the evolution of their confession developed."

"Well, sir, in a case like this, we put the men in different rooms."

"Go on."

"Our purpose is to get a confession to secure a conviction, so we use a particular method."

"What is that, pray?"

"We try to convince at least one of them to admit guilt for that will imply admission of the other man's guilt."

"But as they are in separate rooms, Upton does not know what Featherweight will say, or vice versa? Did you talk to Morrow in the course of these interviews?"

"No sir, we each completed our assignment. Of course, each man can choose to remain silent as he is advised, and then he must hope that his colleague remains silent too."

"Presumably then you do not know whether they trust each well enough for either of them to remain silent, in the expectation that the other man would speak? Did you provide some kind of an incentive for one or other of them to a confess?"

"Yes sir."

"He that confesses is told that he will serve less time in prison if he confesses. He might even go free if we advise the court through counsel to recommend that."

"Provided the jury agree, of course."

"Of course."

"On this method then, a detective has three outcomes; neither of them confess, only one of them confess or both confess. Do you offer the carrot of less prison time to both prisoners, but without the other knowing?"

"Assuming that other evidence is inadequate, the ideal is that both confess, but the incentive of less prison time usually elicits some admission of guilt."

"Now this incentive," said Honeycutt now in full flow and engaging everyone in the court with his line of questioning, "this incentive cajoles a prisoner to rat on his associate in return for a lesser sentence. Am I right?"

"Yes, but if they both testify, then both will get a regular sentence."

"Most interesting, Detective Latterly, for as a method of interrogation this clearly yields results, although in this case, the defendants have changed their plea. Yet the Jury and His Lordship should be concerned with this question:

"Is it the right of the Police to suborn the prerogative of the Court first in terms of the jury determining individual guilt, and second His Lordship's prerogative on determining any putative sentence? To repeat," thundered Honeycutt, "by what right do police have to tell a prisoner in their custody that he will get this or that sentence if he does or does not confess as incentive, when that is surely the prerogative of the Court to decide? I believe they do not have the right."

"We only have the experience of past police practice, sir."

"Yet is it not the case that you are in effect trapping defendants into a confession, avoiding what actually happened in the burglary? The confession, or lack of it, is made solely in terms of the strength or weakness of the two men's trust for each other? Police interrogation then has nothing to do with evidence, which is flimsy to say the least, but the extent to which you can promote distrust."

"But these are criminals, sir."

"Please strike that last remark from the record. No one is a criminal until they have been tried and convicted, and your remark is quite unforgivable and a senior officer like you should not have made it."

"I apologize deeply to the court, my lord. It was made of interviewing suspects in general, not of these particular defendants."

"The Court will accept your apology, Detective, but let your error be a warning to you."

"Thank you, m'lud," said Honeycutt. "Now, Detective Latterly, I urge you not to enter descriptions of other cases in reply which you know is forbidden. But this police behavior looks like entrapment to me."

"I would not call it trapping, sir. We are doing our best to convict criminals, and this is a useful method to secure it."

"That may well be so, Sergeant, but the question is whether trapping a defendant in this way before his guilt or innocence is proved, undermines the legitimacy of the confession, particularly as you are posing to the defendants not merely as police but as jury and judge as well, luring the defendant by the promise of a lesser sentence. I suppose it would be of no importance to you if a judge did not accept that a confession should not mitigate the length of a prison sentence.

"For Detective Latterly, let us suppose you had two defendants in a different felony case, say that of two men raping a young girl. Would you then offer the same kind of incentive, and do you suppose that a judge would be moved to reduce a sentence of a rapist who confessed?

"I put it to you, Latterly, that this method of yours is a crude and uncertain strategy and I, for one, condemn it wholeheartedly, as the job of the police is to bring evidence to a court, not for the police to pose as having powers they do not have," said Honeycutt, his phrases ripe with feigned anger.

"In short, you have trapped these men into admitting a crime, yet you have no idea whether they are guilty or not, not merely because a confession made under duress carries no weight in the courts, but because your other evidence is so paltry."

"No sir, I stand by my belief that these are the men."

"Then in future I suggest you garner more convincing evidence, not subject defendants to such a corrupt practice."

Sir Archibald did not re-examine his witnesses, because he thought Honeycutt's elaborate cross-examination would hold not water with the jury.

Hamish indicated that he would sum up for the jury the following morning and he went home to dinner with Mary very uncertain as to what he would say in his summing-up.

The following morning, Hamish began, "Members of the Jury, I do not need to remind you of your solemn duty to examine the evidence as presented here, quite distinct from any personal predilections you may have about the two accused men in the dock and you should particularly discount the confusion raised by the detective's remark expunged from the record.

"I need you each to separate in your minds two distinct matters.

"First and foremost is the question of the innocence or guilt of these two men. You must decide on the validity of the evidence offered by Mrs. Haworth and Mrs. Cloudless, whether you think their evidence is reliable. You must also weigh the confessions made by the two men accused and decide whether these are authentic notwithstanding whether they were obtained under duress or incentive. If you decide they are authentic, then you must return a verdict of guilty.

"Second, there is the nest of issues raised by Mr. Honeycutt. This is a matter of police conduct and procedures and their justification. I am ordering you to ignore the question of whether this is practice is ethical, sensible or desirable in the pursuit of criminality, but I will speak further on this matter after you have deliberated on the charges brought against the accused."

Within the hour, the jury returned with a verdict of guilty, whereupon Hamish invited Sir Archibald to present any further evidence of criminal convictions by the two men, and indeed, both men had several previous convictions stretching over a number of years, both having been imprisoned for seven years after three successive trials. Hamish then sentenced Upton and Featherweight to five years imprisonment each.

After the men were taken down to the cells, Hamish spoke again.

"I indicated in my summing up that I would address the question of police practice. Mr. Honeycutt argued with great force that confession as evidence was based on their system of breaking down any trust that might exist between two accused persons and that in offering incentives to the defendants separately, the police were suborning the privileges of jury and judge.

"My difficulty is this. In this case, the Court has learned of the men's criminal records after their guilt was determined by the jury, yet such knowledge was in possession of the police at the time of the interviews. This is the core of the matter. It is not the job of the police to treat each person they think responsible for a crime to assume their innocence: That is a matter for the court, judge and jury together.

"On the other hand, if this practice were to be used to elicit confessions from persons whom the police know have no criminal record at all, then its utility becomes impossible to justify. It is where the police extract confessions using this method from those they know to be innocent that the practice would be totally reprehensible.

"For we know only too well that many a man or woman is terrified at being under rigorous police examination and confesses simply to get free of their plight, especially where an associate is being examined in a different location. Yet just as a court must not hear of previous convictions of any accused, so it cannot hear of there being no previous convictions.

"My conclusion on this is as follows and other judges may treat this differently. I advise the police in seeking to extract confessions from those without previous convictions to be circumspect about using the method Sergeant Latterly described, where they propose to indict two persons. On the other hand, it is clearly in the interests of justice that, where the police are aware that their suspects are already criminals, police can use this method as these individuals have already shown themselves to be social liabilities.

"Yet to this I must add a caveat. I suspect that many a jury member will feel that confessions are by their nature suspect as evidence, and the police must work hard to obtain what I will call solid evidence in bringing villains to justice. I suppose we might call the method the detective described as the Prisoner's Dilemma because of the trap set for a defendant by the police, but its results, namely a defendant's confession is inherently weak as evidence, especially when a court will be unaware of how a police examination might actually have been conducted.

"In conclusion, I must thank Mr. Honeycutt most sincerely on behalf of the pursuit of justice for raising so starkly the complexity of issues in police investigations."

Hannah looked at the leg in wonder and saw it as a gateway to her husband's new life. The leg was made from wood covered with pigskin, painted white, and was clearly the creation of an expert. It had mechanisms enabling the wearer to bend a knee, lower legs and foot which a person would operate by simply clicking the mechanism open to bend a knee or flex an ankle. The genius of this leg was that when the knee was bent, the foot tipped upwards so the wearer could sit in some comfort. It was connected to the wearer's body by a complicated set of straps and was as near a match to Tom's other leg as was possible. To Hannah's great relief it was the right length.

She had never seen Tom with his human leg, of course, so it was a startling novelty for her to see him standing up on two legs like any other human being, and she gulped with delight. Tom was delighted too, and being Tom, soon wore himself out practicing walking. He had very rarely used a wheelchair to move himself around, insisting that his perspective on the world should be from his accustomed height. Once he had mastered the leg, his gait was not really close to that of most people. It looked as if he had something very heavy attached to his leg such he was obliged to swing the leg to make any progress, though he would get over that in time, using a stick temporarily so as not to lose his balance.

After a month he felt supremely confident. His one disappointment was that, although he had a new leg, he did not have any nerves in it, so the use of a pedal in an automobile could be difficult if not impossible but Hannah was prepared to learn to be an automobile driver. That was for the future.

Tom, Hannah and young Hector had been away from the Clumber Plantation for six weeks during which Tom had been able to read De Beaumont's book on Ireland and his novel Maria. He resumed his contacts with the tenants when they returned in mid-August. Even though the tenants no longer lived in misery, with little cottages being more sturdily built, with land being cultivated more carefully, and with rising confidence, the social status of the tenants was still that of second-class citizens, if not quite as dire as de Beaumont described.

Tom could ride much more easily now and he resumed his weekly visits to each family. By holding on to a tree, he could stand on the wooden leg on a platform, throw his right leg over the horse and into saddle, then drag the wooden leg after him. Dismounting was more complicated and he needed help which he received one morning from Cóllin Maguire.

"Hallo there, Cóllin," he called from his horse, seeing the man at work on his cottage.

"Hallo there, Mr. Hesketh, I'se been a wanting to talk with 'ee, as my wife and I come to a decision."

"And what's that?"

"Well, see, both my Ma and Da and hers, well, see, they've passed these last two years. You know we inherited this patch from hers, and we's thinking we'd like to go to Canada. I've heard tell of a place called Vancouver, far away, I'm told."

"Yes, it is, but there is now a train right across the country. Takes a while, I'm sure, Cóllin, but I'm told Canada is a friendly place, very large indeed and welcoming to all who want to live there. There is a consulate in Dublin and you should visit them."

"What's a consulate?"

"That is a Canadian Government office which will help any Canadians in Ireland who need it, but it will also help Irishmen with emigration. The Trust will play all your travel expenses and give you thirty pounds which you can change into their dollars when you get there."

"Oh bless you, Major, bless you. I'm only twenty-five, you know, and so is my Mary. We thought it easier to go while we only have two little ones."

"You're right. Do you have the money to get to Dublin?"

"Well, that's a problem too, Major."

"Alright, I'll pay your fare from Derry station. And money for you to have two nights in a hotel."

"What will happen to our cottage and our plot here?"

"The Trust will decide, but we may plant trees."

"There's many a folk who'd give an arm and a leg, begging your pardon, sir, who'd like to live on Trust land as you'se such good landlords. My cousin from County Galway for one."

"We'll see. Come to the Lodge tomorrow and I will give you the money for Dublin."

"Mary, Mary," Cóllin shouted as Tom rode off, and he explained the offers that had just made. She sat down on an old barrel and wept.

Tom was pleased by developments of this kind, though still anxious that the Board give him direction. He now faced the question whether new tenants should come from elsewhere as the Trust as landlord was so attractive to other folks; news of its policies had spread rapidly across Ulster and the rest of Ireland. Yet as he read De Beaumont slowly and carefully, he realized that with every century, every decade from the thirteenth onward the plight of the ordinary Irishman had got worse. It made him feel that the Trust's work, though valuable in itself, was no more than a flash of lightning in an unwinding six-hundred-year-old tragedy.

One evening after dinner in early September, as they sat in front of the smoldering peat fire in the Lodge, Tom said, "Darling, I've been re-reading parts of this book, and you must read it to understand what this benighted island has come to."

"I will, I will, but what do you conclude?"

"I am not sure, but for me, it seems to present us with a choice between my trying to carve a political future here to try to influence politics, or secretly join the Fenian rebels and give them military advice and support on their tactics which are, to say the least, very crude. Since the Phoenix Park assassinations sixteen years ago, they have achieved nothing through violence."

"If you feel like that, we will pack our bags this very night and leave Ireland to sort itself out."

"The trouble is that I have come to think of the rule of Ireland as a vicious tyranny in which a complaisant British government had enabled the rich and powerful to enslave the country under the guise of religious hatred, but tyranny it certainly is."

"But there must be elements of sanity searching for solutions."

"Perhaps, and Parnell was the most promising of them, and look what happened to him: Wrecked on the shores of Home Rule as well as his personal indiscretions. Yet, as usual, when a minority of any kind is attacked or threatened, especially if it is terms of how they see themselves, they become more intense in defense and more defiant in the face of their rulers."

"If that is the case, Tom, then there is no hope for Ireland. While Parliament is incapable of a finding a solution, and Home Rule is the obvious best, then we will see more intransigence and increasing violence."

"There is a feature in the make-up of human male that wants power more than companionship and in some institutions, like the army, that power is codified. Sometimes, as with absolute monarchs, that power is inherited, or, of course it may be won and sustained by force of arms as it was in the Wars of the Roses. Yet there is a spark of that lust for power in every male and it is also institutionalized in marriage, and in non-marital arrangements."

"That is certainly true and for many a woman it is not the distinction of power and companionship, but a surrender of power for protection. That is obvious about the days before civilization but is now a piece of every woman's mental fabric and, as a woman, I can readily see it myself."

"Yet here in Ireland, Hannah, whatever our friends the MPs think, that power is extraordinarily corrupt. The de jure government is not seriously concerned with the fate of the Irishman and his family. The de facto rulers are for the most part absent, leaving control to a segment of religious enthusiasts, the Protestants. It is obviously within the power of the de-jure government in Westminster to change this, but for the most part they are unspoken allies of those who continue the corruption. It makes my blood boil, Hannah, for the outcome is this deep hatred between the controllers and the controlled such that it is difficult to see any sensible or moral path forward."

"There are two ways to think about the work of the Trust here. In your present mood, Tom, you see the Trust as a mole trying to move a mountain, an enormous task, without help and with no chance of success. On the other hand, it could be seen as a small light in the darkness which will grow brighter slowly it is true, but it will not be snuffed out and it will provide a guide for others.

"Two neat metaphors," said Tom with a grim smile, "if we are moles, we must leave. If we are lights, we must stay, and if so, we need to have a strategy. Let's hope that our tenants see it as a light ahead."

"Why not work out now what the light strategy is and take it straight to the Board?"

"I will, my dear. I will, but we have the meeting in December which we need to attend. So we will go to London for Christmas and the New Year. Matters here are simply ticking along until we get Board decisions."

"I'm afraid I get frightened and dismayed, Tom. I try to keep a calm presence in discussion with you, but Ireland is beginning to terrify me.

"I will protect you both, darling."

"I compare our lot with that of my parents which actually sustains me. My beloved father and mother courted far greater dangers than us. Imagine that strong man born in the marshes of Kent, wounded in the chaos of the Crimean War, preacher in a despairing industrial environment and then a missionary in a continent of massive uncertainties and tribulations, disease and illness which had captured the life of his wife and my mother, that daunting woman of such internal strength and willpower, quite apart from her love and her passion for her family, knocked sideways by the sudden death of her eldest child," and here she dissolved into howls of dismay.

Tom got up and put his arms around her, saying, "That's true, my dear, you see the dangers are not as great as we fear. Come to bed now."

Sleep came gradually as she continued to think about the Gargerys. They all seemed to be carrying some kind of burden in their lives, whatever the vagaries of their marriages. It was if God had given to them the burden of struggle, of struggle to pursue the good, to follow their conscience, while beset with challenges to their moral selves.

She was a Gargery. She could meet any challenge put before her. God would approve: Not that anything was resolved by that.

It was a Wednesday in the second half of September, a half day in the Eton College calendar, that Mrs. Elizabeth Egerton responded to an urgent call to discuss the progress of her younger son, Oliver. She threaded her way across the cobbles, to the admiration of miscellaneous aristocratic youth, and was shown into a rather grand study by a porter from the College Gate to meet Oliver's tutor, Mr. Algernon Threewits, a middle-aged man with a pronounced paunch and a dirty pince-nez. It was clearly the room of a bachelor with academic pretensions, books strewn haphazardly over mahogany tables, two worn-out leather chairs, and an inlaid mahogany sideboard on which were busts of Plato and Aristotle, a decanter half full of sherry and a half dozen glasses. Oliver was not present.

The contrast could not have been more pronounced between these two examples of the human species. Elizabeth was not only of outstanding beauty but was dressed in the height of fashion whereas Mr. Threewits's tweeds had seen better days, acquired perhaps during the Great Exhibition, his gown had patches of green on the sleeves, and his whiskers and moustache badly required the attention of a barber.

"Welcome, Mrs. Egerton, please sit down."

Elizabeth was tempted to pull a kerchief from her purse to dust the aging leather chair before sitting down but felt this would be impolite.

"I gather I am here to receive a detailed report on my son's progress and behavior," she said, almost as if she was addressing her dressmaker, "for your letter suggests that all is not well. You will know, I assume, that his father was murdered recently in his room at the Foreign Office."

"Oh dear me, dear me, Mrs. Egerton, please accept my most profound condolences and apologies. The only news we received was that your husband had taken his own life."

"That is what was at first announced: It was put out for information as a political disguise for his murder, but please be so good as to give the account I asked for."

"Well, Mrs. Egerton, this really falls into three categories. On the first, his schoolwork is mediocre in attainment, particularly in Greek Prose and Translation and his Latin is only slightly better. We believe he could perform much more adequately were he to devote his attention to these tasks."

"I presume there are other individuals falling into his category: He is not an Eton Scholar of course."

"No indeed, gentlemen of his year seem particularly prone to intellectual mediocrity."

"Or is it laziness?"

"Perhaps, but that leads me to the second matter, and I will put this as delicately as I can. Young gentlemen here form close attachments and it is desirable that they should do so that when they confront the harsh reality of the world, the school companionships will prove of inestimable value. In their formation, some of these attachments, those between older and younger boys, can be particularly intense."

"Thank you, Mr. Threewits, I am well aware of the way in which Eton and other schools are sinful hotbeds of youthful homosexual enthusiasms as my husband suffered from its blight when he was here as a Scholar."

"Ah," said Threewits unable to contain his blushes, "in your son's case, it is rather the opposite. That is, he has been seen outside the school by proctors on at least two occasions with young women, and it is conjectured that one of them was even offering services for payment."

"Tim a rake?" she said with astonishment, "how delightful!"

"I beg your pardon, Mrs. Egerton, such behavior is a direct breach of the school rules."

"And homosexual attractions are not?"

"Oh no, they are indeed forbidden, but viewed more charitably."

"Might that be because so few of the tutors here are married?"

Mr. Threewits now found himself most uncomfortable at this powerful inquisition and felt sweat beginning to course under his stiff collar and his cheeks developing an undesirable purple.

"Whatever the situation, I fear that I am simply the custodian of the rule book which I have had no say in constructing," he said crossly, hoping to get the upper hand.

"What then do you propose to do about this young man discovering the attractions of the other sex for the first time, a matter true for most of the human race, but forbidden at Eton?"

"I will come to that when I mention the third matter. In recent weeks there have been several incidents which have surprised even startled the College community and go beyond mere pranks."

"And what, pray, are these?"

"During the morning service in the chapel last Sunday, two pigeons were released into the nave, apparently from one of the escutcheons in the chapel ceiling. I am now informed that these wooden objects are quite light and can be raised from within the roof, of course, and it is thought that a person or persons had sequestered themselves within the roof for the purpose of releasing the pigeons. I need not elaborate the effects of such birds flying around during Mattins."

"The pigeons were not part of the service, I assume, though they must have distracted the congregation."

"Indeed, and it appears that Egerton and one other boy were absent from chapel on that day."

"I see."

"But let me go on."

"The porters regularly arouse the College of a morning and last week found several sheep grazing in the quadrangle. How they could have got there is a matter for detection except that Henry continued throughout his class on Thucydides to make sheep-like noises disturbing Dr. Handelschmidt's exposition."

At this, Elizabeth could hardly contain her laughter, but she said with a smile:

"Do you think there was any significance in the fact the animals were sheep? At least they were not snakes or elephants, though I suppose neither of those would be readily available."

"Indeed, but the sheep were marked as being royal property, so were probably abducted from Windsor Park."

"There is more?"

"I fear so. You will be aware as the mother of an Etonian that for many years now we have our Wall Game."

"Indeed, I witnessed it in progress when we brought Oliver to view the College. It looked simply daft to me, boys wrestling in mud."

"Ah, you are not privy to its subtleties ... "

"Of which there are none," rejoined Elizabeth.

"The Wall was defaced the night before last. Across the central part of the Wall in large letters were painted the words 'UT SUFFRAGIORUM.'

"My Latin is not up to much: what did this mean?"

"It is Latin for 'Votes for Women.'"

Elizabeth burst out into helpless laughter.

"What a splendid joke!" she exclaimed.

"What on earth is funny about that?" Asked Mr. Threewits. "It can only be regarded as disgraceful. However, the Provost and lesser authorities are satisfied that the perpetrator of these irregularities is your son. I asked him to be outside the door at this time, as I propose to tell him he is expelled in your presence."

With that, he rose from his chair, walked to door and called "Egerton, come here."

Oliver came into the room and seeing his mother rushed over to her and flung himself into her arms, weeping.

"Oh, mamma, mamma, how wonderful to see you!"

"There, there, darling," she said, "Mr. Threewits has something to say to you."

"Mother, I am so sorry."

"Not at all, my darling, Mr. Threewits has told me of your activities and I congratulate you on all of them, though I think you should have written Votes for Women in Greek as well."

"We were going to, but we could not find a good translation."

"We, did you say we?" Asked Mr. Threewits astounded by this mother's attitude.

"Indeed, sir, you don't surely think I could have done this all by myself, do you sir?"

"Would you be good enough to let me know the names of the others?"

"I am afraid that won't be possible, but the four of us were fortunate that one of our number knew his way around Windsor Park, Her Majesty's back garden."

"Goodness me. We must cease this interview now, Mrs. Egerton, and I must consult with higher authorities. No further action will be taken on Oliver until I have explored this further."

"That is kind of you, Mr. Threewits, but there is no need to trouble yourself. I am withdrawing him from the College forthwith. Clearly he needs a very different environment in which to exercise his talents than the classrooms and playing fields of Eton."

"Oh thank you, Mamma, thank you."

"Now we will have to find out what to do with you," she said as they crossed the Quadrangle to her carriage.

XII

Antonia was excited to host a meeting of the League of Women which Estella Pirrip and Charlotte Mudge had founded several years before. It was July 1898 and in attendance were Victoria Pirrip, Emma Smythe, Margaret Brandram, Anne Masterson, Alice Levy, with Mary MacDonald and Honora Brandram and Eliza Culpepper, Margaret's mother, whom Antonia dubbed the 'old guard. Elizabeth Egerton was especially welcomed, though she knew only Mary. Victoria was determined not to be hostile and greeted her sensibly, if not warmly, for here, after all, was the apparent object of her husband's desire. Harriet planned to come, but London weather had given her a very bad cold. All the women were surprised to find such an elegant building as the Penoyre home outside London in what was now being called a suburban district.

"How is Philip, Victoria? I gather he had a nasty accident."

"We don't know yet, Mary. His body is in general unharmed, apart from a few scratches, but it seems as though he fell on his head from the tree," and she briefly recapitulated what had happened to murmurs of distress from the women listening.

"Of course, in this piece of ill fortune, there is at least the fact that Arthur did not fall on top of my Philip, though he landed next to him. I suppose I have to think no one is at fault. Arthur had no experience of trees and he simply did not understand that little Philip is light, he could sit on small branches without risk, but when Arthur reached up to the branch it could not then withstand the extra weight. He lives in the marshland where trees are few and far between. An accident, but I steel myself not to blame the boy."

"Well Victoria," said Mary, anxious not to prolong this discussion or get into matters of blame and responsibility, said, "let us all hope he recovers and we will think about him."

"He is certainly in my prayers," said Eliza which surprised her daughter Margaret.

But it was Antonia's family that caused polite astonishment. To begin with, Aubrey was clad in various exotic garments and he greeted each of the women by shaking their hands and placing a gentle kiss on their left cheek which made the younger women blush, apart from Margaret who returned the kiss with gusto.

Yet it was the noise of children pervading the house that left them all aghast, for this group of women were brought up with strict conventions about children's behavior and place in a family. Many women, particularly the elderly, warmed to the belief that children should be seen but not heard, mainly for the benefit of their fathers and that their care should be in the hands of a nanny. Yet here were six children between twelve and two obviously playing an elaborate version of hide-and-seek throughout the home with such cries and screams of delight that some of the guests were unnerved. Once Aubrey completed his greetings, he raced up the stairs to join in.

"If we all go into the drawing-room," said Antonia, "the children can get on with their games," as if, thought Honora, the children's games were of much more importance than the adult women's conversation.

"I am so delighted to entertain you all," said Antonia, "but, as you can hear, my children make great demands on my time. While I am thrilled we are starting up the League yet again, and it is a pleasure to host you all, I will not be able to exercise a leadership role."

"Might we begin then," said Mary, "with the procedure we used at Numquam House many years ago, which is that each of us to put forward a topic for the agenda? I am happy to act as Chair for this meeting," an offer that was immediately accepted with noises of enthusiasm, "so, let us develop an agenda and then decide where to start. You do not need to think that you must put forward another topic if your item is already on the agenda."

Unlike the results of the Numquam discussion where many different concerns were put forward, only one topic emerged this time – votes for women, so Mary then asked which items within this topic should be discussed. Immediately there was a cascade of questions and suggestions from each woman in turn.

"Should it include the ability to run for Parliament?"

"Might there be an age limit, say a woman has to be thirty years old to vote?"

"How about a property qualification or is the claim for all women? I should say I am for the latter, but it can be a topic for discussion."

"Might it be approached gradually? I mean should it be for upper class women first, or for people of property before people like those prostitutes the Trust worked with getting the vote?

"What should be the strategy? Work with men in Parliament? Have meetings and processions?"

"My goodness," said Mary, "a cornucopia of ideas. What indeed should be our strategy?"

Emma then brought the meeting to a practical question. "Can I change the direction a little," she said, "I suppose most of us do not follow the progress of associations or organizations that have supported women's suffrage. I noticed this very month that Mrs. Millicent Fawcett, that Cambridge lady, has founded the National Union of Women's Suffrage Societies which intends to offer all groups like ours a partnership with other such groups. I was not aware that in 1869 single women who were ratepayers could vote in municipal elections, so there is a precedent there; and of course three years ago, Parliament generously decided," at which there was mild laughter, "that women could vote in local elections and indeed hold office."

"Really?" Said Anne Masterson, "I did not know that. My sister is single and owns a house. It has never occurred to me to ask if she votes."

"Exactly, women do not take advantage of what they can do, probably because they are too subject to their husbands. Of interest, how many of us know that our husbands will support votes for women? My Clarence does guardedly, I think, as he is worried about being left behind."

Most of those who were married thought their husbands would be in favor, except Victoria.

"My husband Albert is becoming an old stick-in-the-mud. He is a very prosperous businessman, deep in such matters as cost and benefit, and he seems now to be very conservative," a statement which attracted Elizabeth's attention.

"That often happens to a man who has had a wild and undisciplined youth," confided Mary, "oh dear, perhaps I should not have said that."

"Not at all," volunteered Elizabeth, "such histories always provide context."

"Certainly," said Emma, "husbands are the most interesting of topics for conservation, I mean conversation," at which there was general laughter once again.

The doors suddenly crashed open and two little girls burst into the room followed by a young toddler and rushed to their mother. The toddler, Emily by name, stopped and looked carefully around the room before giving a huge smile and followed the rush to her Mother.

"The boys won't let us join in their new game, Antonia," at which there were gasps of astonishment around the room that children were calling their mother by her Christian name.

"Now look, my darlings," she said as the girls clambered on to her knee, "those boys are just behaving like men do. They don't want to let girls join in, which is what my friends here are talking about."

"But why won't they let us?"

"I have told you since they were little that they must learn to play all their games with you little ones, unless of course it is a dangerous game for your age."

"What are the boys playing?"

"They have gone into the garden," said Margaret, the six-year-old, "and they are having a race."

"What sort of a race?"

"It's a bit silly really. They have to run round the garden and touch each tree."

"Is that all? I don't see why you couldn't join that."

"No, but they have to take their clothes off when they reach a tree, and then they carry their clothes to the next tree where they put them on and move on to the next one."

"Well, if you think that is a silly game, then why would you want to join in?"

"I don't really want to play but I think they should have asked us if we wanted to race," said young Estella.

"Rather than just telling you that you couldn't join in, right?" Asked Antonia inquisitively, "I think that would have been better, but my darlings, I need to continue talking with my friends without you all here."

"Alright Antonia, we'll go," said Estella, the four-year-old, "boys are like that with their silly games, aren't they?"

Once the children had left, there were bursts of laughter and comments around the room, as the women had been spellbound by the conversation and, for that matter, the game the boys were playing.

"What is the middle one's name?" Asked Honora.

"Estella, after the woman we knew."

"I must say, she sounded like her namesake," said Mary laughing, "and how important that they are learning the ways of the male sex so early."

"It is interesting, isn't it," said Alice, "how much of their conversation could be attributed to a discussion of wives about their husbands too, or about women and men in general. It is a sobering thought that even in this gentle and open family, boys are already behaving like men."

"You mean playing silly games and excluding women?" said Emma and everyone laughed.

"Exactly," said Alice, "just like the issue we are discussing."

Antonia had ordered an impressive lunch and two cooks from outside her household served the meal in the dining room. Discussion continued and certain decisions emerged. First, that the League should affiliate with the Fawcett group promptly. Second that it should widen its membership arising from their unanimous decision to reject any property qualification or other impediments to all women have the vote. Put to one side for a further meeting was how they might proceed beyond widening the group. Emma offered to become Chair which was accepted with delight, and she was asked to establish the League formally, no doubt with Clarence's advice, and she intimated that the next meeting would be held at her London house.

Elizabeth was proud of Oliver's rebellious character, but she was at a loss to know what to do with him now that he had been at home for the best part of three months. She decided to call on Emma for advice.

"I must say, Elizabeth, I am amazed at one level by this lack of discipline, but full of admiration for the pranks on another. It sounds to me that here is a boy eager for adventure."

"He has talked about joining the army, which his father always discouraged hoping that he would become a serious student."

"I have an idea, Elizabeth. Do you know the Gargery family?"

"Not in their present form. When I was young, as you know, I had a long affair with Albert Pirrip, and he had spent some time as a child with that old blacksmith Joe Gargery and his wife. I met Estella of course, but I don't know well the man who was called Young Pip, now Pip, nor do I know his children."

"So you never met Clara whose husband Sam was killed in the National Gallery Explosion and then married Malcolm Gargery?"

"No, I fear not. I think we must have been in Washington at the time."

"I am asking because Malcolm and Clara are in South Africa. He's in the Gordon Highlanders but was wounded in India and lost an eye and is now in some kind of liaison role there which I expect means he is a spy! I wonder whether Oliver might find South Africa of interest, especially with these Boer people being so difficult."

"What an interesting idea. Perhaps they would have him stay with them and see where it goes from there?"

"I will write to Clara. She is one of my oldest friends and I simply adore her. She is very beautiful and very passionate, apparently aiming to found a regiment with her children."

"You mean like Antonia?"

"Oh my," said Emma, "wasn't all that a surprise! I mean, I have known her slightly and I knew she and Aubrey were free spirits, but really!"

"I know, but I do admire them. Sometimes I do wonder whether this convention and these proper behavior rules dampen the human spirit, not enhance it. I mean it is obvious to any thinking person that society has rules, but does that goes as far as wearing a hat to church? It will be most interesting to see how their children turn out, though those little girls will not be browbeaten growing up in that household. But, back to Oliver, it would be so good of you to write to this Clara, Emma. What about your elder boy? What do you expect him to do?"

"Young Clarence? Probably follow his father into the Law. He is a dear and nothing would convince him to emulate Oliver and get into such escapades. Sober as a judge. The girls are wonderful, beautiful and well-behaved. I am expected to have them come out as debutantes as I did, but Clarence and I agree it is quite unnecessary as we hope they will educate themselves further, especially now that there is a university here in London. Coming out is merely to say they are ready for marriage, quite apart from the expense of all that palaver."

With the delay in correspondence across six thousand miles, it was mid-November when a reply came from Clara indicating that they would be delighted to welcome Oliver but she would like to have a letter from him explaining what he might do. He could have his own room in their house and she added that her infant son Charles Joseph Samuel had recently arrived, to their great joy.

To say that Oliver was ecstatic would be an understatement and the Egerton family had a long discussion one evening after Emma had called with the news.

"Would you join the army there?" Asked his brother Henry, "if so, be prepared to get into combat quite quickly."

"I wish Father were here to help us," said Charlotte mournfully, "what will you write to Mrs. Gargery?"

"I don't know yet, but anything could be better than Eton and I am so grateful to dear Mamma for understanding that. If my acquaintances there are anything to go by, the army generally attracts the brave and the dumb," at which the family laughed. "I don't expect to share anything of Major Gargery's work, but I will get my cues from them both before venturing out, and I do expect to write about what I see there, as well as write letters to you all."

"We will be so excited to receive your letters, my dear," said Elizabeth, "but keep a diary too. Perhaps you might send regular reports and get them published in a paper here."

"I will certainly do some exploring. I cannot expect to loaf around their household; indeed I would not want to. But South Africa sounds to be such an exciting country when you consider these fighting Boers, a British administration, and scallywags like Rhodes, let along the gold and the diamonds flowing free. I think I will stay here for Christmas and depart early in the New Year."

Conversation continued but it was too much for Charlotte, who suddenly realized she might not see her favorite brother for ages and, in tears, she failed to elicit a promise from him that he would return soon which he skillfully avoided as he had really no idea what he would find in South Africa when he got there.

Harriet had not written much poetry since the period after Pip and Susanna had left for Africa. Thereafter she worked hard to produce two small volumes with thirty or so sonnet-like constructions in each. Her experiments were with form as much as content and it surprised no one who knew her that the poems conveyed a powerful sensuality and in one or two cases unrequited love.

Nevertheless, she was an avid reader of poetry and particularly enjoyed the work of a young poet, Michael Field, and she now knew that 'he' was Katherine her friend and her niece Edith.

"How are you, my dear? Asked Katherine when they met for lunch that week. "You met Edith when we heard Alice Peake at the Browning Society, didn't you?"

"Yes indeed, it is pleasure to meet you again, Edith."

"Tell us about yourself. Are you well?"

"Oh, I am quite well. My husband Pip was wounded in a violent brouhaha in Ireland and thank God he is no longer engaged there."

"How awful. Why was that?" Asked Edith.

"It is a long story which is tragic, as indeed everything about Ireland seems to be. The Jaggers Trust bought a large estate from Clara Gargery. Pip and I went there to manage the estate but when I was back in London, Protestant villains murdered one of the tenants working with Pip and assaulted him."

"Is he alright now?"

"Yes he has recovered and continues to work with the Trust on other matters. But what about you? Are you both writing?"

"Yes, and I am glad the public in general is unaware of our relationship," said Edith quietly.

"Why should the fact that you are lovers as well as close relatives make any difference? I must say I get quite angry when I consider all these conventional limitations on how love may be expressed."

"I know, but I suppose people might regard us as somehow incestuous."

"No, surely," said Katherine, "that arises only as a matter of the biological reproduction of the species, where individuals mating are too close in blood relations to produce healthy offspring. That is not the case with us."

"I am thrilled for you both as I have always been an advocate of free love, but now I am disappointed not to have any close female relatives! I dread to think what my upright husband might think of it."

"My dear Harriet, it has become a story about those of us who live in the Victorian age, for what of a better term, that we are so upright, prudish even, and that the common practice is for families to contain an indelibly faithful husband and wife with children brought up with rod and birch where needed, and that Sundays are spent in prayer and contemplation of our sins. Indeed one anticipates historians writing about our century in those terms."

"Yet," added Edith, "but it is all such utter nonsense. The century has been extraordinarily creative, not simply with artists, novelists, painters and poets but in inventions and industry, men like Brunel or Balgazette. Under this surging power of creation lies the matching power of men and women's sexuality."

"Take Dickens, for example," said Katherine, "such a marvelous writer, or so I am told for I find him almost too depressing to read. Yet he kept a mistress, something that never appears as a theme in his novels, and what of Parnell or Dilke, or even dear Oscar. Tips of the iceberg in my view."

"We live in this time of shifts in our moral perspectives," continued Edith. "What is it about people that they shrink in horror at a relationship such as ours? Not that we care, of course, except that we would be sure that there are women, perhaps thousands of them who would, if they could, break free of their dour marriages and enjoy love for a woman which would fit their nature and their desires. Sadly, we can do nothing for them as we are not missionaries. We are not like that woman who acquired notoriety as Gentleman Jack."

"Do not forget your financial independence. Katherine. What I find it so interesting about you both, now that I have listened to this is that you find love only in a woman. I am sure from meeting you that neither of you could or would contemplate infidelity, and certainly love for a man. Am I right?"

Both Katherine and Edith nodded.

"I think that is itself a victim of the prudery of the age you criticize," Harriet continued. "I regard living and intimacy in general as a marvelous experience and my desires, though settled now, have in the past been for women as much as for men, but my free love was vastly different from mere promiscuity. This is not to criticize your relationship, far from it, but I think you are both in thrall to an ideal of there being only one love in a life, the epitome of romantic love, whereas I think I have breached conventions in a far more radical way."

"So you see us as a married couple, incapable of infidelity, just like the image of the Victorian family, for better for worse and so on," said Katherine laughing.

"Oh I don't really know you that well, do I? Perhaps both of you secretly harbor lust for other women, even men."

"Never, never, never," said Edith, almost in tears, "I have loved my dear Katherine exclusively since I can remember."

"I find that very interesting, Harriet," said Katherine, "but perhaps our love is unique and steadfast because we came to love each other through my looking after Edith when her mother could not. Our bond of love arose through unique circumstances."

"In any event," said Harriet, "I am full of admiration for you both and I am sure that your writing is enhanced by this bond of love as you call it."

"Now listen to me," said Katherine, "I have read your early poems and they are delightful, but you must take up your pen again as you need fulfilment and maturity in your writing."

"I fear not, Katherine," Harriet replied, "the well is empty, and I occupy my time in other more practical pursuits."

With that the lunch ended. The three women embraced and said their goodbyes, Katherine and Edith feeling challenged in their relationship by Harriet's comments and Harriet wondering whether she might share this exchange with her beloved Pip. On balance she thought not, but their conversations did reflect a certain smug self-satisfaction which she did not like, but then they seemed completely absorbed in each other.

"My dearest," said Pip over breakfast, "Hannah has written to say that Tom, baby Hector and she are coming to London for Christmas and staying over the New Year, primarily for him to meet with the Board, but also for him to get his leg."

"Since my improved relationship with Hannah, I will be thrilled to continue to build on this new beginning. We both adore Tom, of course, not just because he had made Hannah so happy, but because he is a man of such manifest integrity and courage."

It turned out to be an especially joyous Christmas as the only child was Hector, emerging as a person in his own right at eighteen months old and with the occasional stern look which reminded everyone of Tom. He toddled around the house, speaking a few words, with just the faintest tinge of a Scots accent, so said Pip with a strong element of wishful thinking. After all the festivities, the walks in the park with everyone snugly dressed to keep out the cold, and Hector in bed, the four of them went to bed very contented. On the morning of New Year's Eve, the conversation turned to Ireland.

"Ireland gives us enormous opportunities for explorations on all kinds of subject matter, especially our families. The other night, we had a serious discussion about whether we should give up on Ireland, but if we did not, whether we should not in effect join the radical Irish, the Fenians, who want to see an end to rule from London. You see, we are convinced that only a departure from Ireland will enable them to govern themselves and tackle their own problems in their own way. But how to get there?

"I see," said Pip, "so you are Home Rulers, a viewpoint with which I am in strong sympathy."

"We are indeed, but we want to learn from your experience. It seems to me that the Gargerys have something of a burden, given by God as I would see it," said Hannah.

"Do you mean a vocation or a conscience, for that is often a burden?"

"Vocation, I think, but it is more than that. I mean, you did not have to go to the Crimea, but then you picked up the burden of preaching both in Salford and Africa, knowing that your burden was that you would rarely be listened to."

"I am not sure about that," said Harriet, "in Salford, he was listened to on the streets, but I think he was mainly helpful in pastoral activity, as he was later in Africa."

"Father, I've been thinking about Mother and you recently and trying to compare my life with yours. I suppose Tom and I want to know, if you were our age, whether you would accept any such burden as the work in Ireland, the chances of success being so infinitesimal, and if so, would not those slight chances drive you to more radical activity to achieve what you believe is just?"

"Ah, just, now there's the word: Just. My judge friend Hamish and I discuss justice a great deal. He is knee-deep in the conflict between the Law and justice. He has to struggle, not in every case that comes to his court of course, with how to strive for justice where the law can be so unjust. And is burden the right word? I don't think we saw Africa as a burden, though it became one when you mother fell ill."

"H'mm, that is perplexing but a great privilege and Ireland is replete with unjust laws. You see," she continued, "I was also thinking about Malcolm. Our colonial experiences as a nation have different histories and different applications. I don't think he yet realizes he too is carrying a burden, the challenge of doing right in the face of difficult odds."

"Good heavens, Hannah, you are sounding as if your life is a religious mission," said Pip.

"We are surely not unique in having a burden as you describe it," said Harriet.

"No, of course not," replied Hannah, "it is just that the three of us, Father, Malcolm and me have chosen lives in which the burden of seeking justice, of struggling against evil, seems to be our lot. Perhaps less so, for Malcolm and me. We are not, for example, businesspeople concerned only with feathering our own nest."

"I have to repeat this," replied Pip, "the motive in our own religious mission was a delusion. I have told you how your mother thought we had trapped each other into going to Africa. Don't let that happen to you two with Ireland."

"Let me interrupt you, Father. It does not matter how you came to be there, but what you did with it when you got there. Selfless, carrying the burden of putting your children away from you for God's work with a people whom you never really managed to convert, did you?"

"That's very harsh, Hannah my dear."

Harriet and Tom listened very carefully to this exchange.

"No, it may be harsh but it is correct, isn't it? You see, I want to learn from you. I am trained medically, though I am not a doctor. I can see this or that needs healing and I may or may not succeed in achieving that healing. I suppose medicine is very, how can I put this, very short-term, certainly compared to resolving the Irish problem," and they all smiled quietly but soberly.

"I suppose I want success in what I do to be like healing a wound. It gets done, quickly," she concluded.

"How about you, Tom? Do you share Hannah's perspectives on Ireland and the idea of their being a family burden?"

"Not really, Pip. After years in the company of soldiers, I realize that I never understood just how complicated and fascinating life would be until I encountered this wonderful woman whose intellect and moral sense leaves me struggling. I suppose in my simple way I see life as having a fork in the road, two roads one can pursue, simply put, one road in which one struggles to do good for others, and the other road as one in which one pursues personal satisfaction.

"Of course the cynic will argue that pursuing the first of these is just one version of pursuing the second, but I do think the distinction holds. For Hannah and I hope for myself, it is the first road we want to pursue but it presents immense challenges along the way."

"That seems correct," said Harriet, "though I must confess I have found the second road more attractive. Yet you can see the sort of challenge directed at those on the first road: Hannah, for example, pursuing the mission weighed in the balance against keeping Hector close to them."

"That may be true, Harriet," said Hannah, "but although I was not there to see it, I believe Lachlan's death hurt my parents grievously, a death from they never recovered, and I suspect my father never has. Is that true, Father?"

Pip got up from his chair and walked to the window, beginning to weep copiously, turning to them, throwing up his hands in despair.

"Tell me, Father, I have never heard the story, you know."

Pip returned to the settee and Harriet went to sit by him and hold his hand, his tears still falling down his cheeks.

"Lachlan had a bad cold from which he recovered as children do. A month later, Susanna and I had come back from a marvelous dinner party. We went to his bedside to say good night and he complained of being ill and he had a fever. Then he coughed, and I had heard that cough before in Salford. Susanna stayed with him and I went to bed praying I was wrong. I woke at dawn, went into his bedroom and saw that he was very ill. Susanna asked me to get Dr. Grant.

"When Grant arrived, I watched him bend down to examine Lachlan's throat and I saw him recoil from the atrocious smell coming out of his mouth. My worst expectations were fulfilled. He had diphtheria."

At this point, Harriet was weeping, and Tom had tears in his eyes, but Hannah looked stoically at her father recalling the death of the elder brother she never knew.

"It only took two days for our bonnie laddie as we called him; he was fighting an unwinnable war against this foul disease. The grey mass grew in his throat such that he was unable to speak, his neck grew to the size of a grapefruit, but he fought, oh my God did he fight, till it finally finished him. There he was, lying on the bed, his beautiful face ravaged while we sat on the bed together watching our first born, this splendid little fellow, pass from our lives.

"Yes, my dearest daughter, he was on our conscience from that moment, and, for me, he still is. It does not matter that we could do nothing, we still felt responsible. We should, I should, have prevented it. We were never the same. It is not helpful to be told we could do nothing. I cannot erase the sense of responsibility. He was so like your mother, funny, intelligent, loving and caring for his brother wee Malcolm who followed him around as if there was an invisible rope tying them together. Burying that lovely boy, product of our loins, was like watching our lives go into the ground with him.

"And yet. In fact hundreds of children were dying annually and there was no cure. Of course, as many as died, a few recovered. We understood in theory that we could not be held to account for his death. We were not guilty. Yet reason was trumped by emotion: of course we felt guilty, deeply, profoundly, unremittingly guilty and it was on our conscience."

At which there was silence.

"Be careful with Hector," added Pip quietly.

"We will, most medical experts are starting to believe it is passed from child to child, so we will need to be careful to understand medical resources at his school which, of course, could be part of our decision about Ireland: A crowded school in London or Aberdeen or a country school in Ireland. But to return to what we might learn from your life..." she continued when Pip interrupted.

"I don't think you can, my dear. Our set of circumstances were unique to us as yours are to you. You have some general principles on which your life is led. Just follow those and make your choices. You are both people of immense quality and judgment, but no one can avoid mistakes if you are trying to do something worthwhile."

"Of course that is true," said Hannah, a little impatiently, "but we must do all we can in medicine to prevent these diseases, as we have with smallpox. It raises an interesting question, I suppose."

"What is that?"

"If there is a disease which is easily spread from person to person and if there is some kind of treatment, what we might call immunization or vaccination, should everyone be obliged to take the preventative? Can we force people, perhaps against their will?"

"I see what you are after, Hannah, I might be prepared to take the risk that I or my children could catch a disease and I suppose it would be the government that would demand it, or in cases of schooling, the Board or the school itself."

"As a medical person, I would make it compulsory certainly for children. Why if chemists and biologists develop something that will save lives, surely every child should undergo whatever is needed, not just for themselves but for others."

"That will be a bone of contention when it happens, I am sure, probably because some children will die from the vaccine. On another subject, did you all know," Harriet continued, "that there has been an accident at Numquam with Arthur Fletcher, Nellie's grandson, who fell from that old elm tree taking young Philip Pirrip with him. Arthur has a broken leg, but Philip landed on his head and is not yet recovered."

"Oh dear, oh dear, it is always so tragic when children die or are wounded in some way," said Pip, "there was an African boy in the Mission who landed on his head when he fell out of the tree but it wounded his neck and he was paralyzed. Nothing anyone could do out there, of course."

172

Sleep beckoned for each of them, but Hannah insisted on their singing a verse of Auld Lang Syne before four very somber people went slowly to their beds with no thought of waiting for 1899 to begin.

The following morning Mary MacDonald came to call on Harriet and was delighted to find the Hesketh family there.

After introductions and expressions of good will for the New Year, Mary asked:

"Hannah, how long will you be here?"

"We return in a fortnight."

"It struck me that with your knowledge of Ireland and all the discussions in politics about Home Rule, you might come and talk to the League of Free Women while you are here about your experience."

"If it can be arranged, I would be glad to, but we return to Ireland immediately after the Board Meeting, postponed till this month. Perhaps in the summer."

1899

XIII

Clara sat in the drawing room in Clyde Street, reveling in her open and interesting correspondence with Emma which was much like their conversations when she was in London. She shared the letters from Malcolm too, and the story of Elizabeth's admirers in particular left him almost unable to control his laughter, as he pictured Clarence's demeanor and Albert's aggression in declaring themselves to her. Clara was radiant with maternal love as her third boy, Charles Joseph Samuel Gargery made the celebrations very exciting, especially for little Susanna who had begun to see the baby as her pre-eminent occupation in this New Year.

Malcolm had not met Elizabeth, though these letters made him feel as though he had, but her second son Oliver was due in Port Elizabeth soon on a boat to from Tilbury. The child of such interesting and distinguished parents would not cause his household any distress, he thought, notwithstanding the pranks at Eton, all of which Emma had described in detail.

Malcolm waited at the dock on a Wednesday evening and Oliver was not difficult to spot as he came down the gangplank, dressed in a sporting attire as if he were about to play lawn tennis, with white trousers, a blazer with a badge which Malcolm assumed to be from Eton, and a large straw hat, sitting on his head with a rakish tilt.

"You must be Oliver," said Malcolm.

"Indeed, sir, not difficult to single you out too, look for an officer with an eye-patch I was told."

By the time they reached home, it was the hour for a pre-prandial drink which was always a choice of South African wine which both Malcolm and Clara had come to appreciate, young but bold, and a way to escape the problem of

French wine traveling such a distance. Both had decided to avoid strong liquor, apart from Scotch whisky.

Oliver was introduced to the children and young George pestered him with questions about the voyage, comparing them with his:

"Did you eat at the Captain's Table? My parents did, though children were sent to bed."

"I was invited, but declined, George."

"Why?"

"Usually one accompanies a lady to such a dinner, and I had no taste for being seated next to someone I don't know, so I played quoits in the dark on the deck with a fellow traveler."

"George," said the motherly Clara, "there will be plenty of time to talk with Oliver. Prepare yourself for bed now," at which George kissed his mother, then his father, and left the room.

"Tell us about England, as it takes time for us to get any news."

"Everyone thinks there will be another war with the Boers, and there is a great deal of jingoism in the newspapers, promoted by the politicians. I am afraid that I heartily distrust such displays of patriotic sentiment. I came across a recent novel by Mr. Hardy before I left called Jude The Obscure and read it while at sea. There was a story at Eton that when the copy arrived a new young librarian had catalogued it under Old Testament Criticism, but it is very fine and a very sad tale. I won't reveal the story but there is an interesting line which caught my attention in which a character compares the excessive love of parents for their children to patriotism, saying it is just a form of exclusiveness."

"That is surely mistaken," said Clara whose love for her children was the core of her life.

"I agree," said Oliver, "but I think the author must have had in mind those who support their country right or wrong; but you would enjoy the book, nevertheless."

"I'd love to read it. By the way, I want to talk with you about Eton as we were thinking of sending our boys there."

"I will explain why I suggest that you consider that most carefully, but not in their presence, and you will understand that I have certain prejudices against the institution. Etonians will tell you a grand tale about the College, but 'it is a tale told by an idiot, full of sound and fury, signifying nothing.'"

"Ah, so you did some studying at Eton. Indeed, you read seriously, I can tell."

"Yes, I do, but I found that it is only possible in those subjects with teachers who clearly enjoyed their teaching."

"Do you have ideas about what you might do here?" Asked Clara, "as your letter did not make anything clear."

"I do, actually, I do. I feel like an explorer. I saw the docks as the ship came in, and I want to wander around there and see what people do and keep a diary about what I see. I have written a great deal on the boat."

"You will need to be very careful," said Malcolm, "there are all manner of races near the docks and many very undesirable characters."

"I know, but my mother, bless her heart, was quite aware that I would get into some rough spots, so she sent me here with a Remington revolver and plenty of ammunition," he said sipping his wine. "She refused to tell me where she had got it, but I expect it was my father's."

"Can you please ensure that you never show it to the children and keep it hidden, preferably in our small safe?" said Malcolm.

"Most certainly, I will keep it in your safe if I may. I don't expect it to be of use, though my mother was most anxious for me to have it, probably because she could not bear losing me after my father's death."

"We were most sorry to hear about that," said Clara, "it happened before I left."

"I don't think my mother knows this yet but his murderer was tried in camera and hung for treason. I discovered that through a friend at Eton whose father was involved in identifying the man, a despicable human being as well as a colleague, an Etonian of course."

"But did your mother know the man?"

"I am not sure. My father must have kept him at arms' length but they may well have met socially."

"What a tragedy," said Clara, "and how are your brother and sister coping?"

"To be quite candid, Mrs. Gargery, Charlotte weeps incessantly; I love my sister dearly and I understand that as my father doted on his only daughter. Henry my elder brother worries me as he seems bent on vengeance though he has no idea what that might mean. He has talked to me about wiping out the man's family as well, though we are not aware of his identity."

"That won't solve anything of course, but who is this murdering swine?" Asked Malcolm.

"Ah, we believe without evidence that it is George Fortescue, and I heard my mother once tell of a Monty Fortescue. Interesting story actually. She was at an Embassy do in Paris and she and her gentleman friend of the time were in the garden and heard this Fortescue behind a rhododendron bush engaged in a plot with a woman. She was whisked off to meet the Head of Chancery almost immediately and grilled about the conversation. I'd bet this George was that man's brother. Filthy bunch, those Fortescues, but we don't really know it was one of them."

Oliver then put his head in his hands and began to weep.

"Excuse me," he said trying to stem his tears, "the loss just comes over me from time to time. My father was the kindest, gentlest of men with such profound love for my mother and his children. He was brilliant too, but I will never forget the warmth of his arms around me as a little boy and his smell. As I grew up, we were all so proud of him. Do you know, he never failed to kiss us good night, something I will miss every night until I die."

"Oliver," said Clara, "I share your grief as my first husband was murdered."

"What?" said Tim, startled and shocked.

"Yes, Sam died after being blown up by an anarchist bomb at the National Gallery. But while I do share your grief, the loss of a parent is quite different from the loss of the person you are married to."

"I lost my mother to disease," said Malcolm, "though my relationship to her was not as close as yours to your father. I was quite young when my parents began their mission here and I was grown up when she died of yellow fever."

"Life is so odd," said Oliver sniffling, "I had a number of friends at Eton, but any conversation about parents was to be avoided. If they visited, boys would be mortified if their mother showed any sign of affection. I was puzzled by this schoolboy attitude and it never stopped me from hugging and kissing my mother which has always been such a profound delight, though I was mocked thereafter."

"That happened to me too," said Malcolm, "though I think they visited me only once, preoccupied as they were with their religious duties."

"Of course we know expressions of love in childish behavior were not allowed to grow, don't we?" said Clara, "educational institutions want their charges to become independent of family and, as you said earlier, Oliver, focus their emotions on the institution and its members, not their families."

"I knew boys who regarded their mother as an object of ridicule and were terrified of their fathers. The school gave them a substitute of a sort."

"Malcolm," said Clara smiling at Oliver, "we have here a very interesting and lovely young man who is going to stimulate our conversations and whose company we are going to enjoy greatly. As your mamma is not here, Oliver, I will kiss you good night in her stead," at which the young man again began to weep again.

"You are bound to be homesick, Oliver," added Malcolm, "it is the most gut-wrenching feeling I remember all too well. We will understand."

As they went to bed, Clara said:

"Is he not a fascinating creature? I hope our children feel as close to their parents as he does when they get to his age."

"Me too," said Malcolm, "and I was quite surprised to hear him talk so personally and openly, rather than be a stiff upper lip person which Eton and many other schools seek to breed."

"We need to think so carefully about our little ones, don't we? Do schools foster distance from and disdain for parents?"

"I don't know, but I do think that while the phrase 'in loco parentis' is intended to indicate the school's special responsibility for the child, it has a dark side where a school specially one which boards children, seeks to impose itself by becoming the more dominant object of affection."

"We must hope that when our children marry, Malcolm, their love for their husband or wife is stronger, though different from their love for us, their parents; but that is quite different from that primitive regard for an institution, school church, university or army which can become a lifelong habit."

"My goodness! Does that not explain so much about some of the friends young Oliver and I have had? There was one man in the Regiment whose name I forget with a very dull wife who seemed to be unable to talk about everything except his life at school. Every damn conversation was either about a teacher who was like a pedagogical Messiah, or about some special occasion in which he had played a part, or about how often he returned to the school to meet old chums, such emotional immaturity as I have ever witnessed. Moreover, he managed to turn every conversation around to his recollections. He was the most colossal bore."

Before Tom and Hannah returned to Ireland, both were invited to a discussion by the Board in the New Year at which all the members still hoped they could finally agree on a strategy. Albert was asked how his son Philip was faring and all were glad that there was considerable improvement and that his stay in the London hospital, on Withington's advice, had yielded considerable progress.

"My son can speak, if only for short periods much as he had done before his fall," he said in reply to persistent questions from Mary, but the Board members sensed that Albert did not really want to discuss his son further so no one replied, though there were murmurs of sympathy around the table. That upset Mary who wanted an outlet for her sadness and she sensed too that something was wrong with Albert's health and she made a mental note to ask him.

Tom had not yet completed his report but Aaron Levy made the running by speaking first after Clarence had opened the meeting.

"As a member of a race that has endured constant persecution, I am thoroughly in sympathy with Irishmen, even though their religion seems to be primarily responsible for stories which have created the waves of persecution and pogroms over the centuries from which my people have suffered. I think the religious hatred, the *odium theologicum*, that exists in Ireland is primarily a British cover for their rapacity in taking over their land by one method or another. I suggest that the Trust can best act as protector of individual families by continuing to own the Clumber land, but to divide it the original parcels that we have discovered in those documents, and to create leases for 999 years at a penny a year. As the Trust owns the freehold it will then be very difficult indeed for any entity, Government or others, to control it without our express permission."

"What of the parcels which are, so to speak, empty?" Asked Pip.

"We offer them to existing tenants or where there are no takers, we plant trees. But there is still much for Tom to do in terms of supporting tenants using Trust funds to hedge their parcels, to create clear tracks, to provide cattle, horses or sheep for those who require it, and to seek to create a satisfactory relationship with the local church and where possible the Protestant Community."

"Thank you very much, Aaron," said Clarence, "how do members of the Board react to these suggestions?"

"These proposals are a quite unnecessary encumbrance on the Trust, I believe," said Albert testily. "The peasants must fend for themselves. I'd put the whole estate on the market so that the money could be used by the Trust nearer to home."

"Oh Albert," pleaded Pip, "how about a little charity for these poor people?"

"May I remind you, Albert," said Mary, "this Board is specifically established to help the poor, not to treat its work as a business."

"I know but I don't see why at least some business practice cannot be worked into the Trust's activities," Albert replied with annoyance. "For instance, the Trust should reimburse everyone for whatever amounts it has cost them to come here today as members of the Board."

"Oh nonsense," said Pip, "we are here precisely as a charity to which we are pleased to donate our time and our resources where necessary."

"For the life of me, I do not understand this," Albert replied with some vehemence, "we have been readily supporting those of our number who have been on these jolly trips to and fro Ireland, so why am I not supported in the way I have described?"

"Jolly, what on earth do you mean?" Exclaimed Pip bristling at the suggestion. "I was badly wounded in a fight and poor O'Sullivan was murdered. Nothing jolly about that."

"I suppose I am quite out of sympathy with the work of this Trust..."

"Of which your step-mother was a primary architect," added Mary.

"Yes, and she was mistaken in many ways. I do not now understand why anyone ever took her advice seriously. She was a woman with grievous faults."

"I am utterly astonished by this, Albert," said Harriet sorrowfully, "as far as I can tell from what you say, you are certainly quite out of place on this Board."

"Wait," said Clarence, anxious to calm the situation down, "we have got miles off track from Aaron's interesting proposal. We have only heard Albert's response. Tom, what do you think?" At which Albert began to sulk at having lost the attention of the others.

"I think Aaron's suggestion is excellent. I have arranged for the Maguires to emigrate to Canada as they have asked for help to do that. I can amend my survey to include reports on how individual families react and what the reaction is in the community at large. I am convinced that we need to retain control to protect the leaseholders."

"May I suggest," said Pip, "that we make the lease 99 years renewable."

"That seems right to me," declared Hannah, "but I have another suggestion. I would like to see a cottage hospital established within the Clumber Estate, perhaps with no more than a dozen beds, two nurses and a presiding doctor, and that these should preferably be Catholics. The health of these leaseholders and their children is of the utmost importance. Tom can work out costs and perhaps the building should be on the site of the Plantation House and, of course, as a hospital, it should be open to anyone who requires it services, not just those on the estate."

"That is a wonderful suggestion," said Mary, "and we should create some kind of hospital board with members of both communities. Tom could investigate that possibility."

"To be sure I can and that could be a small step in bringing the communities together. Who cares if the doctor repairing a broken limb is a Catholic or a Protestant?"

"I'd not be so confident, if I were you," said Pip, "nurses in Ireland tend to be nuns, Sisters of Mercy for instance."

Discussion continued around the proposals from Aaron and Hannah such that at the end of meeting, Clarence was able to announce that the Board accepted both proposals, that Tom was instructed to handle the tenants and Hannah the hospital. Albert alone voted against both proposals. After these results were announced, Albert offered his resignation, but Pip, Mary, Harriet and Clarence strongly argued he should stay because of his historic connections with the Board and its foundation.

At this point, Emma spoke up.

"For my part, it does not seem valuable for the Board to have a member who is clearly quite out of sympathy with its purposes. I want to ask you, Albert, are you really as much out of sympathy as you appear to be, or are you just creating argument for the sake of it?"

"In fact, I am in two minds. I accept this historic obligation deriving as much from my father who was Mr. Jaggers' partner as much as my step-mother. On the other hand, I believe that we as a nation have reached a point at which, while moral sentiment is desirable up to a point as I show in my management of my corporations, but business ethos and its practices are a good discipline for an organization such as the Trust."

"Understanding that position, as Chairman, I hope you will stay."

"Let me be clear," said Emma, "business rather than conscience? There will be nothing worse for the Trust to have a Board member who does not share its moral position and who will be constantly carping and complaining in the way you have done today."

"Hmm," said Mary, "I see your point, Emma. While we would like Albert to stay with us, we want his full-throated support which does mean that he has the right to criticize any proposal. Certainly we would not wish him to sit silently, like Patience on a monument."

"May I take some time to consider my position in terms of that has been said?"

"Of course, Albert," said Clarence, "we would not wish any decision to be precipitate. In fact this Board rarely rushes to make a decision," at which everyone laughed and moved gradually into the hallways at Old Square to collect coats, hats and gloves and to wait for the brougham to take them to the Cheshire Cheese.

"You would have very much enjoyed today's meeting of the Board," said Mary to her husband as they sat at dinner.

"Albert revealed himself as a man of business, quite different from his father or Estella. He did not quite pour scorn on charity, but it was close. I also think he is unwell, and I watched him closely, but I could not tell."

"I am not surprised," said Hamish.

"How so?"

"It's quite simple, I think. Once a man begins to think of the significance of prices and profit, he realizes he can think of nothing else. He has a wife and children to support, his self-respect becomes locked into his successes at selling and this affects his attitudes to other human beings whom he starts to see solely as customers. Everything but profit pales into insignificance. It happens to the best of men."

"Yet is it not true that people like yourself, a public servant of a special kind, do not face such problems of survival?"

"It is true that the public purse supports me now I am no longer in practice, but the point I am making is that the source of a man's earnings will determine his character."

"Does this profit-seeking behavior influence the upbringing of the man's children and, indeed his relationship with his wife?"

"I am sure of it. Now, I am not saying that the search for profit is undesirable, far from it. What a man does with his wealth, or the loss of it, is for him to determine, but it is not a priori immoral. When I was a student in Edinburgh, we were in the storm created by a couple of long since dead Scottish professors, Adam Smith and David Hume. We studied a couple of Smith's books and he quite brilliantly shows in one of them that wealth creation by individuals is a vital part of society and in the other that this has to be governed by what he calls moral sentiments."

"Presumably, someone who seeks to make a profit on his business may be more tempted, if he is in danger of losing wealth, to take an immoral course of action, like not paying his creditors, or being fraudulent in other ways."

"Indeed, the temptations must be much greater than those of us in public service, which I think is what Smith is after in his second book, and cases come before the courts where financial fraud is the topic from time to time."

"What would that other man you mentioned, David Hume say about such matters."

"In my time he was unpopular, because he was most certainly not a believer in God, and he thought that all our moral views derived from our emotions."

"Well, don't they? I would not hurt someone whom I cared about, would I?"

"I will look it up, but he has this remarkable comment which our tutors used to present to us as the thinking of a mad man. It goes something like this: 'it is not contrary to reason to prefer the destruction of the whole world to the scratching of my finger.' I suppose he means that mere reason without emotion can have very strange consequences. But enough philosophy," Hamish concluded. "I think we should have a dinner party or a party of some kind to celebrate us. We will have been married twenty-eight years in June. James promised he would return this year, didn't he?"

"That would certainly be cause for celebration. He has been a treasure writing to us so regularly, but he has been something of a surprise, our son, hasn't he?"

"Over the years since taking his degree at Edinburgh, I have wondered whether we should not have asked more of him."

"No, we should not worry," said Mary. "We wanted him to be independent. He met this American student whose father had business in Scotland, you remember, and off they went to New York."

"We could not have stopped him, and one thing has led to another and they have virtually gone around the world together since. Maybe he will come home and settle down."

"I do hope so. I see all our friends in close touch with their children and grandchildren and we don't have that experience, yet."

"I will write to him at his last address as he said he would be in Peru for a while, and I will urge him to return."

"Yes, now is the time," mused Mary, "to take the businessman's view and cash in our investment on our beloved son, we have had enough of our teaching him to be independent."

"Quite so," said Hamish.

For Malcolm and Clara, Oliver was proving a delightful companion. Within a week, he had discovered the beaches near Port Elizabeth, where the Indian Ocean made bathing a delight. During February he tried each day after his discovery to attract Clara and her children to beach pleasures and the family soon got into the habit of taking a picnic, sometimes with and sometimes without Malcolm.

George and Alice took care of the little ones as they paddled in the shallows, while baby Charles gurgled in his perambulator or played with his parents on a rug between their chairs. Matilda sometimes came to care for the baby, but Clara was not initially attracted by the sea and she usually sat in a deck chair which Oliver carried down for her from Clyde Street. Malcolm was a very strong swimmer, having been to a school in Capetown where sporting excellence was at a premium and he had chosen to swim in preference to football and he swam in an ocean whenever he got the chance. Such outings invariably became a picnic.

The sea in the Southern Hemisphere was delightful for the Gargerys, and Clara gradually became less apprehensive. Moreover, unlike England, the proprieties associated with dress and a secluded beach hut were not observed and beaches were very rarely well populated: indeed, a family might have twenty yards between them and other people. The sea was usually calm, with gentle waves lapping the shore, so no danger was expected, though any ocean has its dangers.

One such Sunday afternoon in March, the weather seemed to presage a storm in the late afternoon, but the family spent an enjoyable time, swimming and playing French cricket. The boer-hound puppy named Rufus had finally arrived from a kennel several miles in the country north of the city and was soon rolling around with the children on carpets or sand.

Oliver had acquired two friends, Harry and Simon, from his regular visits to the beaches and they were running around playing tag between bouts in the ocean, behavior typical of growing young men and indeed of Rufus. The three of them had gone back into the sea and were swimming thirty or so yards from the shore, quite out of their depth. A squall appeared seemingly out of nowhere and the turning tide suddenly became very rough. Malcolm and Clara were engaged with the young children and at first did not hear the cries for help from the sea.

Malcolm glanced at the sea, realizing that the surf was strong even with his limited sight.

"Clara, look at the sea."

"Where are the other boys?" she cried, as Simon stumbled out of the waves and flopped down on the beach exhausted. Now they could hear the cries for help from Harry and Oliver who seemed to be quite close to each other from what she could see.

Malcolm threw off his outer garment, towel and eye-patch and rushed into the sea, swimming fast in search of the two boys.

"Help, help," Oliver shouted, "I'm drowning. Malcolm, Malcolm, I'm over here, I'm over here."

Ignoring Harry nearby, Malcolm shouted, "I'll get you," and he grabbed the boy, put his strong hands round his waist and dragged him back to shore until he could get a foothold in shallower waters.

"Where is Harry?" Cried Oliver standing now firmly in the shallow water and looking out to sea, "he was out there with me."

"I must get him," Malcolm shouted, plunging back into the surf while Oliver struggled up the beach to where Clara was waiting anxiously, her children in tears at the commotion.

Shouts of 'Harry, Harry' could just be heard from the shore as Malcolm swam strongly through the turbulent sea. A few spectators were gathering to watch this drama unfold and they could now see Malcolm hauling the young man out of the surf and swimming strongly toward the shore. Stumbling out of the sea exhausted, he laid Harry on the sand, and without knowing really what to do, held him face down over his knee and pumped the boy's body where he thought his lungs were, as Harry seemed unconscious. Suddenly volumes of sea water were vomited out of the boy's mouth at which Malcolm turned him back over on the sand, thinking the boy was dead.

Clara looked on in horror, paralyzed with fear. All her children were crying loudly at this scene. A Malayan man-servant nearby saw the events and he rushed over to Harry and put his mouth on the boy's, blowing furiously as if he was pumping a balloon of great size. Gradually, life seemed to be reappearing and the servant turned the boy over and he vomited again and started to breathe. Rufus ignored all this and splashed around barking at the sea.

A policeman had noticed the commotion and pushed his way through the small crowd of spectators gathering.

"Get off that boy, you bloody kaffir, get off, get off," and he ran up to the Malayan and punched him in the face and dragged him away from Harry.

"What the hell are you doing?" shouted Malcolm who had watched the servant with admiration. "He has just saved this boy's life, you stupid oaf!"

"And what's your name," said the policeman, now standing face to face with Malcolm and staring into his eyes.

"I am Major Malcolm Gargery of the British Liaison Force."

At this, the policeman withdrew and without comment walked back to his station on the promenade. Harry was now resting prone on the sand, shocked but alive.

"Thank you my friend," said Malcolm, shaking the Malayan servant's hand. "He is not our son, but I am sure his family will be much in your debt. What is your name?"

"Abdul, sir, and I am house servant to my lady Waterhouse who is resting over there. I see problem and I know what man can do when boy drowning."

"You certainly did. Clara, have you your purse with you?"

"Of course, darling?

Malcolm pulled a five-pound note from the purse and handed it to Abdul, who expressed his thanks so excessively that Malcolm wished he would be quiet.

"May I talk with your mistress?" said Clara.

"Please for me to accompany you," said Abdul.

Mrs. Waterhouse and Clara conversed for almost a half hour, and as they were parting she said that she and her husband were about to return to England to get away from what she called this dreadful war.

"Will Abdul then be without a job?"

"I fear so, as he will not accompany us."

"Then I will employ him as soon as you leave. May I speak with him?"

"Of course, of course."

It was soon settled that Abdul would join the Gargery household immediately the Waterhouse family embarked, in about two weeks' time.

Malcolm sat disconsolate on the sand, exhausted by his efforts and amazed at Abdul's speed and determination. Simon knew where Harry's parents lived, so a message was sent and within half an hour his mother, Mrs. Ellsworth arrived with her two younger sons.

She gazed at Harry, now sleeping, and then knelt down to kiss him.

"I suppose there was nothing you could do," she said to Malcolm.

"He could do nothing, Ma'am," said Simon who was standing near, "I managed to get free of the turbulence in the waves, and then Major Gargery came in bravely and grabbed Oliver, but Harry was out of reach at that time, but the Major went back to get him."

"I suppose Oliver is your son," she said, staring at Malcolm.

"No, he is just a son of friends in London who is staying with us."

"Well, of course, you had to save him first, didn't you?" she said getting angrier and beginning to weep and then coming close to Malcolm she began to beat him on his now covered chest, breaking down into sobs and tears that seemed to shake the earth.

"You should have saved Harry first, you know."

"Mother," said Harry weakly, "I am alive thanks to my Malayan savior."

"I went back into the sea, Ma'am," said Malcolm, "as soon as Oliver could get a footing in the shallows, but Harry was already unconscious. I brought him as quickly as I could to the shore but I did not really know how to revive him but Abdul did."

Mrs. Ellsworth was not to be comforted, even when Harry got up and led her with her younger children away from the beach.

When they got home, Clara took Malcolm in her arms.

"You did all you could, darling. Harry is alive. She was just terribly upset by the possibility of losing her son and so lashed out at you."

"But is she right? Should I have tried to save Harry before Oliver?"

"Oliver was nearest to you from what I could see and you had no time to engage in deep moral thought about which you should have saved first."

"You are right, of course. But should I have gone for Harry first?"

At which point, Oliver walked in.

"Malcolm, thank you from the bottom of my heart for saving my life. I am incredibly relieved that the Malayan knew what to do for Harry."

"So am I, but should I have tried to save him before you, as his mother seemed to imply?"

"I cannot face that dilemma: You just grabbed me in the turmoil we were in."

"It would have been on my conscience if either of you had been drowned, I must say."

"And there's an end to it," said Clara.

That night Malcolm went into Oliver's bedroom to say goodnight:

"You have today experienced mortal danger, Oliver. Learn from it that the world is a dangerous place, especially when it looks its most attractive."

"I will, I will, and thank you again."

XIV

It was a fine day in June so Hamish was glad to return home early on Friday as the case was concluded before lunch, so instead of going to his club, he came home to Cheyne Row. Harriet had taken Mary out to lunch and he knew she would not be back before tea, so he called the maid to bring him lunch and he waited in his study, glancing at the newspapers. Lunch had still not arrived, when the doorbell rang and he heard a man's voice he was sure he recognized.

He leapt from his chair, knocking some books on the floor and there was his son James with a woman standing in the hall.

"Good afternoon, Father," James started to say before he was engulfed in his father's arms.

"My son, my son, my dearest, how are you?" said Hamish with tears in his eyes.

"I am very well indeed, but I want you to meet my wife, Stella, formerly Stella Gilmour."

"Good heavens, really, well, well, welcome Stella, welcome indeed," and he shook hands with his daughter-in-law, almost James's height, with blond hair and the palest of blue eyes. Both of them looked travel-worn, with brown cheeks from the sun and dark arms as if they had travelled a desert.

"I did not expect to find you home yet, but I thought Mother might be here."

"She is with Mrs. Pirrip for lunch but should return in an hour or so. I am sure you should not tell me everything and then have to repeat it. Tell me first, what are your immediate plans?"

"None really. We have come home and intend to relax for a month or so and hope we could stay here."

"Of course, this is your home, my dear. Your bedroom awaits you, so why don't you both make yourself comfortable and unpack before Mother comes home when we can both hear all about it."

"It's been a frightfully long journey, so we may rest a while."

"Off you go, then," said Hamish trying to avoid showing his shock at his son bringing home a wife, as Mary and he had not had a whisper or a hint about a marriage.

Hamish returned to his study and sat in contemplation. When Mary came home, he took her right hand and led her into the study, sitting her down in the old leather chair.

"What's this, Hamish, a confession?"

"No, my dear," he said laughing, "there a couple upstairs in the spare bedroom and I want you to guess who they are."

"A couple? I have no idea, Tom and Hannah? Malcolm and Clara? I give up."

"James Irving MacDonald and his wife Stella, nee Gilmour."

"I am glad I am sitting down," said Mary more calmly than Hamish expected.

"Yes, he arrived after I got home as the case ended before noon, and I was more than surprised when they came in, though delighted of course, but astonished at his having a wife."

"I sent them upstairs to rest as I told them I did not want to hear their stories before you came home."

"How sweet of you. I will go and raise them."

She got up, went into the hall and called out "James, James, your mother is here."

"Hallo, Mother darling, we will be down directly."

"What a pity his sister is not here."

"I am sure Emily will come from Liverpool when we send a note. I'll write one now."

James came down the stairs first and enveloped Mary in his arms which made this stoical woman weep copiously.

"Oh my darling," she said through her tears, "five years is far too long. I do so hope you have done enough travelling to want to settle down here in England now."

"I think so, Mother," he said as his wife came downstairs with a casual elegance that pleased Mary.

"Mother, this is my wife Stella."

"How completely lovely," said Mary, kissing her daughter-in-law on both cheeks.

Meantime Hamish had informed the maid and the cook that lunch would be for four, so the maid brought sherry and they sat in the conservatory for although it was June, this was England and it had now started to rain.

"Stella," said Mary, "you can tell me about your travels later, but I want to know first about you two."

"Ah," said James, "we met my last year in Edinburgh at a small student party and I noticed this charming medical student."

"We met from time to time until I left with Jimmy for America, but returned after a month to my family," said Stella, "but we corresponded."

"So," said Hamish, "did you study under Mrs. Jex-Blake?"

"Indeed, but she was something of a tiger, you know. I don't see myself as a pioneer, but she certainly was. Wonderful person, drawing women into medicine and it is now firmly entrenched at Edinburgh."

"You will meet Hannah Hesketh, formerly Gargery, at some point. She did not train at the University but at a small hospital. She did not complete her studies," Mary continued, "and she is now in Ireland with her husband Tom Hesketh at the moment. Your name is Scottish too, I think."

"That is right, but my father was a lawyer in Durham and my mother is English, so I am afraid I have no Scottish mannerisms."

"Before my husband waxes lyrical about Scotland, I want to know more about these two," at which Hamish smiled.

"We corresponded regularly as I said, Mother, I was in Chile when I wrote asking Stella to come to America and think about marrying me. I could not have done this without Father's monthly allowance and I was able to live within its confines."

"Good gracious me, how come we knew nothing about this, James?"

"I did not know whether she would accept and it took two years. I returned to a state called California where I got a letter saying she would come to Boston arriving for Christmas 1898, last year indeed. I had been across by boat to Japan where I was not welcome and China which is very poor and strange, and at least in Boston they speak English so I was glad to come across the country by train."

"Let me continue, Jimmy," said Stella, much to Mary's discomfort at hearing a diminutive she disliked intensely.

"We spent three days in Vermont last December, where it did nothing but snow but the people seemed to love it. Confined to the lodging we had nothing to do but talk, and we then returned to Boston and got married."

"That is such a romantic story, James," said Hamish, "we will celebrate by going to the Savoy for dinner. I will send them a message promptly."

"So," said Mary, "here you are, my dearest son, but without a career, I assume?"

"Not exactly, that is so, but part of my reason for return at this point is that I met a man in Boston who works for The Times, and he said that my travel experience stood me in good stead for a job there. I am not convinced as I am most uncertain about travelling again. Stella and I want to settle down."

Over lunch Mary and Hamish listened to tales of adventure they found difficult to imagine. Their incautious son had traveled extensively in South America, even going to Cape Horn and looking out toward the Antarctic. He spent two months with the Welsh people in Patagonia and had taken a boat from Ecuador to the Galapagos Island which he knew had been visited by Charles Darwin.

"This is an extraordinary happening, my dear," said Mary as they retired to bed that night.

"I am much surprised, I must say, but Stella seems a charming young woman, obviously prepared for the hazards of travel and exploration."

"Thank goodness," Mary concluded, "but we should be proud. He is an adventurous soul but with a sound head on his shoulders."

"I will be fascinated to see what he does next."

"Me too, but I do wish she would not call him Jimmy."

Harriet sat in her drawing-room after Mary had come and gone and her thoughts turned to the Gargery family of which she was now a central part. Pip came into the room from his study and sat down in his usual chair.

"You seems to be musing, my dear. May I ask on what?"

"I was just thinking about your children, how surprised Joe and Biddy would be by them and what they are doing. I suppose the fact of your family experience of Africa has not made them cautious about travel or the experience of other nations."

"Indeed, but Malcolm is in much more danger again with this trouble with the Boers. These rumblings in the press and elsewhere suggest another war. He is there. He will get caught up in it, I know. I wish they'd come back to England, though their letters suggest they like Port Elizabeth."

"I have not been concerned or troubled by our argument with Boers," grumbled Harriet. "War annoys me so much that I don't really want to know what the problem is, which I suppose I should."

"I follow it closely as Malcolm is there with our grandchildren. The fundamental problem is that the Boers are a farming God-fearing people whose families are originally Dutch. We British are colonizers of a different kind. We want to use the natural resources of the Empire to make us top dog in the world."

"That would be a conflict solved only in Heaven," said Harriet with a dry laugh.

"It has become very serious since diamonds and gold were found ten years or so ago in the Witwatersrand, Boer country, but some sixty thousand Tom Dick and Harry's went out from England seeking their fortune. They were called uitlanders by the Boers, but they were not allowed any formal rights by the Boers, like voting. They lived near the mines but inside the South African Republic. We have recently been negotiating with Boers at a town called Bloemfontein which has just failed."

At this, Harriet's interest was aroused and she plied her husband with questions, "What are they negotiating about?"

"Politicians on both sides simply were unable to compromise. I see it as money versus religion."

"What on earth does that mean?"

"The battle over the diamond and gold mining industry itself and who controls it. Malcolm was there in the very early days."

"Doesn't Rhodes control it?"

"No, he has long since gone after that foolish attempt to take over the Boers by force. Another matter is our Government's wish to drag the Boers who live in the Transvaal and the Orange Free State into some kind of federation run by us."

"Why would we want to do that?"

"Control once again, but also to prevent the Boers siding with the Germans or anyone else and allowing them into South Africa."

"So the Boers won't let these uitlanders vote?"

"No, and you can understand why. They are a very religious, even simple people who cannot tolerate a bunch of freebooters and gold-diggers drawn from the dregs of British society influencing their politics."

"Don't the Boers still have slaves too?"

196

"I think so, but they don't buy and sell them as far as I know. As Susanna and I found in Africa, white people do not care about the Africans, Xhosa, Zulu. Most of the white people she and I met there, and you saw some of it too, thought we were mad, that Africans were savages and simple-minded. Such an awful attitude."

"That all sounds terrible to me. I always thought that man Rhodes was a scoundrel, not that I knew much about him."

"Apparently our new man in the country Sir Alfred Milner is a very tough egg and likely to make demands on the Boers that they won't accept which will give him, or the Boers, the opportunity to begin a war. My money would be on the Boers starting a conflict. Then we will be drowning in jingoism once again."

"Do we know much about Malcolm and Clara's area of the country? Would it be near the fighting?"

"Probably not, as they are on the east coast in a British colony, nowhere near the mining area. I read a piece some months ago now saying that as the railways have expanded everywhere, the harbor at Port Elizabeth is very busy with imports and exports. The article called it the Liverpool of South Africa, and it has multitudes of different origins there, Africans and folk from Asia too."

"I wonder what Malcolm really makes of all this. His letters are always all about his family, which is a delight, but we are left without knowledge of his work. Do you think they will come back if war starts?"

"Only if he resigns his commission. Otherwise he is at Milner's beck and call and he is responsible to the Commander of the Army. It used to be Roberts, but is now Kitchener, I think. Of course with his injury I think combat is unlikely, but we will have to send thousands more troops to the country."

"What a curse. I hope Clara is able to cope."

"That lady can cope with anything, I am sure."

With the afternoon mail came a letter from Clara telling the tale of Oliver's rescue and Harry's savior which shocked both Pip and Harriet such that she felt obliged to call on Elizabeth directly to share in her good fortune at her son being saved from the sea. It was a straightforward journey from Chelsea as Elizabeth continued to live in Eaton Square after Timothy's death in an elegant house as befitted a senior Foreign Office man.

"It is odd, is it not, Harriet," said Elizabeth, after they had gone over the details of the beach incident, "just how many children die before their time. I wonder if it is divine intervention, or survival of the fittest as Mr. Darwin might offer as an explanation or just fate to luck or whatever you want to call it."

"None of those, I think," said Harriet. "Of course with Lachlan the disease was insuperable. But that Harry was a foolhardy risk and very lucky to escape death. Should we be surprised that children suffer the same as older people do? I think not. It just seems unfair somehow that they are deprived of a full life."

"With children it is the parents who must suffer, and too often accept blame for their child's misfortunes."

"True of my husband, certainly."

Plans for the MacDonald Party went ahead and the arrival of James and Stella made it a great celebration. Hamish and Mary felt that their children had been well brought up and that they were a loving family, but once their education were completed they had both disappeared on various expeditions, writing home of course, but largely out of touch and now they were returning like prodigal children.

Mary thought occasionally that she had driven them away, which was nonsense as Hamish told her, but grandchildren were at last no longer a distant dream. Yet, as they told each other, we are mildly unconventional people and we brought our children up to be imaginative and independent, so why should we be sorry, anxious or bitter that they become imaginative and independent? Different upbringing though from Antonia and Aubrey's brood.

The date for the party was fixed for Saturday July 24th and James and Stella had gone off to the National Gallery to see the portrait of Mrs. Estella Pirrip. For Hamish, it turned out to be a dire week. Norman Thereabout was to be hanged in Wandsworth Jail the following Wednesday morning.

"It was not the first time that I have had to wear the black cap to send a man to the gallows, but I was troubled both by the man's weak intellect, but also because too much emphasis was placed on a confession, even though there was much more evidence than there had been in many other such cases. I find the most difficult part of being a judge is when my conscience is rattled by a conflict between the law and what I take to be just, especially when that involves hanging a man. In this case, I will constantly bear the sense that what I ordered to be done was wrong, morally wrong."

"Was Thereabout weak in the head then?"

"Yes and in a peculiar way. Thereabout showed under questioning that he knew what he was doing but did not understand the consequences as he was too simple-minded. It was as if he hit the woman with this blunt instrument and intended to do that, but then he was surprised she fell to the ground, bleeding to death. He seemed to me not to really understand the connection between means and ends, as that philosopher Mill described it. The jury had no patience with any defense, shocked as they were by the brutality, and I could not issue any contrary direction."

"Did he go into the witness box then?"

"No, his counsel was inadequate as he had confessed but he really needed to be questioned to reveal his real mental state. I was sorely tempted to call him to the stand myself after the verdict."

"Look, darling," said Mary, "you must realize that the law is imperfect, it is a human institution that cannot produce perfect justice and moreover, you are not the Solomon in the court, the jury and the counsel are all necessary to the system. Moreover as you know perfectly when you became a judge, when you condemn a man to death, it is not a matter for conscience, you are simply doing your duty according to the laws of the land."

"I know that, but I am puzzled and distressed by this man. If a person intends to do something, say, taking an axe to a tree, he will know that the consequence of his striking the tree with the axe will cause the tree to fall. Actions have consequences. With Thereabout it seemed as though he would know what he was doing in taking the axe to the tree but he would not understand that the consequence would be that the tree would fall."

"But you didn't sentence him to be hung because he chopped down a tree," said Mary laughing.

"Of course not, dear, but be serious, this still worries me immensely. Do you think it is possible that a man in some of his actions simply does not always understand that an action has a specific consequence? Of course, many things we do in life have unintended consequences, so it cannot be claimed that in every act we perform, we know the exact result. What if Thereabout was in a mental muddle about intended and unintended? Certainly if he was somehow mentally disturbed in ways we are not yet aware of, he should not have been hung."

"He could not function in life if he did not understand that what he does has a consequence, could he? But there is another side to this," Mary continued, "this man was almost fifty: What does society gain by executing him?"

"Ah, the question of the punishment fitting the crime is surely different from the detail of my case."

"Indeed I think it is a relic of barbarism that we execute people, and, though I recognize the reasons our society has, you know, tooth for a tooth, it will deter others, and so on, these all seem specious to me."

"I agree actually, though I must abide by sentencing conventions," he said as they heard someone in the hall, and their daughter Emily waltzed into the room.

"How delightful to see you, my darling," said Mary with a kiss after which Emily immediately went to her father's arms.

"Oh how lovely you are, we are so thrilled that you are here," said Hamish. "Pray tell us what you are up to since you left."

"Well, Father, life is treating me well. I don't think I have yet found my place in life. I have been very busy during my time in Liverpool, getting very interesting experiences in volunteering in hospitals and working with various organizations, but now I want to come home to my distinguished Papa and my darling Mamma and spend three months exploring possibilities in London."

"Ah, is that not wonderful as your brother is also back from his travels?"

"That is exciting too, and your letter telling me of his arrival soon made up my mind for me to come down to London. I gather there is a party in the offing."

"Yes, on Saturday."

"You have been very quiet, Emily, about what you have actually been doing in the past couple of years."

"Have I? Yes, I suppose I have. I will keep it for another time. I think it may shock you, Father, more than you Mother."

"Let us wait then until James can be with us too, and you can meet his wife."

"Wife? Really, who is she?"

"Stella Gilmour."

"Oh I have met her; she is a splendid woman. I saw her when I visited him in Edinburgh when he was a student."

"Odd, isn't it," said Hamish later, "how our children have had lives we knew little or nothing of, once they went off to the university."

Parties are a common meeting place for renewals, remembrances and gossip. Harriet and Mary spent time discussing Estella, the well-known lady with her eccentric guardian.

"She told me once in all seriousness, Mary, that she had plans to kill Pip's first wife Beatrice, but that she saw that Nature would do it for her."

"Plans, not mere fantasies?" her voice rising in shock, even horror.

"That is exactly what I asked her," continued Harriet, "but she seriously entertained two methods, poison with weedkiller which she had had her gardener buy or pushing Beatrice down the stairs at Numquam."

"Oh, my goodness, how terrible for her to be in liege to such a frightful desire."

"In one way, yes, but she added that both her mother and her father had been murderers."

"Of course, of course. Nature and Nurture once again. What an extraordinary woman she was."

The Pirrips arrived and Mary left to greet them with Hamish who introduced them to his children, James and Emily.

"What handsome progeny, Hamish, I am not sure which of their parents has contributed the most to their looks," Albert said as if he was reviewing racehorses, while his wife turned away in disgust. Fortunately no one took up Albert's remark, because everyone saw it as being in very bad taste.

"What might one expect from a man of business?" murmured Hamish to his son as they moved away to greet the Brandrams, "you're not attracted to commerce, are you, James?"

"Good Lord no, Father, I can think of nothing I would rather do less."

With people moving around, Hamish and Mary's daughter Emily, an attractive woman at twenty-three years old found herself in conversation with Albert.

"Tell me, my dear, how is your social life?"

"I am not sure what you mean, Mr. Pirrip. I have a variety of friends."

"Oh I suppose I was meaning whether you had a particular friendship, whether there was a man in your life."

"Oh to be sure, I am immensely fond of my father and my brother," Emily replied, feeling she was entering a trap as he was maneuvering her with some skill to an area of the garden which was more private.

"No, surely a lovely woman like you must be enjoying the delights of a close male friend, surely."

"I am not sure that it is any of your business."

"Ah I see, you have something in your life you want to keep secret, but you can share it with me, as indeed perhaps we could share more than secrets, could we not?" he said with a leer.

"I must get something to eat, Mr. Pirrip, forgive me."

Holding up his hand, he almost grabbed her arm, but decided in the last moment to refrain from doing so, but she had noticed his right hand was covered in a rash.

"Will you not come to the table eat too?" She asked, trying to extricate herself from this situation with as much tact as possible."

"No, my dear, I find I am not very hungry these days but, of course, I would invite you to a private dinner," at which he touched his brow which Emily recognized as a mild fever.

She quickly managed to escape from this singularly undesirable man, and then it struck her. No appetite, a fever and a rash. She turned white and rushed indoors to wash her hands as she had been obliged to part with a long handshake.

What a boor of a man, she thought, I must tell my mother.

Returning from the washroom, she walked slowly up to Mary, still deep in conversation with Harriet.

"I have something really important to tell you and as Harriet is here I can share it with you both."

"What on earth is the trouble, Emily? You are quite white," said her mother.

"I have just had a most unpleasant experience with that Mr. Pirrip whom I don't think I have ever met before. He badgered me with personal questions, maneuvered me away from the other guests and, I think was about to make an indecent proposal to me."

"Yet you have escaped his clutches, so do not be alarmed. Is there something else?"

"Yes, and I hesitate to say this, but I think he has a disease, probably syphilis."

"Oh no, Emily," said Harriet, clapping her hands to her mouth, "I am sure not. He was Estella's step-son and after an infidelity before he was married, he is happily married to Nellie's daughter."

"H'mm. Was Estella upset by his infidelity?" Asked Mary, continuing the conversation with Harriet and putting Emily's claims to one side.

"Indeed, she upbraided him and told Elizabeth to break with him because of it."

"Then we know he has been something of a cad in early life. His success in business has made him rather uncouth, I think, and we heard him at that Board meeting basically condemning charity and its institutions."

"I have volunteered in hospitals," said Emily, "and in particular at a seaman's hospital in Liverpool for a few months and I am telling you he has all the early external signs of syphilis. Of course we cannot examine his body for the other tell-tale signs, but it is the coincidence of these three symptoms that is very suggestive. I must say I am led to this partly because he is clearly a wanton creature too, pressing his desires on me, whom he does not know, in a context such as this, all that is surely indicative of a man whose lusts are quite out of control."

"What can we do? How did he get it?"

"Doctors have much evidence to indicate that it is transferred when a man or a woman with the disease can transmit it to the other when a couple copulate. Of course it is frequently conveyed by prostitutes, some of whom show no signs of the disease at all."

"I did not know all that," said Mary, wincing slightly as she took in this information.

"If so," said Harriet somewhat in shock, "Victoria is in danger."

"I am afraid so, and mortal danger too."

"We must somehow warn her," said Harriet, "it is another curse of the way women are treated. If he knows what is his complaint, he will keep it his wife in ignorance."

"Why should any woman have to endure such a fate? If her husband won't tell her, I will," said Mary firmly. "Either of us have a reputation for taking bulls by their horns, Harriet, but I will invite her to lunch and I hope you will join me."

"As long as you don't take this particular bull by its horns," said Harriet with an infectious giggle which soon had all three women laughing.

At that Mary hurried off to seek Victoria, noticing Albert sitting alone on a garden bench smoking a cigar, but she found his wife in conversation with her two young daughters.

"What a beautiful family you have, Victoria dear, and they are so grown up. I am so sorry we have not had time to talk. Would you take lunch with me soon?"

"We live at Numquam, as you know, but Albert is in town on business and we have a comfortable pied-a-terre near Covent Garden. We are only here for another two days."

"Why not come tomorrow? It would be fun to share remembrances of your mother, and I have not heard about her when she came to you. So we can chat about her and other matters."

"I'd love to, and I don't have to get permission these days," she said laughing.

Albert's illness apart, war with the Boers now seemed inevitable and Harriet was mightily concerned about her husband's soldier son, beside which Albert's tribulations were trivial indeed. She walked away from Mary to find Pip and put her arm in his for their mutual protection from any calamity that might befall them.

XV

Victoria postponed the initial plans to meet Mary made at the celebration. She was at Numquam for the remainder of the summer and there seemed to urgency especially as she did not know Mary well. This grieved Mary a little as she thought she was under an obligation, given what Emily had said, to tell Victoria of what was thought to be Albert's condition. She had thought of writing, but after a discussion with Hamish she felt relieved of the responsibility, as he thought it would be an intolerable interference in the private life of a family if she were to travel to Kent with intent to tell a wife about a philandering husband with a mortal disease. Words like busybody would be bandied around.

Messages were exchanged in the autumn and Victoria wrote to say she would be glad to meet as she would be at their London lodgings for a few days in October. Mary invited Harriet to join her for the meeting as she had been there when Emily suggested Albert had syphilis.

Victoria arrived, admired the house and they sat in the drawing room each with a glass of sherry before lunch.

"We were reminiscing the other day about Nellie, your mother, and oh my goodness what a marvelous woman she was."

"Oh Mary, we were like friends when I was growing up and before I was married; she told me all about her life, particularly when she was whoring, and she was full of stories about that time before she married my father. So many funny stories and some very harsh ones too. Did you know about that Whistler man?"

"The one who was killed at Numquam?"

"Yes, though they knew it was necessary, it was always a shadow over their lives, killing a man."

"Oh that's right, Estella told me the story," said Mary, "I only knew parts of it."

"It must have been so dangerous being a whore, what with disease and all that," said Harriet.

"Oh dear me yes, and she was so funny about that. This is not really a polite conversation for us though."

"Not at all, do tell us. We are beyond being shocked."

"There was this big boat docked in Chatham and, you remember how she talked, 'and all these sailors running ashore to find it,' she said, 'and I hooked up with one of 'em, and when he was ready, I saw all them warts around his you know what, and I said, sorry mate, but you's got the clap and I ain't getting it,' which left Harriet and Mary in stitches laughing at the way Victoria imitated her mother.

"Oh she was such a lovely woman," said Mary, "but I want to talk to you seriously, if I may, how is your marriage? You seemed somewhat discontented at our July party."

"Oh my goodness, does it show? Albert and I have become distant ever since we moved to Numquam. We are never intimate these days; he has changed so many of his attitudes many of which I find very unpleasant. He works very hard so is rarely at home and he says his Chatham business requires it," and she began to weep quietly. "He's been working himself to death all summer, and he is not very well. He has had this rash on his hand for a long time and when I ask him to get it treated, he just says it's nothing,"

"There is no good way to say this, Victoria," said Mary, "but we care for you very much and we think you are in danger. Women who are in danger need each other for protection."

"What do you mean?" Asked Victoria, in a mildly truculent tone.

"We believe Albert has syphilis."

There was silence for a moment or two.

"I know, I know," said Victoria, "the shame of it, it is simply terrible. He won't go to the doctor. I can hardly get myself to admit it."

"You knew?"

"You do not get to be the daughter of a whore and not know about diseases a woman can get through being intimate. My mum went through a whole catalogue of these infections one afternoon, though actually we laughed and laughed at the way men get afflicted. You know, I think she was determined that she and I be friends as her mother died early and she was badly treated by her father and her brother."

"And what a friend she was, but tell us, has Albert been a philanderer then?"

"Some time ago he seemed to want to get near his old love, that Elizabeth."

"Oh, she came to me about that," said Mary, "but she told him to leave, and he was boorish in his feeble attempts to pursue her."

"What do you mean?"

"As we are being blunt about him, he threw himself at her, physically."

"Shame on him: A cad, a philanderer and my rotten husband. There would be something really ironic, wouldn't there," she said with a kerchief in her hand to stifle her tears, "if my husband got sick from a whore in Chatham."

"Now Victoria, you do know, don't you, that we are engaged in this conversation about your husband not to pry into your marriage but to protect you."

"I am my mother's daughter, Harriet, I can deal with him. But tell me how you found out?"

"My daughter Emily has been on her own in the north of the country," said Mary, "and she worked for a while at a seaman's hospital. Albert also made unwanted advances to her at my party and she recognized three of the symptoms."

"Clever woman. Oh dear, tell me, Harriet, Mary, tell me, what should I do?"

"The really important matter is to protect yourself and never, ever be intimate with him again. There is no real cure, though it is said that mercury can still the disease."

"I know and I suppose I am looking at becoming a widow sooner than I might have anticipated, but what will happen to his business? Hackney is fine, but Chatham seems to be another story. I know nothing of his finances either."

"H'mm, my husband Hamish might agree to talk to him. They have known each other since Hamish joined Jaggers, they like each other and Hamish is nothing if not compassionate. I will get him to have lunch on the pretext of a Board issue."

"I cannot thank you enough for this lunch and conversation, both of you. It has been such a help. I mean I think most women would regard your wanting to discuss this with me as the most horrible intrusion on my marriage. But my mother was so open about her past and so willing to share everything about herself with her family, and of course with Estella, that it has rubbed off on me. I don't mind talking with women about intimate matters."

"That is exactly what the League of Free Women is for," said Harriet, "and your ability to do this will help others."

"Anyway, can't be hangin' around 'ere all day, as my mum would say," at which the others laughed with their fond memories of Nellie, "but I am glad to know of your help and support."

Albert was surprised to be invited to lunch with a High Court judge but, on the other hand, he was a very old friend of the family so he assumed there was no particular agenda. Albert had contemplated switching his company lawyers to Courtisone and Jaggers but he intended to stick with Henderson and Henderson of Hackney, as they had known the former practice from the company's inception. Perhaps Hamish intended to invite him to change.

A meeting was finally arranged for Friday November 3rd as the Courts rose before lunch, three months after Emily's initial suspicions had been voiced. Albert was especially pleased to be asked to the Athenaeum as he was still eliciting support for his idea of a gentleman's club in Chatham. To be able to view the inner workings of the most prestigious gentleman's club in London was a great opportunity. He often stayed at his lodgings in Covent Garden but felt feverish overnight and very uncomfortable which he diminished with a dose of laudanum.

He was still groggy that morning, but he was not going to miss this lunch arrangement. His cab put him down at the end of Pall Mall as he thought a little walk to the Club might steady him.

Once inside, he was led to a side room where Hamish was reading a newspaper.

"Albert, my dear fellow, how good to see you. I missed a long chat with you at our party as I was preoccupied with both my children arriving suddenly, and as we known each other well over the years. I even remember when you asked about my long-forgotten proclivities soon after I arrived."

"Thank you so much for inviting me, Hamish. I am not well these days, but still able to conduct my important business."

"I am sure you have been a great success and we admire you for it, but what is your illness?" said Hamish with just that degree of dissembling that a judge could tolerate.

"A severe matter, I am afraid. Since I have known you for a very long time and I know you will keep my secret, I regret that I have contacted a mortal disease, syphilis."

"Oh my dear fellow, I am so sorry."

"It is my own fault entirely."

"Do you know where it came from?"

"I was feeling especially down at heart after a major row with Victoria some time ago and began using a whore which I have since done every now and then. I work late at my Chatham office, you see, so the opportunities regularly present themselves. I have been aware that I was in trouble, though it did not affect Victoria at all because we were not on speaking terms and I have been careful to avoid her."

"Have you told her?" Asked Hamish, scarcely able to disguise his shock at these admissions.

"Yes, but she knew the signs, being Nellie's daughter."

"Well, I hope you can get treatment and that it is successful."

"I will try, but it is so embarrassing to talk to my doctor."

"Try Harley Street first. Go to a London hospital which specializes in the disease after that if you need to."

"Sound advice, Hamish."

"There's another side to this, of course. The disease puts you in mortal danger, but it also can have devastating effects, the loss of a nose for example."

"What do you mean?"

"I read a case some years ago in which a woman was suing for divorce as she had been infected with syphilis by her husband. The report said that in court she was permitted to wear a veil because her face was covered in warts and her nose had disintegrated."

"How awful! Could that happen to me?" He said, clearly shocked to the core.

"Perhaps you would then confine yourself to your house, but have you sorted your affairs in the event of your early death?"

"You can certainly be frank, Hamish, but then you are a lawyer," said Albert with a smile, "and you are right, I do need to review all that."

"Forgive me for being so frank, then. As you say I am a lawyer and we have to tell a client exactly what one thinks without embellishment, and of course matters are discussed in the deepest confidence. You see, if you become progressively ill and unable to run your businesses, the business might become unstable and your wealth would then be in jeopardy which would obviously affect Victoria, your children and their future. I know something of the trajectory of the disease, but I would urge you to think about these possibilities sooner rather than later."

"Yes, let me see. My brother-in-law Horatio and my wife Victoria jointly own Numquam House," said Albert, "but he has no interest in living there, so at least she has a home. I have made trusts for the children but if my businesses were to collapse, that would be of little use."

"Consider this, you have a mortal illness which will eventually kill you unless there is a miraculous cure, and again I am sorry to talk so bluntly but I think your situation demands it."

"It is such a relief to able to talk about this to someone prepared to understand it."

"One possibility is to sell your businesses, which would enable you to rest and try to recover from your illness while at the same generating capital which could be wisely invested. I don't think you need to feel any particular obligation to the Pocket family, none of whom have shown any interest in you, your family or the company."

"Am I to be like my father then, very sick, a drawn-out death, punctuated by doses of mercury?"

"I asked a senior physician at St. Thomas Hospital who was a client at the law practice and he told me that one possible effect of the disease is that it is impossible to avoid mental deterioration, the ability to see matters clearly. Physical deterioration may come with paralysis too and he did say that he indicates to patients that critical decisions should be made earlier than later."

"Thank you, Hamish, for this help which I sorely needed. I would be inclined to arrange the sale through your firm if that is what I decide."

"You would have no better lawyer than Aaron Levy who is a tiger in such matters. Just call on him and say I suggested him."

"If it comes to that, I will."

"One final issue: Will you discuss all this with your wife? My sense is that you will feel much more comfortable if you do."

"As she knows of my condition, that may make sense too, but I am utterly confused about myself. I am not going to rush into seeing doctors, however, for

I do not feel myself yet to be in decline, merely ill. I am keeping up with my business and I am not incapacitated."

Famous last words thought Hamish as they said goodbye.

Between the autumn of 1899 and the middle of 1900 the Second Boer War stirred many a patriotic heart in Britain but the cost in men and materiel was an encumbrance the British public was not accustomed to. Apart from colonial skirmishes in India and elsewhere, the country had not been at war for five decades and the Crimean War was not the cause célébre that the wars with France had been at the beginning of the nineteenth century.

Catastrophe in South Africa was imminent. Both sides had stuck to their guns and the Bloemfontein negotiations in June 1899 collapsed in mutual recrimination and by September the British had demanded full voting rights and representation for the uitlanders, the large number of British residents working in the mines and thus residing in the Transvaal.

The President of the South African Republic Paul Kruger had issued an ultimatum on the ninth of October 1899. It was very hostile and also a sign that the Boers had never expected negotiations to succeed. The British were given a mere two days to withdraw all their troops from the borders of the Boer states, Transvaal and the Orange Free State, although British troops were a long way off in garrison towns. At the same time, Boer commandos had been sent to the border of British Natal in early September. The British government rejected the South African Republic's – the ZAR - ultimatum, resulting in the Boer States declaring war on Britain.

Malcolm got the news from Brigadier Motley-Millard.

"Bad news this, what, but we knew it was coming, didn't we? Those Boers are a crafty lot and I think we'll have a devil of a time fighting them."

"Do we have any orders, sir?" Malcolm asked.

"Merely that we have to be more concerned than we have been with what is arriving in the port."

"But don't the Boers now have their own route now through to Delagoa Bay?"

"They do. Neither you nor I will be involved in combat, of course, but we have an important job to do here, Gargery."

By early December the British Army had begun a scorched earth policy which was leaving increasing numbers of families, mainly women and children, destitute, and the Government decided to establish camps where such civilian casualties of the war might live. Wandering families were said to be supporting the enemy, so, to try to bring the Boers to heel, wives and children of notable British enemies from towns and cities were also interned in these camps, a punishment with a base in force, not the Law.

In late November, the Brigadier called his staff together to announce the start of a camp for Boer women and children in Port Elizabeth.

"Gentlemen, I have received this day information from the authorities at Bloemfontein that we will see a camp established on the Racecourse with its buildings and additional tents to house women and children aiding the enemy. In the past we have housed some of the uitlanders there so these should be comfortable enough to house these people who will almost certainly be Boer women and children."

"Will there be Xhosa and other African families needing accommodation if their farms have been destroyed too?" Asked Malcolm.

"Quite correct, Major Gargery, but for the moment, we are to anticipate Boers only. My own view is that this location will not prove satisfactory and others will be needed. However, we are to give all support to the authorities and we may be called to be responsible for its operation in due course."

The preparation of accommodation was rudimentary and by December prisoners began to arrive, and Malcolm was impressed by the Brigadier's powers of organization which now seemed in full flow after his sedentary life at the Fort, as he told Clara when he got home one evening to report:

"I was shocked, I must say, though I had to steel myself as an officer. I saw women and children with babies, worn out, unsmiling, so distressed and with very sad expressions, many with clothes almost in rags. Some were carrying little valuables, but the old Brigadier is proving his competence."

"Am I right that our army has so destroyed Boer farms and livelihoods that it is the women and children who suffer? If so, how is it to be managed?"

"The Brigadier has been told that a superintendent will arrive shortly. From what I saw today women were doing some cooking and there seemed to be a few pastors there to make sure they behave themselves I suppose. Yet they are really captives which is a new policy for civilians.

"To be quite honest, I doubt the wisdom of the policy and I fear the consequences, but once you destroy their lives and you regard them as supporting the enemy, rounding them up seems the only thing to do. The Brigadier mentioned other camps being established elsewhere, starting with Bloemfontein.

"Presumably the need for camps will be almost infinite and across areas of Boer country in those parts of the Orange Free State under our control."

"Indeed, and I am not convinced we are making much progress."

Malcolm knew that the army was unlikely to be short of officers, so he did not expect to be drawn into combat but what precisely would be his role in this war escaped him. Together they read with dismay the defeats inflicted on the British Army by the Boers so that they did not expect Christmas 1899 to be a celebration, but a mixture of joy and apprehension. During the late autumn the war was now growing in intensity and mortality, and the British public was very concerned at Boer successes. The Government indicated its determination to subdue the Boers first by changing leadership and then by committing some four hundred thousand men, a very large army. Malcolm and Clara received this ongoing news with continuing alarm.

"How come we cannot win this war? Is our army inefficient?" Asked Clara one evening

"The trouble is the Boers will lose pitched battles with the Army, though they occupy cities in the ZAR. But they also know the lie of the land and the Brigadier regales me with stories he has heard of brief attacks on troops after which they melt into the countryside. They call them guerilla attacks. Then our troops burn their house and crops, either kill or confiscate their animals, and then they get attacked again. If that continues, the situation will be frightful."

"Why don't the Boers surrender?"

"Why should they? They are hoping we will simply give up, the price being too high to pay, but that has brought out the worst in our generals who dare not stomach anything but victory. The Brigadier told me today it could not be much longer before we senior officers in Port Elizabeth would be required somewhere else. So prepare yourself my darling, I might have orders to leave within twelve hours. Much more complicated is the matter of food since our troops are destroying Boer farms, houses, crops, livestock to make the Boer farmers give up the fight."

"How simply awful. It sounds as though we are cutting off our nose to spite its face. How can they be fed if crops are being so willfully destroyed?"

"Precisely, and that is problem for feeding the army, though they solve it by promoting this plundering of farms, ignoring the problem for civilians. I surmise that the harvest in March will be non-existent, what with the destruction. We are fortunate that we do not seem to be encountering any shortages of anything here as we are away from the battlefields at a port where food will be imported."

A week before Christmas, Malcolm was called into the Brigadier's office.

"Gargery, the Generals seem to have found some use for you at last," he said with a smile, "though it will involve a great deal of travel, I expect. You are ordered to report to Capetown immediately after Christmas. You will be acting as some kind of covert army liaison to a woman called Hobhouse who is coming from England to view conditions in these new camps. You will report for a briefing in Kitchener's HQ on arrival but that must be before the 27th when she is expected to arrive by boat."

"It's only a day's journey, but what on earth is this about, sir? It seems very odd to me."

"We have heard reports that there has been a bit of a to-do in England as some of the camps are getting outbreaks of disease, measles for instance. Not in our small camp here, however, yet. Apparently she is coming to survey what's going on, and she has some title or other, let me see, I have it here. She is Secretary of the Women's Section of the South Africa Conciliation Committee."

"That sounds very grand, I must say."

"Let me hope for your sake that she is an attractive person not some interfering harridan busybody. Your orders are to keep at a distance, not act as her escort, as I understand it, as Kitchener wants unbiased reports. How you do that you will have to work out, I am sure."

"Indeed."

"She will have to get Kitchener's permission first, I am sure, and goodness knows how she will be able to travel. She'll be well connected which will be her passport, but I am sure the Generals will regard her as nothing short of a damn nuisance, so I can well see that they need someone like you to check up on her. You are an ideal candidate as you cannot be engaged in combat with that one eye," a remark which made Malcolm quietly seethe with indignation. "I don't think the Boers can hold out much longer so I expect you'll be back before you know it."

Malcolm got back home to tell the news to Clara.

"For your sake I am glad you have an assignment that is more interesting," she said grabbing his arm, "but I am mortified that you will be not with us for some time."

"I know, I know, but this woman cannot be here for long."

"What is her name?"

"Miss Emily Hobhouse, I am told."

"She is probably related to Arthur Hobhouse."

"Who's he?"

"He has had an odd career, well known to my father, as both were judges. I believe he did some sorting out of the legal systems in India, a nice man as I recall as I met him at dinner on a couple of occasions."

"So may I mention that if I meet her?"

"Of course, darling. I hope you will leave Abdul with me. I don't think you'll need a batman, will you?"

"I sincerely hope not as I won't be in that kind of formal responsibility."

"I will have Oliver to look after me too, and the children of course."

"I will tell him how important his care for you all will be while I am gone."

At that moment, Oliver entered the room, looking somewhat bedraggled.

"There is something going on at the Racecourse," he said.

After Malcolm had explained it all, Oliver said in a pleading voice, "Can I come with you, Malcolm? I'd love to see Capetown and more of the country."

"I'm afraid not, but you are now almost eighteen and must be here to care for Clara and the children while I am gone. I am sure Clara will give you many assignments, especially with regard to the children. You also need to think more carefully about your future, Oliver. I don't know how long this war will go on, but I suspect we will return to England when it is completed. You have the world before you not least because so much of it is now in the orbit of the British Empire."

"I know I must make such important decisions which really hinge on whether I want to go to the university or not. If I do, then the path forward is straightforward. If not, then there is an array of opportunities, none of which for the moment spring immediately to mind," he said laughing gaily.

"They seem quite clear to me," said Clara, "Do you want to commit to a life of service or a material life of profit-seeking? By service, I mean the professions of course, and by profit-seeking, I mean following such denizens of wealth as that Cecil Rhodes, here or at home."

"My father's influence leads me to the professions, but I have no interest in the military, nor am I religious enough to consider the church, so in that direction lie the civil service or the law, for both of which the university beckons."

"While I am gone," said Malcolm, "seek out information by writing to universities and, you know, there are now other institutions than Oxford and Cambridge, although if you wanted to follow your father, the latter would have to be your destination. Moreover discuss your future with your mother and with Clara, of course."

"I will, I will."

Clara created the most wonderful Christmas for the children while sailing through another pregnancy. She reminded her two Eustace children, George and Alice of their father Sam, telling stories about him from time to time and showing him his photograph, but the family's move to South Africa had shifted the children's minds away from Mayfair and those memories.

As they sat together watching their four children playing with their little presents after their singing around the tree on Christmas Eve, Clara said, "it is so marvelous that you have become such a father to them and to George especially. You know he worships you."

"Thank you, darling, and I feel a special bond with him too. My earnest hope is that neither he nor young Andrew will become soldiers. I cannot imagine us in the future, sick with worry, about either of them on some foreign field fighting for King and Country."

"You do not know what a relief that is to me. I rarely think about them as men, preoccupied as I am with bringing them up, but I have shivered with the thought from time to time that you might want them to follow in your footsteps."

"On the contrary, dearest Clara, it is the very last thing I want them to do. I do not think I can resign my commission as we are now at war, but when it is all over, and indeed now, I want us to think about returning to London."

"I love being here with you, and with the children young, but I will be ready to go home."

"What we do not know, of course, is how this war will turn out, but next week I must leave for this new assignment."

XVI

It was now six months since it became clear that Albert was quite ill. He had returned home after his discussion with Hamish a chastened man remembering all the while the advice to get his affairs in order which had served to concentrate his mind, but he was still unable to confront a doctor. Whenever he was at home, which was a rare event in itself, the atmosphere at Numquam was so tense that he put off discussion with Victoria until just before Christmas when he plucked up courage and found Victoria in the dining-room sitting thinking about redecorating the bedrooms with samples of damask on the table.

"Victoria, I need to talk with you about my disease."

"I am getting accustomed to you and your debaucheries, so what is the problem?"

"I don't know whether you know anything about it but let me confess that after one of our arguments I was working late six months ago and was accosted by a young prostitute in Chatham. That must be the source of my disease as I have not actually been unfaithful to you apart from that terrible mistake, for which I am profoundly sorry."

Victoria looked at him knowing he was lying about the number, but no matter.

"Just the once, I am sure," said Victoria in a tone dripping with sarcasm. "I see. What do you want, forgiveness? I cannot forgive you now and I do not know whether I will be able to do that later."

"The fact is that I am now feeling much worse than I was.'

"That is quite obvious."

"Please, Victoria, if you cannot forgive, please sympathize."

"Go on, then."

"I had a long talk with Hamish recently whom I have known since I was a boy and he is concerned that if I continue with work, my deterioration could lead to problems in the running of the business. I could make foolish decisions because my brain is affected."

"I see," said Victoria, now assuming a more emollient tone. "Tell me what you think will be best."

"I have asked Aaron Levy to sell the business both in Chatham and Hackney. We will then have a considerable amount of capital. We will live here at Numquam and we will have the wherewithal to pay for a full-time nurse for me and the children's education of course. I think we should consider talk again about sending Philip to a boarding school but send the girls to a day school in Chatham or Rochester."

"What about me, Albert? What do I get out of this mess you have landed us in? Why should I remain here watching you die, if that is what happens when you are paralyzed or mentally-dead? How can I hold my head up with friends? Tell me why should I look after you?"

"But you are my wife, and we have had good times together."

"That is true, but now I have to be a slave to your immorality, to your disgraceful behavior and its results."

"I cannot apologize enough, my dear."

"I know, but there was this bit of tomfoolery with that Elizabeth, then this Chatham whore, or is it whores? Had you any conscience at all, you would never have dreamt about taking a whore, you stupid evil man. If you had not got this disease, would you be as penitent as you are now or would you continue turning into a husband I hardly recognize?"

"Probably not, but I am not bedridden yet. I will start investigating a sale of the business though I am not going to abandon this gentleman's club idea."

"As long as you don't put money into it. I told the maids this morning to move your bed into the second spare room as I cannot allow you near me."

"That I understand. I have decided to go to a doctor recommended by Hamish in London after Christmas and I believe I might be confined to my home. If so, so be it," said Albert with that touch of despair apparent where a man is beginning to lose hope. He realized he deserved her withering criticism which magnified his desperate unhappiness. Would anyone pity him?

Major Gargery walked into the offices of the British Army in Capetown at midday on December 27th, 1899. The journey that was supposed to last a day had taken two and a half as trains were involved in troop transport and regular timetables thus did not apply. A subaltern showed him along a corridor of rooms all packed with men with maps, each room representing a different area of the huge arena in which this war was being fought.

The Field Marshal's staff occupied a set of large offices and Malcolm was shown into the office of Colonel Andrew (Sandy) Williamson, an energetic fellow from the Coldstream Guards.

"Gargery, how good of you to get here so promptly. We were harassed on Christmas Day by the shortage of plum pie, but with care and good fortune we will at least bring that to a satisfactory conclusion next year - unlike this war."

"How does it look from here, Williamson?" Asked Malcolm.

"Between ourselves, Gargery, we are a long way off from anything resembling a victory, a view not widely shared among the Field Marshal's staff. For my part, even with this immense amount of troops in the field, the Boer is an excellent tactician with these guerilla movements. We have far too many logistical problems with such a large army and our scorched earth policy has made feeding our lot almost as difficult as it is for them. There are only certain foods we can easily bring from the old country, don't you know?"

"Nothing but frank, eh, Williamson?"

"There is no point in my not telling you my view on our situation, don't you agree?"

"I do, and I wish someone would tell me what it is I have to do."

"Ah, to your responsibility."

"As I am sure you know, there are elements of the great British public disturbed by reports about conditions in these camps we have had to establish as we can't have miscellaneous women and children adrift in the countryside, helping their troops. The problem is that the camps have filled up dashed quickly and I am second to none in admitting that conditions are not ideal."

"How are they run? What do they look like?"

"Varied, very varied. Most have barbed wire and tents, buildings where possible and food is rationed as it is for us, though we do not admit it. Sanitary facilities are problematic and there is some instance of disease which I know has led to mortality among children."

"Is this the official picture or your own view of the matter?"

"The official view, of course. I suspect conditions are much worse. I was not there when a suggestion was made to Kitchener that someone should shadow a Miss Emily Hobhouse which seems a fanciful assignment to me. However, he agreed and she is coming from a London organization to which the Field Marshal gives little or no respect but which is concerned about the camps and the women and children within them. Of course, there are johnnies like that Conan Doyle fellow who seems to be covering himself in patriotic bunting and telling everyone things are fine, but that doesn't help us, don't you know."

"Tell me, Williamson, what does shadow mean?"

"That is what I said at the time, Gargery. Is the officer to commune with the lady or is he to follow her, literally like a shadow? How on earth will that be possible? The old man wants to know exactly what she is doing and he grasped at the suggestion and left me to define the job."

"I see, so it is pretty much up to me?"

"As long as you get us reports from time to time, although I suspect that the lady herself will issues quite enough reports and badger Kitchener with them. I sometimes feel that armies can do quite well in combat but their administration is another story."

"How did my name come up?"

"We were looking for an officer here in the Cape who was unable to take part in combat for whatever reason, so we sent a round robin to all the various outposts, like yours in Port Elizabeth and your Brigadier thought you might like a change."

"I am glad to be of service and given your remarks I will make the best of it."

"Good man. Kitchener will not meet with her formally though she may get to meet the High Commissioner. I am sending a young officer to meet her at the dock with others like yourself and he can tell her that trucks are being provided with guards, but there will be limits to the areas she can visit, basically where there are areas of conflict those will be off limits. The problem for us is that she is creating a real stink in London about these camps, so she is getting in the way of our war."

"I see, but those limits apart, she's free to go where she wishes."

"Yes. She will certainly write some kind of report and we want to know what her criticisms are before she releases them, for I am confident she will find many."

"Go to the Commissariat and get anything you might need. I suggest you get combat gear rather than the dress uniform of the Gordons. A kilt out in the veldt does not bear thinking about. You can have your stars put on your lapels. Get such protective clothing as you can as it can be damned hot out there. There will be three guards around her, reliable soldiers from the staff here, a sergeant and a pair of lance-corporals whom I have asked to meet with you here at 1400 hours, but they are not under your command."

"Presumably we do not yet have mechanical transport?"

"Good Lord no, but Sergeant Mistle is a horse wallah. Sorry, that phrase always springs to mind following my time in India."

"India, really? I lost my eye at Chitral."

"You know, I thought I had heard your name," said Williamson. "I had a friend at Sandhurst long ago, Tom Hesketh, but the last I heard of him was a letter describing his journey home. He lost a leg, you know."

"I know Tom very well as he married my sister."

"Good heavens, what a coincidence. But then we army men are in fact quite a small band of brothers. How is he?"

"He resigned his commission and has been active on behalf of a philanthropic trust in Ulster which is very challenging, as I understand it from my sister's letters. He has acquired an impressive prosthetic leg and they have a son, Hector by name which I hope does not mean he will end up before the walls of Troy."

"That is excellent news. I will seek him out when this business is concluded."

"Thank you, Williamson, for all your help. I think I should now be meeting Mistle and his men."

"Indeed, they will be in room 4 on the floor below us. The Hobhouse boat is due the day after tomorrow, so you have time to get organized before you meet her."

Malcolm realized this assignment was going to be a challenge from what Williamson had told him, partly he was not bound by a set of detailed orders and he could go quite wrong, especially as he had not followed Miss Hobhouse's activities in London. He walked down the stairs and into room 4 to meet the men he would be close to, but not a part of, though he was not that confident that the whole assignment was of any value. Why was the top brass so worried about a single woman coming to see camp conditions? Were they anxious to conceal something?

The men saluted as he came in but he indicated there was no need for ceremony.

"Gentlemen," he said, after they had all introduced themselves, "this is an unusual commission. The main task to ensure the safety of Miss Hobhouse who has come here to inspect conditions in the camps and report back to her organization in England where I am sure that what she writes will be important in the court of public opinion. I will be shadowing you as a group, and you are not under my command, but how much I make myself known to the lady will depend on her situation as much as mine. Damned confusing, eh? Questions?"

"Thank you sir," said Mistle, "may we ask how you lost your eye?"

"I was in the battle for the relief of Chitral and my company was guarding the perimeter of the huge camp before the final push and in the early morning, a rebel got lucky with his jezail. I hope to get a glass eye when I return to England."

"I was not there," said Mistle, "my regiment was at Simla at the time."

"Did you like India?" asked Malcolm.

"No sir, to be honest, India ain't 'arf hot, and at time I had no idea what we were supposed to be doing there."

"What of you two?" said Malcolm, addressing the two lance-corporals.

"I am Lance-Corporal Thankston from the Durham Lights, and this is my first posting out of England. I'd rather be fighting the Boers, though."

"And you?" Said Malcolm addressing the other soldier.

"I'm a novice, sir, Lance-Corporal Blimble from Somerset. Joined up three years ago and been on duty back home but was given a stripe when we was sent here."

"Excellent to meet you all," said Malcolm, "the boat is due at 1700 hours on the 27th, but I do not expect to meet her then. Remember, I am not your commanding officer."

"Very good, sir, "said Mistle. "We will ensure that the trucks and the appropriate provisions will be ready for her as the Field Marshal ordered."

"Good man," said Malcolm and he left for the simple quarters which had been assigned to him, a far cry from the comforts of the bed he shared with his adored wife.

Trying to think about the matter, Malcolm saw that Kitchener wanted as much dirt as he could to disparage the lady and any conclusions she published in London for those would embarrass the government. Quite why the Field Marshal could not just get information from Mistle and his NCOs was a mystery.

On the other hand, he was very keen to see these camps as there was obviously a serious controversy about them. On the face of it, he thought, herding Boer and Black women and children into camps was hardly in the British fighting tradition with its respect for civilian populations.

Pocket and Pirrip was sold to the firm's main rival, Hunter and Son, a large concern on the other side of the Thames near Deptford for a munificent sum as its very steady profits and efficient management made it a very desirable purchase. The legal detail would be completed in January and Aaron Levy confirmed the contents of Albert's new will by letter which left all his possessions to Victoria with trusts for the three children.

Young Philip had made great strides and was almost completely recovered. Just as his son's condition improved, Albert's got worse and it occupied his days in his new Hackney lodgings and his condition was such that he was glad not to have to tend his businesses. The thought of his face disintegrating which he had read about in a medical journal plagued him day and night, though there was no sign of it as yet. Finally he consulted a Dr. Thaddeus Peaceworth at his office in Harley Street just before the New Year.

Peaceworth was quite unlike any doctor Albert had previously encountered. He was a bull of a man with a huge face and an immense beard and a belly to match, somewhat like the famous cricketer W. G. Grace.

"You should go promptly to the Dreadnought Seamans Hospital in Greenwich, very close to the Kings House built on the site of one of Henry VIII's palaces, don't you know, where doctors are more familiar than I am with these afflictions."

"Thank you," said Albert, after which Peaceworth revealed statistics about the disease to Albert that he did not want to hear, but then concluded:

"I am sorry, Mr. Pirrip, but I cannot sympathize with men or women who contract diseases which result from illicit fornication. You have what you deserve. Please leave now."

Albert left the surgery to pay the fee to an elderly clerk but he amused himself slightly by thinking that this doctor was so built physically that there was never any danger of his being in a position to contract any disease arising from intimacy. Yet he was shamed by the doctor's fierce implication that he deserved it. But then of course he did, as he knew full well; the sympathy he needed most from other human beings would not be forthcoming.

He hummed and hawed for a month or so as to whether to go to the Seamans' Hospital. After a painful night following his visit to Harley Street in which all the terrors of the disease kept him awake and made him feel seriously ill, on New Year's Eve he determined to visit the Hospital. He could reach Greenwich quickly from Hackney through the new Blackwall Tunnel under the Thames opened a couple a years earlier, so he committed to go. He used his small carriage the following morning and was surprised how easy and convenient the journey to Greenwich was.

Peaceworth had notified a doctor who specialized in diseases of the venereal kind about this patient Albert Pirrip. On arrival he was obliged to walk through the hospital waiting-room along a long dark corridor to the office of Dr. Samuel Warburton, like a journey he imagined is made by the rejected after passing through the gates of Hell, for the dregs of humanity were present every inch of the way, men with the grossest of diseased faces, limbs and arms, lying in bundles on floors, the now decaying 'hearts of oak' of Her Majesty's Navy with which Britannia ruled the waves.

The stench was stupefying, and he held his handkerchief firmly over his nose.

Warburton welcomed him profusely, partly because he rarely attended a gentleman, especially one whose features did not yet betray the complaint which was beginning to ravage his body. After introductions and a bodily examination, and after giving Albert an account of the origins and progress of the disease, Warburton said:

"I am glad you decided to come as this letter from Peaceworth had me intrigued. I will come straight to the point, Mr. Pirrip. The fact is, Mr. Pirrip, that I believe you have contracted a particularly virulent form of the disease, and I will be in touch with the Chatham authorities to try to locate its cause. I say that because of the relative speed with which your symptoms have developed. I suspect some sailor from a distant land brought it to the woman or women you engaged with.

"You are almost certainly going to die of this disease, earlier rather than later, but you are going to experience a decline wracked with pain and mental distress. I am sorry to be so blunt, but there is little point in my view in trying to conceal their situation from patients."

"How long can I expect to live?"

"You could live quite a long time, but it will not be the kind of existence you would want and certainly not one to which you are accustomed. Within a year, I am sure you will not want to show yourself to your friends as I believe facial disfigurement is probable, let alone the social stigma that attaches to the disease. Your cheek bone is already showing an early indication of that, though I am sure you have not noticed it. Your mental deterioration will follow. Now I could administer the mercury treatment, but the cure is worse than the disease in my estimation as mercury is most dangerous and I find few persons taking it who have stayed the ravages of the disease, especially in such a case as yours."

"I see," groaned Albert, stunned by this diagnosis.

"Of course, this deterioration is likely to be felt most keenly by your immediate family. Unless you choose to live elsewhere, I fear it will be a tremendous burden to them."

"What then is your advice?"

"You have just walked through the hospital where you have seen, if you could bear to notice, just what a devil this disease is, and the tribulations it causes. Parliament stupidly tried to prevent disease among sailors and soldiers by attacking prostitutes in this country, as if such men did not consort with women of that ilk in ports overseas. My advice is to go home and tend your garden, ride your horses as long as you can and arrange for a nurse to come and tend to you, if you can find one."

"I will take up no more of your time, doctor, and thank you."

Colonel Williamson from Kitchener's Headquarters, Major Gargery, and Mr. Septimus Brindley-Bland from the British High Commissioner's office were standing waiting in the morning sunshine for Miss Hobhouse to disembark from the SS Hawarden Castle. She was alone, apart from the tons of clothing funded by public subscription in England which were to be unloaded from the ship's hold. Malcolm tried to stand in the background with this small welcoming group but the 'shadowing' notion was blown away almost immediately as she ignored Williamson's welcome and surveying all around her caught sight of Malcolm's eye-patch. Immediately she cut through the other men and spoke to him.

"I am Emily Hobhouse," she said.

"Welcome to South Africa, Miss Hobhouse, I am Major Gargery of the Gordon Highlanders and I hope that your needs are met and your interests here are protected."

"Thank you, Major. She turned to the other officers and men and said in a loud voice, 'but does the fact that you have only one eye mean that you will be blind to my activities here?' a question that caused a ripple of laughter and mild consternation as the men realized that this was a lady who could be very difficult to handle.

But she then looked at Malcolm carefully and said quietly, "forgive my impertinence, Major. Tell me, where did you lose your eye?"

"On the North-West Frontier, Ma'am."

"And to what do I owe the pleasure of your company?"

"My assignment is a confidential one, Ma'am, but let me say," he said with some guilt about his dissembling, "that I hope to ensure that any communications between you and either Lord Kitchener or the High Commissioner's office are not misinterpreted."

"Young man, there will be no misinterpretation as I will speak to Milner directly and to Kitchener if he will meet me, which I doubt."

At that point, Colonel Williamson introduced her to Sergeant Mistle who in turn introduced Thankston and Blimble as her accompanying party, and he then left with a nod to Malcolm indicating that he should now assist Miss Hobhouse in starting her mission, which left Malcolm nonplussed as Williamson had apparently misunderstood what Malcolm's 'shadowing' assignment was.

"We must get you on your way, Miss Hobhouse, but you will appreciate, however," said Malcolm, as Mistle and the other two listened, "that the urgencies and trials of a sustained military campaign are such that individuals at all levels are focused on their strategies, tactics and ambitions such that distractions often do not get the attention they deserve."

"I am a distraction, then?"

"Frankly, Miss Hobhouse, I must answer in the affirmative. I have been briefed on your mission, yet I have no firsthand knowledge of the camps in general. I am based in Port Elizabeth and have seen the camp there where conditions were quite satisfactory: It was housed on the racecourse, but the number of women and children there is quite small, and I see no reason for there to be any serious inconveniences to them as things stand at the moment."

"My information is that Port Elizabeth is what one might call a show camp."

"Meaning?"

"That it is the camp where conditions are acceptable so that the authorities can direct inquisitive busybodies like myself or even that dreadful man Conan

Doyle to view it without visiting those camps where conditions are not as delightful."

"I see," said Malcolm, as Mistle, Blimble and Thankston stood by looking most uncomfortable.

"Let me tell you this, Major. If I find conditions as ugly as I anticipate, I will be more than a distraction, I will become a confounded nuisance, here and in London. But I will not engage in further discussion with you or anyone else until we have actually seen a camp. I have an introduction to Sir Alfred Milner, so I will go there first, but if you are to be with me, let us ensure that we are on the same ground."

"Indeed, Ma'am."

"You are a military man, Major, and you have seen combat, but are you aware of the Hague Convention of 1899 about the conduct of war?"

"No, Ma'am, only of the Brussels Declaration, 1874 I believe."

"You must then know that this Convention to which our country is committed not only prohibits pillage but states that no penalty, financial or otherwise can be inflicted on the population who are not responsible for the individual actions of others, i.e., their generals. But I am also aware of the Military Law of 1899 which states that any action beyond that which might disable the enemy is needless cruelty."

"I should think so too," said Malcolm, impressed with the force of character shown by this interesting and passionate woman.

"But may I ask," he continued, "what is the status of your visit and its purpose? Forgive me, I have been posted to Port Elizabeth for the past years and have not kept up with English politics or public opinion."

"I am Secretary of the South Africa Conciliation Committee and am here on their behalf to examine conditions in the camps which have so concerned liberal opinion in England. Many people I know are fundamentally opposed to this colonization of the Boer states and dislike intensely that breed of men embodied in Cecil Rhodes. You see, Major, this is not a war on behalf of some just cause, like slavery, but occasioned by imperial greed pure and simple. But now I must go to see Milner, whom I am sure will be delighted to give me every assistance," she said with a hollow laugh.

"I will keep closely in touch, Miss Hobhouse."

"Thank you, Major, I am sure we will have an interesting time together if you are to join me."

Malcolm was furious with himself as she left. His brief was to shadow the woman, but now she was treating him as a companion. Once she started to talk to him, because of her solicitation for his lost eye, he had to conjure up a conversation which would not make him seem to her an idiotic simpleton.

1900

XVII

Tom Hesketh was used to having conversations with Father McGowan who saw that the Trust was here in Clumber to stay and was therefore active in his support. Moreover he liked Tom who was sincere, tough-minded and appalled by the history and the situation of Ireland in relation to Britain.

"Have you heard of Douglas Hyde?" Asked the priest when Tom had called at the Presbytery to give the priest the compliments of the season.

"No, should I have heard of him?"

"He's a very interesting fella for a Protestant. He's become fascinated with the Irish language and many people have started to follow him since he founded The Gaelic Journal and wrote an excellent piece in it, oh some years ago now."

"What was it about?"

"I have a copy of it somewhere," said Father McGowan and he rustled through papers on a side table, "here it is. The article is called 'The Necessity for De-anglicising the Irish Nation.' He argues that Irish people should follow their own traditions, especially in language."

"How interesting, and that presumably means in literature and song, anywhere that language is used."

"Yes, and he also means dress too, though quite what that means I am sure I don't know."

"He also founded The Gaelic League, in Irish Conradh na Gaeilge of which I am a member, though I am not going to send in my subscription again as there are people using it for politics. Not that I mind politics, but I think it is confusing to adulterate the original purposes of the League."

"I wonder how difficult it would be to learn Irish from scratch. I did not trouble myself in India, but I know officers who learnt to speak Urdu."

"They say Irish is a difficult language to learn, but somewhere there must be various textbooks to help."

"But what of your parishioners, Father, how many speak Irish and how many write it?"

"I would say most of them have a smattering of Irish words and phrases, but English dominates social intercourse, as England dominates everything else. As for literacy, no; they cannot usually write anything but their names in English or, for that matter in Irish."

"Is that so? Is there a stigma attached to being literate?"

"Yes."

"That seems a tragedy, as I'd be sure there are wonderful songs and books which are in danger of being lost."

"That is the point of the Gaelic League, Tom. You see while the authorities have made many people literate in Ireland, at any rate as far as reading is concerned, there has been no emphasis on Irish language and literature. Loyalty to political authorities is taught and it is all British. The textbooks were the same as those used in British schools."

"So the ordinary child in the Trust's estate will be literate?"

"Not at all, at all. Though the schools are there, teaching is in English only by law, but many children do not go to school, in part because it is not free and never was."

"If we had a free school for all children, I suppose we could teach Irish as well."

"If, of course, some way was not found to stop you. Some small schools are often regarded as hotbeds of sedition, you know."

"Huh. The Trust has been active, giving its tenants a living wage, providing fares for those who want to emigrate, and we have plans to plant trees which will provide a source of employment. Yet, that all seems to me unsatisfactory. What do you think we should do, more than this?"

"Let me be candid, Tom, and I think you and your lady wife are doing wonders with our people. Until Ireland is rid of British oversight, until there is Home Rule, I see no practical way forward. Here in Ulster, the situation is more complicated because it is a Protestant stronghold and those men would prefer bloodshed to a partnership with us Catholics.

"Now, while Irish people prefer to work on the land or with activities part of it, I have been amusing myself from time to time with the thought of Ireland being industrial, you know, like Lancashire or Newcastle. But for the life of me I cannot think of anything that it would be economic to manufacture here."

"H'mm, what an interesting dream, Father. Of course, in Ireland flax is grown for linen, but that is agricultural. You have no natural resources like coal nearby, so transporting it from England would be very expensive."

"That's right. We'd need something that is small, so it can have fewer transport costs per item. Shoes might do, but we have no leather as we don't have many cattle. Clothing is a possibility. Hats, gloves, buttons? Even nails, like that American Jefferson used to have made, though by slaves I am sure."

"That is a very interesting challenge, Father. When the Industrial Revolution started, the very earliest manufactories – there was one at Styal in Cheshire – were small enough for people already living nearby to work there. Then came the Revolution with large factories and people had to move into the dreadful houses provided by the owners, near the coal fields. If we thought about the Styal model, that is a factory within reach of people already here, creating a small, manufactured artefact which reduced transport costs for the number of items to be transported."

"Now you are getting the idea, Tom. I can see you are enthusiastic and could sell it to the Trust as backers if we could identify the right product."

"I never thought of a priest as what the French call an entrepreneur...."

"Oh believe me, Tom, the major part of my work is selling the faith."

"Aye, but not inventing it," at which they both laughed. Tom got up to leave and shaking hands, said:

"I am glad to be your friend, Father."

"Call me, Francis, as you are not a Catholic."

Tom returned home and saw Hannah looking as though she had been waiting for him with two-year old Hector in her arms. He looked at her and knew immediately, gathered her in his arms with Hector and kissed her fervently.

"When?" He asked.

"Sometime in the autumn, I will guess August."

"I'd like a daughter, what about you?"

"Any child of yours will be welcome but I'd like a daughter we can call Susanna."

Albert was in very deep distress for some months after his discussion with Warburton. Victoria gave him no quarter on the two separate days that he spent at Numquam seeing in the New Year and the beginning of a new century.

His children begged him to stay longer, he claimed he had to work to do and left, though his daughter Beatrice was not convinced, sensing her mother's unhappiness. There was no Estella to turn to as he had so often done when she was alive and his sense of shame inhibited any further discussion with Hamish.

How can I possibly go on meeting Victoria let alone living with her? He thought. She bares her fangs at me daily, and it will get worse with this terrible disease. What will we tell my children? If they do regard me lovingly, what will they soon make of me, for Victoria is so hurt, she will tell them everything, I am sure? And my business friends? I'm sure to be the butt of sordid jokes wherever I am or the example of folly for women bringing up their boys.

What happened to me? Was I copying my friends in Paris? Yet I never heard of anyone there with this disease, though when I last saw Caillebotte he said he thought Vincent was sick with it. Intimacy was so easy especially after Elizabeth left me, every woman I met wanted me in bed. I can't even remember whether I enjoyed the whores in Paris. It must be a divine punishment for my sins. I cannot bear any more of this. I will go to Paris and seek out old friends and maybe a French doctor will be able to help. If I have to die somewhere, why not in Paris?

It was after a miserable breakfast the Monday after the New Year that Albert called for his carriage and was driven to Victoria Station. He walked into the station, stubbed out his cigar and bought a ticket to Paris via Folkestone and Boulogne. He had dressed for cool weather, his heavy overcoat with its fur-lined collar, top hat and leather gloves and with a little more confidence, he began to look forward to Paris. He had no luggage, expecting to buy everything he would need once he arrived.

The train crept slowly into Folkestone and Albert walked slowly along the platform to the dock and went on board the La Liberté for Boulogne and took a seat on the upper deck, though most passengers were inside against the cold. Old habits die hard and he sat down with his back to the rails on a seat opposite a very pretty woman travelling alone, whom in days gone by he would have immediately attempted to seduce, but now he just gazed at her with lust but without desire. She smiled at him when their eyes met, but he did not move. He turned around in his seat to watch the boat shift silently away from the dock as she crossed the deck and sat down next to him.

"You looks a bit lonely, ducky," she said with a strong Cockney accent, "I can tell, you know, you'se very sad. I've met lots of fellas as sad as you."

Albert brightened at this encounter and said:

"I'm Albert Pirrip on my way to see friends in Paris," he said in the jocular way that he had not used for months.

"Oh me? I'm Maria Jenkins on my way to the Moulin Rouge as I've been hired to dance there."

"Are you really going to dance the can-can?"

"I hope so," she said laughing.

Pulling a flask out of his pocket, the facts of his disease slipping away from him, he said:

"Congratulations and I am sure the multitude will be delighted with what they see."

"You cheeky devil!"

"Have a drink on me, my dear Maria, and perhaps we can get to know each other better on this long journey to Boulogne."

Albert had heard recently great things about the Moulin Rouge and he was sure Maria was open to seduction so he fell quickly into a familiar routine. By the time the evening sun could be seen approaching the horizon on an easy crossing, she had her hand on his thigh and his arm was around her. Soon as it was getting dark, they were kissing with abandon.

"Oh no, darlin,'" she said suddenly, as his approaches were becoming intimate, "I'm sorry I can't," brushing his hand away.

"Why not? Do you not like me? I find you immensely desirable and you are just the sort of woman for a man like me."

"No, no, lovey, I just can't."

"Are you pregnant or something?"

"Me? Me? With a bun in the oven?" And she laughed heartily, "not bleeding likely."

"What is it, then?"

"I can't tell you. Let's just go on cuddling and think about how lovely it might have been."

"Surely you can tell me. We will soon part and probably never see each other again."

"I've got the clap."

"Oh dear, I am sorry, Maria, but," and he hesitated for a moment, "I am similarly affected."

"Christ Almighty," she said getting up suddenly, "you men! You was going to have me and you've got it and didn't tell me. How dare you?"

"No, I was not," he pleaded calling after her, "I just told you," but she rushed to the stairs leading down to the waiting rooms.

Her departure left Albert sitting on the deck in a state of abject misery. Rejection from a woman was a final blow to his sense of himself. Remorse and guilt now flooded his mind. He had no future, no future at all with a body gradually disintegrating with disease. What was left? Nothing. Nothing at all.

He was utterly disgraced and he cursed himself for his bad luck in consorting with that Millie in Chatham and all of them that followed. He thought of his father Pip, so upright, so gentle, whose example he had not followed, and of Estella who might have been more sympathetic but would not have countenanced his betrayal of Victoria, for that was what it was.

Oh, the shame of it! How could he have a social life again when the disease would be visible for all his friends to see? What sort of a life would that be? Maybe just finish it now.

He looked around him and he could just make out two members of the crew some distance off smoking and chatting, but they seemed to have ignored him with Maria. He got up from the seat with a feeling of lightness, relief and clarity of mind. Like Algernon Sidney walking to his execution in 1683, Albert walked steadily across the deck and reaching the port side of the boat, clambered over the railings, and threw himself into the sea to shouts of alarm from the crew who saw him disappear: "Man Overboard" rang through the ship.

The ship's engines were quickly reversed and the boat ground to a halt but now some hundred yards or more from where Albert had plunged into the deep. The ship turned around, albeit slowly but it was simply not equipped to lower a lifeboat quickly, especially as the light was fading fast, and the gas lights were inadequate to scour the water's surface.

He hit the water with a thump. He could not swim. The water was very cold. His overcoat filled with water. He made no effort to stay alive. His last thought was that he had lost his hat. His lungs filled with water. The turbulent sea at the ship's stern turned his body over and over. It floated for a while, then sank, then rose again as it drifted on a current taking it toward the shore.

After a half hour of a desultory search, the Captain decided to continue the journey.

After the boat docked, Maria stood on the dock looking for him to disembark as she wanted to apologize. Not by nature a cruel woman, she had spent the rest of the sea journey worrying about Albert's situation and a companion in Paris would be delightful, especially as she noted that he was obviously well-to-do.

The ship's Purser was checking off passengers on a list as they disembarked, as the captain needed to get the identity of the man who had thrown himself overboard.

"Is everyone off the ship?" She said to the Purser as it appeared the boat was now empty of passengers.

"All but that man who threw himself overboard."

"Oh dear god, how terrible, what happened to him?"

But the Purser had hurried away to report the incident to the Gendarmerie at the Boulogne Dock and send a wire to his office in Folkstone naming one Albert Pirrip as a man who had committed suicide on his ship. Maria walked away saying to no one in particular that she'd never heard of such a thing and made her way quickly to the train for the Gare du Nord, damaging her best shoes on the cobbles as she did so.

Victoria had spent the morning of January 12th over at the Cottage with her brood of nephews and nieces, idly talking with Horatio and Beth about Albert whom she had not heard from since the New Year. Not that she was seriously distressed as all her expectations for her marriage were now in the dust, and, as she told them, she really did not want him near her.

After riding back from the Cottage, she felt more loneliness than she had ever experienced. Albert was god knows where. Her children were all at school. There was always the garden where she liked to potter but the gardener kept the lawn, the beds, the rose garden and the orchard in good condition.

She went down to the kitchen and chattered with Mrs. Thistledown, her cook. Coming as she did from what are often called humble origins and having lived near All Hallows all her life, cook and mistress were in fact very good friends. She heard a loud knock at the front door and the maid rushing downstairs to answer it, so she left the kitchen and walked along the corridor past the dining room into the hall where stood a tall thin man in police uniform.

"Are you Mrs. Pirrip?"

"I am, indeed, sir."

"I am Detective Wattstown of the Folkestone Police."

"What do you want with me?"

"Is your husband Mr. Albert Pirrip?"

"He is."

"Is there anyone else in the house?"

"Yes, my cook, Mrs. Tumbledown."

"Please call her."

After a few minutes, Mrs. Tumbledown appeared, drying her hands on a towel.

"I have called your cook to be with you as I regret to say I have some very unfortunate information to impart," said Wattstown.

"Oh God, not Albert," said Victoria interrupting.

"I am afraid so. He was a passenger this Tuesday on the boat from Folkestone to Boulogne. Probably about one hour out from the port he was seen by two members of the crew to climb over the ship's railings and jump into the sea which, as far as we can tell, implied a wish to kill himself."

At this, Victoria sat down hard on a bench and Mrs. Tumbledown sat down with her putting her arms around her.

Yet no tears came, no expression of sorrow, in fact no emotion at all.

"Thank you, Mr. Wattstown," she said with a tremble in her voice, "has his body been found?"

"We think so, but it will need to be identified. It was washed up near Le Touquet three days ago. Can you think of any reason why he might do this? The crew reported that he was deep in conversation with a woman beforehand, whose name we have."

Should I tell? Thought Victoria. Not yet, not yet.

"I'm afraid I have no idea at all. I assume he was on his way to Paris to see his painter friends but, Mr. Wattstown, he and I have begun to live separate lives.

"I see. The French authorities are prepared to release his body on condition that it is identified in Folkestone while it is still on board," said Wattstown, aware that the boat would be the one from which the man had leapt to his death.

"I have come in a carriage and will gladly accompany you the forty miles to Folkestone if you wish. The boat is French and arrives later today so if we leave now we should be there before it departs for its late evening crossing. I was in touch with a Folkestone undertaker, so he can also meet the boat."

"You must go, Victoria," said Mrs. Tumbledown. "I'll look after the house and will see to the young 'uns when they get back from school."

The boat had been in dock for two hours and officials had almost completed marshalling passengers for the return journey to Boulogne when they arrived. Wattstown led Victoria on board followed by Mr. Hannibal Smurch, the Folkestone undertaker and were greeted by a French official from the Gendarmerie in Le Touquet. After a brief conversation with the French purser they filed down the iron staircases to the hold in the bowels of the ship, In a small room in the ship's hold Albert's body lay on a metal table covered with a flimsy and rather dirty white sheet.

"Ici, madame, si'l vous plait," said the official to Victoria though she had no idea what he meant. She walked slowly to the table watching the official's assistant draw back the sheet.

The dead face was white as the sheet and he seemed peaceful; but he was a stranger. It was him, of course, but not him. Not because he was dead, but because he was so changed from the lovely handsome man who had courted her and aroused in her passions she did not know she had. Was it the move to Numquam that changed him, or was it his meeting with Elizabeth, or was it because his wealth had altered his outlook on life? As she stared in silence at his remains it was clear to her that those once lovely brown eyes and lovely body had gone steadily through physical changes, caused not so much by disease but by character.

"Please withdraw the sheet so that I can see his whole body."

"Quoi?" Asked the official.

"Je pense elle veut voir tout le corps," said Wattstown whose base in Folkestone Dock necessitated some knowledge of French.

The official shrugged and removed the whole sheet. There was a slight gasp of breath as the onlookers quickly identified the disease by gazing at that part of a body to which one is instinctively drawn when confronted with a naked body, dead or alive. Their disgust was ill-concealed.

"I wanted you to see, gentlemen," said Victoria, her voice cracking, "what was wrong with my husband and why he threw himself to his death."

To try to end the proceedings, the French official said hastily:

"Mais est ce que c'est Albert Pirrip?"

"What does he say?" Asked Victoria.

"Is this Albert Pirrip?" Said Wattstown.

"Yes and No," said Victoria, her lips curling and her face contorting as she broke down into howls of dismay and distress and collapsed on the floor. Wattstown helped her to her feet as she lay her head on his shoulder while the official replaced the sheet.

"I don't yet have any instructions," said Smurch quietly into Wattstown's ear.

"Sign the form the Frenchie needs and take Mr. Pirrip's body to your hearse immediately. We will wait on the dock for you."

Victoria's tempest of grief had softened into long moans of sorrow, the tears now relenting as she wiped her eyes with a kerchief.

"I am very sorry you had to see your husband's body under such circumstances, Ma'am," said Wattstown, "can I ask what you would want to arrange?"

"What do you recommend?" Asked Victoria sniffling.

"Smurch should take his body to an undertaker near your home at All Hallows, as I assume you would like him buried there."

"No, he will have to lie with his father in Highgate," she said regaining her composure, "as my village church won't allow him in the graveyard, will they?"

"You are right and I am sorry I forgot that. Smurch must then find a London undertaker. Give him your Kent address, so that funeral arrangements can be made."

"That is what I would wish, but I will leave it to him. I won't return home now but must go to Chelsea to seek help from a friend."

"I will take you to the train which will go to Victoria Station in London."

One and a half hours later the maid opened the door of Mary's house to admit Victoria.

"What are you doing here?" Asked Mary, "it's almost dusk. Do sit down."

Victoria flopped into a chair and began to weep silently, clearly in deep distress.

"What on earth is the matter?"

"I have just come from Folkestone where I had to identity Albert's body brought from France on a ferry boat from Boulogne. He was on his way to Paris several days ago, apparently, but threw himself overboard, and his body was washed up near Le Touquet."

"Oh dear, oh dear," said Mary, beginning to weep too, her accustomed stoicism not this time at her disposal.

"Oh my dear, how simply awful, what a monstrous calamity for you."

"I am sorry to burden you with my presence."

"Victoria, that is the least of concerns at this moment. You will stay with us for the night."

"May I ask your maid to take a wire for me? I left my children in my cook's care at Numquam and they need to know where I am. I need your advice badly too."

"Of course, of course."

As the maid was leaving with the dispatch, Hamish returned home and on coming into the drawing-room immediately realized Victoria was distressed.

"Victoria, my dear, why are you upset?" He asked at which Mary cut him off, saying:

"There's been an awful tragedy, Hamish. Albert has committed suicide by drowning, throwing himself off the Ferry to Boulogne and Victoria has just returned from Folkestone after identifying his body."

"Good Lord, Victoria, I am so sorry. I had no idea when I met him that he was anything but able to meet his condition courageously."

"I thought he might too, though I could never forgive him, I am afraid," she paused, "though now, of course, I regret saying that to him."

"Victoria, mere words of mine cannot express my profound sorrow for you, your children and your family."

"Please don't be so pompous, Hamish," said Mary testily, "I want to know how we can help."

"He has to be buried in Highgate with his father and Estella. What do you think?"

"Of course, of course, Victoria" said Mary, "they would welcome him with open arms, were they so able. Estella forgave him everything in life which probably was no help to him."

"Should I take a notice in the newspapers which will no doubt lead to a large funeral and then a wake which I do not desire?"

"That is an easy matter, I am sure Mary and I would be pleased to offer our home for the wake. There will be many a friend who will want to attest to his friendship."

"Tell me, Mary, should I feel ashamed?"

"About what precisely?"

"That my husband chose to end his life."

"But why? I'd be sure he did not choose to end his life just because you indicated your marriage was over."

"I agree," said Hamish, "I will try to put this gently, but his conversation with me was utterly about himself, though he mentioned you briefly. That he killed himself is not a surprise, men or women with this disease can be physically and mentally damaged severely and that would be the cause of his suicide."

"This is what happens to women," said Mary, "though totally blameless, the woman is expected to feel guilt or shame or both and the guardians of social morality pity her and consign her to the outskirts of society. Too often men have no conscience in their relationship with their wives."

"I fear that is true, Victoria," added Hamish, "but we and our friends will do nothing of the sort. Moreover, you should not fill your mind with the detail of our relationship with him in recent months or you will brood on it forever. The fact is simple. He betrayed you by consorting with a whore, or at least that is how we must assume he was infected."

"Thank you so much for this," said Victoria.

"Why don't you go now to a bedroom and rest, and we'll have dinner at eight."

Albert's funeral was a stark affair at Highgate Cemetery. Messrs. Simplick and Woolhandler came from the Hackney firm, but there were no representatives from the Chatham side. No one sent wreaths or flowers. Victoria was supported by her brother Horatio, Beth staying at home with Alphabet children, heavily pregnant again. There was a scattering of Pockets, but to Victoria's immense surprise, Elizabeth Egerton came, accompanied by John Sargent. Pip and Harriet, Hamish and Mary, Clarence and Emma, Aaron and Alice, James and Stella also came, so Victoria felt it was a respectable complement of people.

The committal of the body to the grave brought levels of memory flooding into the minds of some of those present, because Albert's body was being laid above that of his father Pip and his step-mother Estella and that grave was almost next to that of his mother Beatrice. For Pip this was a heartbreaking moment. He loved Albert intensely, the son and heir to his 'uncle' Pip, the youngster treated by Joe and Biddy Gargery his own parents, as a grandson. What a waste, what a waste, he thought as the tears ran down his cheeks with Harriet clutching his sleeve tightly.

When the mourners arrived at the MacDonald's house for a reception Elizabeth decided to renew her brief acquaintance with Victoria, having met her at the League meeting.

"Ah, Mrs. Egerton," said Victoria, rather stiffly, "I am so grieved by Albert's passing. I knew him in Paris, as I am sure you know, and he was very kind and helpful after my husband died."

Being her mother Nellie's daughter, Victoria could be nothing if not outspoken.

"Tell me, did you think after your husband died that you could resume an intimacy with mine?"

"Good heavens, no," said Elizabeth, taken aback by this aggression, "nothing was farther from my thought."

"And what about him?" Asked Victoria with ill-concealed hostility.

"As we are clearly being honest with each other, let me tell you this. I was very grateful for his help at that time as he was someone I had known well. When Timothy's funeral was over, I did not expect to see him again, but he came one morning and, quite literally, threw himself at me. I was very shocked and told him to leave."

"Thank you for telling me that yourself as it is precisely what I wanted to confirm. You see, he told me he had met you again at your husband's funeral and I then found no obstacle to his attendance. Yet my intuition told me, quite apart from the humdrum character of our marriage, that he had someone else in mind. He denied it categorically, but I challenged him forcibly. From that moment on, our marriage was to all intents and purposes finished."

"Are you blaming me for this?" Asked Elizabeth, now visibly upset.

"Certainly not. You see, my concern then and until now was that my confrontation with him was just misplaced jealousy and that my intuitions about his behavior were not correct. However, you have proved to me that I was indeed right about his infidelity at that point in time, for otherwise gossips might claim that I drove him away without cause. From that day he ignored me and started to behave badly with loose women, I assume, which led to his death."

"Well, Victoria, I do not know whether you knew this, but it was his infidelity that was the cause of our ruptured relationship in Paris."

"I did not know that. He explained it as your loss of interest in his painting and your infatuation with what he called that 'damned instrument' which I assumed meant your piano."

"Oh no, Victoria, he had not come home to our Paris flat in the early hours and had I not looked out of the window to see him in the arms of another woman, I suppose our relationship would have continued."

"What is it that gets into men like him?" Asked Victoria. "I have three wonderful children. I can only hope Philip does not inherit these characteristics. Albert had no sisters and from what I can discern, until he met you he was in the company of adults only and dreadfully spoilt, especially by his step-mother Estella. When a boy has sisters, they will not allow themselves to be treated like pawns in their brother's universe, so any immature overlordship will be stifled early. Moreover the boy can learn about women."

As that conversation was finishing, John Sargent approached.

"Mrs. Pirrip, I cannot tell you how grieved I am that Albert should die in such circumstances. Quite apart from intimate relationships, I do think that men of business too often develop a coarseness of spirit accompanied by a heightened love of risk, inevitable in their day-to-day work but which then invades their persona."

"You may well be right, Mr. Sargent, but if I understood the community of painters, they are not exactly exemplars of moral integrity, are they?"

Accepting her reproof, Sargent turned to talk to Harriet. Victoria moved to thank her friends as they left the reception, leaving her eventually alone with Hamish and Mary.

"I discovered from Elizabeth Egerton," she said as the three of them sat in the drawing room awaiting dinner, "that I was right about Albert. I had this feeling there was more to his friendship with her after her husband's funeral. She confirmed what you had told me, Mary, that he threw himself at her."

"Yes," said Mary, "she consulted me about that and indeed another man importuning her. Widows, it seems, are peculiarly attractive to some men."

"Widows eh?" Said Victoria, suddenly imitating her mother Nellie, "Crikey, no need to get my arse out on the street then, they'll be lining up at the bloody door!"

Mary wept with almost hysterical laughter at this; Hamish thought he would die laughing, and Victoria then joined in with delight.

"Oh my lord, I haven't laughed like that in a very long time," said Victoria.

After Victoria had gone to bed, Mary was in a ruminative mood.

"Extraordinary, isn't it," she said, "how that occasion provided two women to be disarmingly honest about their experience and their feelings without any attempt to conceal or dissemble? What would the world be like if we actually said out loud what we thought?"

"Well, my dear," said Hamish, "I don't remember any occasion where you have felt unable to speak your mind," and they both laughed. He took his wife's right hand and they went up to bed.

XVIII

"Mary, I have been thinking that the League ought to put together a list of the powerful women of the nineteenth century in this country as a beacon for women to follow. The Queen has achieved a diamond jubilee and we could use her as an example. "

"What an excellent plan, Harriet! Perhaps we could also try to find women who have not achieved fame but have been remarkable. I mean everyone knows Florence Nightingale, but what of the gallant nurses who followed her?"

"What too of poets? My friends Katherine and Emily only appear as Michael Field to the public, thought they are now known to the literati."

"George Eliot too, Mary Evans. Mary Woolstencraft, Harriet Taylor, Mill's wife for a start.

"That's right, Mary. Did you know that Mill credited Harriet Taylor profusely in the introduction to the essay On Liberty? He regarded her as the woman providing the bulk of the ideas. We could hold a day of celebration, too and that could determine our next meeting, though I am sure voting will be the major topic.

"Why don't we put this firmly on the agenda for the League as the first item?"

"Yes indeed. By the way, have you heard from Malcolm and Clara lately?"

"Yes: First she is expecting another baby, of course, but Malcolm is under orders to accompany Miss Hobhouse as she tours the camps that the Army have created there which is a terrible disappointment to her. Goodness me, that Hobhouse woman is another accomplished woman of immense courage and importance, but Clara also talks about returning to England once the war is over, but whether that would mean Malcolm resigning his commission, she does not say."

"But enough of them, what of your son James and his new wife Stella?"

"They are wonderful. I have divided my first husband David's capital and my inheritance between my children, as Hamish is now a wealthy man from Courtisone and Jaggers and from his position on the bench. That means that both James and Emily are now free to determine their future. But I made a condition: that they settle in the British Isles."

"How wise, it sounds to me as both of them have travelled enough."

Pip heard the conversation from his study and crossed the hall to join them, saying,

"It is such a delight for you to have them back and to know they are here permanently."

"Our son Joseph is turning out to be a bookworm, surprisingly," added Harriet. "He entertains friends from school from time to time and they seem to revel in their scientific studies. We don't understand much of it, do we Pip, but he says he want to read Natural Science at Cambridge, which used to be Philosophy."

"Indeed that is a Joseph Gargery who is much different from his namesake, my father, the blacksmith. I remember just how difficult it was for Joe to understand geography. Old Pip told me one day years later how he had used kitchen implements to draw an imaginary map on the kitchen table to indicate where the Crimea was and he was not sure whether Joe grasped it. I thought about that when we were in Africa, trying to teach a few men what a map was. They understood what it was in terms of the village and the water where the elephants gathered, but I was a total failure getting them to understand the location of continents and countries," and he chuckled at the memory.

"Susanna thought I was just a poor teacher, but she tried with the women and she failed. I wish I had more knowledge of the stars then as maybe using the sky would have given an idea of distance."

"But Pip," said Harriet, "country folk don't travel, do they? I mean Joe and Biddy may have spent time in Chatham and perhaps went to Rochester once, but never to London together, though I think Estella told me that Joe went there when Old Pip was ill as a young man."

"For my part, I hope Joseph will choose to do something of service rather than profit. I mean there must be much scientific thought in the development of the automobile but that is really a matter of manufacturing for profit in the end. On the other hand, working on medical matters and discoveries like that doctor Lister who helped old Pip in his cancer surgery, now that's the kind of work I hope would attract Joseph."

"Odd, is it not. Would we have been talking about him like this if he had been a girl? What a lottery life is. However, you should have that conversation with him soon," said Harriet.

⚜ ⚜ ⚜

Horatio had just removed a wasps' nest from the roof of the shed next to the anvil after smoking it out after dusk the previous night.

"Good job," said Beth as he came down the ladder, "Now I can rest that the children won't get stung."

"Nasty brutes," said her husband as he put the nest in a hessian bag used for wood, "I'll throw it on the next bonfire we have."

"I've been thinking," said Betsy.

"Yeah, what?"

"It's a couple of months now since Albert was buried and I've been going over to see Victoria. I'll go over again today to her to see how she is."

"That would be lovely, Bets, as I'll be sure she's lonely. You know, as I told you before, I was surprised when they was married, but I suppose Mum and Estella were such good friends, they encouraged it as a bond between them. But you be careful, it's only a week since young Horatio arrived, the most beautiful of our babies, I think."

"I will, I will be careful, but I always thought Arthur was magic. Maybe Harry, maybe them two somehow got caught in their mothers' trap."

"Funny way to put it, but I knows what you mean."

"Anyway, I'll take the two little ones over there this morning as well and see how she is."

"She'll be right glad of the company, I know, as the girls are at school and Philip is at that fancy school in Rochester."

Victoria was in the bedroom wondering what to do with Albert's clothes when she heard the cart approaching. She went downstairs and was surprised but glad to see Beth whom she was only now beginning to get to know properly.

"I thought I'd just come over, Victoria, and see how you'se doing. Can't help thinking what a terrible business you'se been through," she said with some confusion as her two young'uns were demanding attention.

"Here," said Victoria, "let me take this lovely baby, what's his name?"

"Horatio, though I 'specks we'll call him young Harry like his dad. He's number eight."

"My goodness, I don't know how you do it. New babies are so tiny!"

"I don't know either, but I only have to see him take his shirt off, and you know."

"I remember that feeling dimly," said Victoria laughing, "anyway, come in the house and I'll get the maid to bring some tea."

"Who's your maid then?"

"Florrie Buzza."

"Oh, I know Florrie Buzza, I was at school with her mum. But I really came to ask how you was getting on."

"I suppose I am relieved it is all over really. Do you think that when men get to a certain age they find their wives stale?"

"Cor blimey, I wouldn't know, would I? We're stuck out in the marshes."

"Of course, but I wonder whether getting married is a way we women trap men as they really don't want one woman but as many as they can get."

"No, love, it's alright for men like he wot was your husband as he can gallivant all over town on his own, not like my Harry, stuck with his anvil and me," and she cackled with laughter.

"No gallivanting for me, even if I wanted to. I really love this house and its memories and am completely settled here."

"Maybe you should do summat in the village if you want to find summat to do. There's a new Vicar, you know, and unmarried too."

"Oh yes, I heard old Windnortham had passed on. He must have been ninety."

"Well, you would live that long in that job," concluded Beth, "nuffink to do really except christen babies, marry people, and bury them, with a few happenings of a Sunday," and she got up to go, and looked at a rider coming down the drive.

"Talk of the devil," she said, "though I shouldn't say that should I, but here's the new parson come to call."

"Please stay, Beth, I don't want to meet him all on my own."

They heard the maid open the door and a deep voice said:

"Is the lady of the house available?"

"I think she's receiving visitors," said Florrie.

Victoria got up from her chair as soon as she heard the newcomer and walked into the hall.

"Welcome, I am Mrs. Pirrip, please come in and meet my sister-in-law and her younger children," she said somewhat startled by this tall handsome man, classically English.

"Thank you, thank you," he said somewhat nervously as Victoria led him into the drawing-room and introduced Mrs. Beth Fletcher.

"How d'ye do, I am the new Vicar on my rounds of the parish, trying to meet everyone, my ambition in the first few months. I am the Reverend John Eustace."

"Now, where have I heard that name?" said Victoria. "Are you any relation of Lord Eustace, the judge?"

"Distant cousins, I believe. I will recall the connection, I'm sure but tell me about yourself, Mrs. Pirrip."

"I think I should go," said Beth. "It's nice to meet you, Vicar, a breath of fresh air, I expect, oh, please forgive me, that's a bit rude."

"Not at all, that is how I would like to be seen."

"My husband Harry is the blacksmith and we live out on the marshes."

"I'll call one day, if I may."

"Of course," said Beth, gathering up her children and winking at Victoria, the two women went to the door, with Victoria promising to call soon. They embraced and Beth went to her cart. Delighted with that conversation, Victoria returned to the Vicar, standing at the French windows.

"What a delightful house and garden," he said as she came in.

"Yes indeed, I am very pleased to be here."

"May I inquire about your family?" he asked.

She sat down and was silent until he sat down, but as she looked out of the window, she could have sworn she saw Nellie her mother arm in arm with Estella walking to the rose garden, and she then told her story with the boldness and candor that was her mother's great gift. No beating about the bush, she thought.

"I should say first I am not trying to shock you, Vicar. My dad was a farrier in the Crimean War and he saved the life of a comrade known as Pip whose father was Joe Gargery, the old blacksmith from long ago. My father, Fletch as they called him, came back to work in the docks at Chatham with odd jobs and he took up with my mother Nellie who was then a whore on the streets. The two comrades met up again when Pip, now a preacher, was getting married, and my mum and dad with my brother and me were starving, literally. Pip gave us some money and then had The Jaggers Trust set us up with my dad as blacksmith as the old man, Joe Gargery was dead.

"So the lady I met just now, Mrs. Fletcher?"

"She's my sister-in-law married to my brother Horatio, and our parents were Fletch and Nellie. However, living in this house at that time was a couple, a Mr. Pirrip known as Old Pip and his wife Estella whom he had loved for years, though he had been married to Beatrice Pocket. Their only surviving son eventually became my late husband Albert. Estella had a very eccentric guardian a Miss Havisham who died after setting fire to herself. Of Estella's parents, one was a convict and a murderer, the other a murderer."

"Good Heavens."

"But my mum and Estella became lovers and later very close companions even though my mum loved my dad to bits and he did not mind her loving Estella, provided there was no scandal. Then I went to London to live with Estella in her very grand house near St. James Park and that's where I met my husband."

"Is your husband here, then?"

"No. Ours was a good marriage at first, but before that he had had a very close relationship with a woman when they were both not yet twenty; they lived in Paris where he hoped to be a painter. They broke up because he was unfaithful and later he gave up painting as he had inherited his grandfather's wood firm and became a businessman. But I am going on too long, but don't worry I am nearly done."

"Not at all, this is fascinating."

"My marriage to Albert broke down in part because I felt jealous that he was seeing that same old flame after her husband died as I knew he had this tendency to infidelity. He'd become a fairly rich man with two businesses, one in Hackney and one in Chatham, but he sold them before he died. He consorted with whores, caught a terrible disease and committed suicide two months ago.

"So here I am. My son Philip is at school in Rochester, my daughters are both at school and should be home soon."

The Vicar was wide-eyed as the story developed, but recovered his composure to say: "Oh, my dear Mrs. Pirrip, first my most sincere condolences on the death of your husband, whatever the circumstances."

"Yes, it was a terrible time. You see, he threw himself overboard from the ferry in the English Channel."

"He did what?" Asked the Vicar, now completely baffled by this extraordinary family history.

"Yes, I suppose he was ashamed of his disease. I don't know about his feelings really as we lived separately, and then we buried him in Highgate with his father and step-mother."

"Oh my goodness, and here was I expecting to come to a quiet country parish."

"It might have been nice for the children in the future to see his grave in your churchyard," said Victoria, ignoring that remark, "but I know you don't allow that for suicides, do you?"

"I would. That seems to me one of the more un-Christian conventions in the Church of England. God would quite understand why people are driven to suicide and he would forgive them and reach out with his everlasting arms."

"How nice that is to know, if we get any more suicides in the family," she said with a harshness he had not heard before in her conversation.

"You are not a religious person then, Mrs. Pirrip?" Asked the Vicar.

"We were married in your church, and I had my children christened. I remember going once or twice with my mum and dad but that was more because they'd had a terrible experience."

"What was that?"

"Oh dear, that's another long story. Mum had been kept as the whore of a brutal recruiting sergeant in Chatham when she was very young, fourteen or so. He threw her out and later she got married to my father as I told you. But then he decided he wanted her back after a few years, I suppose that he had seen her looking so beautiful and happily married, and he began to threaten her seriously. He followed her to this house where she was a maid at that time. Mum and Dad were ready for him. He tried to kill her. That was in the dining-room over there, but Dad stabbed him, though he wasn't dead and Mum ran off to get the landlord of the Bargemen for help. Anyway there was then another struggle and he was throttling Mum so Dad stabbed him in his neck and he died."

"Good Lord deliver us, what another terrible story."

"They went up before the beak and he finally said it was justifiable homicide, but my parents felt very guilty so we all went to church helped by a lady friend of Estella's."

"Why did they not continue to go to church?"

"I don't know, but Mum said they were comforted by Preacher Pip and he was a chapel man, so perhaps they saw no need."

"But what about you, Vicar? You've heard enough of me."

"Well, I have nothing like a dramatic history as yours. I have come from London, from a big church in the north of the city where I was the curate and I had been offered a large church in the west of the city, at Chiswick in fact," and here his eyes began to water and he got up and stared out of the window saying, "but my wife Eleanor died in childbirth along with my son. We had only been married a year. That was a year and a half ago and I sought refuge in an Anglican monastery in Yorkshire to try to heal my wounds. So this small country parish helps me to ease back into my work."

"Oh my dear man, how I feel for you, how awful," and she burst into tears at the thought of this nice man losing his wife and child, as compared with her own loss.

The Vicar turned round and put his arms around her shoulder, "How kind, Mrs. Pirrip, to feel such sorrow for me. I still have moments when I am frightened of the world. I feel so alone without my dear Eleanor."

"No, Mr. Eustace, a godly man like you does not deserve such a fate."

"Well, now is not the time to enter into a theological argument about that," he said with a smile, resuming his seat.

They looked at each other and smiled with that mutual recognition of shared grief and loss, though the differences in their emotional states were palpable.

"Thank you for coming," said Victoria, "and do please call as often as you wish. I am almost always here. My sister-in-law is urging me to find something to do in the village."

"Well, there will be all kinds of matters to attend to and I must say I do hope you might consider coming to church."

"I will, I will" she said as she escorted him to the door of the house.

What a nice friendly man, she thought, but my goodness, what on earth was I doing telling him all that? I'd never put it all together like that before. Did me good to get it out. Perhaps I'll go to his church and see what he's like.

Behind the driver of a sturdy but slightly ramshackle cart were a couple of old barrels remade as chairs covered with rugs upon which Emily Hobhouse and Major Malcolm Gargery sat with three soldiers of the British Army riding behind. The cart led a small caravan including two trucks of clothes as it trundled over the veldt toward Bloemfontein, passing villages destroyed, homes burnt out and a complete absence of crops waiting to be harvested in this southern hemisphere, clearly burnt to the ground.

The confusion over Malcolm's role had long since been settled, the shadow now disappearing under the bright sunlight of Miss Hobhouse's investigation. He was to ride with her, but still deliver reports to Kitchener's office. They had visited various camps at Norval's Point, Aliwal North, Kimberly and Mafeking among others and Malcolm avoided discussion in any depth, but this particular journey provided the opportunity.

"I am surprised by how well those camps are run, especially that the schools in each camp were welcomed by the women and the children, and you remember how those people were so ready to praise Lt. Wynne as the 'Father of the Camp.'"

"Yes, I suppose that the military will want to take control and put men like Wynne in as superintendents. But those are the only bright spots and we have no idea how long the war will last and how the civilian camp population will fare. Few of the camps we have seen so far actually have the bare necessities for their populations, especially food, and they will approach starvation levels soon, I am sure."

"You told me one superintendent had told you soap was a luxury."

"Indeed, but cleanliness is essential if disease is to be prevented. Yet what is interesting to me as I meet officers and the British people here is that they believe any sympathy I show for the plight of the women and children means that I support the Boer cause, so I try to be rigid in not expressing any political opinion, not that it matters."

"I must say, Miss Hobhouse, this is a military situation which is probably unique in the history of warfare: the vast distances and the Boers' tactics now make any traditional engagement impossible, and civilians are inevitably being dragged into it."

"Indeed, I have noted several cases of wives and children living comfortably in towns in their own homes being forced into the camps because their husbands are known to be in the Boer army."

"I can see the logic of that, I suppose, but it is still mistaken in the abstract as a policy…"

"and quite heinous in its execution, "she interrupted, "it is as if the British army is at war with the civilians."

"Tell me, Miss Hobhouse, I don't have a clear idea of how long you will stay here."

"Until my funds run out. You will have noticed, I hope, that I am particularly abstemious in my habits here, trying to eat only enough to keep me alive and avoiding anything that I think is a luxury, though I draw the line at soap," and she laughed.

This kind of conversation took place over the few weeks Miss Hobhouse was pursuing her enquiries. Much of their recent journeying had taken place close to, if not beside the railway lines. This provided the essential guide as moving around in the open veldt would have courted disaster. In late March, the small caravan stopped near a train bound for Kimberley that had halted.

"Look at those people, Major," said Miss Hobhouse and she got down from the cart and walked over to the train, "young and old are crammed into open trucks."

"Do you speak English?" she asked the unwilling travelers, and one elderly woman from among the crowd replied:

"What do you want?" She said in the guttural accent of the Afrikaner.

"How long have you been here?"

"All day, no food, no shelter from the sun, and nowhere to, well, you know. The children are asleep, but it is not a good renewing sleep, it is exhaustion and hunger that makes them sleep."

'Do you have water?"

"A little but it is hot and brackish and almost undrinkable and I worry about putting it in my mouth," at which point the train lurched into action and Miss Hobhouse waved goodbye.

"This is monstrous, Major. What Englishwoman surveying this scene would not be overwhelmed with sympathy and have their conscience rattled to find some relief for these poor souls?"

"I agree and must confess to being quite shocked," and he realized in saying that he was expressing an opinion which ran directly counter to the Field Marshal's view and his policy. He was now beginning to see he had a serious struggle of conscience about what he regarded as fundamentally bad policy. Knowing it was bad was one thing; knowing what to do was quite another matter.

They had arrived at Bloemfontein at dusk and found a small hotel still functioning run by a Britisher. The following morning they set off for the camp, the heat becoming quite oppressive. After several days either spent in or close to the camp, they sat one evening in a stuffy dining room. Miss Hobhouse began the conversation:

"Major, my money is running out. I must return to England, but I am just begun writing my report. This is my first paragraph and I would like to ensure its accuracy:"

"Please read and I will act as verifier."

"Let me read what I have written, then:

'My second visit to the camp at Bloemfontein after the lapse of a few weeks was a great shock. The camp population had doubled and had swamped the effects of improvements which could not keep pace with the numbers to be accommodated. Sickness was increasing, and the aspect of the people was forlorn in the extreme. Disease and death were stamped on their faces. Many whom I had left hale and hearty, full in figure and face, had undergone such a change that I could not recognize them. I realized how camp life under those imperfect conditions was telling upon them, and that no impartial observer could have failed see what must ensure unless nurses, doctors, workers and all extra food, clothing and bedding could be poured out in abundance and without delay.'"

"I agree with all that, Miss Hobhouse."

"You know, I think we know each other well enough for you to call me Emily, Major."

"Thank you, I will and when I am not on official duties, please call me Malcolm."

"I had another refusal from Lord Kitchener today. I had asked him to allow me to go north of Bloemfontein but again my request was refused, so that is an additional impetus to go home."

"I suppose there is military action there," said Malcolm.

"Stuff and nonsense, that is just an excuse to prevent me from seeing some of the worst conditions, but no one must know that I said that."

"Surely though, the main question is what is to be done?"

"I think I can do far more campaigning in London now that I see the policy in action and a situation which I am sure will get much worse. You probably do not know that reports in the English papers are so far distant from what we have seen, with even politicians declaring that everyone in the camps is healthy and well fed. We overwork the word 'shock,' Malcolm, but I have never seen such misery and I'm sure the thirty other camps are no exception to conditions here. This Bloemfontein camp now has 1,800 women and children with no limit in sight as each day the military round them up and have them transported to a camp, irrespective of the camp's ability to hold them, let alone feed and clothe them."

"Indeed, and as I understand it, Emily, from my brief conversations with a few women here and at other camps, many of them came from homes which contained material, like clothes, which would be valuable here, but they were burnt as the house was destroyed, and much of its content pillaged by British troops, who are also suffering from disease."

"What do Kitchener and Milner expect?"

"I did not expect this to happen, Emily, and there is an inevitability to what is happening. The Boer Army is defeated in pitched battles, so it retreats to highly effective guerilla tactics. The British Army responds by destroying anything that could be regarded as sustenance for the enemy, families, homes, crops, everything.

"Exactly, and that leaves the British Army responsible for the refugees, though one colonel I met denied they are refugees. Indeed these camps are full of what the Army regards as combatants, though they are not and have not been engaged in combat."

Several days passed as Miss Hobhouse and her caravan returned to Capetown. She had felt harassed by Kitchener but having a sympathetic ear in Malcolm alongside her was a bonus. When they arrived at Capetown, Malcolm wished her good fortune and returned to HQ write his report to Kitchener.

After Miss Hobhouse left in May, Malcolm awaited further orders. He wrote several long letters to Clara about the work he had been doing. A week later, he met with Williamson and gave him two reports, one completely factual and one embellished for the eyes of the Field Marshal. The latter pulled no punches but lacked the vehemence of the original.

"Now the lady is gone, you can return to Port Elizabeth," said Williamson after Malcolm had explained his reasons for writing two reports, "I appreciate more than I can say having the factual account, and Kitchener will probably ignore whatever I send up the line anyway."

"After this experience with Miss Hobhouse, Williamson, I'm afraid I simply cannot come to grips with the army's treatment of civilians in this war. It is not as if this was some righteous cause, like having the Boers reject slavery. It is a matter of colonial greed which is wreaking havoc on civilians in a way that no previous colonial expansion has done. If you could see the conditions in the Bloemfontein camp as it developed over the two visits Miss Hobhouse and I paid, you'd be ashamed to tell your wife and children that you were a party to it."

"I share your reservations, Gargery. I suppose Field Marshals don't get to that illustrious position by being kind to the enemy. You don't pack your conscience in your kit bag when you go out to fight."

"No indeed. Tom Hesketh and I had an interesting conversation when we were both on the ship bringing us wounded back from India. Tom was saying how one must realize that behind the soldier you kill lies a wife and family."

"That is the nature of war, is it not?"

"Of course, but then this war is total from the Boers' perspective, as everything about their livelihood is under threat. I remember at Sandhurst we had to read the book on war by that Prussian fellow, what was his name, Von Klausewitz. He was thinking about Prussia and Napoleon and Russia too. His point was this. In war, if you have one protagonist whose war aims are limited versus a protagonist for whom everything is at stake, that is, their aims are unlimited, it does not matter how powerful the first protagonist is, the second will always win."

"How good that you remind me of that. I read it too. While we are piling in troops, now some 400,000 in number, we won't go on fighting for ever spending our money and our soldiers' lives, while the Boer will fight for ever for his land and his way of life. If that Prussian is right, we will lose, not today, not even tomorrow, but in the longer term."

"It has been good to meet you, Williamson. I am off to my family in Port Elizabeth. This experience has shown me one thing. It is foolish for me to continue in the army. I know I could not be in combat, so my role is a diminished one. I am ambitious, though I am not sure of the direction I should take my life. I think I will resign my commission, not least because I am ashamed of this policy of concentrating civilians in a camp."

"I am fortunate, Gargery. I have been told I will be required up north soon and that means engagement with an enemy who is rarely visible. Good fortune on your return to Port Elizabeth."

At that moment there was a commotion outside the office and a junior offer burst in:

"Colonel, Mafeking has been relieved!"

"Excellent news, now we are getting somewhere."

After various loud celebrations at this news, Malcolm said, "I must say I don't envy you, but Godspeed and when this thing is over, do look us up in London, Down Street Mayfair."

"I will, I will."

With that, the two men shook hands, and Malcolm left for the train, going past the barracks first to collect his belongings and saying goodbye to Mistle, who like other soldiers was whooping and hollering about the news from Mafeking.

Two days later, he walked up Clyde Street and enveloped his wife in his arms and the children rushed around him in one huge bundle of family love and affection.

"I've decided to resign my commission, darling," he said as they sat with a cup of tea, "my experience of those camps has left me thoroughly disenchanted with political and military policy here and I realized that I am neither fowl, flesh nor good red herring with the army with my injury. I love my regiment and do not regret my experience, but I want to move on. I will write today. I know I will have to go to Aberdeen to resign formally, so we should try to get a passage in June or July as I must wind down my work with the Brigadier.

"I am so thrilled, Malcolm. You are a man of many talents and you are wasted here in this outpost of Empire. It has been a wonderful time here, but I am more than excited to return."

"I want to help Miss Hobhouse when I get back. What's happening here is a frightening disgrace and a stain on the reputation of the Empire which we will never live down."

No doubt listening carefully Rufus hauled his huge body on to his feet and nestled his large nose on Clara's knee as if to say he hoped he could come too.

"We could not do without you, Rufus, and you'll love England," she said, stroking his head."

XIX

There was also joy in the streets of London that May at the relief of Mafeking, a town where the British army had been surrounded for several months by the Boer army. Reports from South Africa still worried Tom and Hannah, and Tom thought the difference with the situation in Ireland was only slight. Boers were unwilling subjects of the Empire, as were many Irishmen. The guerilla tactics of the Fenians, the group willing to fight for a united Ireland were similar to the Boers, though they were not continuously active.

In both cases, the population was rural and its livelihood was farming, and of the greatest importance were their respective religious beliefs. For Tom, a soldier used to giving unlimited support to his country's causes without question, the Irish experience was unleashing his passions in more of a civilian than a military frame of mind.

By July, the work of the Trust was stable enough for Tom and Hannah to decide on a three-month break in England. They felt as though they had been back at Clumber for years but it was only six months, it now being June and a spell of dry sunny weather, so unusual for Ireland. Hannah was enduring a difficult pregnancy, so time in London would be valuable.

"It will be a quite different life for us in London for a short while," said Hannah as they were preparing to leave Clumber.

"Indeed it will. I have been wondering recently whether we should not seek to do something different. We really have no friends here in Ireland, have we, as we would have in London?"

"It is somewhat similar to my parents' work in Africa, without the privations they endured, to be sure. With the Trust, Tom, we have changed the grim lot of the folks living here in almost every way."

"Is it too much to say we have set them free?"

"Yes, but they are still British subjects with all that that implies and the threats from living in this part of Ireland with the religious clash are still overwhelming."

"We must use our time in England to examine other possibilities for our energies. I sometimes wonder what it is like to be a politician."

"Good Lord, Tom, you mean in Parliament?"

"Why not? We are not in the thick of national politics out here on the periphery of the nation, but this war in South Africa is igniting many tensions. When the right to vote was extended, working class men and women have pressed the Liberal Party to take up their causes which I admire."

"Our last letter from my father spoke of the turbulence in politics and I suppose that might provide a way for new faces and new voices."

"Like mine, you mean?"

"Indeed, dear Tom, why not? You are the very soul of integrity, of concern for the unfortunate and a man with an imaginative and clear-headed view of solutions to any problems, which I take it should be the basic equipment of the politician."

"Apart from keeping my class in power?"

"Of course! I had almost forgotten I had read Karl Marx. I thought his political solution of revolution unworkable, but his thoughts on our social structure quite exceptional, even brilliant."

"I will read it. Who do we know in politics? I assume it is a difficult process, I mean, one cannot just enter the lists and stand as a candidate without the backing of a party."

"I think my father knows an MP, Sir Clarence Smythe, but we must ask him when we get to London."

"Of course," exclaimed Tom, "dammit if he is not Chairman of the Jaggers Trust I met with. Of course he will help."

That journey from Clumber to Chiswick was uneventful and Pip and Harriet were thrilled to see them. Harriet immediately picked up Hector and sat him on her knee as they waited for dinner.

"There is simply wonderful news in the post this morning, your brother Malcolm and the family are on the way home, so I will have my darling children, the heirs to the Gargery name together again by late August. For a man approaching his sixty-fifth birthday, nothing could be more wonderful, praise the Lord!"

Hannah looked at Harriet quizzically at this expression of religious fervor and said:

"This year, my dears, Pip is concerned that his faith which he encountered first as a child is not being exercised, so we have been attending West Street Chapel."

"It is so wonderful," said Pip, "to renew my acquaintance with God. He brings to my life all that wonder I felt as a youngster listening to the preacher at All Hallows, and He gives me strength to endure the feelings of despair and dread I get from time to time."

"Dear, Father," said Hannah sympathetically, "we have been too embroiled in our lives in Ireland to do more than go to a Presbyterian church in Claudy but irregularly, because the preacher there is one of those fire-and-brimstone preachers which I don't recognize as part of my religion."

"Now," said Harriet, clutching a contented Hector to her bosom, "tell us your plans."

"First, we will be very happy to take lodgings if it will inconvenience you both for us to be here. I am going to need some special care as I approach another labor."

"Yes, please be most careful," said Pip, "but this is your home too, you know."

"I am glad to be back in London," said Tom. "I am going to have to meet with the Board soon as we think our Irish commitment is at an end. A little time ago, when I was still committed to our work there, I thought I would learn Irish and spoke with Francis about it."

"Who's Francis?" Asked Harriet.

"The local priest, Father McGowan, splendid man, too much of an intellectual for a parish priest, I think, but a delightful fellow once you get to know him."

"Roman Catholic, huh," said Pip with a sniff.

"I soon gave up trying to teach myself Irish and that was something of a signal to me that my time in Clumber was coming to an end, and although I will talk to the Board, I do not really see us doing more in Ireland."

"Part of the problem," said Hannah, "is that while we are friendly with the tenants, we have no friends as we have in London and in Scotland. I haven't seen my friend Jeane Macpherson for years, and goodness knows where Alec is. I miss them, though with Malcolm and Clara coming back, that will help."

"But what will you do, Tom?"

"I am considering politics and I thought I would talk with Clarence."

"Clarence?" said Pip, "yes indeed, you've met him and Hamish, of course, a judge who is very well connected. You met them at the Board meeting, but that discussion was limited to Ireland, of course. I'm sure they'd give good advice about politics."

At that point, the maid called them into dinner and Harriet insisted that Hector now three years old, have a place at the table. Her son Joseph came rushing down the stairs when he heard the maid call, abandoning his first encounter with Plato's Republic, and tending to Hector.

Both Arthur and Philip had long been recovered after their fall from the tree. Philip's head had healed and his sight was back, though he had the occasional headache. In the early summer of 1900 the Fletcher Alphabet children and their parents had resumed their regular visits to Numquam House, the memory of the boys falling out of the Elm a distant memory. Victoria was delighted with their increasingly adult company, as were her two girls Beatrice and Ellen who had tired of each other in that period when their father Albert was not living at Numquam.

As was their custom, all the younger children played in the Numquam garden or in the stables when they arrived and Arthur and Philip, now good friends after their experience with the tree, wandered off toward the marshes. One August afternoon Horatio and Beth sat with Victoria in the drawing room as the wind had suddenly started to blow hard off the North Sea swirling around from different directions, exciting the children.

"How are you doing, Victor?" Asked Horatio as they settled in the drawing room.

"Oh you know me, I am supposed to get over things easily, and while I am very sorry to lose Albert, I think about what life would have been like if he had not done himself in. I mean, what does a wife do with a husband who's got the clap, as Mum would have said?"

"Thank God she's not around to see it, she'd have been so upset, wouldn't she?"

"You know, Harry, I now really think she was not so much excited for me marrying Albert, though she was, but for herself and Estella. Somewhat like this: it was if our marriages was their union, not ours, if you see what I mean."

"That's right, Victor, and my Beth said something like that the other day, didn't you, Beth? I remember how much before you was wed, she talked about how lovely it was for you to marry Estella's son. Coming to think of it, she didn't mention Albert that much when you was engaged."

"Of course, it was different later when she lived with us," Victoria replied.

"I'm glad our youngsters are getting on well, it's lovely," said Beth, getting up and watching them all in the garden, "it's getting so windy out there, do you think they should come indoors?"

"Oh no," said Horatio, "they love rushing around when it's windy, it's like they're chasing the wind. Not as if it's very cold either, even though its August, wind coming off the sea I suppose."

"I'm not sure, that is strange, isn't it, we don't often get winds like this and the trees seem now to be blowing toward the sea," said Victoria, getting up to make sure windows were shut as the wind gusted around the old house, rattling windows everywhere.

Outside the children were screaming with joy, especially when some garden rubbish rushed across the grass, chased by the smaller Alphabet children.

"Well, it's starting to frighten me," said Beth, "I'm going to call the little ones inside. Look after the baby."

She crossed the driveway on to the grass and called out to her children, but it was difficult to make herself heard against the howling wind. Victoria and Horatio were standing by the window watching Beth try to corral her children when suddenly there was a loud, long roar as if the earth was opening up, and the old elm was torn from its roots and came crashing down creating a playground of horror. The trunk of a falling tree of this size rarely lies flat on the ground from root to top, for the root end of the tree props the trunk up such that it lies flat only toward its top.

"Christ Almighty," shouted Horatio as he threw open the French windows and rushed out. Victoria followed, holding up her skirts as she ran to find her children among the debris of the fallen tree. Two of its large limbs had driven themselves deep into the ground, and branches seemed to be covering at least two children. Young Beth was crying and screaming as a branch had scraped her arm badly and she was bleeding heavily.

Just visible under the main trunk of the tree were the legs of ten-year old Charlie and his eight year-old brother Ernest, obviously crushed. Horatio crashed through the branches and struggled with all the might he could summon to move the trunk, but that was impossible. Victoria ran back into the house and called her maid to take the cart and rush to the Bargemen.

"Tell Josh we need five strong men immediately. Tell them what has happened."

Beth herself was lying spread-eagled under a group of small branches which had formed the tree-top, howling in pain, "where are they, where are they? Get me out, get me out!"

"They're here, they're here, darlin," cried Horatio, looking around now to see his seven year-old Frank and Dottie his nine-year-old daughter, with Ellen, Victoria's eight year-old. The three of them were crouching together, covered with a branch which almost seemed to be like an umbrella protecting them, but they too were howling from the scratches on their limbs and faces as the branches fell on them.

As Victoria rushed back to the scene of devastation she tried to account for all the children. Beatrice had been slightly hurt, with her mother Beth next to her. Charlie and Ernest were under the trunk, probably, no, certainly dead. That left Ellen her youngest, Dottie and Frank who were also trapped under branches and the cries of the dead children's mother was louder than the wind as she continued to wail in her misery.

Horatio had abandoned the struggle to move the trunk and was struggling to free his wife. He snapped off branches that covered her and together with Victoria, they managed to lift the branches for long enough for him to pull her out.

"What happened? Where are they all?" she cried as he carried her to one of the raffia chairs which the tree had missed when it fell.

"Darlin,'" said Horatio now weeping and delicately holding her face with his huge hands, "I think Charlie and Ernest are done for as they got caught under the trunk."

"Oh Christ, Oh Christ, my two lovely boys," and her ear-shattering wail started up again.

"Wait, my love, I must get to young Beth," said Horatio as he sought a way through the debris and picked up his eldest daughter, still dazed with the shock of the experience and the fact that she was unharmed. Meantime Victoria had released Frank, Dottie and Ellen.

All those who could now sat down on the grass as the wind started to blow itself out. A cart appeared at full speed with five men and a rider behind them. The rider was the Vicar who had been in Bargemen along with the younger Friendly brothers, Tom and Dick, Josh the landlord, Will Longshot and Dan Wilden.

The six men stared in horror at the devastation and clawed their way through the branches to the spot where the trunk had flattened the children.

"Right, lads," said the Vicar, "let's move this trunk to get those boys out."

No time for condolences three of the men stood on either side nearer the top of the tree by the spot where the two boys lay, with Horatio ready to pull on Charlie's legs and Victoria on Ernest's.

The Vicar cried 'heave,' but they could not shift the trunk after three tries.

They waited to recover their strength; then the Vicar shouted, 'This time, men!' and with a monumental effort, they lifted the trunk for just those few seconds to enable the boy's bodies to be pulled out, then silence fell as they dropped the trunk.

Immediately Horatio saw Charlie, he tore off his coat to cover the boy and then his shirt to cover Ernest. Victoria turned away weeping. The damage to their bodies was brutal, their heads and chests had been almost crushed flat, incongruous beside the stark beauty of their young hips and legs.

"Take hold of Ernest, will you, Josh?" said Horatio, "and I'll bring Charlie," as the men then threaded their way to a patch of lawn nearer the house.

The Vicar stayed by the trunk kneeling and saying prayers. When he began to say the Lord's Prayer in a loud clear voice, all the adults fell to the ground with heads bowed, save Beth who was still weeping and quite unable to look at the event of recovery. Then with the Amens, she glanced at the bodies again as the Vicar got up and she let out another howl like that of a stricken wolf and collapsed from the chair on the ground screaming in anger and with sorrow. Horatio came back to her, trying to comfort her. Everyone who was a witness to this dreadful calamity was still, without conversation, staring into their own distance to try to come to terms with the blow Nature had dealt two innocent young children.

Victoria expressed her thanks to the six men as they were prepared to leave, anxious to leave the families to mourn, but she asked the Vicar to stay behind. She then called out to her daughter, "Beatrice, can you take the little ones back to the house? We must get these scratches and cuts seen to."

Horatio and Beth stood on the driveway clutching each other, unsure what to do.

"Might your two boys lie in the church until the undertaker can come from Chatham, Mr. Fletcher?" Asked the Vicar, "I would be pleased to arrange that."

"Thank you, Vicar, we'd like to take them home, but I'll ask my sister to get a couple of sheets so we can wrap them up."

"If I may I would like to do that for you. You stay with your wife."

"Thank you, Vicar."

"That would be very kind, Vicar," said Beth, now quietening down from the heights of her distress, putting her own aches and sores to one side, and trying to understand how the last thirty minutes had changed her wonderful life.

The Vicar met Victoria hurrying back from the house with two sheets and he tenderly wrapped them around the broken little bodies and carried them gently to the Fletcher's cart one by one, Horatio stopped Arthur and Philip as they returned from their walk in the marshes, first puzzled by the fallen tree, but both boys then going white with shock when they were told what had happened.

Arthur, Frank and little Horatio rode up front in the cart with their father, while Beth and her daughters rode behind on their way home to the cottage, their mother unable to take her eyes off her children's bodies lying in white sheets next to her.

The Pirrip children went back to the Numquam drawing-room and Philip told his sisters how fortunate they were and how sad they should be for their Fletcher cousins, while Victoria and the Vicar conversed outside the house.

"I won't intrude on your grief any longer, Mrs. Pirrip," said the Vicar.

"Please call me Victoria, Vicar, I need someone to talk to. I feel quite numb with my husband's death and now this tragedy. How dreadful it must be for Harry and Beth to lose two of their children in this act of God, don't you think?"

"No, Victoria, an old tree fell down in a high wind, not an uncommon occurrence, but nothing to do with the Almighty, I am afraid. He cannot be blamed for it. Nor should anyone else have these deaths on their conscience. It was a feature of Nature, nothing more nothing less."

"No, I know, not that I really believe in Him anyway," she sniffed.

"Perhaps you will find some solace if you seek Him by coming to church," and he smiled at her in such a way that she trembled slightly even in her grief as his smile seemed to carry with it a look from a man that she had not experienced for many years.

As if she had not had enough shocks to last a lifetime already, that smile was a monumental surprise. On the other hand, he was a delightful, interesting handsome widower, about her age, also recovering from a loss. That apart, the thought of being a parson's wife seemed as far away as a journey to the Moon. Maybe he was just being a kind and helpful vicar.

⚜ ⚜ ⚜

It was August 20th, 1900, when two carriages brought the Gargery entourage from Waterloo Station to Down Street, where the house was so sparkling clean that a fantasist might have said that the house itself shared the excitement among the staff that Clara, her husband and family were home at last. With the family were Abdul holding Rufus by the lead, and Oliver Egerton who promptly called a cab and departed for his mother's house after sentimental goodbyes. Meanwhile a vast amount of luggage was being unloaded from the boat and was making its way from Southampton.

That same morning Mary sat at her breakfast table reading The Times while Hamish was upstairs completing his toilet. He had not succumbed, as he saw it, to employing a valet as many of his fellow judges did to ensure an impeccable appearance in court. At the Old Bailey, of course, his clerk Theophilus Mandrake attended to his robes and full-bottomed wig.

He appeared for breakfast just as the morning post was brought into the room. As was the custom, the maid had opened all Mary's letters and laid them on the tray, as she could not easily wield the knife and hold the letter with her withered arm.

A letter from Victoria caught her immediate attention.

She read it and tears flowed down her cheeks.

"What on earth is the matter, my dear?"

"Listen Hamish. This is as sad a letter as I have ever received or hope to have received."

"Well, go on."

'Dear Mary:

Please allow me to share with you my distress. I write to let you know of a terrible tragedy that took place at Numquam yesterday. My brother's family were visiting me and the children were all playing on the lawn.

It was very windy but tolerably warm and the children were all rushing around on the grass when the old elm tree was uprooted by the wind; do you remember that tree? Two of my brother's children Charlie and Ernest were killed as the trunk fell on them. The rest of them had a few scratches and bruises from the branches.

What a start to the century! Please tell my London friends of this happening, and I hope I will see you soon.

Please give my kindest regards to your husband,

I am your ever-devoted friend,

Victoria.'"   Numquam House, August 22,'00.

"How awful, how simply awful," said Hamish, "I cannot think of a worse way to lose a child, apart from the disease that child of Pip and Susanna had."

"Lachlan?"

"Yes, Lachlan."

"What can we do, Hamish? I don't think we have ever met her brother's family. He inherited the old blacksmith's forge, I believe, and I remember Victoria saying they had Alphabet children."

"What does that mean?"

"The oldest child is Arthur and successive children were named with the next letter of the alphabet as the first, no matter boy or girl. Like many ordinary folk, they have lots of children these days, not like when we were young and so many died in infancy."

"I have to leave now, my dear, but do write to her with our condolences and offer any help. I am sure that Victoria can take care of any financial need there since Albert died."

"Oh my goodness, his death had slipped my mind. I am getting old. Two awful tragedies for the poor woman, even though the dead children were not hers."

As Hamish left for the brougham that would take him across the city to his chambers, he saw a carriage arrive at Pip and Harriet's house along the Row and he held his driver out of curiosity. Out of the carriage stepped a tall man with an eye-patch who hurried up the steps. They must be back already, Hamish thought, but decided not to intrude on that homecoming and told his driver to move on.

Mary meantime had completed her breakfast and in mid-morning decided to walk up the Row to tell Harriet and Pip of the tragedy at Numquam, as Victoria had requested.

As the maid opened the door to admit her, she heard animated conversation coming from the drawing room.

"Come in, come in, Mary," said a delighted Harriet, "Look who is here."

"Dear Malcolm," said Mary as he came over to her, and took her in his arms.

"I assume you are all back, that you have not left Clara to her fate with the Boers," she said, laughing.

"No, we are all back, and I have been regaling my parents with various adventures and I am eagerly awaiting the return of Hannah and Tom who are out shopping."

"Tell me, my dear," said Harriet, taking Mary by the arm, "what brings you here at this early hour?"

"I would fain tell you of a tragedy on this joyous occasion."

"No," intervened Pip, "of course you must tell."

"There has been a dreadful accident at Numquam. Victoria's brother and family were there. It was a windy day and the children were all playing on the grass when that old elm tree fell on them and two of her brother's young boys were killed."

Expressions of horror were immediately stilled by alarm at Pip's eccentric reaction.

"I knew it, I knew it," he said getting up and stamping his feet. "That house has witnessed ungodly happenings in that unnatural relationship between Estella and that whore. It is a divine punishment, a divine punishment," said Pip, his preacher voice resonating throughout the house.

"I said at the time, didn't I, Harriet…

"No, my dear, that was before my time."

"Of course, I said at the time that it was a betrayal of my old namesake for his wife to fornicate with that whore and within a year after his death, quite apart from the beastliness of women as lovers."

The room fell silent, as there was mutual embarrassment among the listeners and Pip looked around at the people he addressed with a slightly wild look in his eyes as if he was challenging anyone to disagree. Even Mary was stunned by this outburst and was about to reprimand Pip for what seemed to be a mad assertion about Numquam House, but Harriet simply changed the subject.

"Malcolm my dear, when can we visit you? We would love to see how the children have grown."

"You will be very welcome indeed. We have brought with us a marvelous man Abdul who became our servant after another incident which I will tell you about sometime."

"How old is he?" asked Harriet.

"We have not asked but I would judge he is in his thirties. He is a Malay by racc, and I think he is a Muslim by faith, though he does not seem to practice."

"How can you tolerate an infidel in your house even as a servant?" asked Pip with renewed aggression, "he will be a terrible influence on. your children."

"Don't talk nonsense Pip," said Mary, incensed by Pip's religious fervor.

"In fact the children love him dearly, as we do. We want him to establish himself here and take the opportunity to build a different life."

"You should send him back to Malaya or South Africa or wherever he comes from."

"Father," said Malcolm, getting increasingly angry, "you had better not come to Down Street if you cannot keep a civilized tongue in your head. I have never heard such claptrap. You demean yourself with such prejudice. Do you not believe that all human beings are God's children and entitled to our general care?"

Pip ignored that remonstrance, and said:

"Oh dear, those dead children are the grandchildren of Fletch, the man who saved me at Balaclava. I shall travel immediately to All Hallows to comfort their father and mother and pray with them."

"That is a good idea," said Harriet encouragingly, "and I will accompany you and visit Victoria."

"We will go today," said Pip hurrying out of the room.

"Harriet, what is the matter with my father?" Asked Malcolm.

"I wish I knew, Malcolm. He seems to have recovered his religious attitudes, which I suppose have lain dormant since his return from Africa, and nowadays he can scarce talk of anything except religion and God's will. It seems so out of character. It is both tiring and boring, but I know he is very deeply worried about Hannah and her second pregnancy, for the first was not easy," she said with a smile.

"On the other hand, and I hate to say this," said Mary, "but he may be ill. I think he should see a doctor of the mind."

"I don't think religion is a disease of the mind," said Harriet stiffly, "though I hold no such views myself."

"No, my dear," said Mary, "forgive me, I did not mean to imply any such thing."

"Very well."

"When you visit Victoria, please tell her we hope to see her in London sometime."

"I will certainly invite her anyway, and she will bring her children too."

After she left, Harriet sat down with Malcolm and to his surprise after that interchange with Mary she expressed her concern that Pip might indeed be losing his mind. She remembered vaguely, as she told Malcolm, that a friend of Estella's was married to a parson who seemed to go mad and that he eventually died in an accident.

"Oh no," Malcolm said, "my father is not mad. My considered opinion is that he likely does not have enough to occupy him since his sojourn in Ireland. To be sure he is concerned about Hannah, but we must find him something to do. Saving your presence, Harriet, it is simply not enough for an active man, however old he is, to live a life of leisure with only one purpose."

"Perhaps, but what is the purpose?" Said Harriet.

"To postpone death, of course."

XX

Apart from these irregular religious outbursts, Pip seemed depressingly normal to Harriet, so she decided to stay at home, reflecting on the wisdom of Malcolm's remark that he should find something to do. The idea of his visiting the Fletcher family was grand. As he would not be able to stay at the Cottage, and he could hardly invite himself to stay with Victoria at Numquam after his remarks about the house, she encouraged him to stay for a night or two at the Blue Boar. Meantime Pip himself sent a message to Horatio that he would like to call and had a reply of welcome, so one Saturday morning in late September, a trap brought him down the track to the Cottage which he had not visited since the attempt on Nellie's life at Numquam.

Yet this cottage was where he grew up and the memories of his father Joe and his mother Biddy tumbled through his mind. All Hallows too was the village where he had first encountered God, and the memory of that was now very fresh, so this was a very special occasion and one in which he hoped to deliver God's comfort to these sad people.

Outside the Cottage there was a cart and a horse grazing nearby, and a splendid horse was saddled and tied up to the post.

Horatio had heard him coming, and throwing off his apron, came over to welcome him.

"How d'ye do, Mr. Gargery. I was a young lad when I last sees you, wasn't I, but I knows what my dad did for you in that war with the Ruskies, so you are most welcome. No, wait, you came to help us after we killed that recruiting sergeant."

"I'd forgotten that too, Horatio, and I am thrilled to see you. I hope to deliver some comfort to you and your wife after your terrible encounter with death."

"T'is true. These been very hard times for us but we've been lucky to 'ave the Vicar from All Hallows, him wot helped us so much that terrible day."

"Not Windnortham surely?"

"Lordy no. He's been dead long since. We's having a Mr. Eustace now, young fellow, bit older than me, I suppose. He's talking with my wife Beth now."

At this knowledge, Pip was taken aback. His journey of comfort was obviously a waste, but then this young Vicar would not know the world and God, for that matter, as he did. More confident, he was shown into the Cottage by Horatio.

"This is my wife, Beth, Pip and this is Mr. Eustace as I told you, and this is baby Horatio, and the other children are at school, apart of course from our dear Charlie and Ernest who lie in their graves," at which Beth began to sob.

"Dear Lord," said Pip, abruptly kneeling on the floor and beginning a prayer, much to the astonishment of the Vicar, "shine Your light on this family who have endured such a loss. Comfort them and give them the strength to replace those they have lost. May they always follow Thy word and be examples and witnesses to Your Glory, and may You cast out the evil spirits that inhabit that house, purging it of the iniquities it has witnessed, cleansed by Your peace. This we beg, O Great Lord, in thy name."

After a communal Amen, there was silence.

"Excuse me," said the Vicar as Pip got up, "we have not met. I am John Eustace, Vicar of All Hallows."

"I am Pip Gargery, formerly a Methodist Minister in Salford and then in Africa."

"Were you a missionary then?'

Pip replied by giving an overlong account of his vocation, the Crimea, his marriage, his loss of Lachlan and his time in Africa, though Harriet was not mentioned while the Fletcher looked on listening, though Beth slipped away into the kitchen to feed her baby.

"What an exciting life you have led, Mr. Gargery," said the Vicar, 'but what was your mention of a house?"

"That is the house where these children died. God had punished us, for that house has witnessed great iniquities, a woman murdered who was herself a murderer, an unnatural relation between its woman owner and a servant whore, and the killing of a soldier in the house. And now these poor children. It is the devil's house and it should be burned to the ground."

"But that's my sister's house, Mr. Pip," shouted Horatio, "and how dare you talk about my mother like that! What it's got to do with you?"

"Quite right," said the Vicar, "and perhaps you do not know God's will in such matters. Mr. Gargery, I am an ordained clerk in holy orders of the Established Church, and nothing you say convinces me that a work of arson is justified, nor would God be pleased to hear such words spoken about his good people. Moreover, it would be a criminal offence anticipating several long years imprisonment, were anyone to attempt such a vile deed."

"Sinners must accept the wrath of God and we are on this Earth to execute his will."

"How do you know, pray, that what you have said is not itself the work of the Devil within you? Come along, if you are a man of God, explain how you know."

At this admonition Pip broke down in tears, hurried out of the Cottage, stumbling with his leg, and wandered unsteadily along the marsh track.

"Oh, God," he screamed, "why have I lost my way?" and promptly collapsed on the track.

The Vicar had followed him out of the cottage and watched him as he fell.

"Come now, Mr. Gargery," he said, pulling Pip to his feet, "let me take you back to the Vicarage where you can stay the night." Together they walked slowly back to the Cottage where Horatio was looking out for them.

"Will you take us in your cart to the Vicarage, Horatio?"

"I will, "he replied as the Vicar was tying his horse to the cart, "but I'se surprised at ye, Mr. G. being so nasty. Thought you was us friends. Now get up in the back."

Pip remain silent, climbed up into the cart and sat with his head in his hands, and the journey passed without a word between the three men.

The Vicarage was a large comfortable house next to the church and Pip and the Vicar were put down there by Horatio who left without saying anything.

"You will stay with me a night, Mr. Pirrip?" asked the Vicar, as they got down.

"Thank you, but my bag is at the Blue Boar."

"I will have my maid find someone to fetch it here. After lunch, you should rest and then we will talk."

Pip had seemed oddly willing to be instructed what to do by the Vicar, as if, somehow, he had the divine authority to tell him about his luggage. The Vicar saw Pip as a person badly in need of support, though of what kind he was uncertain.

"That must have been a hard time working in Salford," said the Vicar later in the afternoon.

"Most enjoyable time of my life, actually. The work was hard, the conditions of the people terrible, but I was in love with Harriet. She is now my wife, but at the time she was a free lover who did not want children and when I was back at the Chatham ministry, I met my dear Susanna whom I married."

"Really? In Chatham?"

"Yes, at the Methodist Chapel, though I had started my belief in God as a Primitive Methodist, firmly against all ecclesiastical hierarchy. I still believe that, in so far as I believe anything."

"What do you mean by that?"

"I don't know and wish I did. I have recently come back to God but He is punishing me for not working enough for Him."

"Why?"

"I lost my eldest son Lachlan to diphtheria when he was young, and my wife Susanna to yellow fever, and now my daughter Hannah is having a difficult second pregnancy and I am terrified by the thought of losing her. Though it would be God's will, I suppose. I have also spent a short time in Ireland where those who are supposed to worship him, whatever their large doctrinal differences, seem to be a pitched battle with each other, and there I developed a good friendship with a tenant who was murdered.

"Yes, indeed, I find it difficult to understand too. Do you feel as though your belief in Him must be mistaken or simply false when you witness cruelty and barbarity in His name?"

"Exactly, Exactly, John, I must call you John and I am Pip, I know I have lost my temper in trying to invoke the God I thought I knew."

The afternoon and evening were spent in long theological discussions not so much about elements of doctrine such as the Holy Trinity, but the complexity of how people come to believe in God, what that means in practical terms and just how simple the message of Christ Crucified should be. Pip and John went to bed firm friends.

After breakfast the following day, the maid opened the door and said:

"Mrs. Pirrip to see you, Vicar," at which John leapt to his feet while Pip remained in his chair.

"Victoria, how delightful to see you," said John, "you will know Pip Gargery, I am sure."

"Of course, he was related to my husband Albert."

"Oh yes," said Pip, "but let me express my sadness about your family losses. I saw your brother and his family yesterday, and the Vicar was there. I stayed here at the Vicarage overnight and we have had long and interesting conversations."

"Victoria, you are most welcome. What can we do for you?"

"I have been worrying since we last met about my house. I got to thinking about things that have happened there; the murder of Mollie Magwitch, the assault on my mother Nellie which led to that man Whistler's death, the falling elm tree, quite apart from Estella and my mother dying there. Then there's Albert's death though that took place at sea."

"People have to die somewhere of course. Albert's mother died in the cottage."

"Oh, I know," interrupted Pip, "I was there."

"You were? How astonishing!"

"But this is why I wanted to talk to John as the Vicar but Pip you can also hear what I wanted to say too. Now I don't believe in evil spirits or haunted houses or anything, especially with regard to buildings, nor ghosts neither," she said with a touch of her mother's intonations. "Rather I wondered if you would come and bless the house and the garden. I know you prayed by the bodies of Charlie and Frank, John, and I would want it to be very private."

"In principle, my dear Victoria, of course, but I would need to consult with my friend Pip the preacher here."

"That would be wonderful, a cleansing in God's name."

The following morning, Vicar John and Preacher Pip took the Vicar's trap over to Numquam. Victoria had kept the children home from school for the ceremony. The branches of the tree had been cleared but sawing the trunk into manageable logs had only just started.

Victoria asked the workmen to break for the morning. The Vicar wore his cassock and surplice, with the purple stole around his neck common at funerals. Victoria stood with her children all holding hands. Pip took the hand of little Nellie at one end and at the other end of the line the Vicar held the hand of Beatrice. He then lead her around to form a circle such he now held hands with Pip.

"Bless this house, O Lord," said the Vicar as he made the sign of the Cross. "Keep all who live in it and love it from every danger that can assault mortal man," followed by Pip who said in a tremulous voice:

"Forgive us, O Lord, if we have sinned against thee, but help this house to become a temple of thy love," at which everyone said Amen.

"I must now return to Chelsea," said Pip very abruptly. "I thank you John, so warmly for your friendship and the peace I feel now in my soul, and Victoria, I hope to see you in London at some time."

As the children walked over to examine the tree trunk, Victoria said: "Oh, I nearly forgot," she said, but before she could say more, everyone's attention was attracted by Horatio's appearance on his cart and the children all ran toward him calling out "Uncle Harry, Uncle Harry!"

"There's a letter come for you, Mr. Gargery," and Pip hurried to open it and a broad smile of delight covered his face.

"Harriet writes that my daughter Hannah has given birth to a little girl, Louise Susanna Katherine Hesketh. Oh, praise the Lord," he said as if in ecstasy, putting his arms around everyone, murmuring his pleasure. "I was so worried about her."

"Maybe," said the Vicar to him quietly, "it has mainly been your concern for your daughter that has disturbed your relationship with God."

"Goodness gracious me, you may well be right," said Pip with some amazement. "I lost Susanna and I would have gone mad if I had lost my daughter too. I think I was anticipating that she would die, just as Beatrice had died in the Cottage, and I was blaming God in advance. How foolish."

"Possibly, Pip, but I am delighted to have met you and I hope you will come again."

Pip threw his arms around John, saying "thank you, thank you, my young friend in Christ. I feel a massive sense of relief and joy now my grand-daughter has arrived and my daughter is well. Now I must leave."

Horatio and Pip walked to the house to get his case and were soon on their way to the train station in Chatham, leaving Victoria and John together as the children all ran back to the tree trunk.

"The League has become rather a lazy organization, don't you think?" Said Hamish as they walked along the river in the September sunshine on a Sunday afternoon.

"Yes, my dear. I suppose by lazy you mean that it is an organization in name only punctuated by bursts of enthusiasm. I have convened a meeting and told members by letter that the League should close down or that it should confirm its earlier decision to join the National Central Society for Women's Suffrage."

"Is that Millicent Fawcett's organization of women's groups?"

"Yes indeed, and influence comes with numbers, I am sure."

"I rarely speak with politicians, Clarence excepted, but members of the Athenaeum are divided, the few that are sympathetic but passive and many more are hostile, if also passive, and the overall mood is not supportive. I am more than sympathetic as the fact that you cannot vote in parliamentary elections seems to me a travesty. What applies to you applies to all women in terms of justice."

"I thought you would take this view, dear and I will take it to the League."

A meeting of the League had been delayed twice but it finally took place in mid-September 1900. When the meeting got under way at Mary's house the following week Antonia said firmly, "there is really only one main issue in our struggle for votes; whether we should seek change only through political means or whether we should be more militant in our fight for justice."

"I should say in response to those alternatives that Miss Fawcett's Society seeks change through political means, not through militancy though I must confess to not understanding what militancy might entail," said Elizabeth, a newcomer.

"That would be to demonstrate on the streets, much as the Chartists did to demonstrate to politicians and to the public just how large the numbers are in support of women's suffrage. For my part, my dear," Emma continued, "as my husband is an MP of liberal views, I think he would view militancy with distaste as he would feel browbeaten."

"That means MPs keep control of the matter," said Alice Levy, "the virtue of militancy is that it shifts the control. Merely pursuing politics, and men in particular, means that we have to defer to their way of doing things, their schedule, and their view of the level of importance of the suffrage against, say, a colonial war. I like the idea of marches, pamphlets and vigorous meetings, especially those that can attract working class women who feel like us that they are second class members of the polity. My husband is fervently in support of our cause because, as he puts it simply, he sees no reason why his wife cannot vote in a parliamentary election."

"That suggests," said Antonia, "that we should challenge husbands to explain to their wives why they should not be permitted to vote."

"Now that would be hard for some but not for my elderly dinosaur husband," said Eliza Culpepper, Margaret Brandram's mother, "I expect he would say something very rude about me." Younger members of the group did not know this odd woman, now of advanced years, and something of a curiosity, but of the generation they respected.

"That is disgraceful," said Elizabeth, hoping further explanations of that marriage could be offset as it sounded so grim. "I think my husband Aubrey was right when he said that diplomacy can take you only so far, and that non-diplomatic means are often needed to secure your wants. In the case of nations, this sometimes means war. I agree with Alice, and she stated the position so clearly. The matter is out of our control. We are not here seeking their permission to vote, we are demanding it as it is our right."

Murmurs of 'hear, hear' sounded around the table.

"We must seek control," said Alice firmly. "Now that may be very difficult to secure, as men hold the constitutional cards."

This debate continued over lunch and into the afternoon with a clear majority of the women favoring a more militant approach.

Clara sounded a cautionary note toward the end of the meeting:

"I have listened attentively to the back and forth of this discussion and I sense this group is most sympathetic to what Alice and Elizabeth have said. I must confess to being less confident about militancy, though no one can feel more strongly than I about the justice of women voting.

"My concern is the unintended results or consequences. The political approach keeps us within limits of what we can do, boundaries which are set by law, precedent and convention. Once we start on a militant track, those boundaries will rapidly become porous. Let me use the example of the camps in South Africa. I am sure that four years ago, while we had the first war with the Boers, and were in diplomatic discussions with them, not a soul could have imagined that four years on, there would be thousands of women and children in camps, barely fed, diseased, and living in circumstances of untold misery."

"I heartily agree with Clara's concise and somber warning," said Elizabeth. "I know that in espousing a militant approach, those of you around this table do not envisage physical combat or the political violence of the anarchist with his bombs. But why not? Where are the boundaries? If militancy encourages our opponents to dig in their heels, then what? More pamphlets, more marches? For my part, I can accept that the steady drip of the claims of justice on the consciences of those who are the decision-makers is preferable. To be honest, militancy frightens me."

"Clara," said Mary, "these are timely and very succinct warnings."

"Harriet, you have been silent, can you help us?"

"Probably not. While I dither about such matters, I would cast my lot with the militants. I much appreciate Clara's and Elizabeth's comment, of course, but we are women, not men, and as a sex not attracted to violence."

"How sensible a comment is that," said Alice, "I agree with Harriet that there are, so to speak, built-in boundaries for militant women."

"Before we close," said Mary, "if we confirm that we want to join Miss Fawcett's organization, it will always have to be provisional in my view. For one possible unintended consequence, to use Clara's penetrating phrase, we can envisage circumstances where we might all wish to become militant, or, if the organization became militant, we might wish to withdraw."

"I suppose everything depends on what progress is made."

The result of a vote around the table was unanimous in continued support for the League of Women to participate in the national organization.

"One question," said Harriet, "does this mean that we now ignore the other items on the agenda we developed at Numquam that I thought were particularly valuable, including the issues of membership?"

"No, let us meet again, and soon this time, to examine that agenda, putting the suffrage issue to one side."

"I sense agreement so, Harriet, would you send that list to everyone?"

"I will."

She approached Elizabeth as the meeting was breaking up, "may we have lunch together sometime?"

"That would be delightful Harriet, come to my house, say, next Thursday?"

Some nights, one or other of her children was disturbed by memories of the Elm Tree accident. After a particularly bad night of tears, moans and cries with Beatrice, Victoria heard a horse coming up the drive after she had finished her breakfast and the children were at school. Looking out of the dining room window she saw that it was the Vicar who had come to call, so before he was at the door, she called her maid to bring tea and biscuits and went into her drawing-room.

She trembled very slightly when he came in as she was beginning to see him as much a handsome man as the Vicar. She had determined in her loneliness before and after Albert's death that she would remarry, should the opportunity arise. Opportunity was rare, however, living in the country with young children.

"I came to see how you are faring, Victoria, I hope I am not intruding."

"Not at all, I am delighted to have your company and your solicitation for my welfare. I am very troubled by my children who are very disturbed in the aftermath of the accident."

"I understand that."

"What can I do with the children, Vicar?"

"I hope you will not think it improper if I ask you to call me John. We are friends, I think, and have shared this disaster."

"That is not improper at all, John," and she could scarcely resist small intimations of flirtation when giving her reply to which he responded with one of his wonderful smiles.

"I had no children as you know. I would imagine that they will dream of their own experience and wake up remembering it."

"I am ashamed to say that I have told them that they were fortunate not to be in the position of their cousins who died."

"That is true, on the basis of 'there but for the grace of God,' and you are merely finding a way to express a mother's love, especially as you have been widowed only recently."

"You are correct. You and I share the loss of a partner, but my experience as you know is a very unhappy one from which I am still trying to recover."

"I am very sorry indeed to hear you refer to that again. You told me of your husband's death, so you are bound to feel all manner of emotions. I can offer some general words of comfort, but they will all end as religious comments which I know you do not share."

"No, John, after your earlier visit I have been thinking about coming to church and bringing my children. I think this might be a way for them to come to terms with this horror."

"Perhaps you would come to the Vicarage one day for lunch and I can begin to instruct you so that when you come to church you do not find it incomprehensible."

With another slight tremble, Victoria said as demurely as she could, "I think that would be most helpful."

"Which days would suit you?"

"The children have resumed schooling, so any day of the week."

"Let me see. Tomorrow I have a funeral, but Thursday will suit. Shall we say midday?

"This is really most kind. As I may have told you, living in this house in the country, my only friends are my brother and his family."

"I am delighted to offer you my friendship both to you and to your brother and his family, whom I plan to visit again shortly," said John, again with one of those smiles.

After he left, she could not help imagining what her mother might have said about her lunching with a vicar: 'You just mind yourself, Vic. Them vicars is dark horses.'"

However, Victoria had realized that she was beginning to see John more as her knight in shining armor than a dark horse but, now Albert was gone, her mother Nellie was so much on her mind so that when she was on her own, she'd speak out loud with Nellie's voice, and often as not it would make her laugh heartily which was a tonic for her distress.

With considerable courage and immense trepidation, Victoria called at the Vicarage the following morning, and it was clear to her that John was delighted to see her again so soon after his visit, though he was sure they had fixed Thursday.

"I have had another letter, John, from my friend Mary. She is contemplating holding a lunch party sometime in October and she wondered whether I would be ready to come to such a party. She does not mention my bringing a guest and I am sure she will not find a man to make up her table, my being so recently a widow. I don't want to go on my own so I am of a mind to ask her if I may invite you to be my guest when the date is fixed," and she smiled.

"Goodness me, in London?" said John, his face showing the same surprise as he would show if the man in the moon had come to greet him.

"Yes, in Chelsea. I am sure she or her friends could accommodate us."

"Well, of course, of course. I do have old friends and my brother living near Westminster, so accommodation would not be difficult."

"Let me explain," said Victoria. "I enjoy your company enormously, brief though it has been and under unusual circumstances. I know it is still under a year since Albert's death. I do not intend to leave Numquam and I know you will be here for some years, even if you are later promoted elsewhere. To be clear, I harbor no pretensions about us being anything more than good friends, but I would like to be with you in the company of people I have known one way or another for years. So please come with me when it happens."

"Nothing would give me greater pleasure. I have to say this. We have both suffered the loss of a spouse. I don't know whether I could marry again, but after meeting you I do not any longer rule it out. If that became a possibility, I know we would need to find out much more about each other and meeting with friends is always a good start. So I am thrilled at your invitation."

"How very satisfactory," said Victoria. "The lunch party is sometime in October, I think."

"As long as it is not on the 31st for the Vicar of All Hallows must be in his church on All Hallows Eve."

So many changes occurred in 1900. Mary MacDonald regularly told Hamish she would like to host a luncheon party, and the purpose, or was it an excuse, was a late celebration for the return of the Gargery family from South Africa. Victoria had already replied indicating that she would come but would like to bring a guest which Mary thought was both intriguing and welcome. Clearly, thought Mary, that widow had recovered from her husband's bizarre death, the poor dear woman. After selecting new dining room furniture at Gillows on a breezy September day, Mary went on to Down Street to confirm a date for the lunch with Clara. That was quickly done and, as she was leaving, Tom and Hannah Hesketh arrived with young Hector and the baby, so Mary did not stay long.

Although they had met several times since the Gargerys' return in the summer, that day was especially delightful, a celebration of the Hesketh baby and an extended period of mutual delight as the children appeared and were introduced. Hannah was cock-a-hoop with her baby daughter and felt things had resumed their natural order with her brother's return from South Africa, and it was such a pleasure to see him with Clara and their children. Abdul brought in a bottle of champagne and glasses to wet the baby's head. Even Rufus shared in the occasion in his boisterous friendly way after satisfying himself with their smells and putting his head in Malcolm's lap.

"You should both know," said Clara, "that Abdul is a very special man and our friend," at which Abdul smiled with quiet embarrassment and hung his head slightly. "He saved the life of a friend of Oliver Egerton's and as his employers were about to leave Port Elizabeth, we asked him to come to us."

"How did that happen?" said Hannah looking carefully at Abdul.

"We were all on the beach enjoying the sun and the sea and Oliver and his two new friends Charlie and Harry were swimming. The sea got very rough suddenly, Charlie got out, and both the other boys were in difficulty. My brave husband rescued Oliver and went back for Harry who was apparently drowned and dragged him to the beach. Abdul rushed over to us when he saw Harry's condition and quite wonderfully put his mouth on Harry's and blew air into the boy such that he recovered."

"Congratulations Abdul," said Tom whose initial reaction of some suspicion at having a native servant in London promptly dissipated.

"How very brave of you," said Hannah, now looking warmly at Abdul and walking over to him to shake his hand, "you probably will not know that The Royal Humane Society has just changed its name from the Society for the Recovery of Persons Apparently Drowned."

"Good Lord," said Tom, "how did you know that, Hannah?"

"One learns a great deal from medical journals which I still read. More important the Society is training people to perform the actions that Abdul used, as the Serpentine in Hyde Park frequently has people drowning it as it is such a popular venue in which to bathe."

"Thank you, thank you, Miss Gargery. I learn this as boy in Redang Island in my country before I come to Africa. I live by the sea and we have many accident like boy Harry," said Abdul in uncertain English. "I go now, missus, or do you want more?"

"No, thank you, Abdul."

"What a fine fellow," said Tom.

"He is indeed and our children worship him. He may be small of stature, but he is very big of heart," Clara concluded.

"What happened to Matilda, then?"

"Oh, she is very much still with us too, but I have sent her off to her family in Surrey for a few days as she has been away so long. In fact the two work very well together and seem to be good friends, but thankfully no more than that."

"What about you, Malcolm?" asked Tom.

"I was given leave after my work with Miss Hobhouse which is now complete and I am going next week to Aberdeen to resign my commission. My friend Alec Macpherson wrote some time ago to say he had resigned too and had to return from India to do so. He met with Duncan Urchadan who made him feel like a traitor to the Regiment. I don't anticipate that kind of reception, given the loss of my eye. Alec had married and was becoming a tea-planter of all things."

"Now wonder Urchadan was short with him," said Tom.

XXI

Invitations were sent out for dinner, but as Mary's guests arrived, the presence of so many guests was only a mild surprise compared to the sensation when Victoria walked in with the Vicar of All Hallows. Of the guests, only Aubrey, Antonia's husband was unable to come. As might have been expected conversation was immediately loud and vital throughout the meal and afterwards.

"Is not growing old and enjoying maturing friendship just the most wonderful thing about being human?"

"Say that again, please," said Emma Smythe as she came to talk with the two men, so Hamish repeated his question which he thought was a rhetorical end to his talk with Pip.

"I suppose so," said Emma, "but many a friendship can be very brittle, snapping at a perceived slight, for instance."

"Surely a good marriage must be based on a friendship which matures."

"Of course, and I do find that my husband and I are much more friends that we were when we were first married, presumably because we now know so much about each other. I am especially intrigued to know how marriages break down, primarily because I do not have any friends in that state, but I hear of other such breakdowns quite frequently.

"I mean," she went on, "saving Victoria's presence, what was it in the marriage that led Albert to debauchery?"

"Oh goodness me, don't ask me," said Pip, "I am a total innocent in discussing marriages other than my own."

"Me too, I'm afraid," said Hamish.

"Then I will go and ask Victoria. The fact that she had brought the Vicar with her presumably means she is no longer bound up in swathes of grief."

It soon became apparent that they had all shared differently in the two primary cataclysms in British life at the beginning of the new millennium, Ireland and South Africa, leading to two overlapping conversations, one led by Hannah and Clara and the other by Tom and Malcolm.

"So what will you do when you resign your commission, Malcolm?" Asked Tom.

"My experience with Miss Hobhouse was shattering. The plight of these women and children in those camps really is a disgrace, and I blame our military leaders, Kitchener especially."

"Tell us more about Miss Hobhouse, Malcolm, she is making a name for herself in London," said Hamish.

"She is quite unique, you know, like a gentle battering ram. She ask questions incessantly and jots her impressions down in a small book, of which there must be dozens. But you know, the conditions in those camps are deplorable. Can one imagine one's own women and children subject to such misery, such terrible conditions and such disease? I have already begun to work with her and will do so much more in the near future."

"I don't disagree about the conditions," said Adam Masterson, "but I don't know what an army does when there are civilians wandering around who may be a part of the opposing military."

"That's all very well, but our army has destroyed their houses, farms and crops," Malcolm retorted, "they aren't just wandering around of their own free will, you know."

"We are getting very mixed opinions in Parliament," said Clarence, "though there is no doubt she is having an effect. That letter from Lord Ripon appealing to a British sense of decency had some effect too."

"When I first started to read about these displacements," said Aaron, "I was reminded of the Jews leaving Egypt, but also of Jews fleeing pogroms in the East of Europe."

"The comparison is a good one, Aaron," said Tom. "Odd is it not, just how difficult it is for us as subjects to get away from a notion of 'my country right or wrong' when in fact it is decisions that are made by monied interests, or politicians, or generals, not some abstraction like my country."

"Again, I don't disagree," Aaron continued, "but there seems to be a logic about war, any war if the object of two combatants is to win. Dire events follow. As I understand it, Kitchener and Milner were driven to take the actions they did as the best, not the most moral objective best able to satisfy the political aims for the war. I'd blame Rhodes and our politicians before I'd blame Kitchener."

"How about Ireland, Tom?" Asked Pip, "you and I have experience of it, and I know we have discussed this ad nauseam in Board meetings, but any thoughts?"

"I am sure Irish History is full of such measures as are being used in South Africa. One such burning of crops and small farms occurred in the province of Munster. When people are oppressed by a government they consider illegitimate, their actions will be depraved as a response, hence revolution."

"Interesting, my experience of the Crimean War was, as I now recall, death, destruction and disease, especially on the ships getting there, cholera mostly. While there may be a just war, a specious argument as I find it, wars create injustice much more for the poor soldier or the poor civilian. I remember asking Preacher Whitehouse whether I should fight, and he said I should talk with God, which was not exactly the clearest response, as my inclinations were to be a pacifist at the time."

"South Africa and the Boers; Ireland, our legacy and now Home Rule! What can we do about it?" asked Hamish with a sense of exasperation.

"Tom and I are going into politics," said Malcolm firmly.

"I beg your pardon," said Clarence with surprise. "Do you both mean it?"

"We have discussed it and while our interests are in these different theaters of the British Empire, we both aspire to be Liberal MPs, though Tom might embrace this new Labor Party, he is unsure."

"That is wonderful news," said Clarence. "I will be leaving my seat and not seeking re-election. It is getting far too complicated balancing my work as an MP and as a lawyer. My seat is solidly liberal. But if that does not work out, I would be thrilled to help you both with your political ambitions and I assume you are both Liberals. For our time is coming, not beholden to a Gladstone but with a solid working majority to get things done on the domestic and foreign fronts. We have some good Cabinet material, the Welshman David Lloyd George and that firebrand Churchill. As you are both war heroes, you will easily find a Parliamentary seat."

Simon Brandram was overwhelmingly enthusiastic about this possibility, saying, "It is such good news, you know, when men of character and intellect try for Parliament. We have had too many members without any serious commitment to causes other than those that affect their own welfare."

Mary had just sat down next to Honora and overhearing that conversation said, "Goodness me, would those two not make excellent politicians, especially with their war records. But Honora, have you pursued your plans to move to Cornwall?"

"Since we talked about it all that time ago, I felt I had to stay with Simon and Margaret, at least until Jude was gone to university, and I have been something of a recluse. I have been keeping everything fairly secret, but last month I arranged to buy a cottage in Newlyn, south of Penzance with a pretty address, Primrose Overlook. It overlooks the sea of course and is a good walk to the town with its interesting harbor. Now I would have invited you to search with me, Mary, but much as I love you, I wanted to be on my own."

"Oh my dear, with the way Hamish's social engagements have developed where he demands my company, I am not sure I would have been able to get away."

"I will go to live there before Christmas but come back for the festivities, I am sure."

It was no surprise too that toward the end of the party Elizabeth and Emma sat together as good friends do and Clara had joined them, three beautiful women, different in their ways and experience, and Pip looked at them in awe. He approached them saying:

"You will forgive me for remarking on this, I know, but the three of you are women of such elegance and talent it's a pity you can't run the country."

"Aha," said Clara immediately much to everyone's amusement, "do I sense that my father-in-law is a suffragist in sheep's clothing?".

"It is true," he replied, "as I am constantly reminded by my dear wife, that the cause of votes for women in an urgent matter and I anticipate the matter being settled by a Liberal Government when we get one, but I will leave my elegant and beautiful friends there."

Clara found Pip's remarks mildly patronizing, so she got up and walked to the other side of the room where Hannah was explaining the developments on the Clumber estate to Simon and Margaret.

"Totally intractable, I'm afraid," said Hannah. "To us it seems so obvious that Ireland should be cut from our embrace and regain its independence. We managed to develop good trusting relations with the tenants, some of whom the Jaggers Trust has helped to emigrate, to Canada mostly. But we had no friends, though Tom got on well with the local priest."

"I was very glad when the Trust took the place over," said Clara, "forgive me for interrupting. I have no idea why my grandfather decided to leave me the estate. I suppose he thought I'd go there from time to time, receive a report from the bailiff and then leave."

"Of course that absentee landlord practice, common across the country, is an important matter for the Irish," said Hannah, "but how delightful that you

Gargerys are all back in England too. We must have our children get to know each other."

"Indeed," said Clara, "Port Elizabeth was a delight with its weather, so different from London. We even managed to persuade the owner of our house to sell it to us."

"Really, will you go back?"

"Perhaps when that war is over, though it would only be for a short while. Of course there will be friends who may want to try out South Africa and could use our house. British people now seem to inhabit the ends of the Earth, and we can always get an income from it. But it is a sweet home and I remember it with great affection, so was quite unable to part with it."

Conversations continued well into the late evening and members of the League were to be found discussing children and their schools.

"Elizabeth, what was your experience with Oliver?" Asked Clarence.

"Not much to say really," said Elizabeth, "I withdrew him from Eton as he was reacting badly so they said, but well in my view, to the traditional men-only behaviors and strange attitudes of the English public school. He masterminded a series of practical jokes which indicated he had outgrown the school."

"He was quite delightful in South Africa," said Clara, "a wonderful inquisitive, forthright young man it was a pleasure to entertain. And by the way, a formidable influence on our younger children, who came to adore him."

"Our experience with Jude has been different. He is a quiet sensitive child," said Margaret, who had been somewhat adrift in the conversations, "probably because he does not board at a public school."

"Similarly with Joseph," said Harriet, "it surprises me."

"You know," said Mary with a touch of whimsy, "the education of our boys might be quite different if they were taught only by women teachers."

"I doubt that," said Antonia laughing. "While I can see that most families do not have the time, leisure or money to keep their boys at home as we have been able to do, I find that my boys seem to have innate attitudes which are similar to boys who are in school. By that, I imply simply that their aggressive natures need to be harnessed to something good."

"I am so glad you said that," added Victoria: "Oddly I think that the least aggressive of my brother's seven children is Arthur the oldest. Oh, I know he can throw his weight around sometimes, but the way he cares for his young siblings means that his parents Harry and Beth have somehow managed to teach him to care, to channel his natural aggression."

"We try to do that, certainly," said Antonia, "our philosophy of upbringing is somewhat radical, I suppose."

"I wish I had been there at the meeting," said Clara, "I don't know you, Antonia, but I believe you have a large family and I want one, as I think a large family provides a balanced loving, what's the word people use nowadays, environment."

"That is indeed true of my brother's family," said Victoria quietly.

"I must say," said Emma, "to change the subject, I think I had a good education, but I have learnt more about myself and the world from meetings of the League than I ever did formally. I found an immense release, when I thought about it all afterwards, from women talking so frankly about themselves. Of course, Nellie Fletcher was the diva of outspoken independence," and there was general laughter around the room among those who knew her.

"I wonder if the League might form a meeting place for all our boys as well as for our girls," said Harriet. "I am thinking that if we foster their friendships in our company, that might help them to understand women."

"What a lovely idea," said Emma. "Changing the subject again, Clarence and I are of a mind to purchase a large farm near the sea in the south of France. We have been looking at a chateau with innumerable bedrooms. I am more alarmed at the idea than Clarence as I can't think why we might need such a place with a warren of rooms. But we could all meet there in the summer with our families, couldn't we?"

"I cannot think of anything more delightful for my children," said Victoria, "and I would like to bring some of my nieces and nephews if there was room."

"That provides food for thought," said Clara with a wry smile, "some of our husbands would not be able to spare all the time. I must say I have longed for a villa in Provence."

"If we all think it a good idea, I will talk with Clarence. I know he has workmen there making estimates so it could well be ready by next summer if we go ahead."

Meantime Pip had drawn John into a quiet corner to ensure their friendship and to ascertain whether John thought he was in need of mental rehabilitation still, so he opened up a question of theological and secular interest.

"Tell me, John, I am puzzled by the question of conscience. By that I mean is a Christian's conscience different than that of a non-believer?"

"Now that is a question for after dinner," said John laughing. "But seriously, I suppose the Christian's conscience rests in what he sees as the laws of God, whereas a non-believer's conscience would, I suppose, have rules like 'do as you would be done by' and so on."

"Why do people talk about the voices of conscience? I find my head is full of contradictory voices, always mine, of course, never God's"

"Good heavens, I don't know. I suppose they mean that when one is thinking about doing something which one knows in one's heart and mind not to be the right thing, one imagines one's own voice saying, 'wait a minute,' or something to that effect. I suppose too that one expresses one's remorse as something one did by saying 'it's been on my conscience."

"H'mm. You see I don't think Victoria's first husband Albert, whom I knew all his life either never had a conscience or lost it. Otherwise, surely he could not have behaved as he did. Hamish said once that he thought men of business were so involved with their livelihood and contracts and so on that they found ordinary decent behavior secondary to their wants."

"I suppose they could have a conscience if they broke a contract, but perhaps not."

"The surprising thing, John, is that my two children had most of their education away from Susanna and me, but they both seem to have very sturdy consciences. In war, the opportunity to exercise a conscience seemed to me to be limited, but even there, if I had shot a prisoner that would be on my conscience."

"How interesting. I must try and work out a sermon on the subject."

After the party ended, Simon and Margaret were surprised by how much they had enjoyed themselves. Holding her hand in the carriage, Simon said:

"We must look forward, my dear. Our grief for Felicia will always be with us, but now let us look to the future and meet our friends more often, perhaps also have a continental holiday while Jude is at Cambridge."

"I could wish for nothing more," said Margaret, "and perhaps then we can get back to where we once were," to which Simon had no reply.

The following afternoon Victoria and John caught the train down to Kent.

"Victoria," said John, "that was a splendid a dinner as I have ever had. What fascinating people these are."

"I feel so blessed, as you parsons would say. I have come to think, John, that if you and I are to have a future together, then you must give me some religious instruction and I should become a member of your church before we make decisions about our future. Forgive me if you think I am being too forward, but the legacy of my mother is such that, like Mary too, I speak my mind."

291

"Far from feeling you are too forward, I am now so anxious for our relationship to grow and prosper. I find you attractive in so many ways, indeed you have such beauty in you both in looks and as a person. We have much to discuss, for instance, I must get to know your children, whether I might be seen as their father, and of course financial matters."

Tom Hesketh arrived at Down Street one morning, uninvited. Hannah stayed at home as their younger child Louise needed her mother's attention. Matilda showed him into the library as the children were all playing in the drawing room with their parents. There was a little delay before Malcolm came in to greet him.

"My apologies, Tom, our four year old Charles is somewhat troubled this morning, though the baby is as sober and as quiet as one could wish for. But, wonderful to see you, old friend and brother-in-law, and you are obviously now the master of your prosthetic leg."

"Yes, I now feel it has become a part of me, but the reason for my visit is this. We have had a conversation over several months now about going into politics. I am most anxious to pursue this path, and we talked about this briefly in the presence of Clarence Smythe who said he would not stand for re-election in 1906 or whenever the next election comes. His intimation then was that he thought one of us might take his seat."

"Yes, I remember. I have not thought yet about where I might stand for election. Clara and I have decided that I should do so, and I am sure my sister will support your interests too. I take it that you wish to resolve whether you or I should see ourselves as the successor to Clarence. I know he has had thumping majorities in elections in the past, especially in 1900 and against the general tide of public opinion. So his support for a nomination will carry great weight in his local party and ease the path to the Commons."

"Exactly," said Tom, "you are my cherished brother-in-law and I do not want any sort of competition with you, indeed quite the reverse as we might well both be in Parliament. If we cannot decide which of us it might be, then I believe neither of us should seek the position to ensure the issue does not rankle in our families."

"My sentiments precisely, Tom. I think we can resolve this immediately. You should be Clarence's nominee. Let me explain why: Clarence has a constituency in north London which is largely composed of aspiring middle class people. I would prefer to be a member for a constituency which is predominantly poor, partly because Clara and I want to develop our own philanthropic endeavors alongside that of the Jaggers Trust."

"I see. That makes sense too as you know well that Hannah and I do not have your family wealth."

"Indeed, while I know Hannah had a legacy from our mother, Clara has monies from a substantial family trust, quite apart from Sam Eustace's money, so between ourselves we are, this Gargery family is, shall I say, well endowed."

"Are you then agreed that if we meet with Clarence, I should be the man to seek to succeed him?"

"Absolutely, and I will seek his advice and knowledge about which ring I should throw my hat into. Like my father's experience in the industrial north, it is there or in South Wales that I would wish to find my berth? I am also prepared to wait if I fall at the fence this time."

Clara came into the library and greeted Tom with affection, saying, "we have taken to drinking a cup of coffee in the mid-mornings which carries us through to lunch so would you care to join us?"

Her drawing room was now cleared of children who were upstairs with Nanny Briggs, formerly Clara's nanny.

"Tell me," she said, "what have you two been talking about?"

"Our political futures," said Malcolm. "We have decided to have a long talk with Clarence about it, and that Tom should seek his seat. I am going to look for an industrial constituency with Clarence's help, if he so agrees."

"For me," said Tom, "the character of a constituency is not of overwhelming importance as my interest are focused more on the Empire's foreign policy than the domestic which I suspect is Malcolm's interest, although what each of us do as MPs will be more dictated by events than our predilections."

"That seems admirable to me," said Clara, "and I hope Clarence will both agree and be a bastion of support."

"I have discussed this with Hannah and, if Clarence welcomed the plan, we would move our home to his constituency area to demonstrate our commitment."

"That is something we would not consider, am I right, Malcolm?"

"Yes, although if I were to be nominated for a constituency with the character I have in mind, we would need a base, a small lodging say, but we will cross that bridge when we come to it."

"Meantime, I hope you will allow me to talk about these plans with my dear friend, Emma."

"Of course, darling, but why not wait until we meet Clarence."

"Very well, but she and I are lunching next week, so why don't you take my carriage and go to Old Square now?"

"Are you game for that, Tom?" said Malcolm.

"Surely."

"Let me fetch my warm overcoat and hat, as it is very cold this November."

Their journey from Mayfair to Lincoln's Inn was always a difficult one as London thoroughfares were always full of horse traffic, carriages and horse omnibuses, but in the last five years, the arrival of the automobile with its particular problems of noise and smell had intensified the confusion.

Nevertheless, on arrival shortly after noon, Robert welcomed them to Old Square and introduced himself as neither of them had properly met him previously.

"Gentlemen, I am Robert Gillingham, and I have been here man and boy for forty years, first serving the inimitable Mr. Jaggers; I have recently been raised to the position of Senior Clerk at Courtisone and Jaggers."

"A remarkable achievement, Mr. Gillingham."

"Yes, my dear sirs, and I have heard a great deal of your military prowess and I congratulate both of you on your bravery and you have my sincere admiration. My wife's brother is serving in India."

"How interesting, Mr. Gillingham," said Tom, "but might we be able to meet with Sir Clarence?"

"I think so. Lord Bakersfield has been with him for an hour, so perhaps you would accommodate yourselves to our small waiting room and I will call you when Lord Bakersfield leaves. Sir Clarence has no other meetings this morning, though he will want to take lunch shortly before going to the House for Prime Minister's Questions."

"Thank you, Mr. Gillingham."

A few minutes later, Tom and Malcolm could hear Lord Bakersfield leaving with the usual parting words of lawyer and client, and Clarence came into the waiting room.

"How delightful to see you both. It is almost lunch time, so perhaps we can go to the Cheshire Cheese later but do come into my office first."

As they sat down in deep leather chairs in a room enhanced by the slightly musty smell of law books, some of a great age, Clarence said:

"What can I do for you, gentlemen?"

"Let me begin," said Malcolm. "You may recall a conversation in which we both expressed an interest in standing for Parliament as liberal candidates, and we understood from you that you did not propose to run for re-election."

"That is correct, and I would be delighted to support the nomination of either of you for my seat and for others. It will not take much doing in my constituency, I think, but finding another may present some difficulty, but I see you younger men as my protegees in this regard, so will work hard to have you both in Parliament soon."

"Thank you so much," said Tom. "If it suits you, Malcolm and I have discussed the question of which of us might be your nominee. Malcolm wants to stand in an industrial district as he is more interested in domestic policy, especially what is done for the poor, whereas my interests are more focused on foreign policy. If it is appropriate I would like to be your nominee for your seat."

"That would be most satisfactory. After our brief discussion earlier, I realized I might have to choose between you, but that possibility is now moot and I am sure you will both make excellent candidates and I will be very pleased to help you both."

"My sincere thanks, but we now need to know how to proceed."

"Let us talk about that over lunch."

Instead of the customary jugged hare and claret which had been the staple choice of all Courtisone and Jaggers lawyer lunches, a new waiter recommended venison from the New Forest with a red wine from the Chateau Margaux vineyard which they all found delicious.

"First, you must become active in the constituency party meetings and other meetings the Party holds so that your face and your opinions become familiar. This is a great opportunity, for the Conservatives have been in power far too long, but it is not just time for a change but for a radical change in terms of education, support for poor working families and much else. Moreover we have in the party such powerful men as David Lloyd George and Winston Churchill and I am particularly impressed by Henry Campbell-Bannerman whom I have got to know very well. I will make sure you become acquainted with these men."

"I met Churchill at a dinner in India after I was wounded, Clarence, and we talked about his entry into politics and I then said I would consider supporting him, so it will be a good time to revive our acquaintance."

"How interesting, Malcolm. He can be a formidable speaker and you will have him speak in your constituency when the time comes. He and Lloyd

George make a formidable pair. As to your possible seat, I will need to do some work. The election is some way off, three years, so members who have decided not to run again will be close to making up their minds. It will be difficult, I think, given how much the trades unions are developing, for you to get a seat in South Wales as we already having working class members and will have more, I am sure and indeed hope."

"I see, so I would need to burnish my credentials for such a seat."

"Being a war hero goes a long way," he said with a smile, "but the question is whether I can find a retiring Member who would support you as I will be doing with Tom, or a seat held by a Conservative with a narrow margin. An alternative would be a seat more akin to my own but bordering an industrial area. H'mm, I must give it some thought. Meantime you must both join the Party if you are not already members and become very active. This is a good time to do that for an opposition party with an election three years hence is in the doldrums of activity and needs to be stirred up."

"Tell me, Clarence," said Tom, "how did you become a Member?"

"Much as you will do. A cousin of my mother's held my seat for several years, and we were at a family gathering when he asked me if I would be interested. We had been married a couple of years, and Emma was enthusiastic, so that was that. It is not incompatible with my being a lawyer, of course. With the increases in the franchise and an expanding population, I foresee a time coming when inheriting seats as I did will become a much more difficult task."

"And your knighthood?"

"I have no idea, Malcolm. It came quite out of the blue, though I had a case in which I represented the Government as both the Attorney-General and the Solicitor-General were not available for different reasons. The case was a civil one, involving complex issues of taxation in the dominions and the knighthood came a year later. The complexity of the case was such that it was never likely to be a matter of public interest, unlike a good murder."

They stood on the pavement after lunch and Clarence said:

"I am really delighted at both your intentions. It breathes new life into me and gives me something to look forward to in the New Year. I am getting stale, both as a lawyer and an MP, but now I have a very exciting project advising and supporting two of the best men of conscience I know who want to serve their country through politics. "

Both men expressed their sincere thanks, and Clarence called a cab leaving the two friends standing in Fleet Street, both thinking of a Parliamentary destiny.

"Tom," said Malcolm, "I never heard him say it, but my grandfather had an expression which he constantly used with my father when he was a boy to express his reactions and hopes for any event which might be both dangerous and exciting, like politics."

"What was that?"

"What larks, eh Pip?"

⚜   ⚜   ⚜

At Osbourne House on the Isle of Wight, a tall gaunt man could be seen walking down the gates one evening and pinning a sheet of paper on the notice-board with the typed message:

'Osborne House, January 22, 1901, 6.45 p.m.

Her Majesty the Queen breathed her last at 6.30 p.m.,

surrounded by her children and grand-children.'

After a reign of sixty-four years, the last of which had brought many personal sorrows, Her Imperial Majesty, Alexandrina Victoria of Saxe-Coburg and Hesse, Defender of the Faith, Empress of India, Queen of England, Scotland, Wales and Ireland and her dominions beyond the seas, Duke of Normandy, was dead. On January 24th her son Albert Edward made the oath of accession at a meeting of the Privy Council in London and stated that he wished to be known as Edward VII.

Pip and Harriet had walked up the Row to lunch with the MacDonalds, and inevitably conversation turned to the nation's loss. Across the Empire, millions were wondering what her son would be like as a monarch as he was so popular a figure.

"That is the end of an era which I suppose we will call Victorian," said Hamish.

"I doubt whether we will see a woman as monarch for centuries," said Harriet, "there are so many men in that family."

END

Characters in 1900

Note: To emphasize that wives are not appendages of their husbands, each living married woman among the Principal and Secondary Characters has their own entry below.

PRINCIPAL CHARACTERS

Pip (Philip) Gargery b. 1837.
    m 1.   Susanna (née Urchadan) Gargery 1865: d.1883.
           -   Lachlan Finlay Joseph (dec'd) 1867-1877.
           -   Malcolm Philip 1869.
           -   Hannah Emily 1873.
    m 2.   Harriet (née Middleham) 1893.
           -   Joseph Gargery (father: Aristide Bruant) b. 1878.

Malcolm Philip Gargery b. 1869.
    m.   Clara Eugenia Eustace (née FitzCuthbert, widow of Sam Eustace) 1895.
           -   Andrew Edward Samuel b. 1895.
           -   Susanna Eleanor b. 1896.
           -   Charles Joseph Samuel, b. 1898.

Hannah Emily Gargery b. 1875.
    m.   Thomas Hesketh, 1895.
           -   Hector Thomas, 1896.
           -   Louise Susanna Katherine, 1900.

Harriet Gargery (née Middleham), b. 1838.

        -   Joseph Gargery (Father: Aristide Bruant).

m.   Pip (Philip) Gargery, 1893.

Clara Eugenia Gargery (née FitzCuthbert, widow of Sam Eustace) b. 1871

   m.   Malcolm Philip Gargery, 1895.

        -   Andrew Edward Samuel b. 1895.

        -   Susanna Eleanor b. 1896.

        -   Charles Joseph Samuel, b. 1898.

Thomas Hesketh. b. 1862.

   m.   Hannah Emily Gargery,

        -   Hector Thomas, 1896.

        -   Louise Susanna Katherine, 1900.

Albert Pirrip (son of Pip and step-son of Estella Pirrip, deceased) b. 1852. d. 1900.

   m.   Victoria Ellen Fletcher. b. 1859. m. 1880.

        -   Beatrice, b. 1886.

        -   Philip (Pip) b. 1887.

        -   Ellen (Nellie) b. 1892.

Victoria Fletcher. b. 1858. m. Albert Pirrip, 1880.

        -   Beatrice, b. 1886.

        -   Philip (Pip) b. 1887.

        -   Ellen, (Nellie) b. 1892.

Hamish MacDonald Q.C. (later Mr. Justice MacDonald) b. 1840.

   m.   Mary MacDonald (née Hamilton) b. 1838 m.1871.

        -   James Hamish b. 1872. m. Stella Gilmour 1897.

        -   Emily Mary, b. 1875.

Mary MacDonald (née Hamilton) b. 1838.

   m.   Hamish MacDonald, 1871.

        -   James Hamish b. 1872. m. Stella Gilmour 1897.

        -   Emily Mary, b. 1875.

Honora Brandram, b. 1842.

    m.   Husband Frederick, b. 1830, d. 1885.

            - Simon b. 1860 (father unknown.)

            - Jude, b. 1860, (twin to Simon,) drowned 1878.

            - Jane Margaret, b. 1874

Simon Brandram (father unknown) b. 1862. m. 1875.

    m.   Margaret Culpepper b. 1863 (d. of Randolph and Eliza Culpepper.), m.

            - Frederica (b. 1877, murdered 1894.)

            - Jude b. 1879.

Margaret Brandram (née Culpepper) b. 1863.

    m.   Simon Brandram, 1878.

            - Frederica (b. 1877, murdered 1894.)

            - Jude b. 1879.

Nellie Fletcher b. 1835. d. 1896.

    m.   Horatio Fletcher b. 1835 m. 1855 (dec'd 1892)

            - Horatio Joseph Fletcher b. 1856.

            - Victoria Fletcher b. 1859.

Horatio Joseph Fletcher b. 1856.

    m.   Beth Horsfield, 1885.

            - Arthur, b. 1886.

            - Beth, b. 1888.

            - Charlie b. 1890, d. 1900

            - Dorothy (Dottie-do-da), b. 1891.

            - Ernest b. 1892 d. 1900.

            - Frank b. 1893.

            - Georgiana, b. 1897.

            - Horatio, b. 1900.

Beth Horsfield b. 1867.

    m.   Horatio Joseph Fletcher 1885.

            - Arthur, b. 1886.

            - Beth, b. 1888.

- Charlie b. 1890, d. 1900
- Dorothy (Dottie-do-da), b. 1891.
- Ernest b. 1892 d. 1900.
- Frank b. 1893.
- Georgiana, b. 1897.
- Horatio, b. 1900.

Sir Clarence Fotheringaye-Smythe, Q.C., b. 1840.
   m.   The Hon. Emma Sophia Victoria b. 1842 (d. of Lord Eustace) m. 1878
- Clarence Arthur Fitzherbert b. 1879.
- Sophia Margaret Louise b. 1881.
- Alexandra Mary Charlotte b. 1885.
- Elizabeth Anne Henrietta b. 1889.

The Hon. Emma Fotheringaye-Smythe, b. 1842 (d. of Baron and Lady Eustace)
   m.   Clarence Fotheringaye-Smythe, 1878.
- Clarence Arthur Fitzherbert b. 1879.
- Sophia Margaret Louise b. 1881.
- Alexandra Mary Charlotte b. 1885.
- Elizabeth Anne Henrietta b. 1889.

Elizabeth Egerton (née Fitzroy), b. 1852.
   m.   Timothy Henry Tatton Egerton. b. 1851 d. 1896 (murdered.)
- Henry Tatton, b. 1879.
- Oliver Charles, b. 1882.
- Charlotte Elizabeth b. 1885.

The Hon. Samuel Eustace. b. 1869. d. 1894.
   m.   Clara Eugenia Eustace (née FitzCuthbert) b.1869.
- George Henry Eustace b. 1890.
- Alice Clara Eustace b. 1893.

Timothy Henry Tatton Egerton b. 1851 d. 1896.
   m.   Elizabeth Egerton (née Fitzroy) b. 1852.
- Henry Tatton, b. 1879.
- Tim(othy) Charles, b. 1882.
- Charlotte Elizabeth b. 1885.

Antonia Letitia Penoyre (née Wheeler) b. 1866. m. 1877.

    m.   Aubrey St.John, b. 1866, m. 1887
- Aubrey, b. 1888.
- Rex, b. 1890.
- Charles, b. 1892.
- Margaret, b. 1893.
- Estella, b. 1894.
- Ellen, b. 1895.

SECONDARY CHARACTERS

Katherine Bradley and Edith Cooper (aka Michael Field.)
    Katherine, b. 1846.
    Edith, b. 1862.

Alice Margaret Peake, b. 1858.

Aaron Levy b. 1841.
    m.   Alice Jane Steinhardt, 1886

Alice Jane Levy (née Steinhardt) b. 1844.
    m.   Aaron Levy, 1886.

Adam Masterson b. 1847 m. Anne Bright, 1869.
- Henrietta, b. 1871.
- Arthur 1873

Anne Masterson (née Bright) 1869.
- Henrietta , b. 1871.
- Arthur b. 1873.

Jeane MacPherson, friend to Hannah b. 1876.

Alexander (Alec) Stuart MacPherson, b. 1869 Gordon Highlanders.
    m.   Cecily Horniman-Heath, 1896.

Cecily MacPherson (née Horniman-Heath) b. 1863.

m.   Alexander Stuart MacPherson, 1896.

Abdul, Malayan Servant.

The Reverend John Eustace, widow, b. 1858.

John Singer Sargent, b. 1856.

Colonel Duncan Urchadan, DCM, Gordon Highlanders.

Eliza Culpepper, mother of Margaret Brandram.

Mr. Algernon Threewits, Teacher at Eton College.

HRH the Prince of Wales.

Henry Chilton, pupil at Marlborough College, Wiltshire.

OTHER CHARACTERS IN CONTEXT

Ireland and the Clumber Plantation
Mrs. Darcy, housekeeper.
Colleen, maid.
Beth, maid.
O'Donovan, groom at Clumber.
Cecil Brown, butler.
Tenants: Seamus and Marguerite O'Sullivan,
            Michael and Maggie Flaherty.
            Sam O'Leary.
            Cóllin and Mary Maguire.
Desmond McAfee, Londonderry lawyer.
Father Francis McGowan.
James McAfee, traveler from Belfast.

Timothy Egerton Murder
Detectives Monroe and Strayman.
Robert Cecil, Marquess of Salisbury, Foreign Secretary.

Arthur James Balfour, M.P.

Harry Montague, Foreign Office Security.

Richard Dalrymple Foreign Office Lawyer.

South Africa

Brigadier Henry Motely-Millard.

Colonel Bruce Williamson.

Sgt, Mistle.

Privates Thankston and Blimble.

Septimus Brindley-Beach.

Colonel Williamson.

Miss Emily Hobhouse.

Mrs. Ella Makepeace, owner of No 7 Clyde Street, Port Elizabeth.

Harry, boy saved from drowning.

Mrs. Waterhouse, Abdul's mistress.

Albert's Suicide and Business sale

Doctor Thaddeus Makepeace.

Dr. Cyril Warburton.

Millie Smith, Chatham Prostitute.

Detective Wattstown.

Hannibal Smurch, undertaker

French official.

Maria Jenkins, Moulin Rouge dancer.

OTHER CHARACTERS

Cases before Mr. Justice MacDonald

Theophilus Mandrake, clerk to Judge MacDonald.

1. Prisoners' Dilemma

    George Honeycutt Q.C.

    Detective Sargent Latterly

    Mrs. Charmian Haworth and Mrs. Denise Cloudless

    Harold Upton and Tom Featherweight, burglars

    Sir Archibald Hamilton-Dawes,

2. The Bigamy Case
   Cynthia Blackstone (née Naylor)
   Husbands: Thomas Bladon Cooperston, Daniel Jones, and Richard Andrew Blackstone.
   The Cooperston sisters: Connie, Dottie and Fanny
   Desmond Droitwich barrister,
   Sir Ralph Standby, Solicitor-General.

3. Offences against the Person Trial
   Thomas Butterworth, sentenced by MacDonald

Lady Emma Fotheringaye-Smythe's dinner party guests
The Bishop of Middlesborough and Mrs. Dorothy Trotter.
Winston Churchill, MP, journalist and cavalry officer in Delhi.
The Hon. Henry and Mrs. Sarah Eustace.
General and Mrs. Bindon Blood.

The Three Jolly Bargemen
John Steppings, landlord.
Sid Butterworth, customer
Samuel Hubble, (son of Orlick, assailant of Georgina Gargery in Great Expectations)

Others

Sir Marmaduke Stewart-Campbell, Equerry to the Prince of Wales
Mrs. Charlotte Bowen-Thomas, Peake's accuser.
Sir Henry Stuart Arbuthnot. Tim's eulogist
Alfred Buzza, customer at the Forge.

Sources:

Elsabé Brits.(2018) Rebel Englishwoman: The Remarkable Life of Emily Hobhouse. Robinson Books, London.
Winston S. Churchill. (1930/1906). My Early Life, 1874 - 1904. Scribner, New York.

Emily Hobhouse, (1902) The Brunt of the War and Where it Fell. Methuen, Books, London.

Rudyard Kipling, (1990) Plain Tales from the Hills. Penguin Books, London.

Fransjohan Pretorius. (2014) A History of South Africa. Protea Books, Pretoria.

Fransjohan Pretorius. (1998) The Anglo-Boer War 1899-1902. Struik Publishers, Capetown.

Various Internet Sources.